The Firehandler

The Dreamcatcher Chronicles

Jason Lee Willis

Lura Publications, LLC.

Mapleton, Minnesota

Lura Publications, LLC
803 Silver Street E
Mapleton, MN 56065
lurapublications.wixsite.com/books
jasonleewillis.wixsite.com/novels

Author's Note: *Since the setting of the book is the late 1890s, and involves the cultures of the Oceti Sakowin and Anishinaabe, the historic nomenclature for these cultures are used in this novel. Although Hiawatha County and the Wijigan Clan are inventions, please refer to the index for an overview of indigenous names and terms.*

Book Layout © 2017 BookDesignTemplates.com

Library of Congress Cataloging-in-Publication Data
Willis, Jason Lee, author.
Eckman, Raven, editor.
Hudson, Becca, designer.
Lyka Marie Toledo, designer.
The Firehandler / Jason Lee Willis. – revised edition.
Summary: A young Native American woman in 1890s Minnesota
must uncover the secrets of her ancestry as an ancient evil stirs.

The Firehandler/ Jason Lee Willis. – revised edition
ISBN: 979-8-9891198-3-7
[1. Historical Fantasy – Fiction. 2. Native American – Fiction.
3. Mythology – Fiction. 4. Action & Adventure – Fiction.]
Library of Congress Control Number: _ _ _ _ _ _ _ _ _

For my grandparents.

A Note from the Author

I never knew my grandparents. All four were gone before I was old enough to investigate my roots. Would they have taught me about Love, Respect, Bravery, Truth, Honesty, Humility, and Wisdom? I'd like to think so, but like many modern Americans, my heritage is like seed scattered on rocks—my roots are shallow. The Great Melting Pot left me with little understanding of my German, Irish, French, English, or Norwegian ancestry. My family records indicate that I traveled a very similar path as the Anishinaabe, beginning in eastern Canada, passing through the Great Lakes, then out onto the prairie, before settling amongst the 10,000 lakes of Minnesota, but this is a legacy that is foreign to me.

In this regard, *The Firehandler* is a story that goes beyond a summer of self-discovery to an epic journey into understanding legacy and heritage. The characters in this novel, and series, come from contrasting heritages. Minnesota's heritage has the blood of the Dakota, Anishinaabe, French, and countless other settlers and immigrants. While history records the conflicts between these cultures, I hope to show the shared beliefs. As an English teacher, my favorite topic has always been mythology, for in myth, we can find common ground.

So even though this tale begins in 1897 Minnesota, it is a fantasy involving monsters, heroes, and quests. Like my characters, you'll learn about a horned serpent, known by such names as the Mishi-Ginebig, the Unktehi, Jormungandr, and Leviathan, depending on who you ask. The Little Men of the Forest? Oh yes, they're known as the Memegwesi to the Ojibwe, Pukwudgee to the eastern Anishinaabe, Canoti to the Dakota, Puck to William Shakespeare, Fossegrim to the Norse, Leprechauns to the Irish, and for lack of a better word, demons in the Bible. As a writer of fantasy, I want to share similarities rather than differences.

I first met my character Lily Weber during a research unit in my English 10 class. Paired with a unit on Native American folklore, my research unit included a variety of historical articles on Minnesota history. Having grown up in South Dakota, I knew details about the Dakota Conflict of 1862, but I'd never even heard of the Battle of Sugar Point in 1898. As I read about the Dawes Act, logging rights, boarding schools, and the arrest of Bug-O-Nay-Ge-Shig, I encountered an anecdote about a young woman in a single canoe paddling between the Anishinaabe sharpshooters and General Bacon's soldiers at Bear Island on Leech Lake.

Who was she? Where was she going?

Why was she willing to risk her life?

During my time as a student and teacher, I'd met plenty of teenagers whose personal problems overshadowed any "real world" issues happening around them. So from the chaos of Bear Island, Lily Weber came to life in my mind. Although I have no tribe or clan, I've spent a lifetime attempting to understand my Lakota classmates from South Dakota, and upon moving to Minnesota, my Anishinaabe neighbors. When the State of Minnesota introduced Language Arts standards that covered Native American literature and nonfiction, I was ready to teach them (with gusto). While most of my students were descendants from pioneer families, each year, I'd have a handful of students with Native American ancestry, most of whom preferred just to fit in with their peers. While I avoided shining a spotlight on my students during these units, I discovered that while they knew their indigenous ancestry, many were generations removed from the myths, legends, and folktales I'd studied.

Even though this is essentially a fantasy, set in a fictional county, with an invented clan and heritage, I wanted to still include some realism. Governmental policy in the 1890s, from mandated boarding schools to the dissembling of reservations, created the very real crisis at Sugar Point on Leech Lake. Just as the Seven Fires predicted, an entire generation of Anishinaabe children was lost to the boarding schools, and the horrors of this practice are still coming to light today. As a child, I was shown cliché portrayals of Native American life; as a teenager, I met public school classmates transitioning from a boys' reformatory school who had come out of the modern reservations in South Dakota who experienced real horrors instead of fantasy horrors. Many other writers have already captured these issues, and while my invented reservation is closer to Hogwarts than Pine Ridge, I have included issues like racism, domestic violence, rape, murder, and broken families to keep this fantasy grounded in reality.

As you will soon discover, Lake Manitou is filled with many types of horrors and monsters, but it is also a place of magic, family, and friendship, where legends come to life in the shadows of the trees. It is a place where the past connects to the future, and the future of all depends on the choices made by our youth.

"Surtr will come from the south,
with a bright light in his hand...
Flames will scorch the leaves of Yggdrasil,
a great bonfire reaches to the highest clouds."
The Prophecy of Ragnarök

"A long time ago,
a really long time when the world was still freshly made,
Unktehi the water monster fought the people
and caused a great flood."
"Unktehi and the Flood" as told by Lame Deer

"And it shall come to pass in the last days,' says God,
'That I will pour out My Spirit on all flesh;
Your sons and your daughters shall prophesy,
and your young men shall see visions,
and your old men shall dream dreams.'"
Acts 2:17

"What the People believe...is true!"
Anishinaabe saying

Contents

White
Earth
Leech Lake
Isle Royale
Duluth
Madeline Island
Bad River
Sault Ste. Marie
Manitoulin
Island
Hiawatha
County
Mille Lacs
Mackinac
Lac Du Flambeau
Morris
St. Paul
Mankato
Detroit

Robin's Photoshop Maps to Help Picture Where
Stuff Happens in 1897-98

<u>Important People from 1897-98</u>

Lily Guerin—The Spider

Fawn Chevreuil—The Poet

Migisi—A Spiritual Guide

Halvar Dobie—The Face of Death

Bjorn Forsberg—The Guardian

Martin Nielson—The Warrior

Albert Fisher—The Intellectual

Kermit Crain—A Leader

Farrell Luning—A Leader

Father Jean Guerin—A Spiritual Guide

For the rest of Hiawatha County, check out the back of the Dream Journal

—Robin Berg

The Firehandler

Brainerd, MN
May 2029

THIS CAN'T BE *true,* Robin Berg thought upon entering the classroom. Not only did it almost take all four minutes of passing time to go from the band room to the civics classroom, but half of the jocks in her grade were also sitting along the back wall when she entered.

Robin looked down and took one of the seats in the front row for the third hour of freshman orientation. The awful gauntlet of middle school ended in a few hours and the possibility of change in high school provided a little hope.

Loud, obnoxious boys never concerned her, but when they began to whisper, Robin tensed. The teacher still stood in the doorway, leaving no protection from softly spoken words.

Is that a boy or a girl?

Did you know her dad is in prison?

She's crazy.

Schizophrenia.

Those were the most commonly heard whispers.

Robin's experience with bullying didn't involve dumpsters like in the movies; her classmates chose to make her invisible. She didn't exist to them. At least public ridicule could garner sympathy. Being ignored was the worst kind of bullying.

The teacher brushed by the front of Robin's desk but immediately started banter with the jocks in the back of the room.

Oh great, he's their baseball coach.

9th Grade Civics was going to be the worst hour of the day next fall.

Instead of turning to drugs or self-harm, Robin found a way to escape her living hell—Hiawatha County. She decorated her drug of choice to look like a typical notebook. It was, however, so much more. It was her dream journal, and inside, she had countless sketches, stories, and random anecdotes from Hiawatha County— which didn't exist, of course. She built it over the top of southern Cass County and Wadena County, bulldozing her real world to create a fantasy world that gave her a different kind of high.

She lived in the pages of the notebook, and the strange creatures and characters of the woods were better friends than anyone in her class. Robin used her arm to shield the dream journal from the prying eyes of the others, but her classmates were too wired to even notice her today.

Summer break was upon them.

While Mr. Allen talked about course expectations and behaviors for freshmen, Robin began with a sketch of a dreamcatcher, a simple loop of willow with crossed ends. Instead of filling in the middle with the webbing, she drew a raven with spread wings. In her dream world of Hiawatha County, ravens brought messages to the characters to steer them on the right path, just like the one in Edgar Allen Poe's poem.

Come find me. Send me a message, too.

And her messenger arrived.

Everyone in the room flinched from the reverberation. Robin caught only a black flutter of feathers, and from the volume of the impact on the glass, she knew it had to have been a bird of some size.

"Dude! That bird just crashed into the window."

The moment Mr. Allen stopped his introduction to step towards the big window, half of the boys jumped to their feet to see for themselves.

"You can see where it hit the glass."

A dozen classmates inspected the smear of saliva, oil, and blood no bigger than the size of a quarter, but with no sign of a bird, Mr. Allen quickly ended the chaos, "Okay, back to your seats."

Robin rose to get a peek for herself before everyone sat down. Past the big window, Brainerd High School's sports complex included open grassy fields, a tennis court, a baseball field, and the football field, all tucked into a bend of the Gitchi-Ziibi, the mighty Mississippi River.

The raven waited in the high branches of a willow tree planted beside the drainage pond.

When the third hour bell ended, Robin bolted for the hallway, down the stairwell, and out the first floor doorway. She hurried across the outfield of a practice softball field, and the excitement and exertion stole her breath by the time she reached the pond.

The raven shook out its feathers, still recovering from its impact with the window.

"Are you okay?" Robin asked aloud.

"Rrrr," the bird made a guttural rattle before barking out two clear syllables, "Robin."

Holy shit…

Robin turned back to the school, just to see if she was being watched. It'd only been less than a minute, and most of her classmates were shuffling between classes, but already, it seemed a world away. "Yes?"

"Find us," a voice came from the raven without the bird opening its beak. "We need your help. Our world is in danger. *Your* world is in danger. Search your dreams, and you'll know where to find Lily."

Lily? Three years ago during her Minnesota History unit on early explorers, she read about Joseph Nicollet's 1836 expedition through the area. With young Nanakonan at the prow of the canoe and wise Chagobay guiding Nicollet's team, the foreigners were told to raise their paddles lest they wake the Horned Serpent that slept below the water lilies. After reading about the strange visit to Lake Manitou, Robin dreamed of Lily living along the shores of the haunted lake. *But she's not real. How can I find someone who's not real.*

"Oh shit," Robin said aloud, sending the raven flying off toward the river. In her hurry to find the raven, she'd left her backpack—and dream journal—in Mr. Allen's room.

So much for saving the world.

The Prodigal Daughter

St. John, MN
May 1897

LILY WEBER KNEW all about monsters, so when she stepped off the train at the St. John Depot, she took precautions.

First, she pulled her green bonnet down so low that she could only see a few feet in front of her. *Not that I don't know every inch of the way home and could walk it with my eyes closed.*

Next, she made sure her matching green cape was tightly closed at the neck and waist. Under it, she wore a cheap striped cotton dress and black boots that climbed halfway up her calves. It also hid her braid that fell down the middle of her back. *No one standing on the platform can know I'm Chippewa under all of this.*

Satisfied, she moved quickly, carrying her satchel in front of her with both hands. Ahead of the crowd, she reached the baggage quickly, spotting her bane—the chest holding all of her worldly goods.

Act like you know where you're going. Move with purpose.

Across the street, she saw locals coming out of the Bonnie Lass Hotel and Saloon to greet the train. Even though the chest weighed almost as much as she did, she found the strength to grip one of the side handles with her gloved hand and drag it along the platform by its smooth metal corners.

"Need help with that, Miss?"

Lily kept her eyes low. "No, thank you. I only have a short walk."

It was a lie to keep monsters away, even well-intentioned monsters.

The train platform stretched fifty yards, with stairs at each end and one at the center. Lily chose the northernmost stairs to avoid the crowd that waited to board. She then let gravity do the work as the chest bounced down the stairs: it took all of her grip strength to keep the large chest from toppling completely. Once down, she made for the church.

Even from the train depot, First Presbyterian Church of St. John could be seen. In fact, its steeple was the tallest thing in the small town of almost 1,000—few of which were Chippewa. *Hurry. Hurry.*

She heard the heavy boots approaching before they entered her narrow line of sight. *Shit.*

Brown boots, leather guards over thick denim pants, and a holstered pistol came into sight. Half of the men in St. John looked like this … but only one used a black walking stick. Only one wore a distinctive vest with black and gray stripes. Only one wore a silver star belonging to the U.S. Marshals.

Jananashins—the Little Englishman.

"Well, look who's back in Hiawatha County. Is that Squeak's daughter?"

Lily paused, not knowing what to say or do. She flinched when the ebony walking stick rose toward her face, but instead of striking her, it gently caught her under the chin, lifting it so she looked right into the face of a monster.

"If it isn't Squeak's little girl, all grown up." Bushy Bill Morrison wore a circular derby hat as black as his droopy mustache. At the end of the ebony walking stick, his hand gripped a metallic skull. "Dressed up like a lady, eh? Looks like the Sisters of Mercy have civilized another pagan. Send your father my regards."

I wish I could. I wish you would arrest him. Then I'd never have to deal with him again.

The silver tip dropped from her chin, and he walked back to the Bonnie Lass Saloon without another word.

Lily hurried away from the train depot, her chest thudding in the dirt behind her. *I'm glad I didn't wet myself right then and there.*

Even though she kept a quick pace, her heart calmed the farther away from Bushy Bill she got. *Hopefully he chased away any other monsters lurking at the station.*

With her last bit of strength, she hauled the chest up the front steps of the church, opened the heavy front door, and called out, "Minister Barrow?"

No one stirred, so she let the door shut behind her as she pulled her bane over to the alcove of coat hangers and shoved it in the corner. "Minister Barrow?"

More silence.

She opened the front door again, looking out at the town of St. John. New sidewalks, new buildings, new streetlamps. Lots of strangers.

Lily closed the heavy front door and walked along the side of the pews. Even in an empty church, she tried to be discreet.

"Minister Barrow?" she called out a third time once she reached the office doorway.

The interior of the Presbyterian church was different from a Catholic church. Fewer statues. Fewer paintings. Everything felt more open. *My chest won't be in the way though.* The chest could stay for a few days, allowing her time to return with a wagon or help to haul it home. It also freed her from the burden of traveling with it.

Accepting that no one was there, she slipped out the back door and darted for the eastern side of town, lifting her eyes only to scan her surroundings before she started on the familiar path home.

In five minutes, St. John no longer posed a threat, and she slowed her pace as she walked on the road heading east. All of the trees had been cut down around the town, leaving grassy fields that provided plenty of visibility. *Nothing can jump out at me here.* To the north, the old forest loomed dark and green. To the south, the shimmering waters of Lake Manitou beckoned.

Finally alone.

With a final glance to make sure no one had followed her out of town, she went about removing her armor—tucking the bonnet and cape into her satchel. She next pulled her cross pendant out so it could reflect upon her chest.

The hard packed gravel road always made the trip to town the easiest part, but when the road sloped down nearer the shore of Lake Manitou, Lily walked down the ditch and entered the dark woods.

After slipping through the brush, she stood under the protection of a tall canopy of pine, birch, and towering sugar maples. Light still filtered through the foliage, but the air was cool and still. *The woods will never change. I'm home.*

A few yards in, Lily dropped her satchel and unlaced her boots. A carpet of pine needles and leaf mulch covered the dark woods, and even though six years of wearing shoes had softened the callouses on her feet, she had no problem keeping a steady pace as she finished the second half of her journey home.

Mother will be baking at her stove, and Migisi will be playing in the river. That thought brought a smile to her face. She began singing one of her favorite hymns, "It is well with my soul …"

So consumed with her own feelings and the vibration of music within her, Lily failed to notice the eyes upon her until it was almost too late.

It took five steps for her to acknowledge her feet.

It's cold here.

She stopped and listened.

No birds—why didn't I notice that?

Her eyes scanned the dark woods, but neither Bushy Bill Morrison nor a pack of boys leering from the shadows of a crease in the earth waited for her.

Her hand clutched the cross at her chest, but her legs obeyed an older tradition and she crouched until she sat upon her heels, listening.

Setting the satchel down, she spread her hand upon the cold earth, trying to understand the pounding of her heart and the warning cries in her brain that left every hair on her neck and arms standing on end.

Jiibay. The old word brought no comfort to her terror, so she turned to her crucifix to recite Psalm 23: *Though I walk through the valley of the shadow of death, I will fear no evil. Thy rod and thy staff comfort me....*

And then no more. The words wouldn't come.

Her eyes scanned the mulch, trying to spot any obvious sign of danger. Yet no physical danger presented itself.

Except for ...

Yellow eyes stared down at her from a branch in an ancient maple, its ears listened to her pounding heart and shallow breathing.

It's not a monster—it's just an owl.

A gookooko'oo warned of evil and death: the forest would go silent, and a cold patch of ground would appear on the forest floor.

Lily could not ignore the omen. She partially rose, keeping her head lowered. When nothing attacked, she grabbed her satchel and slowly backed up while keeping an eye on the owl.

After retreating several paces, she paused to make a decision. Going south meant going closer to the lake and going back made no sense at all. If she went north a bit, then perhaps—

Suddenly, her feet were flying. She ran, leaving the owl and the cold spot upon the forest floor far behind.

The unmarked path took her ever uphill, toward the rocky hills that held the Blue Knife River. As she ran, she tried not to think of the owl or the possible jiibay hiding under the mulch. Instead, she thought of the happy Gray Heron family just a few hundred yards away.

Even though Lily's family was separated from the Gray Herons by the Blue Knife River, they were the nearest neighbors to visit during times of drought. Rose Gray Heron had five older children, including a daughter who was sixteen, a year older than Lily. Fred Gray Heron was a lumberjack, and with saw and blade, he not only crafted the sturdiest home on the reservation but also built a log bridge that passed over the Nicollet Rapids.

Fearing the arrival of the owl's extended talons ready to grab her face and rip out her soul, Lily did not turn around to see if anything followed her out of the dark woods.

The nearer she got to the river, the more patches of exposed stone appeared, thinning the dense forest.

Finally, she came running out of the forest to see the deep channel of the Blue Knife River stretching from the distant pine forests of the north to Lake Manitou just a mile or so away. Her feet rested and her lungs struggled to catch up.

She was safe.

Nothing followed her.

Yet something terrible presented itself before her instead—

The Gray Heron cabin had been burned to the ground.

The Place of Souls

The Blue Knife River
May 1897

ALL OF IT was gone. The barn. The storage shed. The chicken coop. Lily walked around the small perimeter of the house, trying to understand how a fire had jumped from building to building, leaving nothing but charcoal.

While the house had been built on a scenic outcropping of stone overlooking the river, the bridge once stood at the bottom of the hill in a small gully. Not only could Lily see the old posts still sticking up out of the riverbed, but she could also see a lean, brown figure standing upon a rock in the flowing waters.

Migisi.

All of her fears, and even curiosities, vanished when she saw her younger brother perched like a heron in the river. Although nine-years-old, Migisi was more like an older brother. Nothing scared him, including owls or jiibay.

"Hey!" she called out to him, waving her free arm over her head.

"Tew!" he called back, waving his arm, still holding a spear in it.

She ran down the slope of the bluff, hopping from rock to rock rather than taking the path made by the Gray Heron family. Migisi jumped right into the river, sloshing through the water to meet her at the place where the footbridge once stood.

Lily tossed her satchel onto dry ground and rushed into the water to hug her brother, who threw his spear onto the bank and returned the hug.

"Oh, I'm so glad to be home," she said, lifting him off his feet.

"You're early," Migisi said between chuckles.

She set him back down, putting her hand upon his head. "You've really grown this past year. You're almost a man."

"You look like a zhaaganaash in those clothes."

She huffed. "I was traveling, so I had to dress the part."

"You're early. You wrote you were coming on Thursday."

"I needed to get out of White Earth, so I changed tickets. Sister Lynch telegraphed Minister Barrow, but I suppose you didn't get the message, did you?"

"I guess not, or we would've met you at the train station."

"It's fine, I just left my trunk with Minister Barrow." Lily took in the sights of the scenic river valley, only to focus on the opposite shore. "So what happened to the Gray Herons?"

Migisi walked over to retrieve his spear. "They sold their lot and moved up to Leech Lake."

"Sold it? Sold it to who?"

"Triton Logging. Everybody along the western shore has sold their land and moved away. It's really quiet now that they're gone."

"So there wasn't an accident?"

"In a way. Teddy Big Marten died in a hunting accident, but the Gray Herons just moved. Bushy Bill Morrison and some white guys from St. John came and burned it all down."

"Why would they want the lots along the Blue Knife when there is good farmland just outside of town?"

Migisi shrugged. "Maybe they like to fish. Or trap. Or hunt. The river valley is the last bit of the old forest. There's all sorts of stuff living in these woods. I think I saw the Horned Serpent swimming in the river, so I'll protect you while you cross."

Is he teasing or serious… Wait, the bridge is gone. "Did the Triton men tear down the bridge, too?"

"Yep. Mother raised quite a fuss, but they just knocked it down since half of it was on their side of the river. I just walk across, but she goes all the way up to Nimrod Crossing now."

Lily knew the routine of crossing the river, having done it hundreds of times. She would walk over the rough gravel until her bare feet sunk into the wet sand. *It's going to be a cold walk.* The shiver made her remember her fear. "So what happened to Teddy Big Marten?"

"Shot himself in the leg last fall, so his wife took the Triton offer and left with the kids."

"Did it happen west of here?"

"Yeah, Fred Gray Heron found him dead, leaning against a tree. Why?"

"I think I felt a ghost."

"I guess that makes sense. He and his whole family became Christian, just like my sister Tewapa." Migisi gave her crucifix a dirty look.

"What does that have to do with anything? And my name is Lily, now."

"Grandfather says that any of our people who become Christian will be stuck on earth as ghosts instead of traveling to the River of Souls. Teddy Big Marten was a Christian, so you probably felt his ghost haunting the woods where he died."

"Nanakonan is a crazy old man, and you should stop listening to his stories." *Especially stories about owls. Owls belong in the woods. It's normal.*

"You're the one who brought up ghosts." Migisi hopped up onto a rock in the middle of the river. "Go ahead. I'll keep an eye out for the Horned Serpent while you cross."

Lily held tighter to her satchel, and seeing no other choice, walked out into the river. She did her best to gather up her dress to keep it dry, and luckily, the water level was low for late May, letting her cross in knee deep water. "You probably just saw a pike or sturgeon by the way. Not the Horned Serpent."

"It was big!" Migisi stretched his arms wide. "There's no fish this wide."

"And you think you're Iyash reborn now? Are you going to kill it with your little spear?" The thought of the monster of Lake Manitou hunting for victims in the Blue Knife River chilled her. *Maybe I should have gone back to Morris to work with Sister Lynch.*

At her brother's huff, she shuddered. She could feel the magic lingering in the air around her home, and she felt like Tewapa again, a little girl full of fear and doubt.

Once she reached the rocky shore, Migisi came bouncing across the river to join her.

The Blue Knife River's channel cut through stone, littering the shore with boulders and rocks of all sizes, leaving a steep slope that forced them to walk to the nearest gully to climb out.

Soon home came into view.

It looks so small, and sad.

Home was a cheaply built cabin of planks, beams, tar paper, wooden shingles, and a smokestack in the center. Seeing the smoke rising, Lily burst forward. Approaching from the rear of the property, she saw the two windows, both four-paned glass, where the two bedrooms were found. A covered porch faced east, with a new screen door over the heavy old door.

"Hey, Momma!" she called out as she stepped onto the little porch.

The screen door flung open. "Tew! Oh, my Tewapa is home!"

Winnie Weber was forty, and almost as wide as she was tall. To any zhaaganaash, she was just another Indian, but to both the Sioux and Chippewa of Minnesota, she was an outcast, born of two enemies. During a battle between the rival tribes, Lily's Chippewa grandfather had claimed a Sioux woman as slave after defeating a camp of trespassers along the edge of the Big Woods. Winnie was the result of that.

"I have Sioux cheeks," her mother had often bragged, "and also Chippewa cheeks." These remarks were often followed by a slap on her round backside. Although once a great beauty, her skill as a cook had ruined her figure.

But she gives the best hugs.

"Come, sit, let me feed you. I was just making lunch for your brother." Her mother prodded her through the doorway. "Sit, sit."

LILY DIDN'T SIT for long and soon stood side-by-side with her mother as a simple lunch turned into a feast. In ten minutes, nine months of events were summarized, for both women, and by the time Migisi joined them at the table, even details like her trunk had been discussed.

"If things went so well teaching at White Earth, I don't understand why you didn't sign another contract for next year. What are you going to do here?"

"I want to be a regular teacher."

"There's no way they're going to let you teach white children."

"Not at first, but Sister Inez at St. Marie's Catholic Church in Split Rock said I could assist her for her Sunday lessons. Apparently, most of these white kids skip school to help out on their farms, and the only education they get is after church on Sundays. She says she has her hands full."

"Does it pay?"

"No, but with a year's experience at White Earth, and a year working with white children, I'll have two legs to stand on if a good position does open up. Teaching white kids pays twice as much as working at White Earth."

"You know how things are around here. For all I know, your father could be in jail right now."

"I'll help you with the garden, then," Lily replied. "If I don't take a risk, how am I supposed to get ahead in life?"

Her mother hummed. "It would be nice to have some help, and you could help tame those squatters upstream, as well as your brother."

Migisi's busy fork stopped. "I don't need a teacher. Grandfather Nanakonan is teaching me all I need to know."

Mother and daughter shared eyerolls.

"Yes," Winnie said, "I think it will be nice having you around."

"Tew saw a ghost," Migisi announced and then continued shoveling food in his mouth.

Winnie straightened. "You did?"

"Oh, it was nothing. I was just nervous walking through the woods."

"You never used to be afraid of the woods."

"It's probably the ghost of Teddy Big Marten," Migisi remarked around a mouthful.

"Quit putting words in my mouth. It was nothing, Momma."

Winnie leaned back in her chair, eyes wide. "It wouldn't surprise me if you did encounter a ghost. It rained for three straight days."

"What does that have to do with anything?"

"Long before your father's people called this place Lake Manitou, my people once guarded these shores. Wars were fought over it."

"They protected the wild rice fields?"

"They didn't protect, they guarded. You see, to my people, this was not only a sacred place but also a cursed place. It was known as Wanagiyata, the Place of Souls. Lakes with wild rice fields are plentiful, but this place, Lake Manitou, traps any soul that dies near it, whether Chippewa, Sioux, or even Zhaaganaash. My ancestors guarded it to keep folks away from it, but when it rains, some of the souls wander away, trying to find rest in the afterlife."

"You're making this up just to frighten me," Lily said.

Migisi giggled.

Winnie shrugged. "Go ask Adam Thunder Face at the Loose Goose Saloon. Even a brute like him would know this story."

"Nanak said he's a liar," Migisi said.

Samuel Thunder Face is a liar, Lily thought. *He told me his father was taking them back to South Dakota. Otherwise I might not have—*

"Oh, Lily, don't mind me. I didn't mean to frighten you about ghosts. I need to be a better Christian, I suppose."

"Why would you want to live here if it was haunted?" Lily asked, putting thoughts of Samuel away.

"And go where? Your father's people despise me because I'm Sioux, but if I went back to South Dakota, my Sioux relatives would only see a Chippewa. If I'm cursed, I might as well live in a cursed place that nobody wants."

Except Triton.

Lily followed Migisi's example and let food cut off the conversation. When she finished, she pushed the bowl away with a sigh. "Thank you for the wonderful meal. Do you want help cleaning up or can I unpack my satchel?"

"I can manage the dishes, but when you finish unpacking, you need to go visit Grandfather Nanak. Although he won't admit it, I think he misses you."

Swallowing became difficult, so Lily meekly nodded, thinking, *I'd rather go hang out with the ghost of Teddy Big Marten.*

Revealer of Hidden Truths

Turtle Island Reservation
May 1897

LILY WAITED UNTIL just before supper to make the trek to visit her paternal grandfather. Even though he was her closest blood relative, he was strange, embracing the old ways.

"Migisi, want to come with me?"

Migisi nodded with enthusiasm. "Of course, I love visiting Grandfather."

Lily led the way. In just a few steps, they left the nurtured gardens and cabin of their mother to wander into the forty-acres of untouched woods belonging to their father.

She kept her head down, watching her feet on the worn trail. Seven miles north at Nimrod Crossing, the trail connected the land allotments given to her people. Most of the lots were only a few acres wide, leaving the best farmland for white settlers. Lily understood why she walked in shadow: anyone walking upon the trail could not be seen from the Nimrod road.

Migisi ran along the top of the bluff, which overlooked the fertile Blue Knife River. "Migisi, don't get so close."

Lily didn't need to see the Nicollet Rapids; she could hear them. Grandfather lived on the southernmost lot of the reservation, from the Nicollet Rapids to where the valley opened up to dump into Lake Manitou.

Lily spotted the single stone marking the beginning of their grandfather's lot as Migisi gradually angled back to the trail, joining her for the final stretch.

Just past the rapids, a squatty structure stood a few yards from the steep ravine. She knew the spiritual significance behind a sweat lodge, but since leaving home and having stood in several beautiful churches, she felt shame for once having held the lodge in such reverence.

"I'm being trained to be a Fire Keeper," Migisi stated suddenly.

"Don't you have to be a man?"

"Grandfather says I'm special, which is why I get to begin my training early. First, I'll learn how to be a Fire Keeper, then a Mide, and after that, a Jessakkid."

A what? Lily knew Fire Keepers were like Catholic priests, men who performed sacred rituals. A Mide was also like a priest, with duties of a doctor, judge, and historian mixed in also. Typically, it took years of training. "What is a Jessakkid?"

Migisi wrinkled his forehead. "It's someone who has been blessed by Manabozho with the ability to communicate with spirits. Nanak says the reason I can hunt and fish so well is that I can hear the spirits in nature. He says our family has a history of it. Like you sensing that ghost."

The nuns would say he's a sorcerer. "Please don't say anything to Grandfather about the ghost or it'll become uncomfortable. I just want to say hello and leave. His cabin frightens me."

It's a good thing I returned or else Migisi is going to be trapped in the past, too.

A few minutes later, the valley widened to reveal the sprawling waters of Lake Manitou. At a cabin perched on a bluff overlooking the whole seven miles of waterfront, Grandfather normally sat in a wooden chair keeping a silent vigil.

Today, he stood facing the trail.

"So you are the reason the spirits are all astir," he said once they drew close enough.

"It's good to see you also, Grandfather Nanak."

"What did they do to you at White Earth?"

Lily felt a lump in her throat and her heart began racing. *How could he know?* She calmed herself, pushing the faces from White Earth from her memory. "What do you mean?"

"Those clothes? Do they force you to wear them even when you are home?" His eyes inspected everything down to her shoes.

"I'm a teacher now, not a little girl."

"Lily Weber," Migisi said with disdain. He rushed by her and wrapped his arms around Grandfather. "Soon she'll be making me call her Miss Weber, I just know it."

"Lily Weber. Bah! Come, let me get a good look at you."

Grandfather stayed at the top step of his deck, and even with Lily standing a foot below on the first step, he barely managed to look down on her. After seven decades, life turned his skin to wrinkled leather, hunched his back, and took most of his teeth. He extended his worn hands and clamped them onto her shoulders.

She looked down while he made strange grunts and hums, contrasting his worn moccasins and her crisp boots.

"I see you wear the cross like your mother."

She nodded.

He let go and returned to his chair.

Lily and Migisi sat upon the floor of the porch in front of his chair. She glanced once into the cabin, where all manner of disgusting sights hung from the rafters and walls. Dead birds, animal hides, and skulls decorated the walls like macabre wallpaper. The rafters were a gallows of herbs and dreamcatchers.

"Did you meet the son of Tall Birch?"

"Yes, I honored your wish, but I'm not going to marry William."

"You will need to meet John LaBiche."

"John LaBiche?" Lily shook her head. "He's only—he's Migisi's age. And plus, he's our cousin."

"Our clan must be preserved through careful marriage, and a marriage to John LaBiche would produce a powerful child. My watch is almost at an end, and in another decade, our family must be prepared for the return of the Serpent Star."

"Who's John LaBiche?" Migisi asked.

"He's a student at Sacred Heart in Morris," Lily explained through gritted teeth.

"The boarding school?"

"Yes," Grandfather answered, "and in a few years, he will be a man. How does a teacher not understand the importance of preparing the next generation?"

Why does he always put me down? "John won't be able to marry me until he is released, and at the rate he's going, it might be a while." The thought of marrying him was horrible to Lily. "Who says he'd even want to marry me?"

"He will do his duty, just like all of us must."

I have a duty to help my people find a place in the future. Not marry a child. "If I am going to marry someone, it'll be a good Christian man who doesn't have dead animals and birds hanging all over his house."

Grandfather shook his head, dismissing her like usual. "There are those who serve the will of the Great Spirit, and those who dwell in darkness. Can there not be hidden truths shared by all?"

Not according to Sister Lynch.

"Tew saw a ghost on her walk through the old woods," Migisi said with a glance at Lily.

He loves Grandfather more than he loves me. I've been away too long.

Grandfather put a hand on Migisi's shoulder as if rewarding him and Lily looked away. "A ghost? Why do you think it was a ghost?"

"I didn't say it was a ghost," Lily mumbled. "I felt cold and thought I saw something move in the pine needles, but I think it was just the owl in the tree."

"This is why you must stop wasting your time learning another religion and learn the beliefs of your own people. An owl? Point to which bird it looked like." He used his walking stick to point at the dead birds hanging on the nearest cabin wall.

"Maybe it's the ghost of Teddy Big Marten," Migisi offered, receiving a stern look from Grandfather.

"Both of you must be careful, especially after strong rains. While it certainly might have been a ghost, it might have been a Tak-Pei."

No. No, I'm not listening to more of this nonsense. Lily stood. *I spent too much of my childhood terrified of the Little People of the Forest.* She took her brother by the crook of his arm and tugged him to his feet. "As much as I'd like to stay, I'm really hungry after my trip and need to help my mother with supper."

"But we—"

Lily's fingers pinched Migisi, hard.

"Wait, wait. I have something for you. Stay."

Nanakonan rose and scurried into his cabin. "This past winter, once the lake froze over, I traveled across the lake to Jiibay Hollow to gather branches from Old Willow."

Branches from Ghost Hollow? No thank you.

But Grandfather moved swiftly to the door. "Here," he said, holding out a large dreamcatcher. "If there is indeed the ghost of a dead Christian lurking around the woods, this will protect you while you sleep. Hang it in your window and it will protect you."

"I grew up surrounded by your dreamcatchers, Grandfather. I know the stories."

He didn't hand it to her but instead gave it to Migisi. "Once you are a trained Jessakkid, I will teach you how to communicate with the spirits trapped within the web, but until that day, shake the web out each morning. Understood?"

Migisi studied the new web as Lily stepped away. Unlike other dreamcatchers, Grandfather's webs were always teardrop shaped, with the thick end of the willow branch crossing the thin end to create a V-shape above the oblong loom. An assortment of feathers hung from leather straps and bits of wood, stone, and bone hung in the webbing.

Once out of sight of Grandfather, Lily stopped walking. "Tell Mother I'll be coming in about half an hour. Agreed?"

"Where are you going?"

"I'm just going to run up to Lyons to let everyone know I'm back."

"I thought you were hungry."

Lily could see the Loose Goose Saloon in the distance, and thinking of Samuel Thunder Face, her heart skipped a beat. *I am hungry, but not for food, little brother.*

The Loose Goose

Lyons, MN

May 1897

LILY STOOD IN the shadow of the white ice building, waiting for Samuel Thunder Face to step out the back door of the Loose Goose Saloon. Decades ago, the hill had been a logging camp, but the village of Lyons housed one family consisted of several old logging sheds, a small barn, a simple house, and the massive log structure known as the Loose Goose Saloon.

After a year in White Earth, she now understood why her mother insisted she never set foot near the bar. *What does it matter now? I'm no longer an innocent girl looking for love.* A few yards from Grandfather's property line and within range of the trees, she stood beside the building used to house huge blocks of ice cut from the lake and stored all summer long.

Samuel Thunder Face was a full-blooded Sioux. He had fine ebony hair that flowed down to his muscular shoulders, and had soft lips that—

When the backdoor opened, Lily's breath caught. Only it was Samuel's older sister that came stomping out, holding an empty crate. Evangeline walked directly toward the storage shed, and while she fumbled with the lock, Lily stepped away from the ice building.

Evangeline flinched when she saw Lily. A scowl settled onto her once placid face before she asked, "When did you get back?"

"Just today. I was wondering if Samuel was working tonight?"

"No, Samuel's not working." Evangeline crossed her arms. "He's at Flandreau."

South Dakota? Lily's heart stopped. "What's he doing in Flandreau?"

"Living there." Evangeline turned and headed for the saloon door. She stopped and glanced back, her expression cold. "Did you expect him to stay and wait for you? You broke his heart when you left for White Earth, and my dad didn't like him sulking. One thing led to another, and after a big fight, my dad threw him out of the house, so he went to live with family at the Flandreau reservation."

A beating had first sent Samuel into her arms, and as she had tenderly wiped away blood from his split lip and bloodied nose, he had leaned in for their first kiss. Now she bit her lip, but he wasn't there to take care of her. *How could he just leave?* "When did he go?"

"October." Evangeline shrugged. "Listen, Tew, he's moved on. He's got himself a woman now, and he's finally free from my father. Now run along before I find a rock."

Lily glanced at the back door, where a dozen small rocks were lined up on the railing of the staircase. Over the past few years, Adam Thunder Face used them to chase away children from the reservation. Migisi had a scar hidden by his hair.

Evangeline, who'd once been a friend and ally, kicked one of the rocks off the staircase toward her as a warning.

Lily retreated for the trees. After a hundred paces, she flopped down under a cedar tree and began sobbing.

The first tender kiss from a bleeding lip.

Later, the way the straw refused to let go of their hair and skin afterwards …

Did he find out what happened to me?

No, he left in October because his father drove him away. But why did he find another?

Lily heard something approaching. In that moment, it didn't matter if it was a ghost, a Tak-Pei, a serpent, or a group of drunk boys, she needed to let it all out.

Grandfather appeared in front of her.

Do the birds really speak to him?

He crouched down as she wiped her face. "They are a family of outcasts and murderers. It is good you are rid of him."

I thought we were the outcasts. Lily looked away. "Why did he go all the way to Flandreau?"

She felt a hand upon her shoulder, a gesture so tender she looked up to confirm it was indeed her grandfather. She looked down at his damaged hand, with twisted pink scars and absent fingernails. *I wonder how he got those scars. They must've hurt.* Her grandfather knew emotional pain also. Her paternal grandmother Little Wolf had died long ago in childbirth. Only now did she understand Nanak's bitterness.

Now I have scars too.

"It is good that the boy returned to the west, where he belongs. The Thunder Face boy isn't worth your tears and heartache. They are all liars and outcasts."

"Thank you, Grandfather."

"Now, stand up. You are a survivor. The blood of survivors flows in your veins. Do not let this boy claim power over you. You are the one with power."

She took his scarred hands and stood, briefly wrapping her arms around him, finding him suddenly smaller than she remembered him as a child.

"Go to your mother. She'll know what else to say."

CHAPTER FIVE

Caught in the Web

Turtle Island Reservation
June 1897

THE SPECTER OF Samuel Thunder Face was soon forgotten, and a week later, Lily had her life back in order. Her collection of cotton dresses hung up on wooden posts with her three pairs of shoes below. Her traveling bane had been retrieved and the heavy trunk now served as a desk for her collection of books given to her by Sister Inez, who'd been her inspiration for wanting to become a teacher.

After visiting her mentor in Split Rock and receiving the books, she had promised to have them all read by the following Sunday, but the nun only chuckled and said, "Assist first, then lead."

In the dresser, the drawers were stuffed by category. Underwear and stockings remained in the top drawer, out of sight of Migisi. Her casual wear used around the kitchen or at the garden filled the second drawer. The third draw held the clothing that no longer fit. The bottom drawer held her Chippewa clothing, some casual and some ceremonial.

A new start. A new me—Miss Weber.

Grandfather's dreamcatcher hung in the window of their shared bedroom and an eight-inch iron crucifix was on top of the dresser.

Balance.

Lily stepped out of her bedroom and kissed her mother on the cheek. "Would you like to plant the squash today?"

"I was just thinking that it is finally warm enough to grow, and with the clouds, we'll be sheltered from the sun. We'll get those seeds in the ground just before it rains."

Farming—the future of my people. Why don't more follow my mother's example?

The garden was tiny in comparison to the acres of open field belonging to Christopher Apple, who farmed right up to the property line of the reservation. For a family of three, the plot gave enough food to last a year, if properly preserved.

Winnie hummed hymns while she worked, and Lily joined for those she knew. Finally, she broke the humming with a question: "Why did you marry Father?"

"Because he was the most handsome boy I'd ever seen."

"But he was Chippewa."

She smiled. "So was I."

"You are only half Chippewa."

"Most of the Mille Lacs Chippewa are mixed blood, also. Or were. Doesn't seem like tribe matters any more. We're all Indians to the government."

"Back at White Earth, I met families coming from closed reservations from all over the place. Will they close this reservation?"

"It's quiet this summer, isn't it? I wouldn't worry. The Turtle Island Reservation wasn't part of the original treaties. It was different because there wasn't a council of elders or a chief to sign it away. Some French family ceded it to your grandfather during the allotment a decade ago. It was private ownership long before the government ruined everything."

So the same white people who gave the Thunder Face family a plot. "And the new law allows folks like the Gray Herons to sell it to White Men?"

"Unfortunately, that is the problem. Chippewa and Sioux had better learn to get along because soon we'll all be stuck on some lousy piece of land together." She sighed. "This will upset Nanak."

"Does he hate you because you're half-Sioux?"

"Nanak holds old grudges, but he doesn't hate all Sioux. He once had a good friend, Taopi, who was Sioux, but the Chippewa and Sioux were at war for generations"

So he probably just hates a quarter of me.

"Your grandfather probably hates Mr. Thunder Face for stealing the southernmost forty-acre plot away from our family. Nanak thinks this land is sacred."

"Why would the Thunder Face family want to live next to people who hate them? How did they end up with the land?"

"The Sioux and Chippewa fought over this territory for hundreds of years, and eventually the Chippewa people won northern Minnesota from the Sioux. A century later, Adam Thunder Face befriended a politician in St. Paul. That's how he stole forty acres from our people."

"No wonder Grandfather is bitter."

"Not that it matters now. The zhaaganaash get richer, and the natives get poorer. Soon, all of these lots will be bought up and we'll end up together in White Earth. Or Canada."

Mother and daughter went back to work, only to be interrupted a few minutes later by the sound of a horse galloping.

"Where is your brother?" Winnie asked with fear in her eyes.

"I don't know."

Her mother straightened her back and stepped forward just as a large black horse appeared from the north. "Keep your brother away."

Lily began walking toward the ravine to look for Migisi but stopped when she saw who approached.

Wearing a blackcoat as dark as his horse, Marshal Bushy Bill Morrison rode forward, his beady eyes looking at everything but the two women. Armed with a rifle strapped to his saddle, a pistol and bowie knife on his belt, and his ebony walking stick, Morrison was also looking for ghosts, but living ones.

"Hello, Winnie. How have you been?"

"How can I help you, Marshal Morrison?"

"There's a rumor that the Black Hat Gang has come south. You wouldn't be harboring criminals such as Pierre LeDuc, the Blackfish, or your husband Big Squeak in your home, would you?"

"I haven't seen my no-good husband for more than a year now, and if I did, I would advise him to turn himself in."

Morrison laughed. "I find it strange that you haven't seen him in so long when the northern plot has signs of many people camping there recently."

The summerbirds have returned, Lily reckoned, picturing the children who migrated south with their families, especially the families of her father's outlaws.

"The Turtle Island Reservation is seven miles long; I cannot be responsible for squatters *staying* on our property illegally, but I thank you for running off any unsavory characters."

"Squeak wouldn't happen to be inside, would he?"

"Feel free to search."

"If he has come south, I'm sure I'll find either him or his illegal alcohol shipments down at the Loose Goose." Morrison chewed on his lower lip as his eyes scanned the area. Satisfied, he spurred his horse. "You girls have a good day and stay out of trouble. I'd hate for you to lose this land by associating with criminals."

Not giving them a chance to reply—not that Lily or her mother would—Marshal Morrison slowly rode down the trail and out of sight.

He's targeting our family. Why does he hate us so? "Should I still go get Migisi?"

"Jananashins is not here for truancy; he assumed your father would come home for a visit now that you've returned. Fool." Winnie held her palm to the clouds, catching a raindrop. "Looks like we got these seeds in the ground just in time." She turned towards the house. "Yes, go fetch your brother."

How can she stuff away her emotions like that?

AFTER RETRIEVING MIGISI, Lily kicked her feet up onto her bed and read while the storm opened up. It continued through lunch and supper, with Migisi watching on the front porch for most of it. Although the storm lessened near evening, the thick clouds brought dusk earlier than normal, and Lily's tired eyes surrendered to an early sleep.

Yet she couldn't sleep. Although the thoughts of Samuel Thunder Face no longer joined her in bed and kept her up like they did the previous summer, the mystery surrounding the death of Teddy Big Marten filled her mind instead.

When the lightning flashed, she could see the silhouette of the dreamcatcher in the window.

Did I really encounter his ghost? Or was it something else?

The owls offered no answers, and the other birds would be silent until morning. There were no wolves or coyotes howling, or even the shrill sound of crickets. *We're all alone out here. If I screamed, who would even hear me? Is that the point Bushy Bill was making? Was he trying to frighten Mother to a reservation with more of her people?*

Lily sighed and closed her eyes to the ripples of lightning in the clouds. The storm was building slowly, and from high above, a few rumbles shook the air. Light gusts that carried cold air swept around the cabin. Instead of violent lightning strikes and blasts of wind, the storm began to boil.

Then a scream pierced the slow crescendo.

Is someone outside in the storm?

She rushed to the window, her nose bumping the webbing of the dreamcatcher. Like a discharge of static electricity, Lily felt a strange surge pass through her body.

"Save us!" a child screamed, but instead of seeing the ravine out the window, she saw past it to Lake Manitou, where children screamed from an island of ice.

In the chessboard of ice chunks, a pair of black horns ripped through the water as the monstrous Horned Serpent circled around them.

At first, the cries for help brought memories of the children she knew at the Sacred Heart Mission. Her hand once supported by the cabin wall transformed and she found herself leaning into the dormitory door.

"Save us, Lily. It's trying to kill us," the children cried out, but they were not her students from the school at White Earth either.

The scene shifted again, cold air and snow greeted her instead of rain as she was once back in the cabin, half leaning out the window.

Blinking, Lily then found herself at the edge of the lake.

"Lily, help!"

Hearing their terror, she began to leap from plate to plate like a game of hopscotch. When she grew near, a chasm too far to leap existed between her and the children.

Then she understood who they were.

Some had short hair, long hair, blonde hair, and even green hair. The clothing was also bizarre and foreign, but all of them, both the boys and the girls—all had her eyes. She stared at a dozen variations of herself. "Who are you?"

"You have to save us," they cried out in unison.

"It's too far. I don't know what to do!" Lily watched in horror as the black horns of the water serpent created a wake that pushed them farther apart.

A young boy stepped forward, standing on the edge of the ice. "Don't worry, Lily. It's better that one of us should die so that the others can live."

To Lily's horror, the boy threw himself into the frigid water. As he fell, the lake turned into a vortex that pulled both chunks of ice closer. Lily reached down to grab hold of the boy, but as she did, his flesh transformed into blue clay that fell apart in her hands.

The distance between her and the smaller children had her gasping. She lept towards them, unable to extract them from the water. "How do I get you to safety?"

They all turned and pointed to the island, which was not a real island but simply the back of a monstrous turtle. At the center of the island, a fire burned beside a small rock that glowed with equal brilliance. In the warm center of the fire, animals gathered, spaced evenly around it like numbers on a strange clock. A sly marten with long fur, a slender doe with regal eyes, a big loon rested upon its thick chest were there. Also a tall white crane stood upon its long legs, a large bear with auburn fur shifted upon its clawed paws, and a raven and a bald eagle stretched their wings yet did not take flight. Lastly a big snapping turtle with spots as radiant as stars upon its shell stretched its long neck to look at her.

The animals began shapeshifting into human forms. Some she recognized as her new students from St. Marie's Catholic Church, but others were strangers—a boy with green hair, two little twin girls dressed in bright yellow, a strawberry blonde, a girl with pigtails, an angry boy with a scar on his jaw, and a calm boy with strange gray eyes.

And Migisi.

"Stay where you are," Migisi shouted from the back of the turtle. "I will kill the Horned Serpent myself."

Instead of rushing away from the water serpent as it neared, Migisi jumped toward it. As if afraid of his approach, the creature vanished below the surface, but then it reappeared from under the large ice island, tossing the stranded children into the water. While Migisi chased after the horns, Lily rushed toward the children, whose arms reached out of the water for her. But each time that she reached down, the children slipped below the surface.

"You can't kill the Horned Serpent," a voice whispered. "You can only set it free."

I don't want to set it free.

Lily reached for a drowning child, only to knock the blanket off her bed. She'd never stood up to look at the window—it had all been a dream.

She rose looking at the source of the chaos—the dreamcatcher.

"What? Who's there?" Migisi called out, not from the waters but from his bed beside where she stood at the bedroom window.

"Lily! Did you hear that?" Migisi asked. "There's someone else in the room."

Lily's flesh tingled as she once again took a survey of the room. Her dresses now hovered like phantoms. The dresser became a dark pit leading to the underworld. At the window—

The feathers moved, and on the other side of the dreamcatcher, she saw a horned figure staring back at her.

A Stopping Place

Turtle Island Reservation
June 1897

FAWN CHEVREUIL OUTLASTED the storm and now knew she had to act. She tossed the wet blanket off her cold body and threw the useless tarp aside, revealing the cold, dark dawn. Her younger sister pulled the wet pillow over her face, using it as a shield from the reality they'd woken to. The campfire had been turned to ash, and the wood black and cold.

On the other side of the dead fire, the LaBiche tent fared better, with its ropes still holding it taut. *They probably slept through the whole ordeal.*

But the third tent, the LeDuc tent, had completely collapsed, leaving four lumps on the ground. Between the lumps, pools of water collected, slowly seeping through to the bodies underneath.

Fawn took hold of the loose ropes and peeled the tarp back slowly, so the water ran to the sides.

"Mama?"

"No, sweetie, it's just Fawn."

The little LeDuc boy looked as if he hadn't slept a wink. "Where's my mama?"

Where are any of the adults?

"Your mama had to run up to Leech Lake, remember?" She tried to smile, knowing Bushy Bill had scattered the adults to unknown destinations. "Now I know it's early, but I'm going to get some hot food for all of us, understand?" At his nod she added, "Help me hang up the blankets so they'll dry by tonight."

"I'm hungry," one of the LaBiche children said from the opening of their tent.

"We'll get food soon. Did you stay dry?"

"My feet got wet."

That figures. Fawn clapped her hands, and soon all seven kids were either sitting, standing, or helping to hang the wet blankets.

"I hate this place," Christine LeDuc said bitterly. At ten, she was second in command but quite worthless.

The summerbirds now look like drowned rats. Fighting a sigh, Fawn said, "I know our folks told us to stay put, but we're all cold and hungry, so I'm going to take you on a little hike, and in an hour, we'll be warm and dry with full bellies, okay?"

I'm in charge, and there is no sense sitting in wet clothes around a cold fire pit.

Looking to the sky, she saw the clouds breaking to reveal a blue sky. They needed to get moving.

The wooded trail was easy travel, and from Nimrod Crossing, it could be jogged in under an hour, but with a flock of agitated children, it took every bit of patience to finish the trek.

Her faith was rewarded with the smell of bacon.

When the children saw the cabin, they ran the final hundred yards, not even waiting to knock on the front door.

Lily Weber stood at the rear of the cabin with her brother Migisi, who ran around the cabin to see all of his kin.

Despite the long night, Fawn smiled at her eldest cousin. "Aaniin."

"Haw mushkay," Lily answered in Sioux with a wry smile. "We heard there were squatters camping upstream. It's good to see that my little summerbirds have returned."

Even in her nightgown, Lily looked like an angel, and Fawn envied her height, her beautiful straight hair, her slender form, and her welcoming eyes. Lily's mixed blood made her almost regal, but Fawn's mixed blood made her ugly in both worlds. Compared to Lily, Fawn almost looked white. She even had dark freckles on her cheeks, and her mother cut her curly, sandy hair short, tucked into pigtails. "I didn't know you were home."

"Well, White Earth was awful, so I'm going to help teach farm kids at St. Marie's for a year until I can find a better job or a husband. And don't ask me about Samuel Thunder Face or John LaBiche."

"Fine, I won't ask," Fawn said. Turning, she frowned, trying to make sense of the scene before her. A spear, broken glass, an eight-inch iron cross, and a broken dreamcatcher all rested on the ground beneath the rear bedroom window. "What happened here?"

"How do I even begin," Lily muttered, picking up the metal cross. "We had some spooky stuff happen during the storm." She pointed to a piece of wood over one of the windowpanes. "Things got crazy and I broke the window by accident, so we had to fix the window before we got breakfast." Lily paused to fling the broken frame of a dreamcatcher toward the ravine. "You look like a drowned muskrat. Let's get you some food."

BY MIDMORNING, FAWN sat on a stone outcropping, dangling legs with Lily as they watched Migisi fishing with his spear in the eddies of the river. Above their heads, the real summer birds flitted in the branches while the herons and cranes fished in the river; all of it was observed by the silent ravens in the oak trees.

"Was my father with everybody else?" Lily asked.

"No, but I think he was planning on meeting his whole gang before Bushy Bill found out. Blackfish, Pierre LeDuc, and my father were the first to arrive. My mom took off for Leech Lake, and the rest of the women went to warn their husbands."

"They'll probably all run back to Canada now. I only saw him once last summer."

"I wish I only saw my father once a year. Your father is really funny, my dad is mean."

"Funny? I guess I've only seen 'mean' also."

Fawn found herself distracted by Migisi, who stalked his prey in the river. Migisi raised his spear behind his ear and froze. A second later, it plunged into the water and vanished. Its butt reappeared for a moment, prompting Migisi to jump in after.

"What an idiot," Lily said.

He's not an idiot—Migisi is amazing. Even though Migisi was younger than Fawn, he didn't act like a foolish boy. He seemed years older than the others. Two generations before Old Nanak, the Weber family and Chevreuil family trees joined, making the reservation their summer home, but for Fawn, Migisi was potentially husband material. *One day.*

A moment later, he emerged from the water holding a fish almost as long as his spear. Fawn jumped to her feet and ran down to see his three-foot trophy brought to shore.

"What is it?" Fawn asked as the bleeding creature was thrown onto the rocks.

"It's a gar." He grinned when he locked eyes with Fawn. "We can eat it for lunch." He glanced at Lily. "Make sure it doesn't flop into the water, Tew."

A moment later, he hopped back out to his perch, looking for another fish.

"So what happened with the dreamcatcher?" Fawn pressed Lily since she was told not to ask about boys from White Earth.

"Migisi and I thought we heard voices coming from it, so I grabbed Migisi's spear from the corner and stabbed it, which is how I broke the glass. Then I threw it outside and put my cross on it until daylight came to drive any spirits away."

"The spirits talked to you," Fawn declared without judgment. "My dad said that's why Squeak will never be caught. He said the water, wind, and earth whispers to your father. He said your side of the family is special."

Fawn's gaze returned to Migisi when Lily scoffed.

"Well, my father's an illegal bootlegger that sells alcohol to his own people, so don't put him on too high of a pedestal. And don't believe the stories all the old men tell around campfires. Once you hear that stuff, you begin imagining things."

From the river, Migisi let out a startled cry, and without even looking, he tossed his spear toward the shore.

"Be careful!" Lily shouted at him, but the toss had only freed him so he could dive into the water.

"Migisi!" Lily called, but Migisi did not emerge.

Ten yards downstream, Migisi popped up long enough for Lily to shout out his name again. Then he was wrestling with something—

A creature emerged with him.

Does he have it, or does it have him?

Fawn picked up the spear, ready to help, and stood beside Lily at the water's edge.

Finally, Migisi came out of the river dragging a monstrous snapping turtle by the tail. *He's so brave.*

"What are you going to do with that thing?" Lily asked.

"Look how big it is!" Migisi beamed, as the creature's long, thick neck reached back across its shell in an attempt to bite at his fingers. "I could make a shield with the shell."

"Why would you need a shield?"

"For when I fight the Horned Serpent," Migisi said, chuckling as the massive turtle dragged its claws into the riverbank. Lily's face paled, sharing no enthusiasm for the omen.

She's changed since White Earth. Fawn offered the spear, but Migisi reached for a rock to crush the monster's head.

One day he'll be a leader of our people. If I married him, my children would be able to fit in.

Lily didn't smile as her brother finally accepted the spear to finish off the wounded monster. "A Jessakkid wouldn't hurt a turtle. This is awful."

"This is the magic I've been praying for," Migisi countered.

"You're hopeless." Lily picked up the gar and walked back up the hill.

"Do you want help?" Fawn asked Migisi.

"Nope, I can carry it ... I think."

Lily stopped a few yards away, and then crouched down.

Fawn walked towards her. "What's that?" She saw something glistening and white in the mud beside where Lily stopped.

Migisi turned to where the mud met the grass. "Turtle eggs?"

"Was that a *mother* turtle?" Fawn asked. *Does a boy turtle have a penis?*

"Grow up. It's not like she was going to milk her babies."

"They aren't eggs." Lily pried one up with her finger and handed one to Fawn. Even caked in mud, it was gorgeous. "I think it's some sort of oyster. It looks almost like a pearl."

"Or a snail," Migisi offered.

"The rain must've uncovered them." Lily grabbed a nearby stick and unearthed handfuls of the shells.

"Maybe some old Mide dropped them here," Migisi said. "Bring them with; I want to show Grandfather."

"Here, put them in the fold of my dress," Lily offered, and Fawn began scooping them up.

Migisi dragged the snapping turtle up the hill as they uncovered two dozen shells.

On top of the ravine, the younger children played in front of the cabin. Seeing Migisi, the LeDuc children hollered and hooted so loudly that even the ravens took flight. Migisi, looking pleased, dropped the monster on the ground so the children could gawk at it.

Fawn picked up the gar under the gills and followed Lily, who still carried the shells.

"What a beauty," Winnie marveled at the fish as she stepped outside. "Put the gar in the sink. I'll make him for lunch."

"Migisi has a snapping turtle the size of a wagon wheel," Fawn said, turning. "He thinks he is going to make it into a shield for when he fights the Horned Serpent."

"The Unktehi?" Winnie said to Lily, using the Sioux name. "Now that you are home for the summer, do your best to keep him away from the river. It's dangerous."

"I'll try," Lily said with a defeated look before lifting the folds of her dress. "Look what else we found." She showed Winnie the pile of shells. "What are they?"

"The Chippewa elders call them megis shells, but they are cowry shells. Where did you find these?"

"Down by the river," Migisi said, coming towards them.

"Curious. I'm going to wash these up," Winnie said, reaching for the shells. "Afterwards, I want you to show your grandfather what you found. I think it might be important."

CHAPTER SEVEN

Bread Crumbs

Turtle Island Reservation
June 1897

MIGISI ASIBIKAASHI REMEMBERED to say a prayer before he gutted the massive snapping turtle, thanking it for its flesh. And then his knife carved the flesh from inside of the shell. The summerbirds watched as his forearms became coated in blood and gore. He handed the good chunks of flesh to Christine LeDuc, who held his mother's metal serving plate.

Two omens in one day, he thought as his arm reached into the cavity of the turtle shell. *This is what Grandfather Nanak was waiting for.*

"I want the guts for the garden," his mother said as she directed the other children on where to bury them. "Fawn, go fetch a pail of water for cleaning."

Tew was still inside, allowing him to clean the turtle without guilt.

With the sacred shell of a turtle as a shield, I'll be a match for the Horned Serpent. And neither ghosts nor the Tak-Pei will dare show themselves.

He scraped the shell clean, formulating a plan on how to cut the shell in half and then reinforce the interior so that the rough top shell would stay together in a battle.

It'll be awesome.

"Done," he said to Christine, putting down the last bits of flesh. She nodded and carried the platter of flesh into the house.

Fawn returned with the bucket and a smile as Migisi gave the shell a pat. It bothered him that she was almost a foot taller than him now and her freckled face was always smiling. "Thanks."

He quickly rubbed his arms until his flesh was visible again and then flicked his arms to shed the water, getting Fawn wet in the process. *That stole her smile.*

Proud of that accomplishment, he strutted into the house, a victorious warrior, only to see Tew at the table with his other prize—the megis shells.

She's going to claim them as her prize—they're my omen.

He scooped up a handful from the table. Now washed, the white shells held all sorts of intricate glory. From the iridescent shimmer on the top of the shell to the tiny ridges in the creased bottom, they were indeed a beauty to behold.

"None of them had borne holes," Tew explained.

"So?" He let his handful of shells cascade back into the pile.

"In order to put them into a necklace, shawl, or onto clothing, you have to bore a little hole into them with a strong needle or pointed knife. These are untouched."

"Maybe it was a colony that got buried by a mudslide."

"These are tropical snails, dummy. They didn't just crawl to Minnesota. Somebody had to bring them here."

A necklace would be cool. "Mother, can you make them into a necklace?"

"Show them to your grandfather first."

Tew had them all drying on a towel, so Migisi reached down, grabbed the corners and gathered them up like a bag. "I will."

And out the door he went.

"Hey," Tew called out and quickly caught up to him, but not before barking at the other children: "You stay here."

Why does she hate Grandfather Nanak so much? It started when she insisted on being called Lily instead of Tewapa. It grew worse after she was baptized, and after going to school, she acted like he was a diseased skunk. *What happened to my sister?*

Even though Tewapa's legs were twice as long, he kept a hurried pace all the way, which kept her from nagging him about anything and everything.

Grandfather also had a small garden, and he was outside in it, leaning on his tall staff as they approached.

"So tell me about the dreamcatcher," Grandfather greeted. "Did you see anything in it?"

"I heard something," Migisi said, "but Tew wrecked it already."

"Wrecked it?"

"She tore the webbing with my spear and then threw it out the window during the storm. I didn't get a chance to ask it any questions." Grandfather shot Tewapa a dirty look, and for a moment, Migisi thought he might strike her with his staff. He held out the shells, uncovering them. "Today we found something along the bank of the river—megis shells."

Grandfather carefully studied each of the white shells in the pile placed in front of him, his mouth forming a deeply ridged pout. Despite his age, his scarred fingers were deft and steady as he handled one. "Do you see the shape of each shell?"

Migisi nodded.

"It is shaped like the back of a turtle to remind us of what we are looking for. These shells are meant to guide us along the path. They were left for us to find them."

"By a shapeshifting rabbit?" Tewapa asked.

Migisi clenched his teeth at the insult. Manabozho was sent by the Great Spirit to teach the Ojibwe, especially about the spiritual path of the Midewiwin. Although the shapeshifting god occasionally took the form of a trickster rabbit in tales, his teachings were at the heart of Grandfather's religious beliefs.

Grandfather's pout turned into a snarl, and he threw one of the shells at her, bouncing it off her chest.

"Heretics are not welcome in my house. I once had a granddaughter blessed with the name of Tewapa Asibikaashi, and now I see only a Christian named Lily Weber standing before me. Who are you?"

She held her head high. "I'm Lily Weber."

"Wait outside, Lily the Christian, until you can respect our sacred traditions."

Grandfather took Migisi by the shoulder and guided him to the cabin, leaving Tew behind.

"It's an omen, isn't it? Does this mean I can begin more training?"

Not answering him, Nanak set the bag of shells upon the table and went for his coffee pot, pouring himself a serving into a tin cup. He sat at the chair, staring at the shells. "Tell me how you found these."

Migisi started the story with the gar, then detailed his fight with the snapping turtle, and then described how the shells were encased in dirt, barely exposed. "Could they be your grandfather's shells? Or your great-grandfather's?"

"Chief Wiyipisiw? It is possible, but any megis shells they wore would have had puncture marks. These shells are unmolested. It means…"

Migisi watched with open mouth as Grandfather suddenly began to cry, the tears running down angular lines in his deep wrinkles.

"What's wrong?"

Grandfather looked at his scarred hands, his thumb crossed over the missing fingernails. "My father Chagobay died protecting the secrets of our family, and he once walked the same riverbed as you, but Manabozho did not intend for him to find the shells. *You were meant to find them.*"

TWO HOURS LATER, hungry for his cooked gar, Migisi left the house with a spinning head. His feet no longer walked upon the earth but seemed to float in the past and future. Tew waited on a large boulder. As children, they shared all their adventures together, and even though she was changing, he wanted to share this one with her too.

She'll always be Tewapa to me. Migisi handed her a shell, which she studied quietly before asking, "Any answers?"

"He thinks it is the fulfillment of an ancient prophecy."

"What is it this time, oh Great Thunderbird?"

Migisi smiled at her sarcasm. "He says it is part of the Seven Fires Prophecy."

"What's that?"

"Apparently, a prediction from a long, long time ago. The shells are some sort of clue."

"Another long-winded story, huh?"

Migisi nodded. "Our people once lived along the Atlantic when they were visited by prophets."

"Let me guess … and a big talking rabbit?"

"Do you want to hear the story or not?" Migisi grumbled. At her silence, he began again. "The prophets warned that doom and destruction would come upon the people if they did not leave their homeland in search of a new home. Each prophecy was called a 'Fire' and it represented not only a time period for our people but also a stopping place."

"A stopping place?"

"Yeah, do you remember that story about the girl with the red blanket who left pieces of bread behind her?"

"Hansel and Gretel left breadcrumbs, not Little Red Riding Hood." She shrugged. "What about it?"

Why does she think she knows everything? "Well, it was kinda like that but in reverse. Our ancestors had no idea where the prophets wanted them to go, but they were given clues. The hunters went out looking for megis shells, and when they found some, they would move the whole village to the new location."

"Wait a second, are you telling me Grandfather believes gnomes or Tak-Pei or Memegwesi left the shells for us to find?"

Migisi raised his eyebrows and gave a little shrug. "You said it yourself … you've never seen a clam or snail anywhere around here with a shell like that, have you?"

Tew shook her head.

"The megis shells led our people to the Six Stopping Places, but none of the elders could agree upon where the actual Seventh Stopping Place was. Some thought it was Mille Lacs, others thought it was Fond du Lac, and others thought it was further west at Turtle Mountain in North Dakota."

Tew sighed. "And Grandfather thinks they were all wrong?"

Migisi nodded. "His great-grandfather Wiyipisiw came here because he thought Lake Wanagiyata of the Sioux was the Seventh Stopping Place."

"You do realize how crazy that sounds? Magic fairies leaving behind a trail of white shells … So what? What were our people supposed to find at the end of the rainbow?"

Who said anything about a rainbow? "I don't know. Apparently, I have to be trained first before he can tell me more."

"Trained to do what?"

"I don't know. He thinks finding the megis shells was a good omen and that I have a powerful destiny ahead of me."

"Yeah, but *you* didn't find the shells," Tew reminded. "You were busy with the snapping turtle. I was the one who found the shells."

Sugar Coated

Old Copper Road
June 6, 1897

THAT SUNDAY LILY Weber did not take "no" for an answer. She stood beside Migisi's bed until he threw off the covers with a huff.

"Fine, but there had better be desserts."

"There will be. Now put these on." Lily handed him a new pair of trousers she'd sewn and a pair of repurposed shoes.

"I hate wearing shoes. Why do I have to wear them?"

"Because you're coming to church with me in Split Rock."

"Split Rock? To the big church?" Migisi muttered as he worked the buttons of the white shirt. "I'll go with you, but only to protect you. Don't expect me to go inside."

A small victory.

Winnie's home church was several miles west, which meant she had already departed. She often became more devout whenever Father appeared, so the rumors of his return fueled a renewed dedication, especially on a beautiful summer morning. Unfortunately, the little country church had no Sunday school classes, which forced Lily to break with her mother's tradition.

Lily and Migisi did not talk much as they walked four miles to the town of Split Rock. She looked up at the rising sun and the golden sky. *Getting him out of the shadow of Grandfather Nanak is good. Bringing him to civilization and church is a good thing.*

Migisi, however, took his protective duty seriously, studying any danger, real or imagined, along the road.

The two steeples in Split Rock could be seen from almost two miles away. Lily smiled at the sight. "You really should come inside with me. From the balcony, you can see all the stained-glass paintings, and the pipe organ is so loud you can feel it on your skin."

"I'll find a tree to sit under. Trees are holier than your stack of bricks."

When they arrived in the logging town, Split Rock was still sleeping, allowing the Weber children to shuffle up the streets to the safety of the two churches. While St. John was predominantly Scottish immigrants who attended First Presbyterian, Split Rock was mostly Scandinavian immigrants, with First Lutheran led by Pastor Krogstad and St. Marie's Catholic led by Father Hebert.

Migisi found his tree, and Lily found her newest church home.

For most farming families, chores needed to be done before hitching up the wagon to come to town, and for that reason, church began late in the morning. A trip to town on Sunday meant the families would socialize for hours, and for the most ardent farmers, it was the only chance to get an education as well.

While the bells pealed, the organ played and the congregation sang, Migisi waited outside as Lily prepared the classroom.

WITH CATHOLIC MASS taking place inside St. Marie's, Lily peeked out the classroom window from time to time. She marveled at how many wagons parked between the two churches, bringing hundreds of residents into a single city block. She located her brother under the shade of a pine tree; Migisi whittled a branch to the nub and then picked up another. *Next time I'll get him to come inside. This is a first step.*

As the closing song began, Sister Inez burst into the classroom in a flutter of black fabric. Even though her dark habit left only her face exposed, she had an attractive one with bright eyes and thin lips. Sister Inez and other nuns often visited the reservation, which is how they first met several summers ago. She took her place at the front of the classroom before the first student quietly arrived.

Sister Inez ran the show, leaving Lily to silently and meekly assist her as she taught the most illiterate children of Hiawatha County. Despite compulsory attendance at the local public school, most of the farm families ignored the law, leaving Sunday school as the sole source of education during the week.

"Miss Lily, run to the closet and fetch some more chalk please," Sister Inez directed once the children had settled into their lesson.

Miss Lily ... The words put a smile on her face.

Even though fetching chalk for Sunday school classes was a step backward for Lily, she hoped it would pave the way for her to become a teacher at one of the local public schools. *With a semester of teaching at White Earth, and a summer of teaching white students at a church, I'll have a chance at getting a real teaching job somewhere besides a reservation. Granted, it'll probably be some small country school, but a year teaching out in the country will open doors to me being able to teach at—*

She crashed face first into the chest of a stranger. The suddenness of it caused her to scoot backwards into the hallway wall and drop the box of chalk.

"Ouf! My apologies," the man said.

Not answering, Lily quickly looked to her toes, then to the box of chalk, and then to the feet of the stranger. She almost ran back to the classroom, but the man knelt down to pick up the box, revealing him to be a priest.

Definitely not Father Hebert.

This priest was tall, handsome, and lean, as if a soldier had simply donned the robes of a priest. His face was decades younger than Father Hebert, and behind his circular glasses, his eyes studied her intently. "You must be the young woman helping Sister Inez."

Young woman, Lily melted. *Not an Indian, not a girl. He called me a young woman.* She felt her ears heat.

As soon as he picked up and extended the box of chalk to her, she snatched it away and hustled by without saying a word. Her heart pounded so hard that she had to pause outside of the classroom just to compose herself.

She returned to the classroom to find Sister Inez standing with a ruler in hand beside the desk of Frankie Auerbach.

"Here is the chalk," she softly announced before walking over to the window.

She glanced out to see Migisi still whittling away. Just as she was turning from the window, she saw the tall priest step outside. He locked his hands behind his back as if observing a painting at a museum. When he looked up to the window, Lily jumped away to join Sister Inez in monitoring the students.

Albert Fisher eyed her cautiously and Bjorn Forsberg called out specifically for Sister Inez's help. Emily MacPherson didn't seem to care about the distinct difference in Lily's skin tone; she asked enough questions to keep Lily occupied.

When the two-hour session ended, and the children ran out to the picnic tables for lunch with their families, Sister Inez transformed from a statue into a mentor. "You did very well today. You stayed out of the way like I asked, but you provided gentle assistance just like I asked, too. Having an extra set of eyes on the boys helps me immensely. What did you think?"

"It was different from White Earth."

"I can imagine. It's hard for me to believe they'd leave someone your age alone with a room full of children."

Lily didn't know how to answer so she began to help clean up. Sister Inez joined her, and in a few short minutes, they were done. Then Lily approached Sister Inez. "Th-there was a priest downstairs by the supply cupboards."

"Ah, you met Father Guerin."

"He startled me."

"He keeps his belongings downstairs. You think he's here stealing supplies from us?" Sister Inez joked.

"No … I … just … What's he doing here?"

"Truth be told, he is a bit of a mystery to me. He's a Jesuit and a guest of the bishop."

"Is he going to replace Father Hebert?"

"I certainly hope not. Jesuits are different from regular priests. A long time ago, Jesuits were more like warrior priests, serving as missionaries and spies. What he is doing here in Hiawatha County baffles me. He mostly sits up in the balcony reading books during the week. From what Father Hebert said, Father Guerin has powerful friends both in St. Paul and in Washington D.C."

A warrior? Why is he here in Hiawatha County? "Powerful friends?"

"A friend of mine at the Diocese offices in St. Cloud said he had recently been sent to the Philippines and Cuba. His most recent mail is being forwarded from a Georgetown address near the capitol." Sister Inez stepped closer. "I don't know if I completely trust the man, so stay out of his way, understand?"

Lily nodded.

THE HANDSOME JESUIT priest crept into Lily's dreams, but not in the way her broken heart might have hoped. She found herself lost in a gnarled, black forest, similar to the woods along Old Copper Road south of Split Rock. The twisted fingers of oak trees reached down, snagging wisps of her hair as she ran. Fighting the trees, she spun around, and soon the road back into Split Rock disappeared.

"Do not despair," Father Guerin soothed, stepping out from behind a tree. "I know the path of the Seven Fires. I can help you find your way home." He bent down, picked up a shell, and showed it to her.

"It's just a stupid shell. It doesn't mean anything," Lily replied. "It doesn't—" Her protest stopped as a neat little white line of shells appeared, making a path.

They followed it, Father Guerin rambling incessantly about each of the stopping places of the Seven Fires, unaware of the shadows following them, until Lily couldn't take any more. "Quiet. Can't you see where we are? We are walking the shores of Lake Manitou, the *Place of Souls.*"

But it was too late.

The wailing women from her mother's tales had found them.

The black shadows of the trees took the shape of a dozen Sioux women, each slightly resembling her mother. But they were not women; they were ghouls holding their own heads like bloody lanterns.

"You should not have come here," one of the severed heads said to Guerin. "Now we have no other choice."

"Run!" Lily screamed to Father Guerin, whose eyes grew wide with terror before he turned.

But he could not outrun the specters following him.

No one in her mother's tales ever did.

Passing by Lily, the crazed ghouls shouted at Guerin, "Give us back the children!"

Running, out of breath, Lily got further and further behind them.

At a clearing in the forest, one of the women threw her head, knocking Father Guerin off balance and onto the floor of the forest. He tried rising to his feet, but the others hurled their heads at him until he fell battered to the ground.

Lily watched, feeling helpless.

He tried rising again. But this time, a black serpent rose from the edge of the cliff, snatching Father Guerin into its toothy jaws and dragging him to Lake Manitou.

"Don't worry," Father Guerin shouted to her. "I know how to save the children."

But then the Horned Serpent swallowed him down its toothy gullet.

GASPING, LILY JOLTED awake. She looked over to see Migisi still sleeping. Her heart pounded and her back was moist from sweat. *I thought I was past this damn dream.* She debated on waking him for a few minutes. *No. It'll only make things worse for him ... for me.*

Lily turned to her side to face the wall and feigned sleep, but instead of pleasant dreams about the young priest, she kept thinking of the children, and how all their faces looked like hers.

CHAPTER NINE

Puppets on a String

Turtle Island Reservation
June 10, 1897

WITH MONSTERS AND ghosts lingering in the shadows, the patterns of summer soon filled Lily's days with menial duties, lots of reading, and too much time to ponder the meaning of things, especially the secrets of her home.

Finding the shells had turned into a catastrophe, as Migisi spent entire days with Grandfather Nanak now. Worse, her little brother was tight-lipped about what was discussed, and no amount of Sunday sugar could coax it out of him. Desperate to keep her brother under her wing, Lily indulged a shared interest—the ghost of Teddy Big Marten.

She thought it went well, until Migisi carried another dreamcatcher home like a trophy—Lily intercepted him before their mother could see it.

"It's probably a good thing you have two names," Migisi said after pulling the dreamcatcher away from her outstretched hand. "I don't understand how you can be Christian Lily one day and Tewapa the next."

"What's wrong with having an open mind?"

"Being cursed. If Teddy Big Marten is now a ghost, it's because the Great Spirit is punishing him for becoming a Christian. Let that be a lesson to you." He handed her the dreamcatcher.

"And if it's not Teddy Big Marten?"

Migisi shrugged. "So what's your plan?"

Lily kept the second dreamcatcher close then turned and began walking toward the river. "First, we hang it on the other side of the river. Grandfather once said something about water acting like a barrier for spirits." She paused. "Oh! That reminds me, I've been reading Psalms lately, a book of song in the Bible, and there is a place of the dead called Sheol, which seems to be either in the water or is the water."

"Huh?" Migisi grunted.

"Our Chippewa ancestors believe four days after death, a spirit ascends into the River of Souls."

"But the River of Souls is in the stars."

"But still a river, just like Sheol."

He shrugged.

"Both times we saw a ghost, it was right after a storm, right? And we know how our ancestors felt the lake had a connection to spirit, right?"

"And a Horned Serpent."

Images of the Horned Serpent devouring both her brother and Father Guerin filled her mind. "Well … forget about that for a minute. In both religions, spirits are supposed to go to the next place, but what if spirits get stuck? When it rains, they can wander away a bit, but still end up right back at the water. What if something keeps them from crossing over?"

Migisi smiled. "Now you're sounding like Tew again."

Lily recoiled at the comment. *Am I?* "Grandfather said the dreamcatcher is designed to trap evil spirits in the net, so they don't harm children, but what if the spirit we saw was trying to talk to us? It tried to warn us about trying to kill the Horned Serpent. I know you heard it, too."

Migisi shook his head. "Which is why you shouldn't have wrecked the loom and thrown it out the window."

"I'm sorry. I heard a strange voice in my bedroom … of course I wasn't going to react rationally." Taking a deep breath, Lily continued. "What if this time we can bring it out in the woods, hang it from a tree, and try again? We can wake up in the morning, before the sun, and see if we've caught something."

A wrinkle appeared on her brother's brow. "Like fishing—yes, I understand."

LILY AND MIGISI crossed the river, which was already lower than days ago, and walked past the ruins of the Gray Heron homestead, deeper into the old forest. Lily studied the twisted willow and sinew that came into view, wondering how the old magic worked the first time. "Is this far enough? Going in any further would just be foolish."

"I suppose," Migisi said, looking around. "But let's hang it over here in the shadows so the light doesn't burn away the evil spirits."

Lily felt goosebumps on her arms as she followed her brother into the cool shadows. As soon as she hung it, she felt relief. "Now promise we'll only check it together, to watch out for each other, so nothing bad happens to us."

"Agreed."

Lily stepped back. "That should do the trick, right?"

"I guess. Grandfather only showed me how to make them. He didn't talk about how to catch things with them."

Leaving the forest, Lily found comfort in the sun.

"It's hot," Migisi said. "We should go down to the sandbars and swim."

"Seriously? You want to swim in 'Spirit' Lake after we had a spirit in our bedroom? No way. Not until we find out if it's evil. I just want to get home."

"What's the difference between wading through the water and swimming? It's all the same water."

"Look, I want answers, too, but I just don't want to press our luck."

A horse whinny filled the air.

Not good, not good, not good.

"Did you hear that?"

"It came from the lake. Let's get out of here."

Lily avoided a full run, but she knew they were trespassing on Triton land now, and horses meant zhaaganaash. She grabbed Migisi by the arm and pulled him back toward the river.

Once they reached the Gray Heron property, she sighed with relief, until she saw the top of hats floating on the horizon of the ravine. Grabbing Migisi again, she jerked him down to hide behind the foundation of the old stable and put a finger to his lips.

Adam Thunder Face throws rocks. These men could do far worse.

Men of the Dawn

The Blue Knife River
June 10, 1897

HALVAR DOBIE PATIENTLY endured the tour of the newly acquired property. Bushy Bill Morrison, the local henchman, dismounted his big black horse and climbed upon a boulder in the river to explain the plans. Walter Stewart, a local merchant, held Morrison's horse along with his own along the shore.

"Wouldn't it be easier to get some dynamite and turn these boulders to rubble?" Ozias Haggard shouted down from the high bank. Like Stewart, Haggard was another local, but of the three Men of the Dawn, his bloodline was the oldest.

The three local businessmen hosted Dobie and Ira Douglas, with Bushy Bill Morrison serving as the tour guide.

"You're missing the point," Phillip Marquette answered. He was the third local businessman who'd married into the family business. Although his bloodline was the youngest, he grasped the bigger picture of what was happening in Hiawatha County. Marquette looked to Dobie before finishing his point. "The dam isn't just to streamline the logging."

"Then why did Triton invest in those pineries up north by Leech Lake?" Walter Stewart asked.

"Appearances, Walter. Everything we do has to look legitimate," Ira Douglas explained.

Douglas had traveled with Dobie by train from Albany, New York. All six of them served the Order of Eos in their own way. Bushy Bill Morrison did the dirty work, hoping to work his way up the ladder; Stewart, Marquette, and Haggard operated legitimate shell companies for the larger corporation, Triton; and Ira Douglas helped Eos maintain its power through its modern business mechanisms. Halvar Dobie served the Order of Eos at its highest level, even though he, too, was only a servant.

"I feel like a puppet," Stewart muttered, holding the two horses.

"You *are* a puppet, Walter," Bushy Bill chuckled. "Isn't he, Dobie?"

Dobie nodded. "Welcome to the family, Walter. Although Morrison should think twice about buying the cow when he's getting the milk for free," Dobie said in reference to Morrison's affair with Adrianna Sinclair. Like the local businessmen, Morrison knew the Sinclair family was the true power behind the Order of Eos. The two sons of Magnus Sinclair did the bidding of Eos in Hvergelmir, with William Sinclair residing in Nova Scotia and Scott Sinclair moving his family to Minnesota. Yet the two heirs produced five daughters but only one son between them. Had the young princling Jack Sinclair not tragically died in the Hinckley Fire of 1894, the two kissing cousins, Adrianna and Jack, would've united the two branches of the Sinclair family in marriage. Instead of returning home to Nova Scotia, Adrianna Sinclair began an affair with Bushy Bill Morrison, three Minnesota peasants married into the Sinclair family, and the heir-apparent became Pierre Delhut, who'd married Scott Sinclair's eldest daughter.

But Halvar Dobie served the Grandmaster of Eos, regardless of who was elected, and gave Morrison daggers in his smile for sleeping with the boss's daughter.

"It's the price you paid marrying into the Sinclair family," Ira Douglas lightened the mood. "The longer you're a puppet, the less you mind the strings."

"Stay single, Morrison," Marquette offered his advice. "Dobie's right about marriage." The man laughed.

Stewart focused on the matter at hand, "Now Philip, explain to me again why I would want to invest half my fortune in this dam."

Dobie didn't care about the minor issues. He'd come out to Hiawatha County for a larger purpose, so he found a cigar in his vest pocket and began to smoke while the businessmen dealt with matters of the present.

The sweet smell of tobacco smoke drifted into the ravine.

"The first phase is to build the Nicollet Dam, which has proven to be a little more difficult than we first thought. Currently, Triton owns the entire western shore of the Blue Knife River, but you can't have a dam without actually spanning the river. That's why Mr. Douglas and Mr. Dobie came out here to acquire the southernmost acres."

"Hold on a second," Haggard interrupted. "I thought the new laws were going to force all the Indians onto one reservation way up north."

"The White Earth Reservation," Morrison answered and spit a glob of tobacco and winced. "You're right about the intent of the law, Oz, but after the tribal property was distributed to the individual, it still needs to be sold by the individual. None of the Indians on this side of the reservation seem willing to sell."

"Not even with a little coercion?" Haggard asked.

Morrison chuckled. "No, Oz. Luckily we didn't have to stoop so low as to lynch anyone."

"I thought you were supposed to arrest one of the landowners for bootlegging?" Haggard pressed.

"Big Squeak is easily spooked," Morrison admitted. "Can't take away his land until there are formal criminal charges and a trial. Adam Thunder Face had been willing to let us put a road through his property, and even a bridge, but we needed this second lot for a dam."

Halvar Dobie exhaled and turned to the nearby bushes. *Did I hear whispers?* Since leaving St. John, they'd been in thick woods with nary a bird or person in sight. The men talked as if they were in privacy.

Haggard continued, "Mr. Douglas, explain to me Delhut's plan again."

"As you know, Triton is not just about the three of you. Three families represent Triton Corporation: the Terronts from France, the Delhuts from Detroit, and the Sinclairs from Nova Scotia. Even though the three of you married Sinclairs, it's still one vote, and *I* represent Mr. Delhut in this matter with the support of the Terronts."

While Marquette and Stewart worried about their wealth, Haggard offered hereditary skepticism. "You're only a goddamn lawyer, Douglas, and you're not getting our help until we understand what Delhut wants once the dam is built."

And that's the same reason I'm here.

To make sure.

Douglas laughed it off. "The Blue Knife River will serve as a glorified log shoot to get lumber from the Leech Lake pineries through the processing mill at Split Rock. All that is a slight of hand. In order for Oz to transition from a brickyard to a full-fledged quartz quarry, we need to regulate the water flow coming into Lake Manitou. Building a dam will allow logs to be wrangled right over these rapids."

Morrison responded. "So this dam will also let you keep spring flooding from overflowing the banks of Lake Manitou into Haggard's quarry. Why did you call it the Nicollet Dam?"

"Mr. Delhut came up with the name."

"A tad arrogant, don't you think? Are you trying to provoke our enemies?" Dobie asked when the others remained silent. He knew what had happened sixty years earlier. The Jesuits took another shot at the prize, bringing retribution from an even older and deadlier enemy, the Priory of Ormus. After Nicollet's death, the Jesuits and Priory weakened greatly as Eos grew stronger.

"This dam would pretty much put an end to the reservation, wouldn't it?" Marquette surmised.

We're being watched. Dobie climbed off his horse discreetly. He took his attention to the river and began to study the bushes and trees. *These morons need to keep their mouths shut. Show us the site and let's get back to town.*

"End the reservation?" Morrison repeated. "No, but they'll lose some land. The water will be at the top of the ravine by this time next year."

Dobie finished his scan of the nearby bushes before speaking his mind. "Before any of this can happen, we need the eastern bank without a fuss. There's a Jesuit already sniffing around on behalf of the Chippewa. So do this lawfully, Morrison, or it'll blow up in our face. Be discreet."

Morrison bent down, splashed some water on his face, and then shrugged. "A few more months, and the Chippewa won't be a problem for us any more. Trust me."

It's not the Chippewa that worries me.

"The Nicollet Dam will certainly be as glorious as the bridge," Douglas said, turning his horse back towards St. John.

"A year from now," Morrison added as he mounted his horse, "we'll be taking a road back into St. John and the Chippewa will scurry back to the woods up north."

Will I still be stuck in Minnesota a year from now? Halvar Dobie wondered as he and the others returned to civilization. *Can we trust any of these Delhut men to do what is needed?*

"What do you suppose that is?" Ira Douglas asked after they'd traveled a hundred yards.

Morrison turned his big steed to investigate. "It's a dreamcatcher. The Chippewa make them."

Morrison smashed it with his ebony walking stick.

If it was only that easy, Halvar Dobie decided.

Biscuits and Blankets

Turtle Island Reservation
June 11, 1897

WHILE AT HER mother's pine table, eating hot biscuits, issues like homelessness, religion, rape, or even ghosts ceased to exist. Like always, by the time Lily emptied the blue tin plate, her anger and terror had subsided. "What would happen if they did arrest Father?"

Winnie brushed flour from the counter. "There is always Migisi's plot of land to the north, and Grandfather Nanak's land to the south of this plot. I suppose we'd move south since the dam would flood most of Migisi's plot, although it would make it easier to access the water."

Migisi's plate remained empty and clean, even though they'd already finished the meal. Migisi had been gone for hours now.

Winnie began to clean up the table, leaving the drama behind as easily as she swept away crumbs. Lily had to keep her focused. "Why would they tear down the Gray Heron bridge and then plan to build another down by the lake?"

"I suppose it'll be metal and concrete instead of logs. I wouldn't mind having a bridge—let them build it. Folks won't have to pass through our property to cross."

Why did I let Migisi go right back to Grandfather? Now Migisi will hate all zhaaganaash. Her thoughts turned to good people, like Sister Inez and… "Do you remember me telling you about the Jesuit priest?"

"How could I forget about your mystery man?"

"Before they left, they talked about him. They acted like Father Guerin could stop them or something."

"Hmm. Interesting."

"What?" Lily asked defensively, not liking her mother's tone.

"I've always heard tales of Jesuits, but I didn't think they still existed. Besides fur trappers, they were some of the first zhaaganaash to visit. Perhaps your mystery man will be an ally." Winnie's dimples flashed.

"So I could trust him with this information?"

"No. Best to just keep your head low. Jananashins is a dangerous man. There are all sorts of stories about him that come out of Canada. I heard he had to flee some cattle town near Calgary because of murder charges, so he came to Minnesota and fought in the civil war when he was your age."

"This isn't his home?"

Winnie shook her head. "Morrison County is named after his grandfather, but there were Morrisons trading along the Mississippi River long before that. Now, he's using the new laws to force us off land that can then be sold to white farmers—or your dam builders."

"Then why does he let Adam Thunder Face sell alcohol at the Loose Goose?"

"Corruption. He gets a cut and inside information from Thunder Face." Winnie turned from the sink, her expression grim. "Now do you see why Nanak hates the whole Thunder Face family?"

Yes, and I slept with the enemy. "I do, but—"

Migisi burst through the door. "There are people coming from the north."

Lily and her mother joined him on the porch in time to see a diverse throng approaching— children and old men.

The children Lily knew, including Fawn Chevreuil running ahead of them.

"What's going on?" Winnie asked once Fawn stopped at the bottom of the stairs.

"There are three old Blanket Men with an escort of younger men to watch over them."

"Are they Pillagers?" Winnie asked.

Fawn shook her head, "I think they're Mide priests. One of them is from the Merman Clan. I don't know where they came from, but they are old."

"What are Blanket Men?" Migisi asked his mother.

"The Blanket Men live in a world where the zhaaganaash does not exist, just like your grandfather," Winnie explained. "They hold onto the old ways, refusing to change."

Lily looked down at her clothing. *And I'm wearing a plaid dress. Here comes more scorn.*

The LeDuc, Chevreuil, and LaBiche children surrounded the old men, who procured trinkets and treats from the many pouches tied to their ornate clothing.

"Greetings. How can I help you?" Winnie asked rigidly with her arms crossed.

"We have come to speak with Nanakonan of the Turtle Island Chippewa."

"Nanakonan is my grandfather," Migisi said. The three elders wore a small fortune within their ornate clothing, whereas the shirtless Migisi looked like a turtle without a shell. Lily wanted to pull him back to the house, but he was fearless in the faces of these strangers.

"We have come to speak to your grandfather about *your* future," the Midē wearing wolf claws said to Migisi.

"What about my future?" he asked.

"That is for your grandfather to decide. Join us." The one with porcupine quills in his hair placed a hand on Migisi's shoulder and they all continued down the trail.

The children went to follow but Winnie called out, "Children, stay." As soon as Fawn obeyed, so did the rest.

"You're letting Migisi go with them?" Lily asked softly.

"These are important men. It's your brother's choice which path he follows."

No, I'm not going to let them taint my brother. Lily stepped off the porch and jogged to the front of the procession as if to lead the way. The oldest man in the group reached over and grabbed her by the chin.

Lily flinched in fear but held steady to show the elders the respect they deserved.

"You have a lot of your mother in you," the man with long white braids declared as he inspected her face. "I see both Sioux and Pillager in you. Does *she* dress you in these clothes?"

"No. I bought them myself from a store in Alexandria."

"A store in Alexandria," the old Mide mocked. "How did you earn the coin of the zhaaganaash?"

"I was a teacher at White Earth last year."

"So you are the puppet, making our children say the words you were taught in one of their schools, right?"

Sister Lynch was right. The older generation will never change. "I'm not a puppet. I'm helping my people learn how to live in this new world."

"This new world." The old man scoffed. "What do you know of the world? When I was your age, the Anishinaabeg roamed the woods free. Soon, all our lands will be sold, and our people will vanish in the winds. That will be our new world."

Lily stiffened as the caravan moved around them, continuing down the path.

"Pay no attention to Little Toad," a tall, robust man wearing wolf claws said as he stepped up beside them. "My name is James Gray Sky. My clan is Ma'iingan the Wolf, so my blood is mixed like yours, and I understand better than other clans how the world can change. If we are to survive, we will need educated youth like you to speak for our people. What's your name?"

"Tew. Tewapa Asibikaashi, but I prefer Lily Weber."

Gray Sky smiled. "Tewapa ... the Water Lily. So Migisi indeed does carry all the hopes of both the Sioux and Chippewa."

"Why have all of you come here?"

"Don't worry, we are not Pillagers, we are old allies. I come from Mille Lacs, Clyde Speaks First comes from Fond Du Lac, and Joseph Little Toad is from Bad River. We're your scattered kin." He patted her shoulder as the others continued walking down the trail. "Nothing is going to happen to your grandfather or your brother. We are going to perform a ceremony to mark your brother for a path of leadership. We hope he can one day unite the scattered tribes of the Chippewa. But if your grandfather is right, he might be destined for something greater."

"He's just a child," Lily muttered.

"Yes, perhaps we have come for the wrong child." At her snort, James Gray Sky winked and continued walking. "But your brother found megis shells, and that cannot be quickly dismissed."

How did news travel so quickly? But then Lily glanced at the handsome young men mingled within the group, who served as a human telegraph system for the elders. *Did Nanak send for them?*

She stopped as they neared the old sweat lodge, where her grandfather already stood, preparing it. *I can't let these superstitious men claim my brother.*

So she waited.

A Wolf in Spectacles

Split Rock, MN
June 13, 1897

THE FOLLOWING SUNDAY, Lily walked to Split Rock alone, leaving Migisi with the Blanket Men. Being alone allowed her to seek out the mysterious Jesuit priest after mass and Sunday school ended. *After all, I need to warn him about the danger.*

She stood beside a large pine tree and watched the families picnic together. As the only native, Lily kept her distance.

At the center of the picnic, she spotted white-haired Albert Fisher. Albert's family owned the sawmill, and despite him being the frailest child in her class, his family was the most powerful, yet showed their power by sharing the wealth in food and beverage.

On the edges of the picnic, nearest the horses and wagons, Lily saw Bjorn Forsberg. Bjorn's family were red-headed Swedish dairy farmers. Between the two families, Lily spotted Emily MacPherson. Emily's family were blonde-haired Scots and also dairy farmers.

Americans are so colorful.

Although Father Hebert, Sister Inez, and a few other nuns mixed with the crowd, the tall Jesuit priest was absent.

Lily then remembered what Sister Inez had said about the balcony, so she stepped back inside, walked to the back doors, and climbed the steps of the balcony. Although the balcony was empty, a foreign chair and a crate of books had been placed at the front row. She stepped closer, curious as to the titles, finding:

Frederic Baraga's *A Dictionary of the Ojibway Language*, William Warren's *History of the Ojibwe People*, and Henry Rowe Schoolcraft's *The Myth of Hiawatha*.

Lily's heart jumped when she heard heavy steps coming up the stairs. *Great, I've trapped myself.* Quickly, she stepped forward and grabbed one of the books, picking it up as if already deep in thought.

"Bonjour," a man greeted.

She dropped the book and panicked on what to say. "You owe the children a box of chalk."

"Excuse me?" Father Guerin shifted back to English, blinking at her.

Did I just say that aloud? Her eyes went to her feet. "A few Sundays ago, you weren't looking and ran into me, and the box of chalk broke into a bunch of small pieces. Do you know how much children love full sticks of chalk?"

"I believe I already apologized for that incident, but I certainly can reimburse Sister Inez for the expense." His smooth face cracked a crooked smile, and when he didn't say anything else, Lily felt her heart begin to race.

Say something. "What's with all of these books?"

"Coincidently, I'm learning about Anishinaabeg culture."

The Beings Made Out of Nothing. It bothered her that the priest used their name instead of Chippewa. "From books?"

"Before I make a fool of myself, I had to get a running head start." He set down a second crate of books that he was carrying. "You're Lily, from the Mizheekay Reservation."

"Yes, I'm from the Turtle Island Reservation. When I was baptized, I took the name Lily Weber. My birth name is Tewapa Asibikaashi."

"Asibikaashi ... the spider." Then he snapped his fingers. "Thus Weber. I can only assume Tewapa means Lily, but isn't the word makopiniig?"

Lily laughed at the way he said it. "It's a Lakota word for a beautiful lake my mother knew."

"Tewapa Tankiyan, of course. The Lake With the Crooked Roots. Joseph Nicollet wrote about it in his report to congress."

Who is this priest? As much as she wanted to warn him about Bushy Bill then bolt out the door from nerves, another question came out: "Why would you know this?"

He laughed, and dimples formed in his clean-shaven cheeks. Despite his height, he was thin, with short black hair and small, circular glasses. *He's a priest, Lily. Don't look at him that way.*

"I'm an ambassador, which requires me to be a scholar. The Society of Jesus sent me here to assess and give aid to the humanitarian crisis happening to the American Indian Reservation system, so I have to read a lot of books." He paused, smiling. "Joseph Nicollet was an astronomer and mapmaker who traveled all over Minnesota, from Lura Lake to Lake Manitou."

Nicollet Rapids, of course. "Yeah, my grandfather knew Nicollet."

"Your grandfather is Chagobay, Nicollet's guide?" Father Guerin's enthusiasm brought him closer to her again.

She moved to stand at the edge of the balcony to remain visible for any parishioner below. "Chagobay was my great-grandfather. My grandfather Nanak was just a boy when he met Nicollet."

"Oh, I'd very much like to meet your grandfather."

"I don't think he'll meet you," she said quicker than she intended. "All of his white friends died, so he pretty much hates all white people now. He barely acknowledges me after I converted, so he'd really hate you."

"He's living on the Turtle Island Reservation?"

Lily hesitated. "He lives on the first lot north of the Loose Goose Saloon. On the Nimrod Road." *Now would be the time to mention Bushy Bill.* "That's why I wanted to come talk to you. There's a group of white men who are trying to buy up all of the land in order to put up a dam."

"Triton Corporation."

"Yeah," she said, surprised. "You seem to know everything … If you're some sort of ambassador, can you help us?"

Father Guerin sighed and sat down on the chair. "These are complicated times, aren't they? Right now, I'm only in a position to observe and report. I've been visiting reservations and communities all across the Great Lakes region before setting up camp here. Perhaps we could help each other?"

Lily found herself chewing on her bottom lip. "How could I help you?"

Guerin looked over the top of his glasses with a smirk. "I don't want to look like a fool, and with your help, I could practice what I'm going to say."

What does that mean?

"I can promise you I do not want Triton to buy any more land, and I'll do everything I can to prevent that from happening, but I have bigger fish to fry, so to speak, and if I am to help find a solution to this illegal land grab, I need to meet tribal leaders. You could help me practice my Anishinaabemowin."

Lily chuckled again at his attempt at a third language. "You want me to be a tutor?"

"I could speak to your parents about it, if that helps."

"Talking to my father might be harder than my grandfather."

"Has he passed?"

"No, he's the leader of the Black Hat gang—bootleggers. He'd take one look at you and make it his mission to torment and humiliate you. He's a bad man, from what I know."

"Big Squeak?"

Good Lord. Now Lily really wanted to bolt for the stairs. "Skwikomik is his given name, but yes. How do you know him?"

"I met with Chief Sweating Stone up on Bear Island. The only thing he complained about more than the theft of pine was the corruption of the youth by alcohol. He seemed to hate Big Squeak the most."

"Well, there's a complicated reason for that." *Why does this feel like my family is on trial? Something is wrong.* "As much as I'd like to be a tutor, I'm trying to find a teaching position this fall, and I have a lot of letters to write. Thank you for the kind offer." *Besides, you're far too handsome to work with on a daily basis.*

Father Guerin's dimples disappeared. "It was worth a shot."

Lily took a step from the balcony edge to the staircase. "I just thought you should know that these men weren't speaking too highly of you."

"I can handle ill-talk."

"I'm sure you can," she said and continued for the door. "Thank you, Father Guerin."

By the time she reached the bottom of the stairs, Lily decided Sister Inez was right about staying away from this man.

WITH A CLUTTERED mind, Lily paid little attention to the real world as she crossed from the road, past Apple's field, and into the wooded ravine of home. Had she paid attention, she might have noticed the horses, or even seen the men lounging in the shadows of the trees as home came into view. Instead, it was the whiff of sweet cigar smoke that gave out a tardy warning.

Her gasp brought chuckles, but only from the men in the shadows.

"Welcome home, Daughter."

Holding On

Haggard Quarry
June 20, 1961

LILY CROSSED HER arms defensively and asked, "What do you want?"

Big Squeak smirked. "Is it a crime to visit my family?"

Unlike the dead eyes of his gang, her father's eyes sparkled with mischief as if a thousand possibilities were passing through his mind. A fresh welt across his cheek almost drew blood to the surface, but beyond that, he looked a decade younger than her mother. Despite being dubbed "Big Squeak," he was compact and coiled like a snake about to strike. Rugged, handsome, and lean, Skwikomik Asibikaashi tried to use his kind smile to charm his way into her heart.

Part of her wanted to rush into his arms, to tell him of her problems, but her stomach churned with anger and disgust. *It's not happening.* "Getting arrested for your crimes could hurt your family," she answered. "Which is why you should just leave us alone."

"Protecting my family is my first priority in life. My crimes provide you with food and shelter. Ask your mother." With the heel of his boot, he knocked hard against the wooden step, creating an echo that seemed to shake the entire house. "Winnie, come out and tell your daughter how I protect this family."

The door opened to reveal two strange sights. The first oddity was her jovial mother wearing a mask of sorrow with red rimmed eyes. Suddenly, the welt on her father's cheek made more sense. "Do what you've come to do and leave," she said, holding the second oddity, the big shotgun she kept under her bed. Both hammers were pulled back as if she was going to shoot a rabid skunk.

"That's not an answer," he said, turning to her, unfazed by the shotgun. "Am I not here to protect this family?"

Winnie nodded slightly and then slammed the door, leaving Lily to her father.

What is going on?"

He patted the step, inviting her to join him.

"Did Mother do that to your face?"

Big Squeak chuckled and touched the welt. "No, this is the work of my loving father."

"Grandfather Nanak did that to you?"

He nodded. "I might be a scoundrel, but I still know my place and took the chastisement, even though my men would have stomped any other man into the ground for striking me. Your brother can tell you all about it, but I chased off those Blanket Men trying to poison his mind."

Thank God. "Where's Migisi?"

"He went down to the river to wash his hands," he said and looked at his own clean palms. When he patted the step again, Lily obliged.

Her father smelled of debauchery, as if the alcohol, vomit, blood, and other unsavory scents from the Loose Goose Saloon all blended together to blanket him in sin.

"Why is mother crying?"

"It seems as if I have a forked tongue. For every word of kindness I try to offer, it ends up just hurting those I love. Your mother cries because she knows I speak the truth."

Lily scoffed, and in that instant, her mockery made her aware of the sinister men nearby. The most frightening of her father's henchmen was called Blackfish, who earned his name by being the best smuggler in Minnesota.

Blackfish LaBiche had grown up along the northern shore of Pokegama Lake—before there was the city, Grand Rapids. Like a black fish, he could swim up any creek, river, or lake in the middle of the night and deliver his cargo before anyone ever spotted him by the light of day. She'd never heard him utter a word.

Then there was Pierre LeDuc, who could barely shut his crooked mouth. Yet his eyes were often more profane than his mouth. He always seemed to be cleaning a pistol, or in this case, sharpening a knife.

The others were expendable members of the Black Hat gang, willing to risk their life for status.

"You made her cry with the truth?"

"You might think I've abandoned you, but I keep my eyes and ears on Lake Manitou at all times. So I know where Bushy Bill Morrison is right now, just like I knew three Blanket Men came to visit here. Care to explain why there were uninvited visitors?"

"It's some strange superstition about shells."

"I spent my childhood playing along this riverbed, and in all of that time, I never found any mystical megis shells. Did your brother really find them?"

"No," Lily snapped. "I was the one to find them."

Pierre LeDuc dropped his knife.

Lily wasn't sure if the sight of a weapon or LeDuc's knowledge of megis shells frightened her more.

"You found them," her father repeated. "Did you tell that to your grandfather?"

"No, Migisi took them to him, trying to please him."

"Yes, I've noticed how he's taken to my father."

"That's what happens when he has no father figure around."

Big Squeak laughed heartily. "I suppose I deserve that." His charming smile faded. "Holding back the truth is the same as lying. You owe your brother an apology."

"What for?"

Big Squeak looked away. "When I heard you were coming home from White Earth, part of me mourned and part of me rejoiced. I hoped you'd make a good citizen of your brother, and now I find him embracing the old ways."

"Better than being a criminal."

"No, crime will continue into the next century, but the ways of the Blanket Men won't. Tewapa, there is a reason why I have come home. I need to—"

"Lily. I don't want to be called Tewapa anymore. I'm Lily."

He shrugged. "Lily, that's good. That's very American of you. The boarding school took a little Indian girl and created an American woman. Look at you."

Is he mocking me? Or have I become what he wanted? "Why are you here? What did you need?"

He ignored her question. "The people in White Earth spoke highly of you, Lily."

"Really?" She felt her heart stop. "Who did you talk to?"

"Some of the elders. They thought you were a good teacher because you were born a Wâbĕnō."

"A what?"

"Ah, I suppose you don't know that word yet. My father would never teach a girl." He chuckled. "They thought you were a sorceress, the way you controlled the children."

An insult within a compliment? "A witch?"

"A witch," he confirmed with a wicked grin. "None of them could understand how you were able to control such wild children at the school. They assumed you put a spell over them."

"Of course not."

"Good. I don't want my father filling your head with nonsense. Do you understand, Tew?"

"Lily. I stopped being Tew when I was baptized."

"Baptized, huh? Did the old nuns force you? Did they beat it into you?" He gestured at the crucifix on her neck.

"I *chose* to be a Christian."

"That's good. So what's the *real* reason you didn't stay in White Earth? Why did you really come back home?"

"I wanted to take care of Mother and Grandfather, and to get some experience teaching white children."

Big Squeak scoffed. "Your mother certainly doesn't look to be starving. Despite what she says about me, I send her more than enough money."

Does he know what I did? Of what happened? "Then perhaps I feel a loyalty to my family, which is something you wouldn't understand."

"In my heart, I was happy my Little Flower left this place, so I just wanted to know why you came home. I heard some things."

Swallowing became difficult, and she felt an old ache. Being surrounded by a gang of gawking men made her fears even worse. "What sort of things?"

"When you're a man in my position, information is a commodity. I heard that some young buck from Fond Du Lac apparently was giving you a hard time. Is that why you left White Earth? Guilt?"

He knows. He has to. Does he know what I did? Lily's fingernails bit into her palms, keeping her focused in front of the men. "No. That's not why I left."

Her father continued playfully. "There are rumors going around the villages, especially in Lac Du Flambeau. Some of the Blanket Men talk about a Great Thunderbird that will rise and usher in a new era. Some Blanket Men from Odanah speak of finding new paths. Crazy old men are bound to talk. Is this why my Christian daughter refused a paid position and encouraged her brother to learn the old ways?"

He's got it all wrong.

"First, no, I'm not any sort of witch, sorceress, or whatever word you said earlier. Second, I turned down the job at White Earth because it's getting worse by the day, and bootleggers like you are no better than the loggers stealing the land. Third, I didn't refuse a paid position. I'm looking to get diverse teaching experiences so I can get a really good job this fall. I'm teaching lessons to white children each Sunday, and I might take a position as a language tutor."

Lily felt like she was back at the Sacred Heart Mission debating with one of the boys.

"Language tutor?" Her father took several seconds to ponder what she said. She was relieved that her angry retort distracted him from more talk of White Earth.

"Is that all?" Lily snapped.

Big Squeak raised his eyebrows and sighed. "I know you don't like me, and I understand, but I want you to know that I'm dedicated to protecting you. If you ever need my help, like with young bucks from Fond Du Lac, you can count on me. You understand that, right?"

Lily looked away to compose herself. "Yes. Now can I go?"

"I suppose it's time the boys and I pay Adam Thunder Face a visit," he said, rising from the porch steps.

The shadows from under the trees rose, drifting towards Big Squeak, Lily watched them with caution.

"Don't forget about Migisi."

She stayed, gritting her teeth and fighting tears, at the steps for a few moments, waiting for her father and his men to disappear. She hadn't wanted to see him, especially now after hearing him speak aloud of things she didn't allow herself to think about privately.

Migisi. I have to find Migisi.

Lily jumped up from the porch and rushed to the ravine. She quickly spotted Migisi's back as he sat upon a stone. As she grew closer, she saw his feet dangling in the water and that he held something of fascination upon his lap.

She dragged her feet so as not to startle him, but he didn't react. "Father Guerin said he's going to make sure nobody takes any of the land on this side of the river. He claims to be helping our people."

No reaction. He's really upset.

Lily transitioned from the bank to the rocks along the water's edge. "He seems to know the story of our family, too: how Chagobay led Nicollet into Lake Manitou and brought him up the river to the spot where the Pillagers—"

"Leave me alone," he said, turning away from her.

He needs you. "So what has you upset? That Father's returned? Or that the Toothless Ones have left?" *Don't blow this. Why did you say that?*

"Can you just go away?"

"I'm just trying to help you."

"That's what Father said, but he ruined everything."

Lily remembered the mark on Big Squeak's cheek. "Did they get into a fight?"

Migisi nodded.

"What happened?"

"He tore apart the sweat lodge before we were even finished, and then he began beating Clyde Speaks First, which is when Nanak began hitting Father with his smoke pipe, which broke. It broke, Tew. Right in the middle of the ritual. I was supposed to be tested, but now …"

Poor kid. How do I tell him it's for the best? She took a step closer. "Father left."

"Is he gone for good?"

"I don't think he's going far. It sounds like he'll be up at Lyons tonight."

Migisi sniffed. "I really thought I was special."

"You are special," she insisted. Lily put her hands on his shoulders and kissed the back of his head. "You should have been named Mighty Turtle Killer."

Migisi chuckled weakly at that. He lifted his forearm to wipe his nose, revealing bandaged hands.

"Did Father do this to you?" Lily claimed the second half of the rock to sit upon.

"No."

"What happened? What's wrong with your hands? I can see blood seeping through."

"Like I said, I'm not special."

"Let me see what's wrong with your hands. Does Mother know?"

"She's the one who bandaged the burns."

Is that why she'd been crying? Her pity turned to anger. "Burns? Someone burned you? Did Grandfather do this to you?"

"No, I … we … we were preparing for the Summer Solstice. I was feasting in order to prepare for my 'path of life' for when the Cedar Trail aligns. Then he showed up and ruined everything."

"So Father stopped it and got in a fight with the Blanket Men."

"His gang beat up the attendants and even hurt Clyde Speaks First. They didn't do anything to me."

"They burned your hands, Migisi."

"No, no, it wasn't like that. After my fast, I was supposed to find out if I was a Wabeno, a Firehandler."

Which is why Father told me to apologize to my brother. It should have been me who got hurt. I was the one who found the shells.

"After Father took the Smoke Straw and broke it, his gang drew their guns and forced the others to go. When I saw that they were going to leave, and that everybody was fighting, I decided that I needed to show them, so I found one of the stones heating on the coals for the ritual ... and I tried to pick it up and bring it to the lodge."

"Oh, Migisi," Lily whispered, pulling him close. "I'm so sorry." He started to sob, and she kissed the top of his head again. "I've got something that might make you feel better. Do you want to hear about it?"

Migisi wiped his tears away from his eyes with his wrist and nodded. He looked to her for answers.

Are the White Earth elders right? Am I a witch casting spells on children?

Kill the Messenger

Turtle Island Reservation
June 14, 1897

THE PAIN IN Migisi Asibikaashi's burnt palms kept him awake most of the night, but the sound of a raven outside his window forced him from his bed at the break of dawn.

They're laughing at me.

His sister slept on the other side of the room, dreaming of chalkboards, textbooks, and noble priests most likely. Turning away, Migisi moved so quietly that not a board creaked as he left the small bedroom.

The kitchen table bench propped the front door closed, and with the door open to his mother's bedroom, he could see the shotgun still ready in case their father returned. He stealthily crept past her to the front door.

As soon as he stepped out on the porch, the cooler air greeted him with its gentle kiss, and for just a moment, he forgot his pain.

Then the raven cried out again.

He's telling everyone I'm a fraud.

With his bandaged hands, he picked up a handful of rocks from the base of the house foundation and marched around to the rear of the house to confront the raven.

Show yourself, you bastard. I dare you.

The challenge was answered within seconds by an ebony messenger as large as an eagle. It stood in the twisted branches of an oak, just inside the upper canopy. The first toss ricocheted miserably, not even reaching the upper branches before dropping to the earth.

The raven quaked again, laughing.

The second toss almost did the trick, finding a narrow path through the branches until it struck the perching branch five inches from clawed feet. The raven launched itself away from Migisi, toward the river, preventing a third throw. Even so, he threw above the oak, wishing for the perfect shot.

The stone dropped into the ravine near his unconscious father.

The shock of seeing a body took Migisi several seconds to act.

Is he dead?

Or just drunk?

Big Squeak sprawled out in the place where the eroding topsoil met the bedrock of the cavern walls. If he rolled, or was pushed, his body would drop ten feet onto jagged rock. Migisi clutched the fourth stone as he approached.

A black slouch hat covered his father's face, but Migisi knew the rest of the details: the American boots, the deerskin pants, and the blue denim shirt, unbuttoned to reveal bruised ribs, red splotches along his neck, and a large bite mark on the flesh above his collar bone. He stank of alcohol and armpits.

"Why are you such a coward?"

A pistol was drawn, cocked, and aimed before Migisi finished speaking.

"Oh, I thought I was somewhere else." The pistol lowered, and the brim of the hat lifted to reveal a bruised and battered face. His father had a swollen eye, blood around his nostril, and a split lip. "Boy, don't assume to understand a man until you've walked a few miles in his boots."

The scent of alcohol allowed Migisi's anger to return. His palms ached. "You ruined everything."

"You don't even understand what's happening," Big Squeak said, and then groaned. "How are your hands?"

"They hurt."

"Hurt, I understand. Hurt helps toughen a fellow up, and with my blood flowing in you, you need to prepare yourself for a tough life." With another groan, he sat up, then grew wide-eyed when he saw where he'd collapsed. "Stay away from alcohol, son. It makes you do all sorts of stupid things."

"What happened to you last night?" Migisi asked, focusing on his father's wounds.

"Exactly ... What happened? You're too young to understand most of it," Big Squeak said with a chuckle.

"Did you get in a fight?"

"Fight? No, I, uh, had to put a bully in his place. I took a bit of a beating, but I found out what I needed. I'd stay away from the Loose Goose for a few weeks." He felt his split lip with his tongue.

"Who—"

"I had the strangest dream just a few minutes ago," his father interrupted. "I dreamed of some strange looking Blanket Man with braided horns on his head standing on the shores of Lake Manitou, right where it drains into Split Rock, and I watched him melt away the stone and drain the whole lake until nothing remained. Do you know what I saw at the bottom of the lake?"

"The Horned Serpent?"

Big Squeak shook his head. "Nothing. Brush and trees grew where the lake stood, the Blue Knife found a new channel, and Lake Manitou just vanished from the map. No St. John. No Split Rock. It all just vanished. What do you think it means?"

Migisi blinked under the spotlight of his father's intense gaze. "It means our people will vanish just like the lake if we don't stop following the path of the zhaaganaash, like you do with your alcohol."

There, I said it.

Big Squeak laughed, causing him to wince afterwards. He sat up fully and twisted his back a bit. "When I was your age, I found a cave somewhere near here. When I told your grandfather, he pulled the same shit with me, bringing in Blanket Men from all over the north. He's a lunatic, your grandfather. Let me save you the time and a pound of flesh. It takes courage to betray your people, your family, and your father, but when you know what's at stake, then you can see if my boots fit."

I'll never walk in your boots. Migisi calmed his breathing as the tale sunk in. "Grandfather Nanak tried to test you?"

"Oh, yes. Once I found the cave, I don't think he had a choice, in fact, that's when—"

Migisi followed his father's swollen eyes to a dark figure but before Migisi could even understand, before he could see it, the pistol flew from his father's lap, aimed, and fired. The cocked hammer, bringing thunder and a death cry to the valley.

Instead of fear or alarm, the death cry that followed the pistol shot sounded aggressively angry, and it wasn't until Migisi turned fully that he saw the dark object was a dying raven.

The black bird had landed on an overhead limb, and when it fell further, it landed with a bounce just a few feet behind Migisi. It stretched its wings widely before going limp. Red blood came oozing out of its broad breast muscles.

"Bastard," Big Squeak muttered before spitting toward the fallen creature. "No wonder I had bad dreams with him so close. Those bastards are always whispering in my ear, trying to make me doubt." He shook his head. "Did you know ravens can speak?"

Migisi nodded.

"I might not be a good father but let me give you some advice: stay the hell away from ravens. If you start listening to them, they'll drive you crazy."

At least we can agree on this. "Grandfather Nanak says that owls are—"

For the second time they were interrupted. This time it was heavy running that caused Migisi to stop as his father's pistol turned toward the wooded part of the upper ravine. Blackfish LaBiche appeared, stopping when he saw the pistol. A moment later, Pierre LeDuc came running up also.

"Damn son-of-a-whore," Big Squeak muttered, motioning to the dead raven.

Both men relaxed and smirked at their leader.

"You should run back to your mother," Big Squeak said to Migisi before he turned to face LeDuc. "Go get the men ready, we've worn out our welcome."

He's leaving so soon?

His father stood and walked over to the black mound that had been his nemesis.

Migisi watched as he retrieved the bird by the feet and carried it back to where they stood.

"Give me your knife," he ordered Blackfish, and once it had been handed to him, he knelt down and sliced off the bird's wings. Shoving the wings into the side band of his slouch hat, Big Squeak quickly wound a leather band around the hat until the wings were secured.

As Big Squeak modified his hat, Migisi noted his bloody but unblemished hands. *If you were tested, why don't you have burns on your hands?*

Big Squeak put the hat back on his head. "That's how you deal with bullies, son."

Migisi understood—his father had become a predator in a world of bullies.

A Snail Without a Shell

Turtle Island Reservation
June 19, 1897

FAWN CHEVREUIL HELD the last megis shell in the cup of her hand, feeling the smooth husk warm to her body's temperature.

A magic shell.

Lily and Migisi had claimed the rest of the treasure trove and brought it directly to the strange old shaman Nanak, but she spent another hour digging around in the mud until she found one last shell, which she kept for herself.

Fawn climbed out from under the tarp and went directly to the cold fire. A handful of pine needles, twigs, and two fresh logs brought the campfire to life. The Black Hat Gang, including her father Michael Chevreuil, had been gone for days, leaving just the women and children camping along the Blue Knife River.

With the chaos of the brief reunion came a bounty of food, and once she was warm, she walked over to the top crate and grabbed a few of the fresh biscuits and then headed north.

North was better for a variety of reasons. The Chippewa communities of Red Lake and Leech Lake acted as her fall and winter home, which meant solid stone and wood walls instead of waking under a tarp each day. There were fewer zhaaganaash in the north, also, which meant she could walk without fear of reprise. And by walking north, she avoided ghosts.

A summer along the Blue Knife River meant hearing the horror stories of monstrous Horned Serpents, epic battles between tribes, Tak-Pei feeding on the souls of the slain, and the brutal murders of women and children during times of war. Old Nanak told the worst stories, but her mother whispered one that only her family told: how three generations of women were harvesting rice along the outlet of Lake Manitou when a crazed Sioux zealot attacked them, with only the youngest, Fawn's grandmother, surviving. The incident almost sparked a war between the Sioux and Chippewa.

For this reason, walking north was much better.

The steep, rocky walls of the Blue Knife River ravine ended a few miles to the north, and where the stone met the floor of the world, the little village of Nimrod Crossing stood. A straight road ran from east to west for miles and miles, crossing the wider Crow Wing River at the massive pine log general store. It also had a collection of tall houses built for the merchants.

Fawn knew her place and remained in the shadows.

But something else lurked in the shadows she soon noticed.

Under the bridge, she saw a shirtless zhaaganaash stretched out along the shore, with clean shaven cheeks and circular glasses. He snapped priestly robes and tried to flatten the wrinkles in the fabric before setting them out in the sun.

Oh, hello there. This must be Lily's mystery man.

Creeping closer as the sun began to appear over the tops of the trees, Fawn studied Father Guerin, noticing a monstrous horse stood tethered under the shadow of the bridge, along with a military grade olive tent.

Without his black robes, he looks like a plucked chicken.

Fawn watched him wash his face, comb his hair, start a fire, and prepare a breakfast from some dried mixture. As he walked around the camp, she noted something quite peculiar.

She'd seen plenty of naked men in her life, from peeking into her mother's tent to drunken buffoons who urinated on trees, but the priest was different.

Are those scars?

A red slash, long enough to gut a man, ran from his right side up toward his nipple ringed with boyish hair. Two more white scars could be seen at his right shoulder, each on the opposite side of where a suspender would be—a sign a bullet had passed right through to the other side.

Maybe Winnie is right about him being a secret soldier?

Soon, he returned to his tent and began buttoning up his shirt, finishing with his priestly collar. When he went to inspect his cooking, he glanced upwards and Fawn locked eyes with him.

Father Guerin rose slowly from his crouched position. "Lily?"

Fawn went to run, but she quickly took command of her fears, and just like him, rose and stepped into view. "Lily is my cousin."

A river stood between them. *I'll be safe.*

"And who are you?"

"Fawn Chevreuil."

"I'm Father Jean Guerin."

"I know. Lily told me about you."

He put his hands on his hips. "She did? Hopefully good things."

He's smiling. Does he have a crush on her?

Fawn walked down to the edge of the river, and as she did, she saw a few more peculiar items. Two revolvers and a sheathed knife sat out with a Bible and rosary beads, all of the items just waiting to be used. "She said you were some sort of ambassador from the Catholic Church, a Jesuit." Pausing, she asked, "How did you get those scars?"

Clearing his throat, he replied, "I assumed I had privacy, my apologies." He tended to his food for a minute before asking, "Would you like some breakfast?"

Lily is right. He's hiding something. "I already had biscuits."

"You must be an early riser. Does that mean I'm pretty close to the Turtle Island Reservation?"

A small hump kept the two rivers from merging, with the skinny Blue Knife on the western slope and the Crow Wing River on the east. "Yeah, it basically starts right on the other side of that bluff."

"I came back from Leech Lake pretty late last night, so when I found this river, I wasn't entirely sure if it was the Blue Knife or the Crow Wing."

"It's the Crow Wing. You could have followed it to Split Rock."

They both turned to watch the current flowing south. When Fawn looked back, Father Guerin was staring at her.

"So you said you were a cousin to Lily Weber. Does that mean your grandfather is also Nanakonan?"

Fawn shook her head. "No, we're distant cousins. Nanakonan's grandfather connects all of us cousins together."

"So what is your doodem?"

Lily is right. He really wants to be an Indian. She shrugged. "My clan? I'm French."

Father Guerin laughed heartily at her flat humor. "Chevreuil? Yes, it does seem obvious."

"My mother's side is mostly Wa-wa-shesh-she."

"Ah, the Antler Clan, the poets."

"My father's side is from the Wolf Clan at Leech Lake." She realized she had walked right up the edge of the water to speak with him. *Why can't all zhaaganaash be nice like him?* "We moved north after they closed the reservation." Then she told him all about her life at Mille Lacs, Leech Lake, and Fond du Lac, and even places in Canada.

"I have a question, Fawn," Father Guerin finally interrupted. "I'm about to pack up camp, and on my way, I wanted to pay Nanakonan a visit. Could you be my guide for the way back?"

"I-I suppose." *Will Lily get jealous of me? I guess she should have invited me to go with them to the festival.*

"Wonderful. Just give me a few minutes to pack up and I'll cross over to your side of the river. Will Lily be home?"

Another strange smile at the mention of Lily. "Um, no."

"Why is that?" Father Guerin asked, continuing to break camp.

"Well, it's Saturday, which means she doesn't teach us."

"She teaches you?"

"She teaches all the little summerbirds. Right after lunch, she gives us two hours of lessons. She teaches us language, math, reading, religion, and even history."

"So today is her day off?"

"Oh, well, no. Today she is going to the festival. She said Sister Inez invited her."

"I see. Will you still take me?"

Fawn nodded. *If I can't trust this zhaaganaash, who can I trust?*

Scene of the Crime

Lake Manitou
June 19, 1897

MIGISI ASIBIKAASHI FOUND himself wearing leather boots with a hard heel, dark cotton pants, a white shirt with suspenders over his shoulders, and work gloves to protect his wounded hands. Each time he paddled, a tiny shock of pain came from his hands, but he kept his focus on the far eastern shore and the bluff of granite Nanakonan called Bleeding Rock.

Sitting behind him in the birch bark canoe, his sister steered and paddled as they crossed from the delta of the Blue Knife River to the center of Lake Manitou. Nothing much remained of Tew, for she was dressed like every other zhaaganaash he'd ever met. She even tucked her long hair into a silly looking bonnet. For his part, he also dressed like a zhaaganaash, but it was all part of the negotiation.

I'll look like a fool in order to get her to come with me.

"What's so special about this place?" Lily asked a mile into the crossing.

It's full of magic. "You wouldn't understand."

"Let me guess ... Grandfather told you some spooky stuff happened here?"

"No!" he said, but she'd guessed correctly. "Do you see the bay in the southeast corner?"

"Yes, what about it?"

"Grandfather said it is the only wild rice field that has never been harvested, which is why it is now nearly impassable. He said that our great-grandfather Chagobay brought Joseph Nicollet through these reeds, but there were lilies around the outlet of the river that had roots that went all the way down to the evil Manitou. That's how it knew they had come. Before Chagobay could share his secrets with Nicollet, the Pillagers came and took them all prisoner, except for Nanak, who managed to hide. The Pillagers had to let Nicollet go, but later, they found and killed Chagobay for bringing people to this unholy place."

Lily sighed. "You're just a kid, Migisi, you shouldn't be fixated on all of these violent stories." She paused, gazing at the fields before shaking her head. "We're not going into those rice fields to look for the Manitou or Horned Serpent."

"Why not? Afraid to get your clothes dirty?" Her silence indicated he may have hit a mark. *Well, then I have another plan.* "We're going to the side of the cliffs, so don't worry about the reeds."

"You want me to take you to Bleeding Rock?"

Migisi didn't answer.

For a mile, the sheer stone walls made it impossible to climb. Soon they found on the southern slope, near the rice fields, a rocky shore with an angled access to the top of the cliffs.

"It doesn't look as scary as I imagined," Lily remarked after they had gotten out of the canoe and climbed up the steep granite cliff along the shore. Much of the terrain was covered in rotting pine needles, with jagged rocks popping up as frequently as towering pines.

Strangely, Migisi didn't hear any birds in the trees. "Just wait."

She's bluffing. Even a clueless Christian like Lily understood the power of Bleeding Rock. He saw his sister take out her crucifix to let it dangle over her chest and hid a grin. Like Lily, he'd heard his mother's stories of Bleeding Rock, but after hearing Grandfather's version, he needed to see it for himself.

The view of the lake improved with their elevation, allowing them to look back at the seven miles of water, where they could even see St. John on the far northwestern bank. Both of their eyes remained on the ground, however.

So it's true. He smiled despite the beating of his heart in his ears. The stacks of stones had been toppled, but upon the large, circular clearing in the pine forest, grooves had been cut into the stone. Migisi followed them all the way to the edge of the cliff, where the water's edge waited thirty feet below.

"Do you see these grooves carved into the stone?" Migisi asked as he knelt upon the granite.

"This is where they killed the women and their children," Lily confirmed, kneeling with him to study the grooves in the rock.

"The blood would collect here and then trickle into the lake as an offering to the Horned Serpent."

"Who would do such a thing?" Lily asked, stopping her analysis.

"Nanakonan said our Wijigan ancestors offered the blood to call the Manitou up from the depths, but the ritual didn't work." Standing, he led Lily away from the open circle and into the trees. He brushed away a coating of pine needles to reveal more moist stone. "Do you see this grainy powder?"

"It's blue," Lily whispered.

Migisi nodded. "It belongs to the Manitou. It comes up from deep within the earth through cracks in the stone. The Evil One knows his time is coming to an end, so he uses his medicine to let his followers know where he is buried."

"Hold on, is the Manitou the same thing as the Horned Serpent?" Lily frowned. "How can it be in the waters but also deep under the earth?"

Migisi huffed, even though he'd asked similar questions. "'Manitou' just means spirit. A Horned Serpent is an evil water monster."

"Like a dragon or snake?"

Why does she have to make everything connect to the zhaaganaash? "I suppose, but those are just simple words. This creature that lives under the lake is sleeping, protected by powerful magic from the dawn, but one day it will wake, and I must be prepared to fight it or the whole world will be destroyed."

"Did the Blanket Men tell you this?"

"No. Since you left, Grandfather has been teaching me. He said that next summer he will teach me how to defeat the Horned Serpent, who will do anything to avoid going to the Land of the Midnight Sun."

"And you think you're the one to send him there? What about your burned hands?"

Migisi looked down, feeling a different kind of pain. "If I'm really not a Firehandler, then I'm probably the Great Thunderbird, and I will force the monster up from the depths, kill him, and bring about the era of the Eighth Fire. He says our ancestors made a pledge long ago to defeat the Horned Serpent, but if I am not patient, I will fail like the others. Next winter, I will learn the Song of the Manitou. Nanakonan said it is my destiny." *My name means Eagle, so it must be true.*

"Let's just worry about learning to read first. Then we'll battle monsters," Lily joked.

"Don't you understand?" He gestured wildly at the evidence, feeling his temper rising. "This is all real. The Wijigan Clan came here, cut these grooves into the stone, and then sacrificed women and children."

"Our people don't make human sacrifices. It's not the Midewiwin way, and it certainly isn't the Christian way."

"The Wijigan Clan did. Why do you think the woods along Old Copper Road are haunted? The Wijigan took prisoners to this place and spilled their blood at each of those places where the stone altars once stood. They cut off the heads of the children and placed them upon their own severed thighs."

He noticed his sister was trembling. "Migisi, this is just awful. Stop telling me about it."

"But our family is both sides of the story. Mother's blood has the Sioux victims. Father's side has the Wijigan Clan. Our own Chippewa people tried to kill our family for what we did here, but don't you see—it's all true. If the sacrifices were real, then the Horned Serpent must be real also."

"Trust me, Migisi. None of this is real."

He scoffed. "The shells are real. The dreamcatcher was real. The ghost in the woods was real, too. You're part of this family, too! You should start acting like it."

Lily kept her hands on her hips for a long time before finally asking, "Which way to town?"

Grandfather was right. She's a lost cause. Maybe Fawn will be the one to help me.

LESS THAN A half mile later, they next stopped at the headwaters of Split Rock Creek where the big lumber mill stood over the top of the fast-moving current to swallow up trees and spit out lumber.

If Bleeding Rock won't convince her, maybe Split Rock Creek will. "The Horned Serpent made this creek," Migisi commented as they descended the granite bluff to the northern edge of town.

"Erosion formed this creek. Weather fluctuated from year to year, and generation to generation. A long time ago, the waters of Lake Manitou were much higher and flowed over these granite rocks until this channel was formed," Lily countered. "It's science, Migisi." She shook her head. "Let's not talk any more about the Horned Serpent, agreed?"

"If the waters were higher, they would have cut a channel through the rice fields by Kanaranzi Creek. That's science," he rebutted. "This channel was made by the Horned Serpent."

"Supposing that what you say is true, why would some all-powerful creature waste his energy defying the laws of physics in order to cut through solid rock?"

Migisi shrugged. "Grandfather says the Horned Serpent is avoiding his fate."

"Avoiding how?"

"His fate is to descend to the River of Souls, which is where I will send him after our battle." At her sigh, he turned to the road leading from the mill to town. "But first I'll have to finish learning the Song of the Manitou to wake it up."

Jubilation

Split Rock, MN
June 19, 1897

WILL THE FESTIVAL *be an excuse for kindness or cruelty?* Lily Weber held her head high as if she belonged, yet she and Migisi lingered at the big bridge for almost ten minutes as one wagon after another rolled into town for the Split Rock Jubilee. The smell of roasting meats filled the air, and in the distance, bands sent music echoing through the valley. Normally, Lily walked into town from the north on a quiet Sunday morning. Today was Saturday, and to reach St. Marie's, they needed to cross the busiest part of downtown Split Rock.

Act like you belong.

Lily stepped off the bridge, knowing that in a few hundred more steps, she'd be in the protective shadow of Sister Inez.

"This is stupid," Migisi whispered as he followed her on Market Street. "They're all looking at us funny because we're Indian."

"You're paranoid, and besides, Sister Inez is expecting both of us." Lily reached down and grabbed Migisi's hand, squeezing it.

Together, they merged with the crowd, and except for cross glances, few people took notice of two "civilized" Chippewa youths walking up Market Street.

Most of the crowd flowed toward Fisher Mansion, the creamery, and the train station to listen to the coronet band, but Lily and Migisi headed up the hill toward two towering spires.

Soon they saw dozens of children filling the lot between the two churches as clergy from both denominations manned stations ranging from bottle tossing to bobbing-for-apples.

"She's not going to want to talk to you," Migisi insisted. "Not with all the zhaaganaash children here."

"Sister Inez loves me. Not all white people are bad."

Sister Inez lit up when she saw Lily and passed off a young child she was holding to a nearby adult woman and walked over to them. "Lily, your ears must be burning; I was just talking about you. Have you found a teaching assignment for this fall?"

"I haven't heard back from any of the schools I applied to yet, but it is still very early."

"I say that because Father Guerin asked me if I knew anyone who would be able to teach him how to speak Chippewa. I know you are very good at teaching Chippewa children how to speak English, but it should be just as easy for you to do the opposite."

He's obviously charmed her. He's persistent, too. "I don't know if I would have time for that. Besides, I really enjoy working with children."

"Oh, I understand. Perhaps when he returns from his recent trip, we can speak to him about the details together." Then Sister Inez turned her gaze to Migisi. "Hello, young man. Do you prefer to be called Migisi or Eagle?"

Migisi scowled and didn't respond.

Lily frowned at him in warning. "Like I said, he's shy."

"Ah. Well, we have some boys looking to put together a baseball team to compete against boys from other towns. It's a Sunday afternoon league." Sister Inez smiled at Migisi. "Your sister told me how athletic and strong you've become, and I thought you might be the perfect fit. Let me introduce you to some of them."

"I-I … um…"

Nudging her brother, Lily motioned for him to keep quiet.

Resigned, Migisi followed as Sister Inez's tour began with the starting pitcher, Willem MacPherson, Emily's older brother. Like Lily, he was fifteen and considered an adult, capable of working at his father's dairy farm full-time.

After the introductions, Willem's father whispered something to his son, and Lily, fearing condemnation and judgment, moved closer to her brother.

Instead, Willem asked, "You look fast. You fast, kid?"

"Fast as a rabbit," Migisi muttered.

"Good, we could use a shortstop."

Lily smiled when Migisi relaxed just a little. *See? A good white family. Migisi needs to see this.*

The tour took them next to the strong third baseman, Bjorn Forsberg. Bjorn's forehead wrinkled during the introduction as he studied Sister Inez and Lily outside of the context of the classroom.

Once the situation was explained, Bjorn stood, arms crossed, asking, "Does he have a glove?"

"That can be arranged," Sister Inez said before whisking them off in another direction. She lowered her voice when she spoke again. "Little Albert Fisher does not bring much to the team as far as athletic ability, but his father purchased equipment for the whole team. We should be able to get an extra glove for you to practice with."

"I didn't say I'd do it yet," Migisi corrected.

Lily glared at him. "When does practice begin?"

"He could play a game as soon as tomorrow. Baseball is pretty simple: you hit the ball, or you catch the ball. The boys will teach your brother the rest of the—"

Migisi let out a little squawk, and when Lily turned, a large zhaaganaash stood holding her brother by the elbow.

"Constable Graham, what is the meaning of this?" Sister Inez asked.

"Truancy, Sister Inez. Do you know who this boy is? This is the son of Big Squeak Weber, a known fugitive." He frowned before bellowing, "Frankie Auerbach!"

A boy of ten with vibrant blonde hair snapped to attention from his game of jacks nearby.

"Frankie, be a good lad, and run to the blacksmith shop and fetch Marshall Morrison. Tell him I have Big Squeak's son."

"Let go of my brother," Lily protested, but the large man simply laughed and began dragging off her bewildered brother. After a dozen yards, Migisi began to squirm and wiggle, which only drew laughter from those standing nearby.

"Do something!" Lily turned to Sister Inez, whose eyes quickly darted to her feet. Knowing she would be of no help, Lily ran after Constable Graham as he walked down the crowded avenue toward Market Street.

"Where are you taking him?" she cried out, but she knew the answer. Migisi was now nine, which was three years older than the legal age for all Indian youths to report to boarding schools by the Office of Indian Affairs.

When Lily saw that Constable Graham ignored her, she ran ahead and threw herself down on the sidewalk. "Please don't take my brother!"

This time, Constable Graham stopped. "Why? So he can become a criminal and bootlegger like your father? Trust me, this is for his own good."

After Constable Graham walked around Lily, she sprang up and ran ahead of him again. Migisi was bawling now like a lamb being led to slaughter.

This is all my fault.

This time, Lily grabbed hold of Migisi's free arm and tried to pull him out of Constable Graham's grip, which caused him to tuck the boy under his arm and lift his feet off the ground.

Once again there was a chorus of laughter. *Why isn't anyone helping?*

The blacksmith shop appeared, with a metal cage being moved out. The cage would serve as a temporary cell for her brother.

Reacting quickly, Lily stood in front of Constable Graham and stuck out her arm. When her hand touched his chest, the crowd gasped.

"Lily!"

"Migisi!"

The pain came suddenly with a blinding flash of white before everything else, including her little brother, turned to darkness.

CHAPTER EIGHTEEN

Under the Willow

Split Rock, MN
June 21, 1897

PAIN THROBBED FROM the base of Lily's skull all the way to the backs of her eyes, and when she opened her lids, the blinding light overwhelmed her, bringing a torrent of vomit. Choking, she rolled to her side and up onto her hands and knees. As soon as it was expelled, her arms gave out and she collapsed to her side.

Where's Migisi?

Painted gray boards came into focus.

I'm not on the street where I fell.

She turned her head slightly, peering through her eyelashes until she realized the object was a white railing. Her numb arms moved, revealing she was covered in blankets.

What have I done?

Lily surrendered to the pain for a few minutes, closing her eyes and taking deep breaths. The silence of her surroundings told her she was nowhere near downtown Split Rock. Finally, she forced her eyelids open again.

Beyond the white railing, she saw a heap of green that focused into the long fronds of a massive willow tree. Surrounding it, a manicured lawn stretched out between short brick walls. Past the tree, the tops of the homes of St. John could be seen.

I'm at the convent.

Her heart jumped for a moment when a figure in a black slouch hat stepped out from behind the willow tree, but only to lift the curtain of fronds. Like her father, he wore denim and his hair pulled back into a ponytail. His frame was even similar, but he was half her father's age, with scaled boots and tattered pants. Once he lifted the curtain of fronds, Lily could see an old zhaaganaash sitting in a metal chair. The younger man closed the curtains of foliage and both figures disappeared.

Am I hallucinating?

Approaching footsteps sounded so loud that Lily winced, swallowing another round of vomit. Afraid, she closed her eyes.

"Oh darling, we need to keep fluids in you. Let me wipe off your chin."

A wet wash rag passed over her chin. *One of the nuns.*

"Keep your eyes closed, and I'll help you sit up so you can get a drink," the woman said, and a moment later, Lily felt hands reaching under her armpits.

Two women then—but still she didn't open her eyes.

The change in posture caused her to see spots, even with her lids closed. Once the world stopped spinning, she opened her lids slightly to see the robes of two nuns. "Where is Sister Inez?"

"She went down to the train station with your mother and Father Guerin."

Nothing about the statement made sense, but Lily forced her mind to work through it. *What happened to Migisi? How long have I been here?* "What day is it?"

"It's Monday, almost noon. You took quite a blow to your head, and each time you wake, you vomit and pass out," one off the nun's replied. She waved the other away. "While we've got you awake, let's get some chicken broth in you."

It's been two days?

Lily stayed conscious for the entire bowl and even drank a bit of juice. "Thank you."

"We brought you out onto the porch because it was cool and allowed you to be ill without making a mess inside."

"I don't mean to be a burden."

"Nonsense. You were known to us before Sister Inez brought you here." The nun smiled and gave her shoulder a squeeze. "Rest your eyes, Lily. Your mother will be back soon, and hopefully, with some good news about your brother."

Lily moved, her cheek now against a soft pillow, and then heavy steps walked away.

Keeping her eyes closed, she pictured the blacksmith shop, with her unconscious body in the street and her brother still in the cage … *Migisi. I'm so sorry.* The jubilee had certainly ended by now, leaving the town quiet. She opened her eyes, the town a distant blur of shapes and colors in the valley below.

Why can't I focus?

She blinked, focusing on the big willow in the front yard.

Then, a pair of legs dangled from the porch roof.

Migisi? Her heart leapt, but the legs belonged to a young woman, not a boy.

The young woman wore only a nightgown and turned her body so that her bare feet caught the spaces in the trellis, and once she put a foot on the deck railing, she dropped to the ground. Lily gasped at how similar the young woman was to herself, except with short, bobbed hair. Their eyes locked. "If you want to save the children, follow me."

How does she know about the children?

Before Lily could answer, the young woman began walking to the willow. Lily tried to force herself to move, but her vision blurred again.

This must be a dream. How else could she know about the children in the ice?

The details of the big willow came back into focus. Then from under the willow, the fronds parted, and the young woman stopped. She picked up a knife from the lawn and cut a few fronds from the tree.

Who are you?

As the young woman climbed back up the trellis, Lily again saw the same young man in the black slouch hat step around from behind the willow, lift the same curtain of fronds, and revealed again the old man in the chair positioned in the same exact way.

Is my brain broken? "Hey," Lily called out.

The young man emerged from the willow. "Lily?"

"I'm on the porch," she answered, still unsure of how she knew the young man.

With fronds of willow in his hand, he trotted to the north, completely ignoring her now.

"Hey," she protested. "Wait!"

Sudden pain swept over her, and she drifted back to sleep.

LILY WOKE TO the sound of a wagon. She opened her eyes to see monstrously large horses, with furry legs and huge manes, pulling a bright green wagon up the drive. Bjorn Forsberg was driving, holding the reins of the wagon with a tight grip. He avoided her gaze as soon as he saw her. Beside him on the bench, Father Jean Guerin looked over to her and waved. Father Guerin then turned, and Winnie popped up from the back of the wagon— she was alone in the back.

No Migisi.

Feeling sick, Lily closed her eyes and wept until she felt her mother's embrace.

Dirty Business

Hiawatha County
June 21, 1897

BJORN FORSBERG KEPT his mouth shut as he drove the wagon to Turtle Island Reservation. With the reins in his hands, he noticed traces of blood in the crook of his right elbow. He'd washed prior to church yesterday, but not well enough. He'd carried Lily, with her head in the crook of his arm, away from the chaos on Saturday's festival. He sniffed at his armpits.

I need a bath.

Beside him, Father Guerin sat sideways on the bench so that he could utter promises and encouragement about Miss Weber's brother.

Annoyed at the talkative priest, Bjorn studied the man's boots, trying to discern from the mud where the priest had taken his father's retired draft horse Goliath during the previous week.

If Nielson wanted to borrow Goliath, he would've had to sign away half of his crop. Is it because the man's a priest?

Bjorn kept the team of horses at a steady trot upon the road.

Goliath better not be covered in mud.

Two of their titans pulled the wagon now: Svadilfari and Sleipnir were monstrous Swedish draft horses from the north country. Whether hauling wagons of milk, uprooting trees, or unearthing boulders, draft horses could do the work of a dozen men. *We might be poor, but nobody has better horses than us.*

Upon leaving the Nimrod road, he found a simple path that led to the ravine of the Blue Knife River. There, at a modest cabin, a handful of Chippewa children helped the Weber women step down.

Bjorn sat stoically while everyone entered the cabin. All the tears and pain had almost been too much, so he was content to wait in the wagon rather than go inside.

At the rear of the house, he spotted Goliath tethered to a tree with a plate of corn at its base. Pleased to see the horse, he dismounted and retrieved Goliath, rubbing the sandy mud from his haunches. *Father Guerin took him north.*

But then Bjorn noticed flecks of blood on Goliath's neck and saddlebag. He studied the horse closely but found no wound. Nor did he see one on Father Guerin. He tied the big horse to the rear of the wagon. With Goliath secure, Bjorn climbed back up into the driver's bench and waited.

And waited.

I'm going to miss the evening milking again.

Since Saturday, he'd only helped his father with two of the five milkings as he tried to help both Lily and Father Guerin. Bjorn knew his father would soon run out of patience and see it as an excuse to get out of work.

Several minutes later, the Jesuit priest emerged, along with a few children who eyed him suspiciously.

"I'll walk back to town when I'm finished, Bjorn," Father Guerin said. "Thank you for all of your help the past few days."

"It seemed the right thing to do," Bjorn said and before the priest could say more, he turned around for Split Rock.

To return home, Bjorn entered Split Rock from the north, passed over the big bridge spanning the confluence of Split Rock Creek and the Crow Wing River, then traveled down Market Street—which reminded him of the dramatic scene from Saturday.

I can't believe nobody stood up to Morrison.

On the far southern end of town, he turned at the sign for the creamery. A newly built trestle bridge spanned the Crow Wing River, allowing him to pass back across to the western bank, where on the granite ridge overlooking the new creamery, his family's dairy farm perched high above the lake and river.

With the house on the high ground to the west and the dairy barn downslope to the east, he drove straight to the horse barn in the rear center of the homestead. His mother stood on the porch and his sisters were walking toward the barn, where his father waited.

Good. Just in time for the evening milking.

Near his father, a male sat upon a pale horse with a two-toned mane.

Martin Nielson.

"There's our little hero," Nielson greeted. The Norwegian farmer had courted Bjorn's sister Britta two summers earlier, and even after he married another local girl, he still looked to Bjorn's father, Gustaf, as a father figure in matters of farming. "I heard you snatched that stick from Bushy Bill and shoved it where the sun don't shine."

Bjorn smirked and shook his head. He'd snatched the stick from the lawman's hand and threw it to the ground. *I didn't shove it anywhere.* But he enjoyed the attention Martin was giving. At eighteen, Martin Nielson served as a big brother for Bjorn and provided most of the joy in his life.

"How's the girl?" Nielson asked.

Bjorn felt his ears grow warm. "Miss Weber is awake now and seems to be getting better. I brought her home today."

"You did good, Bjorn. Now I've got to get back to the little missus before supper. I think your father needs a hand. Better hustle."

"Girls!" Gustaf Forsberg barked from the doorway to the dairy barn, and Bjorn's sisters stopped waving at Martin and ran into the barn.

Bjorn hustled to unharness the horses and release them into the rear corral. He parked the wagon properly then joined his family for milking.

"One at a time," his father was instructing as Bjorn entered the barn. Gustaf lifted the bucket of corn and climbed into the milking chute. He poured out a long line of corn down the chute and then filled up four small buckets of water and set them at the end of the chute.

By the time he returned to the gate, Bjorn and his sisters were standing above the little buckets of water. "Be sure to clean their teats well. It's been muddy the last few days and I don't want to give Van Slyke any excuse to drop the price."

Bjorn nodded and moved to carry his pail next to the milking stalls. Bjorn's older sister, Britta, took the second stall. In the fourth stall, seven-year-old Signe would take almost thirty minutes to milk old Milly, who was the most docile of the herd. Even so, Gustaf had made sure Milly's rear leg was tied down so as not to kick his youngest.

Ten minutes into milking, Britta interrupted the sound of squirting milk and crunching corn with her sweet melodies of "Rejoice all ye Believers," which was her favorite hymn.

Normally, Bjorn rushed through milking in order to free himself to either prepare the horses for a delivery to the creamery or to hunt or fish. Tonight, he took his time, knowing he and his father would finish the cows while the girls helped with other chores prior to supper.

As soon as the girls finished and left the barn, Gustaf said, "So now that things have settled down, tell me the full version of what happened."

"Constable Graham had Migisi, and out of nowhere, Marshal Morrison cracked Miss Weber in the back of her head," Bjorn started, the words rushed. "Folks just stood there as she bled, so I offered my help to Sister Inez, who was the only one raising a fuss." He looked at the stubborn blood stain on his right arm. "I helped carry her to the convent where she could get help, but then Sister Inez asked if I could fetch Miss Weber's mother, which is why I borrowed the wagon. I know I should have found you before taking it, but I knew it was the right thing to do. Again, I apologize."

"I raised you to be a man of action, and your actions made me proud," his father replied. "Folks explained what happened, which is why I didn't need to hear the story until now. Though Nielson told me you disarmed Morrison, that might've been a bit too bold."

"I know, but he hit a woman. I know she's Indian, but she's also a teacher."

Gustaf nodded. "I see you brought Goliath home, also."

"When I got out to the reservation the first time, Father Guerin was there, and both Mrs. Weber and Father Guerin jumped into the wagon with me. It wasn't until later that I realized Father Guerin left Goliath back at the reservation, so I had to bring him back out when I dropped Miss Weber and her mother at their home."

"Feed him well and clean him up tomorrow." Gustaf looked in the direction of the horse stall before returning to the story. "And the boy?"

"They sent him away with an Indian Agent this morning, nevermind the protest from Father Guerin, Father Hebert, and

Sister Inez. They're sending him to Pennsylvania." Bjorn scowled. "It's not right. How can they do that?"

"There are the Laws of God, and there are the Laws of Men. Being lawful doesn't always make it right." Gustaf sighed. "You did the right thing in helping that family."

"What do you know about Father Guerin?"

"What do you want to know?"

Bjorn tensed, afraid to question the behavior of an adult. "The day he showed up in Split Rock, he came to see you. How do you know him?"

Gustaf was silent for a few minutes. "In a way, he's an old friend of the family. Father Guerin is to be trusted."

It was close to his father telling him to shut his mouth, so Bjorn dropped it and went back to milking.

Once they were finished, his father asked, "Why do you ask about Guerin?"

Bjorn shrugged. "There was blood on Goliath, but neither he nor Father Guerin had so much as a scratch. I couldn't figure out where the blood came from."

"Even though you have the strength of a man, you're still a boy, and there are things about this world you're just not ready to know. One day, you'll know the way things are, and you'll wish to be a boy again. For now, just look away and stop asking questions about Father Guerin. He's a good man who has to do some bad things. Understand?"

Bjorn didn't, but he nodded anyway and followed his weary father into the house for supper.

The Last Child

Turtle Island Reservation
June 30, 1897

ONE BY ONE, the other children vanished. Fawn Chevreuil knew it wasn't the Wintermaker or some foul forest monster, like Lily dreamed. She saw the children leave.

First, Blackfish LaBiche had come to collect his wife and children from the summer camp, vanishing within an hour of appearing.

Next, Pierre LeDuc had arrived, offering a bit more of an explanation. "They took Migisi to try to get Big Squeak to step into a trap. They kept him chained up at a train station in Brainerd for a few days, then they took him to Duluth for another few days. They were just hoping Big Squeak would be stupid enough to try to rescue him."

"So they're really sending Migisi to Pennsylvania?" Fawn asked LeDuc.

"A pawn. He'll be safe but quite miserable. He's in a different kind of trap now, and now it's a waiting game. Big Squeak wants us all to get our families someplace far away, so they don't get used as leverage against us."

"Is my father coming?"

"I ain't seen your father in a while, but I'm sure he'll come for you sooner or later. Hang tight until then."

After a week, Fawn's mother left with her little sister to go visit an ex-husband at Leech Lake, but they didn't come back.

After a summer storm left her cold and miserable, Fawn went to live with the Webers rather than look for her mother.

"SO WHY DID they send Migisi to Pennsylvania?" Fawn asked as she worked together in the kitchen with Winnie and Lily.

At the mention of Migisi, Lily's eyes grew a little clouded. "The school in Pennsylvania takes Natives from all sorts of tribes. They do that so the kids can't speak their own tongue and are forced to learn English."

"Why did they send *you* to Morris?"

"The more you fight it, the harder it is on you. The girls who lived with me at Morris didn't care anymore. The girls who fought it were either beaten or sent away. I'm guessing Migisi fought those Indian agents pretty hard."

Both of them seem fine with this. It makes me wonder if Lily didn't bring him to town knowing he'd get taken away. Would she do that? "Is there any chance he can get sent back to Minnesota?"

Winnie was the one who answered with, "Father Guerin is writing some letters to see if he can get Migisi released, but it takes a while for these things to happen."

Fawn glanced at Lily, holding her gaze just long enough to indicate that she had something important to say not suitable for the ears of a parent. When the meal was finished, the two girls stepped outside to talk.

"I meant to say something," Fawn began once they stood near the ravine, "but it was so crazy with you getting hurt and Migisi getting taken."

"What are you talking about?"

"I don't think Father Guerin is a real priest."

"No, he's a Jesuit, it's a different kind of priest."

"I don't think he's a priest of any kind," Fawn insisted. "A while ago, I found him camped by the Nimrod Bridge, and he had his shirt off, so I could see his chest, and he had scars all over his body. He's been shot and stabbed. Plus, after they came to get Winnie, I took care of the Forsberg horse he borrowed. There was blood on it, and in the saddle bags, he had a list of names, including all of our fathers in the Black Hat Gang. What if he's a villain? What if he's trying to capture or kill our fathers?"

"That's Bushy Bill," Lily dismissed, "not Father Guerin. He's some sort of ambassador."

"Are you sure? I walked with him the whole way back because he wanted to visit Nanakonan, and the whole time, he asked me a hundred questions, and it's not just getting to know you questions but really weird questions about our family." Fawn sniffed. "I don't trust him, Lily."

"Listen, the folks in St. John are trying to steal our land. They already have a crew preparing to make a bridge down by the lake. I heard it from their own mouths that Father Guerin was trying to stop them. He's our only ally on this. What do you think we should do?"

Fawn shrugged.

After sitting on their big rock, Lily deflated. "Nanakonan won't even speak to me. My own grandfather thinks I did this on purpose."

"Did you?"

Lily snapped, "Of course not. Why would you say that?"

"Because you seem to hate everything about being Chippewa. Look at you. You're trying pretty hard to be a white girl. Now that Migisi has been sent away, he can't even learn how to be a Firekeeper."

Lily's shoulders fell as she bowed her head. "Migisi and I had something strange happen to us, and I just didn't want it to get worse. I didn't wish this upon him."

"What sort of strange thing happened?"

Lily looked down the valley. "I need you to be very quiet. The last time Migisi and I did this, we almost got caught trespassing … But I want you to see something, understand?"

Fawn nodded and followed her down the ravine, across the Blue Knife River, and up the western slope. Like a pair of rabbits, they lingered at brush and darted between trees until Lily stopped at a tree where broken dreamcatcher rested on the ground.

"Nanakonan gave that to us."

That's all? "Yeah, I see them all the time," Fawn muttered. "It's a dreamcatcher. Mothers put them above sleeping babies."

"Could a spirit have done this?"

Fawn stepped back in alarm. "Why are you being so weird?"

"You don't understand what it's like living next to Nanakonan. Once he puts something in your head, it's all you can think about. He had me and Migisi convinced that his dreamcatcher could capture ghosts."

Fawn fearlessly picked up the broken loom. "I think somebody broke this on purpose. Did you really think there'd be a ghost caught in the web?"

Lily nodded.

So my father's spook stories about my cousins are true.

CHAPTER TWENTY-ONE

Old Scars, Old Blood

Turtle Island Reservation
July 6, 1897

IT TOOK TWO weeks for Lily Weber to muster up enough courage to retrieve her father's birchbark canoe, which was still in Split Rock.

Will it even be there?

Broad daylight or under the cover of darkness? A weekday or a weekend?

Am I putting Fawn in jeopardy?

"I don't care if government agents take me," Fawn had finally offered. "Let's go on an adventure."

Lily wanted to make the trip to Split Rock worth her while, so she brought letters of application for several schools.

The girls took the northern shore to get to Split Rock, avoiding the main road by skirting the shore. It took longer, but it allowed them plenty of cover.

By late morning, they stood on the edge of the woods looking at the sawmill. The outlet of Lake Manitou was Split Rock Creek, which upon dropping over the headwaters, rushed through a channel of boulders until it joined the Crow Wing River a hundred yards downstream. The sawmill's foundation was set upon the solid stone of the creekbank, with the massive water wheel spinning the noisy saws within. Out in the lagoon, lumberjacks wrangled limbless pines into the mouth of the great monster.

"You can hide under the Split Rock bridge while I go uptown to the church," Lily said as they followed the creek to where it joined the Crow Wing. "If you get spooked, just duck into the woods and go wait below Mount Olivet Cemetery."

"How long are you going to be?"

"I shouldn't be too long. An hour at the most," she answered. "Then we'll climb up Bleeding Rock, and on the south side is the Forsberg farm."

"Good luck," Fawn called, hopping away.

Lily straightened her back and walked directly into the world; unlike the day of the Jubilee, the streets were now empty, allowing her to quickly travel the city blocks to the two spires.

As she walked, she thought of Father Guerin. Her tender feelings of protecting the naïve priest from the villains of Triton now felt bitter after learning from Fawn that he was more than his priestly collar and dimpled smile.

Be polite. Smile. Get him talking. Then ask your questions.

When she reached St. Marie's, she didn't knock and immediately darted to the staircase leading to the balcony.

Father Guerin's sprawl covered the floor, a few pews, and his portable desk. He wore the black clothing of a Jesuit but not his robes. "Hello Lily. It's good to see you."

"Why do you have scars?" she blurted out instead of what she had been practicing to say to him.

He looked down, the sign of a liar. Then he stood, glancing to the main church below. "Father Hebert?"

When no answer came, he sat back down, his expression serious. "Did Fawn Chevreuil tell you about them?"

"What kind of priest gets shot and stabbed?"

"An unlucky priest."

Lily huffed. "Are you even a priest?"

"Of course I'm a priest, but I'm not like Father Hebert. I've told you this before."

She looked around where dozens of maps, books, and letters revealed his purpose … what that purpose was she wasn't yet sure of. "So? Why do you have scars?"

"I'm a skilled linguist, which is why my superiors thought I could be helpful in avoiding a humanitarian crisis in the north woods. Are you familiar with Wounded Knee?"

The massacre of the Sioux several years ago. She nodded.

"My superiors think the same thing will happen in northern Minnesota, and when it does, the U.S. government will have an excuse to deal with the Chippewa severely."

"The scars though?" she prompted.

"I received my first scar during my posting in the Philippines. Do you know the Philippines?"

Lily nodded again. "It's in the far Pacific Ocean."

"As part of the church, I was trying to bring civilization to it. As a linguist, I learned the language of the remote tribes upon these islands, to enlist their help. Well, some of the Spanish locals didn't like change and turned to violence to solve their problem. The other scar," he patted his side, "was a misunderstanding."

"So you're some sort of spy?"

"I'll be blunt: I orchestrated chaos. Once I established contact with some anti-colonial militant groups, I helped fund and organize a growing rebellion. I received my bayonet wound doing the same thing in Cuba, another island, but this one is far—"

"I teach geography," Lily interrupted, a bit impatiently. "I know where Cuba is located."

"Again, I was stationed to protect the Cuban people during the growing turmoil, and in a case of mistaken identity, a soldier thought I was an assassin and stuck me with his bayonet before I could explain who I was. Before coming here, I spent several months at a Georgetown hospital."

A war in Minnesota? It seems far-fetched. "So you're here to help start another rebellion?"

"I need friends I can trust, Lily, and I'm putting my life in your hands. I couldn't tell Fawn Chevreuil about my scars, but I think you are old enough to understand the dangers that face your people if things don't change."

His life is in my hands? Uncomfortable at that, she asked, "Why did your saddlebag have the names of the Black Hat Gang?"

His brow wrinkled. "Fawn did a lot of snooping."

Just give me a straight answer. "So?"

"The best way to communicate between reservations is to use systems that already exist, and the Black Hat Gang already has a network of bootleggers avoiding the law. Nothing has happened yet, but I'm getting to know leaders of all sorts, from tribal elders to gang leaders. Before we can begin a defense of your people, we need to establish a network." Father Guerin paused, adjusting his glasses. "That's the honest-to-goodness reason I'm here, and also the reason why I could use your tutoring."

Again with the tutoring? Lily ignored the proposal by asking another question. "Any word from my brother?"

"Yes, in fact. Migisi is at the Carlisle Indian Industrial School. Until the fall, he's working at a Quaker farm for the Summer Outing Program."

"So he's a slave?" *And it's all my fault he's there. Why did I bring Fawn to town?* Lily retreated a step toward the door.

"The government would argue that he's learning the trade of farming, but yes, he's a slave. You went to the Sacred Heart School in Morris, which is run by the Roman Catholic Church, but even that school is about to change. The government has run out of patience and wants to rid tribes of their beliefs. I'm here to help fight this."

"Isn't change a good thing?"

"A diverse world is a strong world; a homogenous world is weak and easily controlled. Preserving cultures, languages, and traditions is important to me. Does that explain it?"

A Jesuit spy sent to protect an oppressed people? It sounds too good to be true. Why was he so truthful with me? Lily felt the sharp edge of her anger dull, and Father Guerin looked down from the balcony to the still empty church. "I suppose it does explain your scars." *Since he revealed his mission to me, perhaps he can be trusted.* "Can I ask you a favor?"

"Absolutely," he said and took a step closer to her.

"I have letters and job applications given to me by Sister Inez, and I was wondering if you'd be able to bring them to the post office? After what happened to Migisi, I've lost trust in the fine folks of Split Rock."

"I'll make sure they are sent." Father Guerin extended his hand. "But please actually consider my offer to be a tutor."

Dread filled Lily as she left the church to return to the big bridge. *A war in Minnesota? It wouldn't be much of a fight.* Yet while walking the same street where Bushy Bill clubbed her made her realize the war was already being fought. *Joseph Little Toad was right. Soon my people will vanish in the wind.*

Her steps quickened. *Why did I bring Fawn here?*

Once she reached the shade, Fawn waited right where she'd been left.

"That didn't take any time at all."

Talk of war made Lily afraid to walk in town in broad daylight, but the alternative path was equally frightening. The wooded ridge loomed beyond the Split Rock Creek Bridge. "Have you ever been to Bleeding Rock?"

Fawn grinned. "No, but I've heard stories about it. It's where the earth bleeds blue."

The earth? Lily was about to correct her when suddenly it all made sense. Blue Knife. Old Copper Road. *Of course... bleeding rocks.* "There's a shortcut to the canoe if we go by Bleeding Rock. Are you up for an adventure?"

"Absolutely," Fawn said.

AFTER CROSSING SPLIT Rock Creek, the girls scrambled up the bluff, which let them look down on the sawmill, the town, and even Lake Manitou.

Of course, Lily almost laughed. *So obvious.* She could see the dried rivulets of blue vitriol that oozed out from deep within the earth. *Bleeding rock, literally.*

The place seemed beautiful as thoughts of beheaded women and corpses of children tossed off the cliff vanished in favor of simple geology. Exposed copper turns to vitriol, which the waters turn to bluish green blood.

Yet her brother would argue this. *How could he? He is in Pennsylvania.*

Their successful trip soon turned into a disaster once they reached the southern slope of the bluff.

Where's the canoe?

It took Fawn a few moments to notice that Lily had stopped. "What's wrong?"

"The canoe … It's not where we left it. We pulled it up onto the bank and hid it behind the brush so no one would see it. It … it's not there."

"Something's there." Fawn galloped down the hill to inspect. "It's a piece of wood with nail scratches on it. Wait, there's words."

By the time Lily reached the bottom of the hill, Fawn was reading aloud: "'Canoe at Forsbergs.' Guess it's not stolen. What are we going to do?"

Despite being gruff, her student had been the only one to defend her from Bushy Bill, or so she had been told. *He must be an ally.* "Let's go find out."

The Forsberg dairy farm was just a few hundred yards from the wild rice field, where Old Copper Road bent toward the Crow Wing River and the trestle bridge.

As they neared the farm, Lily picked up a stick. "In case they have a dog."

Fawn picked one up also.

Nanak once described settlers as "beaver people" for their ability to destroy a forest to build their homes. Carved into the southern edge of Bleeding Rock, the Forsberg farm sat upon a patch of rocky ground now void of trees, which had been turned into barns and sheds. Unlike a beaver dam, the Forsberg farm was clean and orderly with fresh paint and straight fences.

"Hello? Is anybody home?"

Signe Forsberg acted as the family watchdog, running up ahead of the curious adults at the porch. A moment later, the older children, Britta and Bjorn, came out of the house also.

"We're looking for our canoe," Lily said from where she stopped.

Bjorn Forsberg said something to his parents, who didn't budge. The frumpy redhead, wearing overalls without a shirt underneath, waved the visitors to the barn. Signe herded them in that direction.

"You sure about this?" Fawn said under her breath.

Lily nodded.

When Bjorn opened the door, the birchbark canoe rested alongside the green wagon. "I was going to bring it to your house the next time we needed to go to St. John, but we haven't had a reason yet. I saw some younger boys playing in the reeds and didn't want anyone to just take it, so I hauled it up here. I knew it was yours."

Bjorn acted put-off but his nervous manners indicated something else.

"Thank you, Bjorn. You've been more than kind," Lily said. "Fawn, you can grab the nose."

"I can carry it down for you," Bjorn offered and then rushed forward to roll the canoe over before slipping under it from the rear and walking his way up until he found the center. He grunted a bit, but soon had the canoe off the ground.

"We'll carry the paddles and help keep the ends balanced," Lily said, and the trio left a silent Signe behind for the walk down the slope to Lake Manitou.

By the time they reached the water's edge, Bjorn Forsberg was dripping sweat and breathing heavily. When he flopped the canoe down, he stood with his hands on his hips staring at it.

"Thanks for being so kind, Bjorn. For taking care of the canoe and for helping before."

He shrugged. "Of course, Miss Weber." He wiped his face with his forearm before walking back up the hill.

The girls got the canoe positioned and then pushed off into the reeds.

"I think he likes you," Fawn commented.

"Ew," Lily said and both girls laughed, but the smirk wore off as Lily thought more about his actions.

Not again.

A WESTERN WIND blew across Lake Manitou, forcing the girls to keep the nose into the wind with a steady paddle or risk capsizing. The day was pleasant, allowing Lily to ignore the burning in her arms.

It felt almost cathartic.

But it wasn't enough to keep Fawn from talking about boys.

"Have you heard anything from Samuel?" Fawn grinned with raised eyebrows.

"No, and I'm glad he's gone. Seeing him all the time would just remind me of my mistake or cause me to make new mistakes."

"Are you worried you're not going to find a husband?"

"I don't want a husband until I've been a teacher for a few years. If I get a husband, I'll get pregnant, and then I won't be able to teach anymore." Lily shrugged. "Maybe I'll start looking for a husband when I'm twenty."

"Twenty? I almost wish I'd been grabbed along with Migisi so that I could meet some boys. I'm sick of just wandering from camp to camp. I want a husband who could build me a home and get me a nice kitchen like your mom's."

"Trust me, you don't want to go to a boarding school."

"Why?"

"Because the boys are like wild animals. They'd just see you as a piece of meat. None of them are looking for a wife there. You'd just be a feather in their bonnet. A conquest."

Please, God, help Migisi find his path. Don't let him become mean and nasty, Lily prayed and continued her focus on Fawn. "Go find some quiet community, and even if the boys there are ugly, they'd treat you better than any of the boys at a boarding school."

"What if the boys are—"

Lily stopped paddling when she saw men standing on the shore of the Blue Knife River delta. Fawn took note and stopped paddling also.

"What do we do?" Fawn asked.

Bushy Bill isn't with them. She did see one of the Triton men, standing on the western bank, but didn't know if it was Stewart, Haggard, or Marquette. Another of the men was unmistakable— Adam Thunder Face. He stood on the shore with arms crossed, a full head and shoulders taller than any of the others. The rest of the men were well-dressed men, out of place in the wild.

"We'll just wait," Lily said. "They're not here for us. These must be the guys building the bridge. Do you see the stakes in the ground? That's the path for the road."

Her emotions shifted from admiration to hatred. Triton wanted to take their land, but the path for the new road made obvious sense. Instead of the road turning north at Lyons, it would descend down the ravine and cross above the river valley, leaving a straight path to the town of St. John.

Floating in the same place as her icy nightmare, Lily contrasted reality to her dream. *Is this the meaning of my dream?* Lily wondered. *Do the children out on the chunk of ice represent the reservation? Is the Horned Serpent the Triton men?* In both dreams, her heroes were killed by the monster.

Drifting on the lake, the canoe floated between the Blue Knife River delta and Turtle Island. Seeing it again, Lily remembered another part of the dream—the animals guarding the island.

"What do you know about doodems?"

"Huh?" Fawn glanced at her then away. "Not much; my mom isn't a very spiritual person, if you know what I mean."

"My mother is spiritual, but never taught me about the meaning of the old clans." Winnie had chosen the last name Weber instead of adopting the clan system of the Chippewa. Yet at White Earth, Lily learned the old clans were different than just family trees. Each clan had a role within the community.

Lily's thought ended as the men suddenly converged in the shallow waters of the delta, only to point upstream. *Where they want to build the dam.*

"I think the reason they sent Migisi so far away from home is that the northern forty acres is in his name. If he sells the lot to Triton, they'd probably let him go with money stuffed in his pockets."

"Do you think Migisi would sell?"

"Never. He'll get stubborn, and the more beatings he gets, the angrier he'll get."

"Maybe he'll run away."

"Pennsylvania's a long way away. If he does that, he'd turn into my dad before ever returning home."

The voices of the men grew louder, and then handshakes happened, sending the Triton businessman back to town and Adam Thunder Face back up the hill to the Loose Goose. The tender men, however, continued placing stakes and strings as they finished the imaginary bridge right up to the water.

"Let's go," Lily said, pushing the canoe forward with her paddle.

Fawn nodded, lifting her paddle.

The closer they got to the delta, the less intimidating the pack of four men became. The stakes and strings went all the way back up the hill to Lyons and the bend in the existing road.

As the girls passed, the engineers looked up. Lily kept her head down, but Fawn turned, smiled, and waved.

Was I such a flirt at her age?

Lily knew the answer was yes.

Along Thunder Face's part of the river, the walls were wide, but at the place the river narrowed, the water also deepened.

It took twice as many strokes to ascend the river's flow, which at midsummer now reached its lowest point. Once they reached the rapids, they took out the long poles, and standing, walked the canoe up through the narrow parts of the rapids.

The blue knife.

Bleeding rocks.

With the water low, she could see springs in the riverbank leaking stained water: orange water carrying iron and blue-green water carrying copper residue.

It's not sorcery ... it's basic geology. Maybe God sent me symbolic dreams so I would protect my people. He's sent me Father Guerin and also Bjorn. Perhaps he's getting my heart ready for trials to come.

A few miles upstream, the water deepened and the flow lessened, allowing them to catch their breath before beaching the canoe at the big posts that had once been the Gray Heron bridge. Together, they pulled it several feet up the bank.

"I don't know about you, but I'm starving," Lily said, smelling smoke wafting into the valley.

Yet it wasn't a freshly cooked meal that welcomed them home.

"Whose horse?" Fawn asked.

Lily had the answer but didn't say it, fearing the worst.

When they reached the porch, her mother sat with Blackfish LaBiche.

The somber thug looked right past Lily, which calmed her heart. He stared down Fawn as she approached.

"Your mother sent me," he called.

"Why?" Fawn folded her arms.

"Your father was arrested in Bemidji."

Fawn shrugged.

"Your mother and little sister have gone up to Leech Lake to wait for their annuity payments. I can bring you to her if you want."

Lily knew how this was going to go. Fawn's father was a criminal, and her mother was a whore. A dozen men had come in and out of her life, and with each one, her mother's worth grew less. Her father remained a mythic outlaw.

"What if I don't want to go?"

Blackfish remained stoic and reached into his pocket. "She sent you a little money. You are to use it if you need to travel or to give it to Winnie to pay for your keep."

"What's going to happen to my father?" Fawn asked, not reaching for the money.

"That depends on your father, but don't expect to see him for a few months at least." He paused, shifting his weight from foot to foot. "So? Are you coming with me?"

Fawn shot a look at Winnie, who nodded.

I lost a brother but gained a sister. Perhaps God sent Fawn, also.

CHAPTER TWENTY-TWO

A Promise

Turtle Island Reservation
July 1897

HER MOTHER ALWAYS prepared for the worst, which meant Lily's summer days were filled with harvesting and preserving food from the garden in case the men in their lives never appeared again. Berries and nuts were gathered from along the ravine, fish were gutted and dried, and the vegetables were either dried or canned in the manner of other pioneer women instead of the traditional Anishinaabe methods.

But this time, Lily had Fawn.

More and more activity came from Lyons as the road went from stakes and strings to crews of men tearing into the earth and then rebuilding with packed dirt and ditches. A few years earlier, the sound of logs coming down the river would draw Lily to the riverbank. The sound of a horse would draw her to the edge of the woods. Now, those sounds were so regular that she almost ignored them.

So it came as a surprise when Lily saw a rider veer away from Lyons and head to Grandfather Nanak's cabin.

She set down the tub of canning water at the top of the ravine and wandered to her grandfather's lot to investigate. It was an old stallion.

Goliath—the old Forsberg horse.

Intrigued, she kept walking.

When she arrived, she heard voices long before she reached the cabin, realizing the voices came from below the spot where Migisi's ceremonial lodge had been built.

Even though the lodge had been taken apart, she could still see its footings as well as the pile of stones used to heat the sweat lodge.

Superstitious heathens, Lily thought of the Blanket Men who'd visited. One of those stones had burnt Migisi's hands when he tried carrying it from the pile and into the lodge.

A rock shelf overlooked the river, giving her an almost vertical view of the water. Standing below, she not only saw Grandfather Nanak but also Father Guerin. Dropping to her belly, she let out a grunt then held her breath.

They kept talking.

"So you don't know if Nicollet visited the cave?" Father Guerin asked.

"The water was low like this, so I stayed with the canoe as he took Nicollet further upstream. If I hadn't been with the canoe, I certainly would have been captured by the Pillagers too."

"So Nicollet was taken prisoner before your father showed him the cave?"

"I was only a boy, but it couldn't have been more than two hours before Chief Matchigabo found them, so I doubt Nicollet was able to see much."

"Nicollet's journals about what happened along the river were a little vague. He wrote about what happened once he and Chagobay were taken as prisoners to Leech Lake, but we can only speculate what happened here."

"The Pillagers had orders to protect this territory, whether from Sioux or American. When they took Nicollet and my father, I knew the abduction would draw attention to Lake Manitou. Even though it took quite a bit of effort, I managed to cover the opening of the cave with enough rock that no one would accidentally find it."

"If we weren't standing here with you showing it to me, I would not have been able to guess there was a cave."

"I am forced to wash away the pewabic that leaks from deep inside the cave."

"Pewabic?" Guerin asked.

Clay, Father Guerin. Pewabic is our word for clay.

"The blue residue that comes up from the ground. The magic of the Water Drum cannot be contained, even by my crude efforts to conceal it. Our enemies know about the blue earth, which is why they have since focused on this place."

"Perhaps," Father Guerin said and gave a long sigh. "This plan for a dam seems to indicate they haven't put all the clues together. Why would they want the cave hidden under the waters of a reservoir? Their focus seems to be entirely on the western shore."

"Assinikande," Grandfather said.

Flat Rock, Father Guerin. The western shore.

"As much as I'd love to roll away those stones and take a peek inside the cave, we'd best leave things alone, lest we draw unwanted attention. Luckily, both projects will be downstream, so Triton should not have an excuse to be anywhere near here. I've got some men coming to put up the fence along the Thunder Face property line. While Constable Graham and Marshal Morrison are already in Triton's pockets, I think the sheriff might be able to help us if there are any trespassers. I appreciate you showing this to me."

Grandfather and Father Guerin grew silent for a short while before Lily heard footsteps on the rough trail.

They're coming back up.

Lily crawled backwards and crept behind a thick trunk.

With surprising tenderness, Father Guerin patiently assisted her grandfather up the last part of the hike. Even more surprising was that Nanak let him. The two returned to the cabin for a few minutes, speaking things Lily could not hear. After several minutes, Father Guerin returned to the old stallion and deftly saddled it.

Once he was out of sight, Lily boldly stepped out into the open and was almost immediately spotted by her grandfather.

He said nothing, cradled something in his hands, and turned to sit upon his favorite chair on the porch.

When she made no move to come closer, he called softly, "Come, Granddaughter."

No sass. No questions.

Just let him lead the way.

It had been weeks since Migisi was taken, and there still hadn't been a significant conversation between them, but with the mystery of her dreams, she wondered if he had answers for her.

Lily obeyed.

"Do you know what this is?"

The object was made of polished wood, very similar to an ornate walking stick except that it had a flat head with an inlaid metal instrument resembling a thermometer.

Lily shook her head.

"Take it and look at the back."

Lily took it and read the carved inscription:

For JNN

Yours Always,

AVH

"The young priest brought it to me as a token of his dedication. It is a barometer that my father once used while escorting Jean Nicholas Nicollet up the Mississippi River. Even though my father

Chagobay was a savage to most white men, Nicollet understood my father as an intellectual equal. Nicollet shared his science, and my father taught Nicollet the ways of our people. My father was killed by ignorant men, and Nicollet was poisoned by his enemies, but a promise was made long ago, and Guerin means to fulfill it." He looked at her, eyes narrowing. "Should I trust him?"

The question lingered in the air. "You're asking me?" *Oh, Good Lord.* Lily searched for the words to answer. "I don't understand what Father Guerin wants with you."

"When I was younger than you, the Serpent Star appeared in the sky. When I asked my father what it meant, he said it was how the Creator marked time. Each time the Serpent Star appears, a new era begins. The last time, the Serpent Star brought Nicollet, but enemies destroyed the plans of great men like Nicollet and Chagobay." He looked at the barometer. "So, Granddaughter, does the young priest speak truth or does he wear the Face of Death?"

Perhaps this is how I'll save the children from the Horned Serpent. "Father Guerin says he is a Jesuit sent to bring chaos to the north woods to help force the government to stop its policies of removing the reservations." *There, I said it. But did I just betray Father Guerin or help him?* At her grandfather's silence, she added, "He's a priest but he's also some sort of soldier. I think he might be dangerous, but I think he's on the side of our people."

Grandfather rubbed his temples and brow, shielding his face with his hand. "You are avoiding the question—which is a good thing." When he removed his hand, he looked almost frightened. "I am old and might not live to see the Serpent Star return in another decade. You and your brother will have to lead the way for our people. So the choice is yours."

"What choice?"

"You will need to decide if you trust the Jesuit or not. Once you have decided, then your training will need to begin soon."

"What training?"

"You are a teacher, correct?"

"Yes."

"Guerin tells me that they could keep your brother for years, and if that is true, I cannot risk dying with the knowledge I have. I must pass it on, and you then must be the one who trains your brother."

"Me?"

"By the end of summer, you must decide. If you trust the priest as an ally, then I can share the truths with him; if you don't trust the priest, then *you* must carry the mantle to pass on to your brother." At her gasp, he shifted away. "Now, run along."

That's it?

Lily rose and looked at the antique barometer. *What sort of promise was made between Nicollet and Chagobay?*

Servant of the Horned Serpent

Turtle Island Reservation
July 1897

A COLD FRONT broke the summer drought overnight, bringing gale force winds, a ferocious lightning storm, torrents of rain—and spirits from the depths.

Lily could hear the river roaring through the valley while she ate breakfast and finished quickly, rushing to check on the canoe. The nose was tethered to a tree, but she pulled it further up the bank in case the water continued to rise.

There's no way I'm running the rapids today.

As a young girl, Lily used to watch the rapids froth for hours following a storm. A hundred miles of creeks and streams fed the Blue Knife River. Besides the danger of whitewater conditions passing over Nicollet Rapids, Triton would have already released pine logs down from the forests south of Leech Lake.

"I'm going to bring letters into town," Lily declared to her mother once she arrived back at the cabin.

"Can I come with you?" Fawn asked.

I shouldn't have brought you last time. "Not this time. Besides the mail, I have business with Sister Inez and Father Guerin, so I'll be there for a while. I should be home by supper, though."

"Father Guerin, huh?" Fawn sassed.

Lily took a breath to argue but instead walked away.

LETTERS IN HAND, Lily cautiously walked the road leading to Split Rock. With the morning sun rising over the woods to the east, she hastened her step as she passed by the bend in the road at Lyons, where farmers and loggers drank until passing out.

And even worse, where Adam Thunder Face was.

From Lyons, she hiked in the warmth of the sun for three miles.

Hearing the rattle of wheels approaching, Lily hid behind a big cottonwood. Over her heavy breathing, she made out the rattling sound of empty milk canisters and sighed. It was likely Jonas Penny returning from town after selling his family's dairy products for the day. But she wasn't brave enough to look.

Once it had gone quiet, she stepped out from her hiding spot and continued towards town.

A few minutes later, she stepped off the road into the tall grass when she saw a rider on a big chestnut horse approaching at a gallop.

Delbert Grant.

Unlike Jonas, who always gave her a cold stare if he caught her looking, Delbert had shown her unwanted and inappropriate attention during their adolescence, so Lily walked a steady path on the grass, spying where she might run if needed.

Lessons learned from White Earth.

Back at White Earth, she'd nursed Esther Red Eagle, one of her peers, for a week after she'd been beaten and raped on her way back from buying supplies from a nearby mercantile store. When no one was brought to justice, zhaaganaash or Indian, everyone became a suspect in Lily's mind.

But Delbert gave her a mere glance when he passed her.

Best be off the road by the time he returns. His wormy brain might have ideas by then.

When she reached the second curve that turned south to Split Rock, she saw another rider approaching and got off the road to hide in the shadows of the trees.

Except for the prickly wall of pine needles on the outer edge of the woods, the inner forest was cool and inviting. The tall canopy of pines kept weeds and brush from growing and dropped a thick bed of soft golden-brown needles along the ground. Compared to the dark tangle of oak trees along Old Copper Road, the northern shore felt like an enchanted forest.

At least it normally did. Not so much today.

There was something different about it after the storm. A strange fog hung in the air. Images of the headless women searching for their children filled her mind as she recalled her mother's tales of Bleeding Rock.

But it wasn't their eyes upon her.

Nor was it the Horned Serpent, lurking in the waters of the lake.

With every step Lily took, she felt something stalking her. *Only a mile to go. I can do this.* Delbert Grant suddenly didn't frighten her so much. *Keep moving.*

The feeling grew stronger, and Lily pulled out her crucifix, letting it bounce atop her chest as she walked. Instead of feeling the need to pray, though—or even run—she found herself biting her lip and clenching her fists.

"What do you want?" Lily stopped, boldly waiting for an answer.

When she could no longer bear the silence, she huffed. "Haunt someone who is afraid of you," she informed whatever demon, Tak-Pei, or Manido was following her.

She continued walking, the floor of the forest gently sloping downward. *I will not run.* She shivered in fear, but the closer she got to water, the stronger the feeling of doom grew.

Everything is—she stopped in her tracks, unable to move.

There—in the brush—with the sparkling waters of Lake Manitou behind the gently moving leaves, she saw the ghost. It hovered like a cloud of newly hatched mosquitoes, as if the humidity of the bush gave it life.

It's been leading me.

The ghost turned, exuding fragments of its identity. Wearing a deerskin loincloth, with a chest covered in necklaces, amulets, and talismans, the figure had the unmistakable look of a shaman. Upon his head, he wore a strange headdress of fur and feather that culminated in two curved horns.

It's the ghost I saw in my bedroom window.

Lily took a step back, but when she looked at his face, she saw pieces of Migisi, her father, and even Nanakonan, and she paused.

"Come," the spirit whispered through the cool of the pines. "I need your help to save the children. Help me finish the song."

A piercing whistle from town filled the air, taking all strength from Lily's knees. Hearing it so close jarred her from the moment, and she turned to flee, but only managed to smack into an adjacent tree. She spun wildly and ended up on the ground.

When she scrambled to her feet and turned back, the ghost was gone.

Another whistle filled the air and Lily relaxed. The roaring creek, churning water, and high-pitched whistle meant that civilization was only yards away.

Avoiding the bush where she'd seen the ghost, she continued the final yards of her trek until she came out of the darkness and into the light of Split Rock Creek.

The horns? It wasn't a monster. He was just dressed in priestly garb. A servant of the Horned Serpent?

No, he spoke of saving the children.

He knows my dream.

In front of her, the water leapt over a field of stone on its way to the Crow Wing River. Upstream, the wooden giant stood astride the creek. Big water wheels spun in the channel of the swift creek, turning the loud machines housed inside the huge building. Log chutes stretched as far as the eye could see toward the sawmill on the other side of the granite bluff.

But it was more than just a granite bluff.

It was Bleeding Rock.

And then something grabbed her attention; Lily involuntarily flinched, just because of the proximity of the movement.

But it wasn't the horned ghost.

It was a boy.

A living boy.

Albert Fisher.

Lily chuckled with relief. "What are you doing, Albert?"

Albert sat on a boulder in the middle of the current. His face showed recognition, although Lily could tell the boy struggled with context.

"I'm Miss Lily. From Sunday school."

Albert lifted a hand and pointed toward the northern shore of Split Rock.

He focused on the backside of the bush where Lily had seen the ghost. By the time his eyes returned to hers, the boy stood up, and in one sudden motion, he leapt across the current to another dry rock, and then another, before ending up on the southern shore of Split Rock Creek.

He saw the ghost too.

He turned to glance at her again before running off to the safety of his father's sawmill.

If Albert saw it, then it was real. I'm not crazy. Lily collected herself, noticing her shaking hands. After taking a few breaths, she spotted a mill worker staring down with judgmental eyes from one of the windows and turned to avoid the young man's gaze.

WHEN LILY REACHED the big, covered bridge spanning the Crow Wing River, she no longer felt eyes upon her, as if she'd crossed an invisible threshold. On the other side of the bridge, new sidewalks led all the way to St. Marie's Catholic Church.

Civilization allowed her to push the strange encounter from her mind, even though Split Rock offered its own dangers. Even after several trips to town, Lily still kept her eyes low for a smile one moment could mean a club to her head the next.

Soon she stood at the big church doors and knocked, remembering the lessons from the nuns at Morris about customs. Lily's heritage taught to step right into a home, knowing the resident would provide shelter and food to anyone at their door. But the zhaaganaash expected a knock.

So she knocked.

And knocked.

After several minutes, Father Guerin opened the doors with a look of agitation before softening to smile. "Bienvenue! The doors are open. You didn't have to knock. Are you here to see Sister Inez?"

This time, he wore a priestly collar. *If he's a warrior priest, perhaps I could tell him about the ghost.* "Yes."

"Unfortunately, Sister Inez is not here right. I believe she mentioned going to a parish in Wadena.

Lily didn't budge. "I could use your help then."

"Really?" Father Guerin opened the big door wider.

Great, now he's interested. What do I tell him? Why did I have to say that? She thrust her hand into her bag. "I have more letters."

"Ah, more teaching applications?"

"Yes, and a letter for Migisi. Have you heard anything from him?"

"Ah, yes, Father Hebert said he received a letter addressed to you, but I'm not sure about the senders. Let's go speak with him. Come in."

Lily followed, watching the back of his head as he led her through the main part of the church and toward the offices along the side. As she passed by the confessional booth, a stray thought entered her mind: *Am I being punished for what I did in White Earth?*

She stopped but wasn't noticed until Father Guerin reached the doorway. He pivoted with a curious expression.

We're all alone. I could tell him everything. Lily looked at the confessional booth, not even sure of her intentions. "Do Jesuit priests take confession?"

"Confession?" Father Guerin held onto the door frame. "Well, um, that's really not something I do, no. But I'm sure when Father Hebert returns, we could figure something out. I know Wednesdays are when—"

"Never mind," Lily said, shrugging it off. "I was just curious." She doubled her pace and brushed by him as he stood at the doorway.

Father Hebert's office was empty, but in no time, Father Guerin found the letter on his desk.

Lily tore it open to discover it was a polite rejection letter. She slid into the big chair in front of Father Hebert's desk and handed the letter to Father Guerin, who leaned against the corner of the desk as he read.

"They can't even see I'm an Indian, but as soon as they see Sacred Heart and White Earth on my resume, they know the truth."

"It could be your inexperience. How old are you?"

"Old enough," Lily snapped and took the letter from him. "I knew a teacher from Morris who was only fourteen when she got her first classroom. Of course, it helps that she was white."

Did I just say that? He's your ally, not your enemy. Lily found the letters. "I hate to bother you about this."

"Oh, you're no bother at all. It'd be my honor," Father Guerin said, taking the letters and stepping away from the desk.

Lily stood and didn't wait for him to escort her to the nearest door. As she rushed through the church, she suddenly felt as if she didn't belong. *Have my sins followed me here? If I can't talk about them with a priest, will I continue to be haunted?*

She burst out the door without another word as Father Guerin called out, "The offer still stands. I need a language tutor."

Lily didn't stop.

CHAPTER TWENTY-FOUR

Sins of the Father

Turtle Island Reservation
August 1898

FAWN CHEVREUIL LOVED to watch the workers. When August arrived, crews of men began working from dusk to dawn on the road, but on Saturdays, they would drink, and the Loose Goose Saloon filled with action.

Despite Winnie's and Lily's warnings, she'd linger at the edge of the woods watching the spectacle: Fights. Cursing. Silliness. It all thrilled her.

"What are you doing?"

Lily's voice caused her to jump, which brought giggles of guilt. "I'm just watching. Is that a sin, Sister Lily?"

"I'm certainly not a nun."

"Yes, I know. I just don't know why you won't let me have fun when you've already had your fun. And now you've got your handsome priest, but you won't let me come to town with you."

"It's not like that, brat."

"Because it's wrong?" Fawn shrugged. "Why can you get away with things, but I can't?" Her eyes narrowed as Lily's face paled. "'Don't go near the Thunder Face family' and what do you do? You spend all summer rolling around with Samuel Thunder Face.

'Don't come to town with me. The zhaaganaash are dangerous' and then you spend all your free time running to your church. 'You don't want to go to White Earth' but then you won't even tell me about your *boyfriends* there."

"I don't want you to make the same mistakes I made."

"Yeah, but mistakes are fun. Your mom was Sioux and married a Chippewa. Why? Because danger is fun. It's so boring here. All we do is grow food, preserve food, and eat food."

"Do you want to get in a canoe and paddle all the way down the river to New Orleans?"

I wish she was serious. Fawn laughed, thinking of their previous discussion of Mark Twain novels. "Can we? What an adventure. Plus, there are lots of French people down there. I'd fit right in with a name like Chevreuil—when do we go?"

"After supper," Lily said with a wink. "But first let's go eat."

Fawn didn't budge. "Why doesn't your grandfather ever eat supper with us?"

"Do you remember when I told you about *Romeo and Juliet?*"

"Yes, they knew how to be bad and have fun, didn't they?"

Ignoring that, Lily said, "Well, he's Lord Capulet, my dad is Romeo, and my mom is Juliet. He can't get past centuries of bloodshed between the two families … Now do you get it?"

"I guess."

THE IDEA OF Romeo and Juliet stirred in Fawn's brain during supper until she just had to ask: "So how did you meet Big Squeak, Winnie?"

"Fawn," Lily snapped, but Winnie held up a hand.

"Big Squeak ran away from home. He grew up here along the banks of the Blue Knife, but he and his father had a falling out, so when he left, he went looking for his cousins up at Leech Lake. This was before the Black Hat Gang." Winnie's eyes grew darker.

"My father is Chief Sweating Stone, leader of the Leech Lake Band of Chippewa. He's a great warrior, and a descendant from a line of chiefs. When he was a young man, my father defeated the Sioux out on the prairie and took my mother as a slave wife, bringing her back to Leech Lake and our home on Bear Island. When your father learned I was half Sioux, I think he courted me just to upset his father."

"See, Lily, being bad is in your blood."

Lily stuck her tongue out, which made Fawn snort. *There's the old Lily.*

"It felt like love at the time," Winnie continued, ignoring the silliness. "He was very charming at first, but I'm much happier now that he's no longer in my life."

At that, Fawn had nothing to say.

Nor Lily.

A FEW HOURS later, Fawn woke to the sound of horse neighing, but assumed it belonged to either a drunk, lost farmer, or a Chippewa using the trail to travel back north. When the clomping of hooves came from right outside of the cabin, she fully woke up. "Lily, someone is outside."

Lily had to have been already awake and listening, for she slid out of bed immediately. "Stay here."

Fawn watched as her cousin slipped out the bedroom door.

A voice sounded in the darkness. *A man.*

A moment later, Lily called, "Mother, we have company."

Then Lily stood in the doorway of the bedroom again, her eyes shining. "It's your father, Fawn."

Ten minutes later, Fawn Chevreuil was packing her things to head with her father to Michigan. *Finally feels like a real adventure to me.*

CHAPTER TWENTY-FIVE

On a Pale Horse

Turtle Island Reservation
August 1897

LILY WEBER FOUND herself alone this Sunday.

No Migisi.

No Fawn.

Not even the little summerbirds.

And within ten minutes of waking, even Winnie had given her a goodbye kiss.

"Why don't you come to St. Marie's? It's a lot easier than having to go all the way up to Nimrod Crossing."

"A town church? Please, you know better than that. Even at a country church, I sit in the back so as not to remind the good white farmers that I'm an Indian. Besides, I have my friends, and it doesn't matter if we're Sioux, Chippewa, or Metis—we're all dark-skinned Christians."

"Be safe."

"If a woman can't walk in the open on the day of our Lord ..." Winnie began but didn't finish her thought. She kissed Lily on the head, saying instead, "See you this afternoon."

Lily waited around the empty house for another half hour before walking to Split Rock. With the river high and the woods saturated, she had to stay on the hard packed road. At least leaving early meant the wagons of farm families would not force her into the wet grass, nor did she have to worry about Delbert Grant delivering mail. It also meant she'd stay away from the woods near Split Rock Creek—*at least until I can talk to someone about it.*

At the Split Rock bridge, she paused to look down at her reflection. For a moment, she saw herself as an old woman, wrinkled and bent, until she realized it was just the ripples on the water. Bemused, she looked upstream to the sawmill, focusing on the bank where the ghost had stood. *Clearly, ghosts are not just an Indian issue.* Her eyes narrowed on the rock where Albert had stood transfixed. *Albert certainly saw it also.*

LILY WAITED UNTIL the big steeple bell started services to sneak into the back of the balcony. The families with social status, like the Fishers, sat up front while the misfits from society chose the anonymity of the balcony.

Singing a few songs is not the same as confession, Lily decided. Nor did she go join the congregation for the Holy Eucharist, ducking out for her classroom instead of kneeling at the altar.

Arriving early, Lily sat down in the school room to pour over lesson plans, books, and supplies.

Sister Inez swept in just after Father Herbert's mass and, like normal, the kids flooded into the room in a wave of energy after the last prayer. Lily greeted them with a forced smile.

"Good morning, Miss Weber," Bjorn Forsberg said instead of his typical grunt, watching his feet as he took his chair in the back of the room.

Oh dear, Fawn was right about my freckled hero.

Bjorn Forsberg wasn't the only one hiding something. Just before class, Albert Fisher came in on the skirts of his mother, and with his eyes down, he found his way to the front row.

He definitely saw something, but how do I broach the subject without sounding like a lunatic?

All thoughts of the paranormal vanished when Sister Inez began the lesson.

Everything went according to clockwork until the closing minutes, when Sister Inez leaned over to whisper, "Father Guerin has information about your brother. He said to meet him on the front steps after class."

The front steps. Completely in the open, yet all the parishioners will be in the backyard having their picnics.

Lily prepared herself for more pressure about tutoring while the class finished up their writing assignment.

After class ended, she saw Albert Fisher linger for just a moment, glancing in her direction. *Should I talk to him about it? He looks like he wants to talk.* But when she took a step toward him, Albert bolted for the back door. She chose to head for the front of the church instead.

Father Guerin wore his Jesuit cassock and his polished shoes. He was sitting on the top step with his feet resting three steps below. He turned slightly when she came to stand beside him.

"Ah, Lily. When I dropped off your letter, I had two letters of interest for you. The first is from Fergus Falls."

Lily tore open the letter he held out, only to have her heart drop at the succinct words of a rejection from the public school. Her legs crumpled, and she sat down beside the priest.

"Bad news?"

"It's not bad, it's just not good." She grimaced. *And here comes his pitch again …*

Father Guerin reached into the hidden folds of his cassock to retrieve another piece of paper. "This one might cheer you up."

"You opened it?"

"Well, it's a letter from Washington D.C. for me. Before coming here, I got to know Bishop John Ireland during my time in

St. Paul, and as it turns out, he is close friends with President McKinley."

"The President of the United States?"

"Yes. I once had the pleasure of being part of a briefing about the political conditions in Cuba, even though I didn't utter a word. Even though McKinley is a Republican, he's not a strong supporter of the Dawes Act or even Pratt's school. Bishop Ireland explained how your brother was taken out of Minnesota, and that he, and all Indian boys, should be educated in their own home state." He grinned. "The men who broke the law in sending your brother east will soon learn we have the ear of the President."

"But Migisi's still in Pennsylvania?"

"Yes, but getting your brother sent back here would be the first small victory."

Lily thought back to Father Guerin's meeting with Nanakonan and her grandfather's words to her after. *Do I trust him? But if I do, is my dream a bad omen? Will the Horned Serpent take him like it took Migisi?* "Why do the Jesuits care again?"

"Care?" He acted wounded. "It's our Christian duty to care about the welfare of others, and our mission is to protect poor and oppressed populations: the Filipinos, the Cubans."

He seems sincere, as always. "I know my history. Jesuits followed my people from Montreal all the way to here in Minnesota. Why do they support the Anishinaabe tribes over all others?"

"Your Chippewa ancestors were some of the earliest allies of the Jesuit Missionaries. Converting to Christianity is one of the reasons why the Chippewa flourished and so many other tribes withered away."

"And the French supplied them with weapons at the behest of the Jesuits." At his sigh, she rushed to add, "I'm just trying to understand, Father Guerin. I've read about the missionary era, and how you left the Chippewa to the mercy of the United States. Why did they send you back now?"

Father Guerin grew distracted as if sizing up which lie to tell her. "Assimilation and the dismantling of reservations will end up doing the same thing that the Assyrians did to the lost tribes of Israel."

That's not how Sister Lynch sees her duty. "Isn't it better for my people to see ourselves as Americans? When Scottish, Swedish, or Norwegian settlers come to America, they become Americans. I know my brother and grandfather wouldn't agree, but shouldn't my people do the same thing?"

Father Guerin took too long to answer; in fact, he didn't answer at all, which confused Lily even more.

"That's what the nuns at Sacred Heart taught me: 'Kill the Indian, Save the Child.' Isn't that the policy? I can now read and write and I want to be part of America, but then there's Fawn, who's stuck in abject poverty as her parents drag her from up north all the way to Michigan, trying to pretend it's not all part of the United States now."

"Drag her? Did something happen to Fawn?"

Oh, oh. What did I say? He looks angry. "Her father showed up last night to take her way to Michigan."

"Michael Chevreuil?"

"Yes, that's her father." Lily tried to lighten the tone by adding, "Apparently, he escaped from the jail in Bemidji."

"Michael Chevreuil? One of your father's men? One of the Black Hat Gang?"

"Yes? What's wrong?"

Father Guerin looked away. "Confound it all."

Lily felt her stomach drop. "What's wrong?"

Father Guerin suddenly looked like a soldier. "Michael Chevreuil did not escape from jail. He's a cooperating witness for the government."

"What does that mean?"

"He's flipped. He's working for Marshal Morrison now." He turned to face her, his tone urgent. "He was at your house last night? What did he say?"

"He said he was going to take Fawn to Michigan, and that she needed to pack up all of her stuff." Lily's chest tightened. "And that he was meeting my father at Pine Beach."

Guerin stood, took a step down the stairs, and then quickly pivoted back. "Where is Pine Beach?"

"It's on Gull Lake." Lily stood too. "Is Fawn in danger?"

"Fawn? No … Where is Gull Lake? How far away is it from here?"

My father is in danger, though. "East of here. Thirty miles or so."

"Could you show me on a map?"

Lily froze, uncertain. *He doesn't know where to go. This is just like my dream. Is this how I save my family?* "I could bring you there just as easily. Gull Lake is a big lake, and I know exactly where my father used to camp." *My dream prepared me for this moment.* "This is important. I'll take you there."

Guerin seemed to calculate the timing in his head. "Agreed, but this is what you need to do. I need to get a few things ready. Go find Gus Forsberg and let him know that I'm in desperate need of a fast, strong horse. Can you do that?"

"I saw Bjorn in class today. They should be in the park."

"Go then, I'll be back down in a few minutes."

Lily sprinted to the rear of the church, but at the sound of laughter, she stopped. She clung to the corner, and she looked for the Forsberg family.

Bjorn's red hair stood out in a crowd; he was sitting with a group of teens under a short maple tree. Lily calmed herself before approaching him at a quick gait. "Bjorn, can I speak to you?"

His freckled face wrinkled but he nodded, getting to his feet. "What do you—"

"Father Guerin is having a bit of an emergency," Lily interrupted. "He needs a fast, strong horse that can ride for thirty miles."

Bjorn's face filled with panic. "My pa took the team out to the Cottingham farm to drop off a load of potatoes. He won't be back for a few hours."

The blonde young man who had been sitting beside Bjorn stood up. "I've got the fastest horse in Hiawatha County … You want to borrow it?"

His grin was too perfect to be sincere. "Father Guerin said I should speak to Gus Forsberg."

"What's the situation?" the blonde teen asked, grinning a crooked smile.

Ignoring him, she stepped closer to Bjorn. "We need to get to Gull Lake as fast as possible. Fawn and my father might be in danger."

"Trust me," the young man insisted, stepping closer. "I'm a friend of the family. Lily, right?"

Just leave us alone. She looked away.

"I'm Martin Nielson. Bjorn can vouch for me. Isn't Grim the fastest, strongest horse around?'

Bjorn nodded without hesitation.

"A Norwegian Fjord horse will be twice as fast as those lumbering Swedish ogres. If this is an emergency, I insist. Dolly and I can just borrow a Forsberg horse to get us home. Time's a wastin'."

He insists. Father Guerin needs a horse. What am I to do?

The rest of the young people watched from their blanket and when Lily nodded, they all smiled.

Martin Nielson led the way to where all the wagons and horses were kept, and in no time, a pale horse was saddled and ready to go.

They came with Lily to the front of the church, where she caught Father Guerin slipping a revolver into his black cassock.

Is this really happening? Does this mean I trust him?

She stood beside Bjorn Forsberg who made introductions.

"Father Guerin, this is Martin Nielson," Bjorn began. "He's got one of the fastest horses around. You can trust him. He's a good guy."

"Martin Nielson," Father Guerin repeated, extending his hand for a firm handshake. "I'm in your debt. We're riding out to Gull Lake as fast as possible. We might not return until Tuesday."

We … I'm really doing this.

"Forsbergs will take care of me until then. Do you want us to come with you?"

Father Guerin looked indecisive for a second before shaking his head. "It would only spook them. Thank you, boys." He glanced at each of them before asking, "Can you keep this quiet?"

"Yes, we can," Bjorn said.

"What good is a fast horse if I don't know where I'm going," Father Guerin said to himself before turning his gaze to Lily. He nodded as if affirming his thoughts. "Lily and I will ride to your farm and grab Goliath. She's light enough to ride old Goliath, and I'll take Nielson's horse."

"Grim," Nielson said. "Short for Grim Reaper, due to him being a pale horse."

Lily shuddered. *Nielson is a little darker than his dimples would imply.*

A Gaggle of Geese

Gull Lake, MN
August 1897

TUCKED INTO THE southeastern corner of Hiawatha County, Gull Lake ran eight miles north to south. Situated a short distance from Brainerd, it also had access to both the Mississippi and Crow Wing rivers. For this reason, criminals and bootleggers used its many bays and alcoves for secret deals, knowing there were a dozen ways to scurry away if trouble appeared.

Pine Beach was part of a peninsula that separated Wilson Bay from the main body of Gull Lake. Although Lily once enjoyed the sandy beach and warmer water, she now understood its strategic advantages to her father.

"This is where we camped," she said to Father Guerin. "My father met his friends farther up the peninsula."

Father Guerin halted Grim and dismounted. He found a sturdy, dead tree to tie up the horse and then guided her and Goliath to the same post. "This is as far as you go."

He took her hand as he helped her down from Goliath after tying his reins to another limb.

Lily shook her head. "If my dad is waiting, he won't know who you are. Let me come with you."

"Your father will know who I am." Father Guerin turned away when she started to protest. "I set this into motion, so I need to be the one to warn him. It's getting dark, so you just hold tight here next to the beach, where I can find you easily in the dark. Keep quiet and avoid anyone that comes by, friend or foe. Understood?"

She hold of his hand. "My father's a dangerous man."

"It's not your father I'm worried about."

In the dream, there had been ice floating on the water instead of geese, and instead of a peninsula, Lily had seen the distinctive hump of Turtle Island. Gull Lake did not match her dream, but the symbolism remained: The frightened children. The animals pacing on the island. *Is Michael Chevreuil ... a rat?*

Lily patted the horses as Father Guerin slipped away. She thought about the betrayal of one of her father's lifelong friends. Just like Blackfish and Pierre, Michael Chevreuil had come in and out of her life with the regularity of the Canadian Geese that currently paddled around the bay in front of her. Two adult geese led five smaller copies along the shore.

They follow their parents so blindly, but then again, their fathers aren't criminals.

Somewhere, Fawn Chevreuil was nearby.

Does she know her father is a rat? Would it matter to her? And here I am trying to help my father, also.

Lily walked down to the shore and picked up a handful of stones to skip over the surface of the water. The sunset changed the surface to a golden hue.

She pictured Father Guerin in his black robes walking into the camp. Would her father laugh or draw his pistol? What if Michael Chevreuil was already waiting?

Accusations would be thrown, and her father would be more willing than not to trust his childhood friend over the Jesuit.

If it goes wrong, I could save him. My father would trust me over Chevreuil. Lily looked back to the narrow land bridge. Two hundred yards was all that separated the two bays, and despite the thickness of the woods, she could see through to the other side.

Then she saw movement.

She hid behind the horses where a thicket of trees and slight depression kept them all from being seen. Her nose pressed so closely to one of the trees that an ant climbed onto her cheek, forcing her to brush it off.

What are they doing here?

Two hulking thugs escorted an elderly man, who despite being of similar age to Grandfather Nanak, walked taller and faster than others his age. *I remember them.* As if sensing her, one of the thugs looked her way and she pressed further against the trees until they continued past her narrow spot along the peninsula.

Cut Ear and Tall Birch, Lily remembered the names of the thugs from her mother's tales. *Killers, both of them.*

She leaned out from the shelter to see the three figures heading off to where Father Guerin had gone. As she studied them from behind, she confirmed the identity of the central figure. While he did wear traditional moccasins, a beaver hat, and had a few beads and feathers trailing down upon a leather strand, the rest of his outfit was much more modern—a white dress shirt under a velvet jacket and black cotton trousers. On one hip, a traditional beaded bag; on the other, a revolver in a holster.

Chief Sweating Stone, my maternal grandfather.

As the three Pillagers vanished to the tip of the peninsula, Lily watched with a hand over her mouth. *Romeo Montague and Juliet Capulet—two families who'd rather kill each other.*

Besides running from the law, Big Squeak also spent years looking over his shoulder for his father-in-law's Pillagers. Had Lily's father wooed one of Chief Sweating Stone's full-blood Chippewa daughters, a bounty would have been placed on his head, but since Winnie was a half-breed, the slight eventually was ignored, resulting in few family visits through the years.

An ambush inside of an ambush—does Father Guerin understand what is happening?

Behind her, the flock of geese departed, causing Lily to jump. To get airborne, a goose had to start running in the water while also flapping its wings. At the midpoint of this awkward process, both wings and feet struck the water, creating a ruckus that could be heard almost a mile away. While the lake and woods were dark, Lily could see the flock rise against the light sky and bank to the northwest.

But the paddling sounds continued.

She turned back to where the sun had set and saw a dark object coming from the central island in Wilson Bay. It sounded like a hundred geese coming toward her, but its shape looked like a house and floated out from the shore of the island.

A paddleboat.

It was the wheel, not geese feet, which struck the water.

'It's not your father I'm worried about.' Father Guerin's words felt like a splash of cold water to the face.

No sooner had she taken a few hurried steps forward did she freeze in place.

A dozen riders came up the peninsula.

More soldiers.

"Fan out," an officer ordered. "Make a line so no one slips away."

Lily's feet found a hidden path through the trees toward the tip of the peninsula. The sound of the paddle wheel was soon replaced by the sound of her heart in her ears, giving her hope that she'd reach them in time.

Finally, she could see a solitary lantern through the trees. Before she could reach it, though, a pistol cocked in the darkness, and she tripped to a stop.

Blackfish LaBiche pointed a gun in her face. "It's a trap. Soldiers are coming by paddle boat."

The pistol dropped and LaBiche paused for just an instant to listen—

He bolted toward the lantern.

Guns fired, but not from LaBiche's pistol or from Sweating Stone's men.

"You are surrounded! Put your weapons down and lay on the ground or be fired upon!"

Following LaBiche, Lily entered the inner circle of criminals gathered around the lantern. Father Guerin, her father, Chief Sweating Stone, and other men looked at the direction of the ultimatum, which came from Marshal Bushy Bill Morrison across the channel from the peninsula.

"They've got men on boats," Blackfish LaBiche explained, pointing south.

While the outlaws armed themselves, her father stepped close. Lily flinched as he lifted a hand to place on her shoulder. Instead of pulling her closer, he turned her toward Father Guerin and stepped back.

Father Guerin's face twisted with sudden anger, and his hands clamped on both her shoulders and he redirected her away from the scene.

Glancing back, Lily saw her father pointing to a second paddle boat coming into view from the north.

They're surrounded.

A gunshot pierced the air, and a second later, a thunderstorm erupted behind her. Lily tried to look back, but in one fell swoop, Father Guerin knocked her right off her feet—just as a volley of gunfire ripped through the woods.

On Opposite Shores

Gull Lake
August 1897

FAWN CHEVREUIL STOOD alone upon the sand of the point, watching Bushy Bill and his men lash their horses through the shallow waters of the straight. Paddle boats came from the side while another group of riders came from the south.

Her father rode beside Bushy Bill Morrison as they charged right into the camp. Michael Chevreuil pointed to two men: Big Squeak and Chief Sweating Stone.

Then Bushy Bill pointed his pistol at the head of Tall Birch and blew half of the man's head off in a spray of crimson.

Seeing the murder took Fawn's breath away, and when the pistol shot echoed across the water, her legs turned to jelly and she felt her face land in the wet sand.

The spots in her eyes became spiraling galaxies of darkness.

WHEN CONSCIOUSNESS RETURNED, her fingers did not feel the wet sand under her body but leafy fronds. Like a tangle of cobwebs, Fawn pushed them away until she saw a woman dressed in black.

"This isn't what was supposed to happen," the woman said.

Despite the shortness of hair, the plumpness of her features, and the obvious changes, Fawn knew her—"Lily?"

"You lied to me, Fawn. You told me it was Turtle Island. You said it would save him, but now … now he's dead. He's gone. Not even the willow can bring him back. What does this mean, Fawn? Tell me? What does this mean?"

Fawn didn't understand.

"Who's dead?"

Lily didn't answer.

"Who's dead, Lily?"

ANOTHER GUNSHOT BROUGHT Fawn from one nightmare to another. Wet sand clung to her face as she lifted herself off the shore.

The tip of the peninsula was bathed in light, lanterns showed her the truth of her father's betrayal. One by one, the surviving Chippewa were brought forward in shackles. Although none of them wore their hats, Fawn spotted several members of the Black Hat Gang, including the leader himself, Skwikomik Asibikaashi, Big Squeak Weber.

Her father's words echoed in her mind: *'For the people.'*

Michael Chevreuil had justified his betrayal by convincing himself that Big Squeak was a pariah, a parasite which preyed upon his own people. Although her father had also been a bootlegger, he recently convinced himself that ridding the world of Big Squeak meant ridding the reservations of alcohol.

But this isn't about alcohol.

She stiffened as another figure came into view. Having spent her childhood bouncing around from one reservation to another, Fawn knew the diminutive figure that quietly joined the others waiting to be loaded onto the open ramp of the paddleboat.

Chief Sweating Stone came from a line of hereditary chiefs from Leech Lake, who not only led the local Pillager band of Chippewa, but because of his ancestry, also presided over the rest of the chieftains in the region. Seeing him in handcuffs like a common criminal was like seeing a governor in handcuffs.

From across the shallow channel, Fawn watched her father stick to Marshal Morrison's side, helping the soldiers separate the henchmen from the leaders.

This is something much different than arresting bootleggers, Fawn decided as the operation continued while the rest of Minnesota slept blissfully unaware. *What would bring such a strange mix of people together?*

As dawn neared, Fawn got her answer.

Father Guerin—another Judas?

The Jesuit priest walked freely amid the chaos, standing with her father and Marshal Morrison at the center of the storm. The two men in black stood for quite a while, speaking unheard words. Father Guerin jabbed a finger into the chest of Morrison without consequence. Morrison ignored the jabs, and the words, and focused on loading the paddle boats.

The prisoners went on first, and shortly after, both platoons of soldiers loaded back into the boats. Marshal Morrison joined the other men on horses to depart south toward Brainerd, leaving only her father to wade across the chest-deep waters of the channel.

"That didn't go well," her father said smugly. "But now we can leave for Michigan."

Images of Tall Birch's head exploding filled her mind. She'd known the entire family since she was a child. Nanak even tried to arrange a marriage between Lily and William. *He was flat out murdered. Because of my father.* "No."

"Excuse me?"

Fawn took a step away from him and into the water. "I'm not going with you. In fact, I don't want to ever see you again."

"I did this for us. So we could start a new life together."

"No. Take your blood money and go to Michigan, I'll have none of it."

"What? Will you go back to your whore mother?"

"Better to be a whore than a traitor."

"Where are you going?" he asked once she was on the opposite shore.

"Someone must tend to the dead."

But who's dead?

It didn't take her long to find the first two corpses, which were placed side by side. One of them was Tall Birch, and when she saw brain matter in the wound, Fawn turned and vomited.

"Lily?" Father Guerin called out from the darkness. "Is that you?"

"No," Fawn said softly. "It's Fawn."

When he saw Fawn sitting by the bodies, he sighed. "I'm sorry you had to see this ugliness."

"Is it safe?" Lily asked from somewhere in the darkness.

Fawn jumped up in surprise.

"Yes, you can come out now," Father Guerin said.

Lily emerged, enveloping the priest with her arms as she sobbed and sobbed. Father Guerin held his arms up, unsure or unable to comfort Lily. He had to take her by the shoulders and push her away a bit in order to turn her in the direction of Fawn.

"You're … you're … Oh, Fawn. I tried."

Fawn rose and rushed over to embrace Lily.

CHAPTER TWENTY-EIGHT

Women of the Dawn

Gull Lake, MN
August 1897

FAWN SAT WITH Lily beside the embers of a dying fire, with the bodies of four slain men a few yards away. *We should have buried them last night.* Dawn came slowly to Gull Lake, and with it, the sound of loons echoed across the water.

After gathering the bodies, Father Guerin rode for Brainerd, with Lily promising they'd stay until he returned. As they waited, everything had been explained in those first frantic moments of sitting around the fire. Lily told her how Father Guerin saw through the double-cross, and how they tried to reach Gull Lake before the ambush.

And then Lily gushed about how Father Guerin had saved her life.

Her hero …

For some reason, the more Lily talked about how the priest risked his own life to save her from the armed men, the angrier Fawn grew at her father for being a coward. Finally, she curled up to the fire and ignored her cousin.

Now, with the loons welcoming the dawn, Fawn sat back up. "I had a dream about you."

"Just now? I didn't think you were sleeping."

"I wasn't. When Tall Birch was shot, I passed out. I dropped like a sack of potatoes. That's when I had my dream."

"What was it about?"

"You were older like your mother, and … there was a tree. A willow. You told me I was a liar, and … you were crying."

"Why was I crying?"

"You said someone had died."

"Was it Father Guerin?" Lily asked, looking to the south where the priest had ridden.

Are you only worried about the priest, Lily? "No, I thought it might've been Migisi, but maybe it was a premonition about all of this."

"A premonition? What if something is still going to happen to him in Brainerd? Should we go—"

"Stop with the priest!" Fawn shouted. "Your brother was taken, and your father was arrested."

"No thanks to your father," Lily snapped back.

A loon called again, filling the silence.

"You're not the only one with dreams," Lily said. "I've been having dreams about the Horned Serpent. In one dream, Migisi died. In the other, it was Father Guerin. That's why I'm worried."

"Oh," Fawn said softly. "The Horned Serpent?"

"It's more than that. When I first came home, I felt as if there was a ghost waiting for me in the woods, so Migisi and I hung a dreamcatcher."

"The night of the storm, right?" Fawn could still picture the glass and broken loom outside of the window.

"We saw a ghost that night, and just a few days ago, I saw it again, except this time it was in broad daylight. It said something about saving the children."

"What children?"

"In both dreams, there were children, and I was trying to save them. They all had faces that looked like mine, so I thought, you know, that they were my descendants or something. I think it's an omen or a warning about what's going on with Triton. I think I need to help my family fight to keep the land. That's why Father Guerin came. He wanted to keep my father from being arrested."

"Huh," Fawn said. "Why didn't you say something about this sooner?"

"Why didn't you tell me your dream?"

"I just did."

"So what do you think I should do?"

"I think you need to tell Nanakonan. He'll know what to think of your dreams."

"Should I tell Father Guerin?"

Fawn rolled her eyes. *Again with the priest.* "No. I know he's a priest, but you saw him tonight. He's a different kind of priest."

"He sure is," Lily whispered, smiling just a little. Her smile disappeared quickly as she asked, "Will they take my home now that my father has been arrested? Is the fight over?"

"I don't think it works like that, in fact—" Fawn heard splashing, and not from a fish or a loon. It came from the channel. She gasped when she saw a solitary figure crossing through the waters.

Oh no, he's come back to take me.

But it wasn't a small man like her father; the man was enormous.

Blackfish!

In all of the chaos, she'd assumed he'd been arrested with the others ... *A black fish knows how to swim.*

Lily reached for Father Guerin's pistol, but only set her hand over the top of it when she saw who it was. Blackfish LaBiche headed right for their fire.

"Where did Father Guerin go?" he asked Lily.

"He rode into Brainerd to tell others and to get help."

"Church type?"

Fawn nodded, bringing Blackfish's gaze to her. "I'll bring you to your mother. I'm going to Leech Lake to tell others what happened, but I came back for you."

"I ... I'm staying with Lily."

Blackfish shook his head. His stern face was flecked with blood. "Now that your father is gone, you need to be with your family. My wife can help take care of you until we find your mother."

Fawn looked to Lily for help, but her cousin said and did nothing.

The silence almost felt like more of a betrayal than her father's.

Blackfish continued. "I'll speak to your mother. I'll make sure she changes." His gaze bounced between them before he added, "Both of you are too young to have seen this. Both of you need the love of your mothers."

Fawn looked across the channel, where her father had been just a short time earlier—the same direction Blackfish had come from.

Don't ask him—he'll tell you the truth.

The flecks of blood on his face told her everything.

Is he the monster or the hero?

"I'll wait until Father Guerin comes back for Lily," Fawn said softly. "And then I'll go back with you to find my mother."

Blackfish relented with a nod, and Fawn broke into tears for her slain father.

CHAPTER TWENTY-NINE

A Forked Tongue

Turtle Island Reservation
August 1897

AS SOON AS Lily Weber saw her mother in the doorway, she slid off Goliath and ran into her arms. She didn't explain what had happened, only sobbed on her shoulder.

"Lily?"

Father Guerin came into view, and they all sat down on the front steps of the porch as he explained what had happened at Gull Lake, his words sounded like they were spoken into a well or inside of a tin can. Lily heard the ordeal repeated, including how Father Guerin had literally shielded her body from the soldiers' bullets as they advanced into the camp.

Even with her cheek pressed to the ground, Lily had still witnessed the deaths of four Chippewa men, including Tall Birch, who was executed with a pistol as he stood his ground to protect Lily's grandfather, Chief Sweating Stone.

Winnie fanned herself after taking in the story. "Where have they been taken?"

"Brainerd," Father Guerin answered. "But I would bet they will be transferred to another prison and court where Morrison can ensure conviction. Luckily, this meeting was not about bootlegged alcohol, so I doubt your father will be held for long."

"And my husband?"

"Morrison already had a warrant out for his arrest, and if Chevreuil testifies, things will go badly for him. I have powerful friends though, and since I got him into this mess, I'll do my best to get him out of it."

Lily managed to wipe her tears long enough to see Father Guerin riding away with Goliath in tow a few minutes later when the silence went on for too long.

If he saved my life, can I finally trust him?

The chance to answer rode out of sight, and her mother could only provide hugs and comfort food.

AFTER SLEEPING FOR most of the day, Lily went to find answers. She found Grandfather on his porch. He barely gave her a glance when she sat down on the steps in front of him.

How do I tell him this? "My father was arrested along with Chief Sweating Stone. Morrison and the men from Triton will use this to steal our land. You'll be the only one left here."

"Being alone does not bother me," Grandfather said, but his chin began to wobble. "But I doubt if that will happen. I have allies in this fight."

"Father Guerin? He was there trying to stop the arrest." She paused, realization dawning. "Is Father Guerin trying to start a war? Is that why he had my father meeting with Chief Sweating Stone?" Her mind raced. "My father has an underground network of thieves, but to start a war, he'd need the approval of the chiefs and elders, especially Sweating Stone, who would normally have nothing to do with my father or alcohol."

A slight grin appeared on Grandfather Nanak's wrinkled mouth.

"Am I right?" Lily asked, breathless. "Instead of alcohol, Father Guerin wanted my father to arm the Chippewa?"

Grandfather raised an eyebrow. "Have you decided? Should I trust Guerin?"

"He saved my life. He literally threw himself over me when the soldiers began to fire, and later, he kept them from taking me away to be locked up with the others. He stared down a rifle to keep me safe. So yes, I trust him with my life, but I don't know if I trust him with anything else when he keeps things hidden from me." Lily groaned. "What do you think? Is he here to start another war?"

"Yes, he is fighting a war, but not the way you think."

"Then what—"

"Father Guerin is a soldier, but creating a political incident is only the first step in a long journey. He is preparing for the day the Serpent Star returns."

This is not an answer I wanted. "So Father Guerin is using us to start a war. Is that what you're telling me? Is he an agent of the Catholic Church or does he belong to something else?"

"You're focusing on the wrong details. Do you even know what the Serpent Star is?"

He mentioned it last time, too. "No, should I?"

"The Serpent Star has sent soldiers before, and priests, and also a scientist. Father Guerin wears the robe of a Jesuit, but he is indeed part of something else, something larger."

A government agent? One political party tries to grab Indian land, and the other tries to prevent it from happening.

Lily shook her head. "What if he's just pretending to be an ally, Grandfather? He brought you gifts, and suddenly, you open your home to him. Yes, his words say one thing, but the results of his actions indicate something else. Since he's come, Migisi has been sent away and father has been arrested, along with Sweating Stone.

Is he trying to destroy our family? Could he be a double-agent hired by Triton?"

Grandfather laughed heartily. "The only forked tongue belongs to the bartender at the saloon. No, Guerin is not our enemy."

Samuel Thunder Face held me in his arms too and lied right to my face. But I want to trust Father Guerin.

"If a war starts, our people will suffer just like the Dakota suffered in 1862. Like the Lakota suffered at Wounded Knee. Any uprising will bring about the full wrath of the U.S. government, regardless of Father Guerin's political connections," Lily said.

Her grandfather shook his head. "Father Guerin's gift to me was a reminder of a promise made in my childhood, but his name is an even older reminder and promise to our people."

Guerin?

"He risked his life to save you because he knows the story of our family."

"Why would he save me?"

"He knows what must happen," Nanak replied. "The legacy of our family is complex. We were marked by Manabozho the Trickster during the time of the dawn, and your ancestors, both good and evil, have served this destiny. Should we trust Guerin with secrets? Absolutely." His eyes narrowed. "But can I trust *you* with our secrets?"

Me? How dare he! "Or perhaps it is *you* who cannot be trusted," Lily retorted. "Is that why my father left us?"

Instead of anger, a tired sadness covered his face. "Your father still serves the will of Manabozho, even in failure. I've had dreams where my son returns to me to fulfill his destiny as the Firehandler, but now it seems as if the path he's chosen has forever taken him away from that destiny." He looked away, his shoulders slumping. "My son and grandson have been taken away, and I will not live long enough to find another ... besides my sassy granddaughter."

"So?"

"Have you made your decision yet?"

"What decision?"

At her grandfather's snort, she sighed. *Of course I trust Guerin. I just don't know if I can trust myself.* "Yes, I trust Guer-Father Guerin."

"Yet you still hesitate. Neither of us has time for indecision. Go back to your mother and tell her you will be spending a week with me for training."

"A week?"

"It will only be the beginning. If you want to be part of this fight, we'll need the whole winter."

A whole winter? This isn't why I came home.

Lily stood up. "Just so you know, it wasn't Migisi who found the megis shells along the bank of the river." She took a deep breath. "I did."

CHAPTER THIRTY

A New Mission

Split Rock, MN
September 1897

LILY STOPPED AT the doorway to the balcony. "I've decided that I will become your language tutor." She broke into a smile when she saw Father Guerin's enthusiasm but lost it when he went to give her a hug.

No, a professional relationship. She stepped to the side to use the doorframe as a shield.

He took the hint, stopping at the last pew. Behind him, maps of the region were spread out. "That's wonderful."

"With just a few conditions."

"Certainly."

"It needs to be during the week, when either Father Hebert or Sister Inez are working. My mother also wants it to be in a public, open place." *My mother? Now I'm lying to a priest.*

"Father Hebert takes confessions on Wednesdays, and this balcony is as open to the public as it gets." He glanced around before looking back at her. "Will this work?"

Lily nodded.

"I can arrange for someone to pick you up and bring you into town." Father Guerin turned away and returned to a series of stuffed crates.

"Yes, I suppose that would work."

"My schedule fluctuates, and I will be taking trips throughout the fall and winter, but if I'm going to learn a new language, I'd like to try to fit in a few extra practices in a week. Will Sundays and another day during the week work, with proper chaperoning?"

Amusement filled his eyes when Lily nodded.

"Wednesdays." *Where is he going?* Lily stepped forward, keeping her distance. "I told my grandfather I was going to be your language tutor. He asked if I trusted you."

"What did you tell him?" Father Guerin asked, dropping items into another empty crate.

Lily sat down on the closest pew to the doorway. "I told him how you saved my life. You're certainly heroic." She avoided his gaze when he glanced at her. "But Nanak was talking about a different type of trust. He's willing to see you as an ally because of your connection to Nicollet and your name."

"My name?"

"He said your name gave him more reason to trust you as an ally than the barometer you gave him. Something about your family?"

"I'm an orphan, Lily. The only thing my parents ever gave me was my name, Jean Nicolas Guerin."

An orphan? How sad. "So why does my grandfather trust you then? Because you're going to help the Chippewa fight a war?"

He didn't look at her which made her suspicious of his reply. "A war? No. You've got the heart of the matter, but your purpose is a little darker than the truth. The Black Hat gang was going to be a communication network for all the Chippewa bands from North Dakota all the way to Quebec."

"I can't teach you if I think you're going to lead my people into a war."

"I won't lie to you. For things to change, more people might die. My intentions are to find someone to unite your people so that we might make a stand against the governmental policies that are attempting to steal the land and culture of all Indian tribes, not just the Chippewa."

"This isn't about alcohol, is it?"

"Sweating Stone insisted—" Guerin stopped himself. "You're right. These charges won't stick because it was just a meeting. That's all. To change things, I will need to get my allies involved, and that will require a few headlines all the way in Washington and New York." He paused, hesitating. "It won't come to war."

So he is trying to be a guardian of culture. Lily shifted slightly to get a better look at what he was packing. "Nanak said that I'm going to begin training, so I won't be able to start tutoring right away."

"Well, I am about to go on a trip, so I won't be able to begin learning right away," he said with a laugh. "What sort of training?"

"Old pagan rituals."

"Nanakonan said that to you?"

"Well, he didn't say it like that, but he wants to teach me some important rituals passed down by our family." She sighed. "Pretty awful, huh?"

"No. This is a good thing. You should learn these rituals— it could be important."

Unbelievable! Sister Lynch at Sacred Heart would have slapped a student's face for suggesting something so … un-Christian. "Fawn's right. Sometimes I wonder if you're really a priest. The only way to Heaven is through Christ, right? 'Thou shalt have no other gods before Me.' Isn't it heresy to dabble in this stuff, Father Guerin?"

He's grinning. Do I amuse him?

"When the Jesuits first came to this continent, their primary concern was evangelizing the souls of those in the Big Woods. The nations of the Anishinaabe were some of the quickest converts, but that didn't stop these priests from a secondary purpose: recording the traditions and rituals of these tribes. Countless Jesuit priests wrote books on tribes from here to the Atlantic. They became historians, which is what you'd be."

"A historian?"

"I'm heading to Duluth to visit Big Squeak and Chief Sweating Stone, and even after I return, I'm going to be coming and going, but you ... you can learn the ways of your people, write it down, and then share it with me so we can understand it together."

"Why is this happening now? Why not fifty years ago?" Lily asked bluntly.

"You want to know my secrets?" He took a few quick steps and slid onto the pew beside her. If he saw her lean quickly away, he didn't bother to comment on it. "Let me tell you what I was working on right before the incident at Gull Lake: I'd just met with an architect by the name of J. Walter Johnston, who specializes in building granite Romanesque-style buildings. I've also approached a construction engineer to oversee production costs and supplies."

"I don't understand. What are you talking about?"

"My secret agenda—you figured it out after a few months of spying," Father Guerin started with a chuckle. "My assessment is to invest in a private Jesuit school."

"A school?"

"Your words helped me hatch this idea. Current government policy is to forcibly remove children from their homes and send them to boarding schools under the pretenses of civilizing the savage yet in truth trying to exterminate a culture and language. A private school can offer an alternative education, one that does offer a path to the modern world but also protects Anishinaabe culture, customs, and language."

"You're building your own school?" The thought made Lily almost light-headed.

"Right now, it is only on paper. I have the funds, and now the plans, and prior to Gull Lake, I was making progress on acquiring a location for the school." He paused, studying her. "You asked what I was hiding. This is my devious plan ... a private school for the Chippewa."

"But how? Where?"

"A year from now, you could be teaching a classroom full of children in a room designed by J. Walter Johnston. One semester they could learn the tenets of Catholicism, and the next, they could learn the wisdom of Manabozho. All you need to do is hold steady for a year. Stay here, learn from your grandfather, provide me with some language lessons, and this dream of mine could rise up in opposition to the tide that threatens Turtle Island Reservation."

"You'd build it there?"

"A handshake is not a legal document. Before Michael Chevreuil betrayed your father, I'd managed to get Chief Sweating Stone to agree to the school. Now, I have to travel to Duluth to make sure all this hard work doesn't fall apart."

"What's going to happen in Duluth?"

"Even without a lawyer, I should be able to get Chief Sweating Stone released, since there was no evidence of alcohol during the arrest. Your father's release will be far more difficult considering the warrants for his earlier crimes, but I'll be sure to acquire solid legal counsel for him." He smiled. "And in exchange, I'll get his signature."

Lily realized she'd been holding her breath and released it slowly to ask, "In exchange for ...?"

"Your father warmed to the idea of you teaching in a grand, granite school building, which is why he agreed to sell me his forty-acre plot of land, so I could build you a school. All I need now is his signature."

CHAPTER THIRTY-ONE

The Seven Fires

Turtle Island Reservation
September 1897

HER GRANDFATHER HELD his icy gaze on her for almost a full minute before he rose from his porch chair and walked into his cabin with a flip of his hand to beckon Lily to follow.

She followed.

Unlike her own house, which was filled with a warm light from all of the windows, the only light came from the front door and a small window along the back wall.

Nanak's log house was a simple square, with exposed pine logs that rose from the floorboards to a height of seven feet, where the steeply sloped wooden roof met it in a grid of exposed beams. The central stove had a chimney that rose through the rafters to meet the ceiling. Dozens of objects hung from the rafters, from dreamcatchers to drying herbs.

"I am pleased you've accepted this responsibility," he declared, even if his pouting expression did not reflect it. "Since the arrival of the zhaaganaash, many elders have refused to train women, but prior to the time of the First Fire, women served the people. You are Tewapa Asibikaashi of the Wijigan Clan, which not only gives you the right to be trained but will perhaps reveal an even greater purpose." He motioned for her again with his hand. "Sit, Granddaughter, and tell me about this name of yours."

So far, so good. Lily sat adjacent to him in front of the stove face, which allowed her to focus on the flames and coals rather than staring into his wrinkles, age spots, and imperfections. When she was a child, his aloof nature frightened her, but now she only saw a fragile man. "My mother named me Tewapa, which means 'water lily' in her Dakota tongue."

Grandfather shook his head. "It is true you are named after Lake Tewapa Tankiyan, but it was your father who chose the name. Do you know why?"

My father? Lily bluffed, connecting the story Migisi told her, when she replied, "It's also a reference to the lilies that grow near the outlet of Lake Manitou, which is where you and your father Chagobay brought Nicollet." *Did that sound acceptable?* "Are the two stories connected?"

"Everything is connected," he answered, pointing to a dreamcatcher above his head. "Tell me about your last name."

Weber, a family of spiders. "Asibikaashi is the word for spider, a reference to Grandmother Spider from the creation myths. She's also the one who made the dreamcatcher."

"And the Wijigan Clan?"

Lily shivered. *The Skull Clan.* "Migisi told me a little. He said they were the ones who ... were at Bleeding Rock."

Grandfather took over the conversation to tell the tale. "Chief Wiyipisiw beheaded women and threw children off the cliff and into Lake Manitou as a sacrifice to the Horned Serpent. Don't ignore the past. My father was killed for being a Wijigan, even though he had no part in these atrocities, or the atrocities of the past. You carry the crimes and guilt of all the concerned parties: the Dakota, the Wijigan, and the Pillagers. Perhaps that is why

Manabozho has brought you to me. For you to understand the end of the journey, you must first understand its beginning."

Nanak reached for one of the sticks found in an open barrel beside him. "This is a willow branch, which we use for making dreamcatchers. The thick end represents the past, and the narrow end represents the future; you are here, in the present."

He found a cup, which held an unknown liquid. His tremulous fingers removed a slender piece of sinew, which he wrapped around the conjunction of ends, leaving a few inches of the past and future to form a V above the loop.

Lily saw there were other cups, some holding beads, others holding feathers, and others holding long strands of leather. His frail, scarred hands worked steadily as he spoke.

"Long ago, when our people lived along the shores of the Atlantic Ocean, prophets came to warn us of the future. Each prophecy was delivered by a different prophet, who delivered warnings about a specific time, which became known as 'Fires.' The Seven Fires are thus seven separate prophecies." He glanced at her. "Do you understand?"

Lily nodded. *Just like the Bible.* "So these prophets ... were they part of the village or were they visiting strangers?"

Nanak gave a wry grin. "I will explain that to you at a later time. Now, I will tell you about each of the Seven Fires. The wording of these prophecies varies in the telling, and the way it is told upon the prairies is different from how I tell it and how it was told in the east. These differences protect the legend while allowing the people to know their past."

Lily waited, watching him work.

"The first prophet told us, 'In the time of the First Fire, a People Formed From Nothing will rise up and follow the sacred shell of the Midewiwin Lodge. The Midewiwin Lodge will serve as a spiritual guide and the source of much strength. The Sacred Megis will lead the way to the Seven Stopping Places of the journey. You are to look for a turtle-shaped island that is linked to the purification of the earth. You will find such an island at the beginning and at the end of your journey. You will know the chosen ground has been reached when you come to a land where food grows on water. If you do not move, you will be destroyed.'

"At the time of these warnings, many people scoffed at the prophets, for they lived in peace and harmony. Those who believed the prophets, a People Formed From Nothing, departed the Atlantic and became the nations of the Anishinaabe. Those who stayed behind, our Mikmaq brothers, were the first to have contact with the zhaaganaash. As the prophecy foretold, they suffered greatly." He reached for a bead. "Do you have questions?"

Her pile of shells rested a few feet away on his shelf. Her brother had already explained the strange "bread crumb" trail, so she was not taken aback by the supernatural aspect of the tale. "Where did they find the first shells?"

Grandfather's eyes widened at her interest. "The place was known as Mooniyaang, or 'turtle-shaped island,' which is now known as Montreal."

Several hundred miles away. No wonder the Mikmaq thought their brothers had lost their minds. Imagine sending out Migisi to look for magical shells on islands. Tens of thousands of islands. "Were all the Stopping Places islands?"

"Yes, in fact, they were, although not all the settlements developed on the islands themselves. As soon as the new Stopping Place was found, the quest for the next began immediately. It often took years before the path was revealed."

"Where was the second Stopping Place?"

"From Montreal, the Anishinaabe had to defeat the mighty Iroquois nation, which ended with them finding the second Stopping Place near Niagara Falls."

"And once they reached the second Stopping Place, did they get the second prophecy?"

"No, the Anishinaabe left having received all of the prophecies. It wasn't until they reached the third Stopping Place, Round Lake, near Detroit, that they understood the second prophecy. The second prophet warned, 'You will know the Second Fire because at this time the nation will be camped by a large body of water. In this time, the direction of the Sacred Shell will be lost. The Midēwiwin will diminish in strength until a boy will be born to point the way back to the traditional ways. He will show the direction to the stepping stones to the future of the Anishinaabe people.'" Nanak's eyes narrowed.

"So the large body of water ... was that one of the Great Lakes. Lake Huron?" Grandfather bobbed his head, giving Lily confirmation. "What exactly is the lost Sacred Shell?"

"If you prove to be worthy, I will explain the meaning to you, for it is a mystery that your generation must solve. During the days at Round Lake, many of the Anishinaabe either lost faith or grew weary of the quest. Our brothers, the Odawa and Potawatomi, simply made homes in Michigan. The boy spoken of in the prophecy guided the people to the fourth Stopping Place, Manitoulin Island on Lake Huron. From there, the words of the third prophet came true: 'In the Third Fire, the Anishinaabe will find the path to their chosen ground, a land in the west to which they must move their families. This will be the land where food grows on water.'"

"Food that grows on water," Lily repeated. "That's wild rice, isn't it?"

"Yes, from Manitoulin Island, our people found the fifth Stopping Place near Sault Sainte Marie and after, the sixth Stopping Place at Madeline Island, off the shores of Lake Superior. It was during this time that the warning about the arrival of the zhaaganaash came true: 'You will know the future of our people by the face the zhaaganaash wears.'

"The Fourth Fire guided our people in their alliances with the French, English, Americans, the Jesuits, and others. It was during this time that our Wijigan ancestors discovered our sacred quest was known by our enemies, and the long war began for control of the seventh Stopping Place. The Fifth Fire warned that we would 'abandon the old teachings' and trust in a 'false promise' and now those living on reservations understand the meaning of the 'destruction of the people.'"

The dismantling of the reservations and the indoctrination of boarding schools—this prophecy is more likely a retelling of history.

"My father Chagobay believed the arrival of the Serpent Star meant the beginning of a new fire. But are we living in the era of the Fifth Fire? The Sixth Fire? The Seventh Fire? Nicollet explained to my father that the Serpent Star was destined to return, and that with good health, I might live to see it again."

Is he sick? "What does the Sixth Fire describe?"

"The prophet of the Sixth Fire said, 'In the time of the Sixth Fire it will be evident that the promise of the Fifth Fire came in a false way. Those deceived by this promise will take their children away from the teachings of the elders, grandsons and granddaughters will turn against the elders. In this way, the elders will lose their reason for living ... they will lose their purpose in life. At this time a new sickness will come among the people. The balance of many will be disturbed. The cup of life will almost be spilled. The cup of life will almost become the cup of grief.'"

Lily looked down, ashamed of her recent arrogance, but also because of skepticism. *Is he making this up?* "If the Seven Fires Prophecies are told orally, how do we know they are still accurate?"

"Do you remember the Sacred Shell? The original prophecies were placed inside of the shell, to be protected and preserved."

A chest? A box? "But you said the Sacred Shell was lost."

"It will remain lost until the final days of the Seventh Fire, but the Wijigan Clan, and the faithful now known as the Chippewa, kept their own records of the prophecy. While the prophecies are kept by the Midewiwin priests, scrolls of all the sacred ceremonies and prophecies were kept in a 'hollowed out log from the ironwood tree.' These sacred texts were then hidden from our enemies in a place only one man knew.

"It is said that during the era of the Sixth Fire, a young person will once again guide the people to the truth. When your brother found the megis shells, I believed he was the 'little boy' prophesied to discover these sacred texts, but now I believe the truth has revealed that *you* were the one to find the shells."

Lily kept her gaze on the cold metal of the stove. "So what does that mean?"

"I must teach you how to battle the Horned Serpent. Whether or not you are the one who will receive visions of the Ironwood Scroll is to be determined by the will of Manabozho, but your blood as part of the Wijigan Clan demands much more. At the end of the Seventh Fire, there will be a fight that will not only determine the fate of our nation but of all races. This fight will either end in a rebirth or the destruction of all."

The will of Manabozho the Trickster? Lily chuckled and pointed to herself. "The future of mankind will depend on *my* ability to fight a water snake? It won't be much of a fight."

"Yes. With my teachings, the Horned Serpent is destined to be defeated. You will draw it out of the depths, destroy it, and cast it into the River of Souls where it belongs."

That's not what I meant.

"I am glad that you've finally come to me with an open heart and mind, but before your training can begin, I must prepare a sweat lodge. Then we will determine if you are only a teacher ... or a Firehandler."

Two Roads Diverged in a Wood

Turtle Island Reservation
September 1897

A NEW ROAD existed. Lily stood at the place where the road once turned north to Nimrod, but now, the intersection had been rebuilt to send traffic from Split Rock directly west to St. John. Although the workers' camp was still atop the hill adjacent to the Loose Goose Saloon, the workers were down in the valley preparing the pillars for the massive bridge.

Evangeline Thunder Face stepped out of the house with a basket of clothes but stopped in her tracks when she saw Lily standing at the crossroads.

Months passed since thinking of Samuel, but seeing his sister twisted her heart. Lily lifted a hand to wave and Evangeline turned toward the clothesline without returning the greeting.

She thinks I'm a whore.

Memories of Samuel kept her thoughts off her current troubles, and her walk to Split Rock felt like she was walking down a tunnel of nostalgia and regret. Sister Lynch promised her that with confession and baptism, her sinful relationship with her neighbor boy would be forgiven. *But what about my sins at White Earth?*

The bridge on the north edge of Split Rock returned her back to the present, and she studied the banks of Split Rock Creek and the Crow Wing River for signs of wandering spirits or lost boys.

It feels like I imagined it all.

BACK IN THE balcony of St. Marie's Catholic Church, Father Guerin's crates once again poured out into the space.

"Ah, I see young master Crain delivered my message," Father Guerin said with a smile. "Kermit's a good boy. His father is the blacksmith over at Sterling Junction."

I don't care. "Is it bad news?" Lily asked, tense and distracted.

"The news is mixed, with one pleasant surprise," he said as if baiting her into asking more. He moved over on the pew and patted it. Only after she sat did he continue. "Your grandfather Chief Sweating Stone has been released, along with several others unlawfully arrested."

"But not my father."

"No, but I was able to meet with him prior to his trial. I know your father has made a lot of mistakes in his life, but he wants to protect you. When I told him that the Turtle Island Reservation would remain with Migisi and Nanakonan, he agreed to the Turtle Island Jesuit School."

"He sold you his land?"

"No." Father Guerin grinned, though he looked defeated. "He negotiated a different deal for his children. After he heard what Adam Thunder Face did with his lease to Triton, he agreed to do the same thing with his plot, leasing it to the Society of Jesus until April 13th, 1986. Your family will receive annual payments for the next eighty-eight years, enough to feed you and dozens of potential grandchildren. Even though I argued against it, he will retain the deed."

Lily tried to understand her father's random date but gave up. "Why a lease?"

"He understood the legal danger of the trial, as well as the physical danger of being sent to prison, but Migisi is his heir. Building the school makes the Society of Jesus and myself a vested ally. The lease is null and void if something happens to him or your brother, which leads me to my surprise."

Lily rolled her eyes and refused to be baited.

"Your brother is going to be transferred to Sacred Heart in Morris."

Lily stood in excitement. "Really? When?"

"Soon. His time in Pennsylvania is coming to an end. Now, despite all of this, he is still effectively a prisoner, so don't expect him home any time soon, but it should allow me to visit him and to oversee his condition. Triton will be able to exert political pressure, but I'll have allies also. This, of course, leads to the next obvious question: when can we start our lessons?"

"This is all a bit much," she hedged.

"As you know, I have the ride situation figured out. The boy you met, Kermit Crain, comes to Split Rock on an almost daily trip."

"Yes, I understand, and Kermit is a nice boy, but—"

"We need to discuss pay. As I said before, daily lessons will not be necessary because there will be times when I will be traveling, but when I am here, I'd really like to work on my language studies. I would be willing to give you a dollar a day."

Lily gasped. "A dollar a day!"

"I just threw out the first figure that—"

He's clueless. Lily shook her head. "I wasn't complaining. If anything, you are dramatically overpaying. I'd be ashamed to take so much money. A dollar a day? You don't earn your pay by the hour, do you?"

"I have a small salary."

"But the church takes care of everything else, doesn't it?" Father Guerin nodded. "So you would pay me a dollar a day to just teach you my language?"

"Again, it might not be every day, but if you are willing to sacrifice giving up a full-time teaching position to help me, I'd be more than willing to compensate you fairly."

Lily felt a strange chill run down the back of her neck. She leaned away from him and into the corner of the pew. "A dollar a day just to teach you my language?" she repeated.

"In the coming months, I am going to be speaking to many tribal elders all across Minnesota and Wisconsin. I need to be able to speak fluently and understand fully if these negotiations are to be a success." He paused. "And next summer when the school superintendent is hiring his staff, how could I not recommend you? What do you say?"

"About being a tutor? I guess … I'll do it. How can I turn down a dollar a day?" *With the money, we could repair the house.*

Grinning, Father Guerin extended his hand, holding it there until Lily lifted hers and received a vigorous shake. "We have a deal."

Lily found herself staring at her lap after the handshake.

"I'll make a schedule of my travels, so you know when I'll be here and when I'll be gone. I'll make a duplicate for Kermit, so he knows when to stop at your house."

"Will the new school have staff housing?"

"Yes, we will be building new housing for our teachers and a dormitory for the students, but your lease payment should allow you to build a new home, either on Migisi's land or with Nanakonan."

"I spoke with my grandfather. He's agreed to begin my training, but first, he needs to build a sweat lodge for a test. To be honest with you, I'm a little nervous about it."

"Oh, I'm sure your grandfather will be a patient teacher. He has a lot riding on it." He hummed, looking interested. "What has he taught you so far?"

"He's been teaching me about the Midewiwin Way and the Seven Fires Prophecies."

"Ah, the story of the Anishinaabe migration from the Atlantic to the woods of Minnesota."

"You know it?"

"Oh yes, I've read all about it." He turned to his pile of books. "Was it William Warren's book? Schoolcraft? Oh, I know it's in one of these."

"Did you read about the Seventh Fire?"

"Yes, it was the one about two roads. Refresh my memory."

Lily took a deep breath, not just to recite but to decide if she wanted to share. "It begins by describing the final prophet. Did you read about the prophets in your book?"

"Yes, each prophecy was delivered by a prophet."

"Except the Fourth Fire—it was delivered by two."

"Ah, I didn't notice. So there are eight prophets then?"

"Yes, but the Seventh Fire Prophet was different from the other prophets. He was young and had a strange light in his eyes. He warned my people, 'In the time of the Seventh Fire, New People will emerge. They will retrace their steps to find what was left by the trail. Their steps will take them to the elders, who they will ask to guide them on their journey. But many of the elders will have fallen asleep. They will awaken to this new time with nothing to offer. Some of the elders will be silent out of fear. Some of the elders will be silent because no one will ask anything of them. The New People will have to be careful in how they approach the elders. The task of the New People will not be easy.'

"'If the New People remained strong in their Quest, something called the Water Drum will again sound its voice. There will be a rebirth of the Anishinaabe people and a rekindling of old flames. The Sacred Fire will again be lit.'"

"Did he explain the meaning of the Water Drum?"

Lily shook her head. "He said I'd learn more about it and the Sacred Fire after I've gone through the rituals. Nanakonan said that in the era of the Seven Fire, it will be a white person who will be given a choice between two roads. If this person chooses the right road, then the Seventh Fire will light the Eighth and final Fire, an eternal Fire of peace, love, brotherhood, and sisterhood."

"Like the Millennial Kingdom described in the *Book of Revelation*—Heaven on Earth."

Lily hummed. *Not quite.* "If this person makes the wrong choice of roads, destruction will not only come to this country, but death will come to all the Earth's people."

"Armageddon," Father Guerin said solemnly but with a slight depression of his dimpled cheek.

How can he be so casual about the End Times? "Now do you understand how crazy all of this is?"

"While it certainly is not the way St. John described it, there are some striking similarities between the two prophecies. Seven Seals ... Seven Fires. Seven Candlesticks ... Seven Stopping Places. Seven Archangels ... Seven, or Eight, Prophets. The Jewish disciples were once aghast when Paul began evangelizing the Gentiles, so it would not surprise me if God's plan involved people who don't originate in the Middle East. You don't have to renounce your salvation in order to have an open mind." He handed her a fresh notepad. "Could you write down these lessons? That way I could read them during my travels and ask questions when I return."

I'm spying on my own grandfather, Lily thought as she nodded. *I wish Migisi was here instead of me. I'm supposed to be his voice of reason. All of my mentors have obviously lost their minds.*

CHAPTER THIRTY-THREE

Sacred Heart

Morris, MN
September 1897

A FEW MINUTES after Jude Weber climbed into his dormitory bed for the night, Migisi Asibikaashi murdered him. None of the other boys in the Sacred Heart Indian School understood, or cared, what happened.

Some nights Migisi silently strangled him. Other nights, Jude Weber received a knife to the throat.

Once, Migisi rallied the rest of the boys—Luther Pratt, Francis Little Sturgeon, David Loon Foot, Hiram Warner, Samuel Johnson, and his cousin John LaBiche—to hold Jude down by the bedsheets and beat him to death.

Most nights, Jude Weber was killed by smothering him with their shared pillow.

Time to die, you traitor.

Earlier in the day, Jude Weber had pitched a gem of a baseball game in a scrimmage against the white kids from Benson Public Schools. With his short hair and uniform, as well as a strong fastball, Jude looked the part of a modern baseball player. The win helped his popularity with the other boys—Lakota, Fox, Arikara, and Turtle Island Chippewa—making his return to Minnesota much more tolerable than Pennsylvania. Jude Weber now knew the Parts of Speech also.

Nouns can be thrown.

Verbs are what you do.

Adverbs are how you do it.

So Migisi reached (verb) up from the depths of the water, picked up a stone (noun), and violently (adverb) smashed Jude's face until nothing of his other-self remained.

While the other boys slept, Migisi continued his sacred training.

From the depth of his imagination, and the depths of Lake Manitou, he summoned the Mishi-Ginebig, the Horned Serpent. Like the one described in the tales of Iyash, his leviathan had two sharp horns upon a lion's head, except rather than hair, his creation had slithering eels for a mane. Its long neck cut through the water, which hid the rest of its monstrous form.

In his dream, Migisi stood upon a rocky point on Mizheekay Island as the surge of water preceded the creature's attack. With shield and spear, he held his ground, ducking and stabbing.

Some nights, the fight would last for hours. Other times, he would dodge the brunt force of the initial attack and surprise the Horned Serpent with a simple, but fatal, wound.

But with each fight, Migisi died by morning, allowing Jude Weber to come back to life.

CHAPTER THIRTY-FOUR

The Thunderbird and the Horned Serpent

Turtle Island Reservation
October 1897

LILY WEBER WATCHED her mother process the request. *Is she buying it?*

The wrinkles in Winnie's forehead seemed to indicate the obvious answer. "So why is Father Guerin traveling all the way to Turtle Mountain in North Dakota? I didn't even think there were mountains in North Dakota."

Endorheic Basin, Lily remembered the word used by Father Guerin. *Like Devil's Lake, a body of water without an outlet.* "You know how your mother was taken prisoner after a battle with Chief Sweating Stone's Chippewa?" At her mother's nod, she continued. "A whole bunch of Chippewa believed the last Stopping Place must be farther west, since no one could conclusively find the place in Minnesota."

"I thought it was Mille Lacs," Winnie said with a shrug.

"And others think it is Spirit Island by Duluth—I didn't say they were right. The Turtle Mountain reservation is on the border with Canada, and apparently, there are even a few small bands that went into the Rockies." Her mother was missing the point. "Father Guerin keeps a journal that might one day become a book on culture. That's why he's traveling to North Dakota. It's also why I'm going to be staying with Grandfather for a few days—to learn."

Winnie sighed. "I hope you know what you're doing."

Lily held her blank notebook and pencil. "I'm just doing this for posterity. I'm not losing my faith or anything like that. I'm acting like a secretary for those who will come after me."

AN HOUR LATER, Lily's notebook was thrown into the stove at the center of Nanak's shack. "For generations, the Wijigan Clan has passed down its words without paper and pencil. You will write these words upon your heart. Understood?"

Father Guerin gave that to me. Lily watched the notebook burn. *I'll just write them down later on another notebook.*

"Come, there are things I must show you."

He first took her to his new sweat lodge and explained, again, its purpose and construction technique, which she had written down back in her bedroom. Then he took her to a patch of bald stone overlooking the Blue Knife River.

Grandfather looked down at his hands. "Do you see the burns? When I was a boy, Chief Matchigabo of the Pillagers killed my father Chagobay by burning him alive. But before they killed him, Matchigabo gave me a chance to rescue him. They put a hatchet in the hot coals and said to me, 'If you are truly a wabeno, then reach into the flames and pull out the hatchet. You can cut his bonds and free him.'" His face was grim as he added, "I am not a Firehandler."

"Is that why Migisi had bandages on his hands?"

"We are not the last of the Wijigan, despite the efforts of men like Matchigabo. The men who came at the beginning of summer—Joseph Little Toad, Clyde Speaks First, and James Grey

Sky—also carry the blood of the Wijigan Clan. Migisi is not a Firehandler either, although he might still have one of the parts to play in the Sacred Fire. If you indeed found the megis shells, you might play one of the other parts."

"Migisi believes he is the Gitchi-Animikii, the Great Thunderbird. Is that true?"

"It is up to Manabozho to decide who is to defeat the Horned Serpent. My father believed he had found the Great Thunderbird after meeting the explorer Joseph Nicollet. When the Sacred Fire is lit, a Firehandler will summon the Horned Serpent from the depths, and once it rises, the Great Thunderbird will destroy it and send it into the River of Souls and the Land of the Midnight Sun, where all souls must go."

What to ask first? The River of Souls and Land of the Midnight Sun is akin to Heaven. The Horned Serpent is obviously something evil, like Satan. He won't tell me about the Sacred Fire yet. "How does the Firehandler summon the Horned Serpent?"

"Once in a generation, Manabozho will mark a child with strange abilities. A Mide is trained. A Jessakkid is blessed with the ability to see spirits. But the rarest of all the spiritual gifts is the one passed down from the dawn of time. A Firehandler can both command spirits and control the elements, if armed with the right magic."

If Manabozho is also the Trickster, how can I trust any of this? "I don't understand what you mean by the Great Thunderbird. I thought it was some sort of animal that protected our people from evil, like the Binesi, the guardian birds."

"Thunderbirds have always defended the people from evil serpents and Manidos, but the Great Thunderbird is destined to fulfill the Seven Fires Prophecy by destroying the evil Horned Serpent that sleeps below the waters of the lake. This boy will be different from any others who have come before. When my father met Joseph Nicollet, with his boy-like features and wide eyes, he believed the prophecy had come true."

Grandfather pointed below where they stood. "He took Nicollet past the rapids where I tended the canoes up to this spot where the rocks bled blue and green. He would have shown him the secret our family kept if Chief Matchigabo of the Pillagers had not taken Nicollet prisoner." He frowned, impatient. "Now do you understand?"

Shown him what secret? "I'm trying," Lily muttered. "So in Lake Manitou, there is a Horned Serpent. What did it do that was so bad? Why are we trying to defeat it?"

"Manitou is a word for water spirit. The Horned Serpent is a phrase used so we don't utter the spirit's true name."

Satan. Lucifer. Beelzebub. I get it.

"The Horned Serpent might sleep, but it is very real and very ancient. He comes from the dawn of time. Do you know the legend of the Fisher Cat?"

"The story of the Big Dipper? My father told it to me." Lily grinned, remembering an open field. Migisi was just a baby, held in Winnie's arms. She and Father rested on a blanket looking up at the stars. "It's one of the few stories he ever told me."

This seemed to please Grandfather who smiled a little. "Yes, the seven stars of the Big Dipper are part of our constellation for Ojiig, the Fisher Cat. It is a reminder to us that the war with the Wintermaker is as old as the earth itself. Long ago, the Horned Serpent walked upon the earth like a man, the Wintermaker. This man was a powerful shaman who learned how to collect the souls of the dead, keeping them in a cage like pet birds."

"Why?"

"The Wintermaker believed if he could gather enough souls in his cage, he could cheat death and become an immortal."

Place of Souls. Her mother's name for Lake Manitou. "Did the Wintermaker become immortal?"

"Yes, but not as he wished. When the Great Spirit learned what this shaman was doing far off in the lands of the north, he sent a warrior—the Fisher Cat. The battle between the Fisher Cat and the Wintermaker was so fierce that the world itself was almost destroyed, forcing both of them to flee into the stars."

"If the Fisher Cat is the Big Dipper constellation, does that mean the Wintermaker is the North Star?"

"Close," Grandfather said and smiled. "See, perhaps it is your destiny to teach your brother the secrets of our family. You have the face of a woman but the wisdom of an old man."

"Thank you," Lily chuckled. "So tell me more about the Wintermaker."

"The Wintermaker is represented by the constellation you know as Orion, for his spirit rises, descends, and then rises again. He used his magic to keep himself trapped here, and although his human flesh was killed, his spirit remains. If the Wintermaker is restored to life, as is his plan, he will usher in the destruction of the world. If he is defeated, then the world will see the Eighth Fire."

"How is he defeated?"

"The Sacred Fire can only be lit when the time is right—when the Wintermaker is vulnerable. My ancestor Wiyipisiw tried to force the prophecy, only to see his efforts destroyed."

Hearing the name flooded her mind with images.

The Horned Priest down by Split Rock Creek—the one Albert Fisher also saw.

The image in my bedroom window.

'I need your help to save the children. Help me finish the song,' Wiyipisiw had said to me.

Do I need to help fix a mistake?

"For the Wintermaker to be defeated, we must be armed with three weapons given to us by Manabozho: The Water Drum, the Sacred Shell, and the Ironwood Log. You are Wijigan. If the secrets are lost, the blood of your ancestors will be upon your hands and the future of your children will be put in peril."

"I understand."

"When was your last moon-time?"

My menstrual cycle? Is this a joke? "It has been three weeks."

Grandfather nodded. "A woman's power is strong during her moon-time, which is why most are not allowed near the Sacred Lodge and the Sweat Fire. A woman's body purifies itself, whereas men must perform rituals to cleanse their bodies from the poison water called alcohol. For generations, our family has protected old magic known as the Song of the Manitou, which is needed to light the Sacred Fire. If you are to learn the Song of the Manitou, you first must be tested."

"I don't know about this. I just want to learn the words and stories."

"Want? Duty is greater than desire. If you are to learn the Song of the Manitou, you must prove to be worthy. We shall see if Manabozho has chosen you."

The ghost mentioned a song. Lily looked down at her crucifix, which Grandfather saw.

"For evil to be defeated, there must be more sacrifices. You must be willing to make sacrifices, just like your Christ."

"What kind of sacrifices?"

"When your father was a boy, we entered the lodge looking for answers—he did not hear the answers he wanted to. Perhaps you will not hear what you seek."

"I don't understand."

"When your father learned the truth about his past and his future, he rejected his path. Now you come searching for the same answers. The Song of the Manitou teaches that a Great Thunderbird will defeat the evil one, but first a powerful Firehandler must wake it from its slumber, and another will..." Nanak's voice trailed off. "Either way, I do know that when I die, you and Migisi will be the only ones left who know the Song of the Manitou."

"What exactly is the Song of the Manitou?"

"The Song of the Manitou is powerful medicine, or magic as you would call it. Each verse is a separate spell, and when sung in its entirety, it will light the Sacred Fire, bringing the Seven Fires to an end."

"And what are—"

"First, we must discover the role chosen for you by Manabozho. You must be tested. If you are willing, at dusk, we will enter the sweat lodge."

Song of the Manitou

Turtle Island Reservation
October 1897

FOUR DAYS AFTER entering the sweat lodge, hunger had gone from a sharp pain that coursed through Lily's body like electricity to a dull throb. She had no energy to care anymore, not that she was hungry, nor that she was half-naked, even when Grandfather reentered the sweat lodge with more heated stones.

Lily looked down at the moose blanket beneath her as he entered with more stones. He poured a few scoops of water onto the fire and the temperature in the lodge became sweltering again. She pressed her face against the cool of the earth. *Tired. Hot.*

"Are you angry with me?" he asked as he sat down on the other side of the fire. Despite having just gone outside, sweat poured down the side of his face.

His father was a hero; my father is a criminal, but we're both victims of our destiny. "No, I am not angry. You are doing what you have been prepared to do."

"You do not believe our words."

"Perhaps I'm not meant to understand."

"Today is the fourth day. Tell me again, why do we fast?"

Lily sat up, the massive bundle of woven shells draped over her breasts sticking to her skin. "We fast for four days because that's how long a soul takes to reach the Land of the Midnight Sun.

Is that why Jesus remained in the grave for three days? Or why Lazarus stayed in the tomb for four days? Does the Hebrew soul follow the same path as the Chippewa?

Grandfather took a medicine bag and showed it to her. "If you are indeed a Firehandler, your weary soul will awaken after its journey to the place of our ancestors."

"Why did the Pillagers burn you?"

Grandfather looked at his hands. "The Wijigan Clan was once trusted within the nation, for our guidance brought the faithful to the Sixth Stopping Place, but when the war with the Sioux went on for more than a generation, the Wijigan elders grew desperate. In their desperation, they turned to dark magic and initiated a rite involving eating the flesh of the dead."

"Cannibalism?"

"When the people learned of these deeds, our relatives were driven away from Madeline Island. In this time of darkness, my grandfather Makadewaa was born. While Manabozho did not bless me with the gifts of the Firehandler, my great-grandfather Wiyipisiw was born to be both Jessakkid and Wabeno. Despite the dangers of the Sioux, he came to Lake Manitou alone, believing he could fulfill the prophecy. His black heart twisted the Seven Fires prophecies, and he believed if he released the Wintermaker, it would be his ally and help him defeat all those who wronged him."

Is my tormentor evil then? "He's the one who made the sacrifices at Bleeding Rock?"

Nanak nodded. "He tried to impose his will upon the Great Spirit, and instead of waiting for the proper time, he tried to wake the Wintermaker himself. He failed because he did not have the Sacred Shell. He possessed only the Water Drum and the Ironwood Scroll. When the Pillagers and other bands of our people learned what he was doing, they allied themselves with our enemies to crush the Wijigan Clan. Wiyipisiw was slain, along with most of the Wijigan Clan. My grandfather fled north to Canada, but before he died, he told my father about the secrets buried at Lake Manitou. Now, I must pass on these secrets to you."

Wiyipisiw died at Lake Manitou. "So none of the other Mide, Jessakkid, or Firehandlers from other villages or clans know the Song of the Manitou. Only the Wijigan Clan know it?"

"Yes. For the Seven Fires Prophecies to reach an end, the Song of the Manitou must be sung, accompanied by the sounding of the Water Drum."

Is this how I can save the children in my dreams? "The prophets spoke of a boy who would dream of where the Ironwood Log was buried and usher in the eighth and final fire. Do you think Migisi is this boy?"

"That is yet to be seen. Your brother has some gifts of the Jessakkid and has been selected to train as a Mide when he returns, but he was not a Firehandler. Like you, he is already unique because of his blood. I believe both of you will have important parts to play in the days to come. That is why I must prepare you. The fast will find out if you are a Jessakkid, and your soul will return from the Land of the Midnight Sun with answers to guide you."

"And how will I know if I'm a Firehandler?"

Grandfather again looked down at his hands. "The test of the Firehandler is different. A Firehandler is a servant of Manabozho blessed with the ability to handle fire. Only a Firehandler, trained to sing the full Song of the Manitou, can use the Water Drum to wake the Manitou from its slumber."

"That's why I have to learn the Song, in case the Water Drum is ever found."

Grandfather nodded. "Your brother will not be the one to wake the Manitou because he is not a Firehandler."

"I see. But he might still be the Great Thunderbird because he is a Jessakkid."

"Yes. Men like Joseph Little Toad, Clyde Speaks First, and James Gray Sky can still train Migisi in this role, but only I can pass down the Song of the Manitou."

Father Guerin was right about my role. "So you don't need me to do anything more than pass down the knowledge of the Song."

"I know you have cast aside our beliefs, but I want to test to see if you are a Firehandler."

He's going to burn me. "But I don't … I don't … I'm a Christian, Grandfather. I don't believe any of this stuff is real."

His scowl made his face look as if it were about to break in half. "When the Black Robes first walked upon our shores, they understood the truths shared between the Christian God and the beliefs of the Midewiwin. They understood our Kitshi Manido, the Great Spirit, was akin to their God; they understood our Dzhe Manido, the Guardian Spirit, was akin to their Holy Spirit; and they understood our Manabozho, the Mediator made man, was akin to their Christ. Do you think the similarities stop there?"

Jesus is the Son of God. Manabozho is a shapeshifting rabbit, the trickster. Are they two sides to the same coin? "Why does Migisi have to do this? He is only a boy."

"A boy who is pure of heart. The dark medicine surrounding the Manitou corrupted my great-grandfather after decades, and the people cast him and the Wijigan down. The Seven Fires talk of a boy leading the way, yet only the blood of a Wijigan can fulfill prophecy. A time of trial is upon us. It must be Migisi." He paused, studying her. "Perhaps you will be the one to wake the Manitou."

"What if I'm not?"

"Then I will teach you the Song so you can pass it down, but I can only teach the Song to one committed to learning. For me to teach you the Song, you must be tested. I chose to put my hands in the fire to save my father, and Migisi chose to pick up a hot stone. This is your choice alone."

Lily relented with a defeated nod. "Then I will learn the Song of the Manitou to help my brother. I will teach him everything you teach me."

"Once, the Wijigan were part of every village, but only the chosen ones were allowed to learn the Song of the Manitou. Now we will find out if your body and soul are strong enough to endure. You will eat this paste, and then we will go outside. If you can hold a stone, then you are worthy of learning the Song. If you can carry the stone into the lodge, then you are a Firehandler."

From the pouch he began to mix strange compounds together in a wooden bowl. One of the compounds was a blue paste.

In the Gospels, Jesus asks Peter to walk on water to him, even though Peter already believed in Jesus. My grandfather asks the same of me, even though I don't believe.

But I promised Father Guerin.

And I love my little brother.

And I owe it to all those who came before me.

When Grandfather extended the bowl to her, Lily looked down at her pink, unblemished palms and accepted it. The paste coated her mouth like chalk dust, choking her until her saliva helped it pass. She stood.

Outside the sweat lodge, a pile of heated stones sat upon a fire, along with the fork Grandfather had used to lift them.

He began to sing.

The heat radiated off the stones as Lily bent over the flameless bed of coals. Her hands hesitated above the pile, the heat pouring off the closest one.

She scooped one up …

… and became a Firehandler.

The Lesson of Jonah

Split Rock, MN
October 10, 1897

HALF A DOZEN hands instantly shot into the air when Sister Inez asked the question. Lily's eyes scanned the Sunday school class, even though she wasn't the one to call on them. Britta Forsberg's entire arm vibrated with enthusiasm. Competing for attention, Lindsey MacPherson whined like a hungry puppy. Sylvie Berg calmly raised her hand, even though Lily doubted she knew the answer.

Sister Inez's attention finally focused on two boys in the back of the room, Frankie Auerbach and Albert Fisher. The two looked like brothers; the only difference was the birthmark peeking from Albert's hairline. Neither had raised his hand, but Albert dared to look whereas Frankie looked away.

"Frankie?"

"What?" Frankie almost jumped, and the accidental sass made some of the other boys smile.

"Can you explain why Jonah boarded the ship bound for Tarshish?" Sister Inez repeated.

Frankie blinked as he searched for the answer. "He was running away."

"Running away from what?"

Again, half a dozen hands shot up.

Lily looked down at her own hands, then her palms, before putting them behind her back. There was not a burn mark or blister to be seen, but she still felt scarred.

Cynthia Van Slyke answered, "Jonah didn't like the people in Nineveh because they were pagans, so when God sent him to preach to them, Jonah disobeyed by getting on the ship."

"Very good, Cynthia," Sister Inez praised. "Now as we heard, Jonah did not get very far before God caused the storm to stop him from running away from his purpose. What happened to Jonah because of the storm?"

Most of the children raised their hands, except for Albert Fisher.

"A whale swallowed him," Monte Crain shouted before being called on.

"How did he even end up in the water, Mr. Crain?" When he shrugged, Sister Inez called, "Britta?"

"The sailors threw him in the water when they heard how he had disobeyed God."

"That's correct." Before another question could be asked, Brisco Miller raised his hand, forcing Sister Inez to acknowledge him.

"What kind of fish was it?"

"It was a big fish. I'm not quite sure what kind it was."

Then each child spoke over the top of each other.

"My dad said it was a whale because they breathe air."

"What kind of whale was it?"

"A blue whale—they're the biggest."

"Was it a Terrible Dogfish like in Pinocchio?"

"Or the Manitou?"

"I bet it was a sperm whale."

Sperm. One word threw the discussion into complete chaos as all the prepubescent boys, and a few girls, burst into laughter, causing Sister Inez's face to turn red. "That is enough of that!" And the yardstick that appeared in her hand ended all snickers.

After that, the lessons continued in absolute order until Sister Inez dismissed the children.

As Lily tidied the room, she took a moment to clarify a few thoughts rattling around in her head.

Father Guerin was still in North Dakota, leaving her no one to share the unholy miracle that had happened a few days earlier. "Sister Inez, I have a question about today's Bible story."

"As long as it isn't identifying the species of fish that swallowed poor Jonah."

"No." Lily smirked as she tended to the chalkboard. "God sent the big fish to swallow up Jonah and carry his body back to the coast, right?"

"Yes." Sister Inez straightened her notes.

"Was Jonah dead?"

"No, the point of sending the fish was to keep Jonah alive. God demanded that he go to Nineveh, so the fish brought him all the way back."

Lily accepted Sister Inez's authority and didn't ask anymore.

"Is there something bothering you?"

"Why would God spare Jonah's life?"

At this, Sister Inez stopped collecting pencils and turned to face Lily. "To teach him a lesson about obeying God's will."

At first Lily went to meekly accept the answer, until she remembered she was an adult and countered with, "Do you remember how Jesus referenced Jonah when telling his disciples about his impending death on the cross?"

"I believe it was in Matthew."

Matthew 12, Lily amended silently before continuing. "Yes, Jesus said he would be dead for three days and used Jonah as a comparison for the disciples to understand."

"Yes, at the end of three days. Jesus was alive and Jonah was alive upon returning to the shore after three days."

"God wanted Jonah to preach to the Ninevites, right?"

"Yes."

"But Jonah didn't think they were worthy of salvation. In a way, he would have let them burn in the flames of Hell instead of bringing them salvation."

Hell. After finishing the confirmation program with the nuns at Sacred Heart Indian School, Lily thought that she had a clear understanding of Heaven and Hell. The righteous souls went up into the sky while the evil ones were punished with the flames of the underworld. The simplicity of her adopted religion made her a quick convert, but it wasn't until after Nanakonan revealed her abilities as a Firehandler that she began to realize Lake Manitou shattered her beliefs.

After holding the hot stone long enough for absolute confirmation, she had dropped it at Nanak's feet and ran back to Winnie.

"I see your point," Sister Inez said, clearly placating Lily. "Jonah is being racist by refusing to preach to the men of Nineveh."

"What if God wanted to teach Jonah a lesson by showing him, either in a vision or in spirit, what waited for the Ninevites if Jonah did not preach to them?"

"What do you mean?"

"Jonah gets swallowed by the big fish, but a few verses later, Jonah is seeing the depths of the sea, including the mountains of the ocean floor. How can he see such details from inside of the big fish?"

"Perhaps this is what he saw before the fish swallowed him."

Sister Inez wasn't cooperating. *How could the souls of the dead gather in a place like Lake Manitou?* "Then why does Jonah say he cried out from the 'Belly of Hell' and mention the bars shutting behind him? What if this watery Hell is the destination for all human souls?"

"Jonah was a prophet of God. Of course he would not go to Hell. I think he compared it to the awfulness of being inside the fish, which was a miracle itself."

Lily surrendered and turned away, unable to ask what she really wanted to.

CARRYING THE SUPPLIES downstairs, she almost knocked over Albert Fisher as she came around the corner at the bottom of the stairs.

"Oh, are you all right?"

Albert nodded but didn't move. The boy had big eyes so deeply set they looked like puppy-dog eyes. Unlike the farm boys, Albert was frail and thin. In the months she'd been assisting Sister Inez, the boy had only uttered a few words to her.

"Could you get the cabinet door for me, Albert?"

He nodded and walked over to grab the knob, then he just stopped. "Did you see it?"

The somber tone in his voice sent chills down the back of her neck. "See what?"

"In the woods. By the bushes of Split Rock Creek."

"That's right … I was walking through the woods and spooked a deer." Having spooked several deer along the path, it was a half-truth. "Is that what you saw?"

Albert shook his head. "You need to make it stop."

"Make what stop?"

"Him. You need to make him stop. Don't let him trick you."

The Old Tree Sighs

Hiawatha County
October 11, 1897

HALVAR DOBIE TRIED to imagine another world from another time. His feet stood upon solid stone, but his heritage taught him that the world was ancient, caught in a cycle of destruction and rebirth. Beneath the surface, the remains of the old world existed.

He knelt down as if he were in a church. *If we have truly found you, then I offer my life to restore yours. Guide me. Give me wisdom.*

Dobie's god didn't answer, which didn't shake his faith in the least. The Order of Eos took root following the destruction of the previous world, and for countless centuries, it grew closer and closer to its final shape. Now the fruits appeared on the branches.

If we are to break the cycle, sacrifices must be made.

Dobie rose from his silent prayers and dusted off his knees. Ozias Haggard and Ira Douglas approached him. While Douglas worked on all the business and political maneuverings to set up the next stage of the old war, Dobie had taken measure of Hiawatha County.

"So?" Ira Douglas asked. "Do we proceed?"

In the east, Lake Manitou grew dark. In the west, the setting sun illuminated the field of rocks with pale red light. Dobie ignored the question and walked over to the depression in the stone. "So this is where it happened? This is where you'll make your quarry?"

Ozias Haggard, unlike his ignorant brothers-in-law, took his responsibility seriously. "I'm ready. I know what is at stake. I will reward your trust in me."

Dobie kicked the toe of his boot against the smooth stone. "We pin our hopes on this little patch of stone?"

"I know I can't prove it, but this depression was made by the Philosopher's Stone," Haggard argued.

"How? I know all the rumors about LeSueur and Lahontan, but that was two-hundred years ago, and since that time, Eos has spent considerable resources chasing down countless lies."

"The Delhut family has never wavered in their steadfast belief of what lies here. The truth cannot remain hidden. The earth bleeds blue, once again, for a good reason," Haggard pressed.

"It's a crazy story," Douglas added, "but the circumstantial evidence Delhut has collected does seem to indicate some validity."

In 1758, spurred on by the heavenly appearance of a comet, an outcast clan of Chippewa known as the Wijigan took Lake Manitou from the Sioux. According to the lore, they sacrificed a dozen captives to the lake in order to the Horned Serpent that dwelt in the waters. Ten years later, the same priest attempted to summon a god buried in stone with an ancient relic referred to as a Water Drum.

Back then, the Order of Eos was clueless about what was happening at Lake Manitou. Nor did the Jesuits, the Periphery, or even the Priory of Ormus have a hand in what happened next. A young Sioux chieftain took it upon himself to build a coalition, including the Pillagers, to wipe the Wijigan off the face of the earth.

Here, at the place where Halvar Dobie now stood, a Wijigan priest transformed solid stone to create the beginning of a tunnel. However, the Sioux-Chippewa coalition stopped him that day, killing every last man, woman, and child they found camped along the shores of the lake.

"So what happened to the Water Drum in the battle?" Dobie asked. "If the Wijigan did somehow find LeSueur's lost prize, what became of it."

"They hid it," Ozias Haggard quickly added. "It explains the blue earth—the vitriol, the ormus—that Professor Nicollet observed when he visited both Mankato and Lake Manitou. The Philosopher's Stone refused to be hidden down at Mankato, and now somewhere in Hiawatha County, it again refuses to stay hidden."

"I'll be frank with you, Haggard," Dobie added. "William Sinclair is focused on the Rocky Mountains. He's convinced Baron Lahontan's map describes the upper Missouri River. Hell, Sinclair is convinced Joseph Nicollet intended to return to the upper Missouri before his untimely death. He thinks his brother's theory about Hiawatha County is a dead end, but after visiting Lake Manitou, I think a further look is warranted."

"So we're proceeding?" Ira Douglas asked.

Do I tell them about the bad dreams I had last night? In his dreams, Dobie pictured the earth cracking open at Lake Manitou and an army of giants emerging from the void, bringing death and mayhem to the world in the endless. Beneath the roots of the world tree Laerad, the three Norns sang their song of doom. *We must break the cycle of destruction.* "The history of the Order of Eos has taught that impatience leads to disaster."

"The Delhut family has been patient for two hundred years," Haggard contended. "With or without the Philosopher's Stone, we will discover what is lurking beneath Lake Manitou."

"Ira, go back and let Sinclair know what's happening here. I'll be staying to properly vet Stewart and Marquette to make sure their families understand our ways." He turned to speak directly to Ozias Haggard. "Progress will be slow and patient. You'll have the backing of the Order of Eos behind you, but know that our enemies are just as powerful."

Dobie walked toward Lake Manitou, knowing that he'd now play the part of Heimdall, the ever-watchful guardian of Asgard.

ACROSS LAKE MANITOU, a shadow stirred in the reeds, but Frankie Auerbach ignored it. All the animals came out at night, he knew, and dusk was the perfect time to catch bullfrogs.

On the northern shore, Lily Weber looked over the notes she'd written about the Firehandler ritual she'd endured. Her unblemished hands held the pen that recorded the foreign syllables taught to her by Nanakonan. As she wrote them, her mouth practiced saying them.

Trapped in the depths for countless centuries, one of the twelve shadows fed upon the faint song whispered on the air. It rose slowly to the surface, where a young boy waded closer and closer.

Skipping School

Old Copper Road
October 11, 1897

SOMETIME AFTER SUNDAY school was dismissed, Frankie Auerbach vanished. Bjorn Forsberg sat on the wagon outside of Dutch Boy Creamery, listening to Burt Van Slyke tell Mr. MacPherson all about it.

Frankie made the sperm whale joke, Bjorn remembered. It was now Monday morning, and even though Frankie had been gone for less than twenty-four hours, a chill ran down Bjorn's spine.

John and Christine Auerbach, residents of Split Rock, had reported their son missing the previous night. Frankie had taken his fishing pole down to the beach near the Split Rock Creek outlet. Constable Graham had found the boy's footprints in the mud, along with his fishing gear, but there had been no signs of foul play.

"We should muster a search party," Mr. MacPherson said to Burt, who was better at gossip than running the family creamery.

Van Slyke nodded. "Constable Graham is going to keep searching. If the boy doesn't turn up soon, the church bells will ring to call everybody into town."

Once the milk canisters were exchanged, Bjorn Forsberg moved his wagon into position.

"You hear about the Auerbach kid?" Van Slyke asked as his brother Stefan walked to the rear of the wagon. Bjorn nodded, and with a shrug, Van Slyke went to the back of the wagon to help unload.

School started in two hours, and the students would go crazy about the talk of a missing classmate.

I should just skip school and start looking for him now. Frankie's so stupid he's probably lost in the woods of Bleeding Rock.

Bjorn wanted to imagine Frankie sitting in a duck boat, hunting. If not for school and the farm, that's what Bjorn would be doing. But the terrible dreams that plagued Bjorn all night, leaving him lethargic and bitter, led his mind to darker places. As much as he loved fishing, the thought of water repulsed him now.

The wagon's tailgate closed, causing him to jump.

He signed for the delivery and turned his wagon for home.

By the time he pulled onto Old Copper Road, the MacPherson wagon was already at the top of the hill, turning south toward their farmstead. A few yards to the east, the big iron trestle bridge spanned the Crow Wing River.

That's where I'd begin if I were Graham. If something did happen, the current would pull Frankie's body into Split Rock Creek and down the Crow Wing River. By this evening, Frankie could be heading toward the town of Staples.

The trip home lasted a few minutes; Bjorn prepared his monologue for his father.

"I want to help search for the missing Auerbach boy," he began, and with each question, his father led to the inevitable answer.

"I suppose, if he doesn't show up, we'll have done our part already," Gustaf agreed. "We can't go running around this evening when it's already dark and there's milking to be done."

"So the girls can collect my schoolwork?" Bjorn clarified.

"Yes, but I don't want you going through the woods, or sticking your nose around the mill. I'll search the Crow Wing River, but I want you to take the rowboat and check the shoreline from the bluffs all the way down to Buffalo Slough. Be sure to check Kanaranzi Creek while you're down there."

Bjorn's dream returned—*hundreds of bodies floated like lily pads in Lake Manitou* ... "I will."

TO REACH THE waters of Lake Manitou, Bjorn had to walk the steep trail that led from behind the house all the way down to the rocky shore. Although not as steep as the bluffs at Bleeding Rock, he still had to clutch a few branches along the way when his feet slid.

He and his father had built a simple pine dock, which allowed the boat to be tied up during the summer, and when winter came, it could be set onto the platform for storage.

He's sending me to the wrong place. Does he want the glory of finding the body for himself? Or does he think seeing a body will frighten me?

Bjorn's odyssey began with a trip north along the tall bluffs. Once he reached the sawmill, he turned the rowboat to the west, making a full circle around Deadwood Island, which was filled with dead cottonwoods left behind after a spring flood. While the brush and young trees quickly grew back, Deadwood Island had a much more sinister atmosphere than Turtle Island and its turtle shell hump that protected its trees.

No Frankie.

By the time the sun was high in the sky, he'd reached Buffalo Slough, filled with its fields of wild rice.

Bodies don't float upstream.

With a fairly dry summer, both the slough and the secondary outlet had all but dried up, which meant Split Rock Creek was now the primary outlet.

The slough was almost a half-mile wide, beginning where the shallow waters came up and ending where the MacPherson barn stood on the last bit of bluff. The Bordeaux farm sat on the other side of Kanaranzi Creek, built on a location that rankled his father whenever they drove past it.

Wild rice reeds reached six feet above the surface of the water, and grew thick as a rainforest jungle, so Bjorn paddled along the edge of the field until he found the deeper channel leading to Kanaranzi Creek. Soon, he was surrounded by walls of vegetation that closed in on him.

Filtered by the tall plants, the water was clear and calm, allowing him to see all the way to the bottom, where tiny green spirals reached for the sun. Lily pads marked the place where the failed current allowed the strangers to grow in the crease of the two fields.

Bjorn Forsberg cursed in Swedish when he saw the unmistakable hump of a human back floating in the still waters.

He'd found Frankie.

CHAPTER THIRTY-NINE

Freezing Moon

Turtle Island Reservation
October 1897

LILY WEBER RUSHED to the window as soon as she heard the grind of wagon wheels. Kermit Crain steered the milk wagon up the road to the reservation instead of continuing back to the Haskins farm.

Father Guerin is back.

I can't wait to tell him everything.

Lily moved aside for her mother to peek out the window, stepping outside onto the porch. Falling leaves filled the October air, and in the distance, Christopher Apple harvested his fields, making the approaching wagon appear like a painting.

As always, Kermit Crain slouched on his seat of the wagon, making the eleven-year-old boy look even smaller. When he saw Lily, he vigorously waved.

It's good to see him doing better, Lily thought as she stepped off of the porch. After Frankie Auerbach's death, Kermit had stopped talking like a chatterbox on their trips to Split Rock. Even with her prompting, Lily could only get a few grunts and single word answers.

She was no Sister Inez—the veteran nun had done her best to explain death to the class, and most were red-eyed even before they came to church. Each time one of them asked a tough question about mortality, Lily flinched even though Sister Inez answered both poignant and silly questions with grace. After a few weeks of deep sorrow, the class eventually returned to normal.

"Guess who's back in town?"

He's teasing. "Father Guerin," Lily answered. *My mysterious hero.*

"You guessed it. He wanted to let you know that he's free for his language lesson tomorrow, so I'll pick you up at the crack of dawn. He also wanted you to have these letters."

Winnie appeared on the porch.

"Hello Mrs. Weber," Kermit greeted. "I've got letters for you."

Lily stepped aside as her mother claimed three letters.

"Thank you, Kermit. I'll see you in the morning," Lily said, excusing the helpful young man.

"Be sure to dress warmly," he said. "It's getting colder and colder in the morning."

The first letter was from the Minnesota Territorial Prison, where her father wrote that he'd been transferred from Duluth to a town east of St. Paul called Stillwater.

The second letter came from Morris, where Migisi wrote that he was behaving and learning a lot—it didn't sound like her brother at all even if she could tell it was written by his hand.

The third letter was a surprise. Fawn Chevreuil had been unable to find her mother, but the LaBiche family had been kind and hospitable in letting her stay with them.

Winnie spent most of the evening reading and re-reading each letter, with a series of new questions after each study.

Lily went to bed imagining Father Guerin on his horse, wearing a hooded duster over his priestly robes as he wandered lonely highways, crucifix on his chest and pistol in his pocket.

BY THE TIME dawn came, Lily was waiting on the porch, dressed warmly.

Once the normal greetings were exchanged, Kermit began with other bits of gossip. Lily understood why the boy knew all the gossip; Charles Crain, a gifted English blacksmith, had customers from all over the county visiting his forge in Sterling Junction. "My dad says the Blue Knife bridge will be finished by November."

So soon? "That will make your trip a lot quicker, won't it?"

"Reckon it will cut off twenty minutes from my day," Kermit said. He glanced at her then away. "So what were the letters about?"

Sensing danger, Lily studied him as if for the first time. Physically, the eleven-year-old boy was as average as average could be: short brown hair, a round Caucasian face, wide eyes, and an unblemished complexion. His clothing was drab and common. Father Guerin vouched for the family, but how well did he know the local families? The Sinclair sisters, whose husbands now ran Triton Corporation, lived on the western shore of Lake Manitou, just a short trip from Sterling Junction. If the Crain family stood to benefit from the endeavors of Triton, could she trust any of them?

"They were just letters from my family saying everybody is doing well."

TODAY I'LL TELL him. Before the lesson starts, I'll tell him everything. Someone needs to know. Inside of St. Marie's Catholic Church, she wasn't a Firehandler—she was just Lily.

Before running up the stairs to the balcony, she wandered into the sanctuary, pausing at the stained-glass portrait of the resurrected Christ with Mary Magdalen at his feet. The scandalous woman had confessed her sins and became one of Christ's most ardent followers. Mary hardly knew Jesus yet confessed. Lily hardly knew Father Guerin ... *So why can't I tell him?*

Turning, she looked up to the balcony, her breathing heavy. She trusted Guerin but doubt still lingered. *How do I bridge this subject when he won't be open with me?*

"Aaniin ezhi-ayaayan?" Lily asked as she entered the balcony.

"Bendigen," he answered, looking up from his pew covered in scattered papers.

Lily paused just inside the doorway so as not to look too eager. "How was your trip to Leech Lake?"

"Successful. I met with Chief Sweating Stone."

"You did?" Lily's voice lowered. "Y-you didn't speak to him about the Song of the Manitou, did you?"

"Of course not. That's just between us. I went to Leech Lake on business."

"Your revolution then continues without my father?" Picturing her father side-by-side with Guerin somehow inspired her, but instead her father sat in jail while Guerin continued without him.

He sighed. "Yes, your grandfather is a powerful man, and even though the government doesn't officially recognize his authority, the people do. Despite the arrest of your father, Blackfish LaBiche and Pierre LeDuc not only continue the illegal bootlegging operation but also have become allies in the effort."

Lily left the doorway and moved to stand beside the closest pew. "And the school?"

Guerin raised his eyebrows. "All my efforts are tied to the school, which is why I crossed ten miles of icy water to Bear Island to let him know about several proposed laws."

"What kind of laws?"

"There is a Kansas lawman who wants to create a law that will abolish tribal governments entirely. All Indian children will be forced into public schools and the individual landowners will be left to fend for themselves."

"Can they do such a thing?"

"They are already drawing up plans, which will steal an entire state from the Five Civilized Tribes. But it will impact all Indians. It will be a federal law and could be the final nail in the coffin."

Lily sunk down onto the pew. "If they pass this law, won't it defeat the whole purpose of having Turtle Island Jesuit School?"

"Oh, no. We need the school in place to offer an alternative. The atrocities at the boarding schools are coming to light, which is why the public school policy is being offered, as if to sweep dirt under a rug. Both the public school system and boarding school system are cultural genocide for your people and all tribal nations." He smiled. "This spring, once the ground thaws, building will begin. My travels not only rally support for my 'revolution' as you call it, but also to find pupils for the school."

And warriors? "Sweating Stone is not just an old man like Nanak; he was once a proud warrior. What if you get a full-fledged war instead of a few protests or conflicts?"

He shook his head. "I know what I'm doing, Lily. The protection of your people has always been my priority."

But if Bushy Bill had dared, the revolution could have ended. "You're just one man."

"Yes, which was a lesson I learned in Cuba." His expression was amused until he grew serious again. "Trust me when I say I have powerful friends. I have newspapers, lawyers, politicians, and businessmen in my pocket. I am prepared to help the Chippewa fight these changes, but I have plans in place to keep things from escalating. I do not want a massacre like Wounded Knee, but if the Chippewa are going to keep any of their land from the hands of the greedy, they will need to rally behind a hero."

"Chief Sweating Stone?"

"Thanks to Blackfish LaBiche, news of Gull Lake has spread already, but strangely, the inglorious treatment of Chief Sweating Stone is talked about even more. He had to walk all the way back to Leech Lake from Duluth after he was released. He complained about ruining a pair of his favorite moccasins."

Lily grinned, wishing she knew her maternal grandfather better. Relaxing, she looked around his room and saw most of Guerin's belongings still packed. "Aandi ezhaayan?"

"I am going farther north to the Bad River Reservation in Wisconsin."

"Ikidon miinawwa?" she demanded.

"I am going Giiwedinong to Gaa-Waabaabiganikaag."

Lily chuckled. "You can't just mix English in whenever you want. When are you leaving for the 'North'?"

"Ishww-anami'e giizhigad," Guerin said, indicating Monday. "I won't be getting many lessons this week."

"Well, you need them," Lily teased, but he didn't react. "What's in Bad River?"

"A rumor. Apparently, there is a Mide who claims to have found something called the Gitchi-Animikii."

Lily's heart paused. "The Great Thunderbird."

"You know it?" At her look he amended, "Of course you know it." He shook his head. "Apparently, this Mide has created a bit of a religious revival in some villages. I'm going to find out more information about him. I should return by Baashkaakodin Giizis"

Freezing Moon in November. He'll be gone for so long.

"Have you been writing down Nanak's lessons like I asked you to?"

"I have." *In secret ... afterwards.*

"That's excellent. You are recording vital information for your people. I cannot wait to see what you have gathered."

Talk of the Great Thunderbird derailed her planned conversations, so she surrendered to her prepared lessons instead. During the lessons, she had his undivided attention, even if it was only on the words and situations she prepared. While learning, Guerin seemed younger, more earnest, a student, and didn't wear the trappings of his office. He smiled through most of a lesson, but when it ended, the smile went away, and he returned to being Father Guerin.

"I've been thinking," She gathered her thoughts after putting away her materials. "What do you mean someone found the Gitchi-Animikii? Someone is claiming to be the Great Thunderbird?"

"That's why I need to make this trip. I need to understand. I'm fighting a political battle, and the last thing I need is for a zealot to stir things up like Wounded Knee." He rubbed a hand over his face, his shoulders slumping. "So what has Nanak been teaching you lately?"

"No," Lily said strongly, even though she wasn't sure why. "No."

"No, what?"

How do I bring this up when I know he's keeping things hidden from me? I need him to trust me as much as I trust him. "No, you do this all the time. I ask you a question and you squirm away before I can get a straight answer. None of this makes any sense. The school. Your revolution. Your interest in the Great Thunderbird." *I'm so tired of the secrets.* She glared. "Why are you *really* here?"

"I've been as open as possible. I've confessed things that are almost treasonous. You know more about my mission than anyone else I can think of."

"Fine," Lily said, crossing her arms. "Play your games." *There are things I haven't confessed either. You're not the only one with secrets.*

"What games?"

"The school gets built. Grandfather Nanak gets a dozen young apprentices. I get a job. Migisi comes home. My father is released. My mother gets a brick house. My grandfather Chief Sweating Stone takes a political prisoner, blows up a bridge, or burns a building down—just enough to get the attention of your newspapers. Your 'powerful friends' then jump into action, preserving the reservations." She jumped to her feet, turning away. "Why? Why do you care?"

"It's a humanitarian mission, Lily."

"Excuse me for saying this, but you are full of it." At his snort, she turned around.

"Hold on a second."

"I'm acting as your spy when you already seem to know what you're looking for. You knew more about my family than I did, and now you're off to Bad River to look for some zealot. What's next, Father Guerin?" His title passed her lips bitterly. "Why are you obsessed with my family and our dirty little secrets?"

"I'm beginning to understand why Joseph Nicollet was so taken aback by your Great-Grandfather Chagobay." He sighed. "Your family is full of people with keen, discerning minds. I want to answer you, but I need more time. Yes, I'm an investigator, and yes, I'm a real Jesuit priest, but I'm part of something beyond the Society of Jesus. I think your Grandfather Nanak understands this, but for now, both of us are trying to understand if we can fully trust the other side. Both of us are trying to answer the same questions. When I have my answers, I'll lay them at your feet, understood? Give me just a few more months, and I'll tell you everything."

Lily shifted her crossed arms. *Do I accept that?*

"Agreed?"

Next time. Always next time. "If you're going to Bad River, you can't be mixing English and Anishinaabemowin words together. The folks there are even more set in their ways than Grandfather Nanak. Be very careful what you say. And don't bring up anything about the Seven Fires, or they'll slam the door in your face."

Or worse.

Job Opening

Split Rock MN
October 1897

AM I TOO *handsome?* Martin Nielson carefully combed his blond hair in the small mirror hanging on the living room wall. He checked his teeth to make sure they were clean before stepping back to inspect his clothing.

Mother was right. I grew into my clothes.

When he crossed the Atlantic from Bergen, Norway, he wore his prized outfit so it couldn't be stolen. After all the felling of trees, plowing of fields, and harvesting of crops, Martin Nielson was now twice as thick as when he'd come. His white dress shirt pulled at the buttons, and his expensive jacket, with the bright green lapels, barely closed.

"You're going to get me jealous dressed like that," his wife, Dolly, said from a distance, holding his matching green top hat in her hands.

"I have to impress Mr. Van Slyke so he knows that I'm serious. I need to convince him that he needs an extra set of hands at the creamery this winter. I don't want to twiddle my thumbs all winter."

"Oh, I understand we need the extra money, especially with the baby coming early next summer. Promise me you'll save all your charm for Mr. Van Slyke and spare none for your former sweethearts in Split Rock."

Martin kissed her on the lips, pulling her close enough so that the small bump on her belly pressed against him. "After I get the job, I'll bring back some fabric for baby clothes."

"That would be lovely." Dolly planted an even harder kiss on his lips. "Please stay away from the Forsberg house, at least until Britta finds a beau. She gives me the evil eye whenever I see her."

"I'll be on my best behavior." Martin Nielson placed his hat upon his head and winked.

Outside, Grim waited, already hitched to the wagon filled with surplus walnuts, acorns, apples, fruits, and corn that didn't fit in the packed root cellar. Martin and Dolly were ready for a long winter, but they lived harvest to harvest. An influx of cash would help them develop the land quickly.

I'm a married man with a child on the way, Martin reminded himself as he climbed onto the wagon bench. *I'm no longer a boy shivering in the cold.*

The eighteen-year-old farmer eyed his home and compared it to the other farms along the road to Split Rock. A few years earlier, the lot was all he could afford, and despite the thrill of living off the land, he barely survived the first winter. Having bought the most worthless plot of land surrounding the lake—a rocky point overlooking Turtle Island—Martin and Grim had cleared countless trees and boulders that first year to eke out enough tillable land to survive. Three years later, Martin meant to keep the momentum going.

Grim snorted as they passed through the thick oak forest at the turn of the road. Now that the leaves had all dropped, the woods revealed its secrets: gnarled trunks and twisted branches that looked like clawed fingers.

The Grim Reaper isn't afraid of a few ghosts. "Are you, boy?"

Grim raised his head, slightly picking up speed.

Martin used the popularized view of death, the hooded skeleton carrying a sickle, when he had named his beautiful colt. Nielson's Nordic roots taught him that before the Grim Reaper, Odin once disguised himself with the hood of a mortal man to walk openly in the world of mortals as Grimnir. The strangers that harassed Grimnir were cursed while the only one who helped him, a boy named Agnar, was blessed as the Lord of the Goths.

So don't mess with me or Grim, Martin told the shadows among the trees.

Once Old Copper Road turned north toward Split Rock, his mood lightened. At Buffalo Slough, where the Auerbach boy had drowned, he passed by the farm owned by Jeremie Bordeaux and his unfaithful wife. She'd once managed to get Martin's shirt off before he ran from her clutches. Of Bordeaux's bevy of children, half were rumored to belong to men from the county.

Next, Martin passed by the MacPherson dairy farm, with its domed roof towering above everything else on both sides of the valley. With sons and a flock of healthy dairy cows, MacPherson could afford the finest amenities money could buy.

One day I'll have a big red barn also.

Finally, he reached the corner where the road turned east and downhill toward the Crow Wing River bridge. Tucked into the woods of the corner, he briefly looked over to the Forsberg's house and then turned his gaze to the road, knowing how Britta often stood on the second-floor balcony to watch as wagons passed.

The Dutch Boy Creamery was nestled along the river, just before the bridge. In the morning, wagons from a dozen dairy farmers would line up to offload their milk, with Nielson usually having the smallest load. With farmers milking twelve hours apart, the loads came in during the wee hours of the morning, bringing

the evening and recent milking before the warmth of day spoiled
it.

So there were no wagons when Martin arrived midmorning.

Even so, Burt Van Slyke, the elder of the Van Slyke boys, came
out with empty cream cans. "Got a wedding or a funeral today?"

Martin shook it off. "I was wondering if I could speak to your
father."

Burt put his hands on his hips. "Sure, follow me."

In the past three years, Martin had never seen past the doorway
where the Van Slyke boys collected the cream cans. The interior of
the creamery was filled with monstrous metallic tanks.

A sudden release of steam drew his attention away from Burt.

"Pay attention, Stefan," Burt yelled to his younger brother.
"You're going to ruin a whole batch."

"Something's not working right." Stefan turned one of the
wheels to release the pressure in the boiler tank. "It keeps
overheating."

"You want to haul cream cans and I could do your job? Turn
the knobs when the needles reach the numbers. I've written
everything on the pipes for you."

"I know, but when I open the release valve, it's like the water
doesn't leave. I think the valve is defective."

"They are brand new. Are you sure you're turning them the
right way? Look, turn left to open, turn right to close." Burt spun
the metal wheel and watched as the pressure dropped immediately.
Fresh water from Lake Manitou came in through the intake tube,
passed through the filters, filled the boiler, and then was released
out through the outtake tube that dumped into the Crow Wing
River, cleaning the machine at the same time.

"That's exactly what I've been doing." Stefan pouted.

"Are you feeling well? Your eyes look funny."

Stefan had dark bags under his eyes like the remnants of a fist fight and the veins in his eyeballs made the whites of his eyes look almost pink. "I'm fine, if this machine would just work."

"Be quiet and just do your job, or we can find someone who can." Burt then looked directly at Martin, causing him to grin.

Burt led Martin through the noisy processing room into another chamber, which was where the milk was processed for bottling, cheese production, and other dairy products.

"Forsbergs have sick cows," Burt announced as he led them to a distant office.

"Any of them die?"

"No, but three of them have some intestinal problems. But don't worry, we sterilize all the cans. Keep an eye on your cows, though." He glanced at him, smirking. "Are you looking for a job?"

"I am."

"Jeremie Bordeaux is divorcing his wife. I guess he caught her in bed with Delbert Grant ... again. So there's a job opening with the post office, but we just hired Loren Larson as our new milkman."

Martin felt his hopes sink. "I'd still like a word with your father."

"Burt! It won't shut off," Stefan shouted from the far side of the creamery. Burt sighed and took off jogging for the creamery.

Just as Burt reached the doorway of the creamery, an explosion shook the air and building, sending glass and debris everywhere and knocking Burt off of his feet.

Hot clouds of water filled the room, but Martin still ran towards it.

Burt had landed on his back, but looked no worse for wear, so Martin kept running. Just inside the doorway, Martin found Stefan on the ground, gasping, a large piece of metal stuck in his chest. "I turned it left," he whispered as blisters began to form on his scalded skin.

Burt rushed in moments later, collecting his dying brother in his arms.

Stunned dairy farmers rushed over also, as helpless as Martin.

The explosion had blown a hole in the wall large enough to drive a wagon through …

Grim!

Martin stepped through the rubble and out into the cold wintry air.

Both Grim and the wagon were fine, although a dozen yards from where they'd parked.

"Don't fret," Martin said as he rubbed the horse's quivering flank.

Grim continued to snort and shift as if standing on hot coals.

"What is it? You hurt?"

A strange cloud of cooling steam rolled out of the opening in the creamery, and with each passing second, it shrunk in size. It appeared as if the warm air escaping from the creamery created a draft that pushed the cloud uphill toward the woods. By the time it reached the trees behind the lot, the cloud condensed to the size of a cow, but the smaller it got, the denser it got.

Then it began to crawl with long, slender arms up the hill toward Bleeding Rock.

Waking the Great Bear

Turtle Island Reservation
November 1897

LILY WEBER LEANED against the headboard of her bed, trying to make sense of all the fragments of syllables in front of her. Each piece of paper had phonetic syllables upon it, along with simple musical notes and phrases for proper emphasis. Each one also had a date written upon it, chronicling months of lessons from Nanakonan.

Pieces of a puzzle.

Ignoring the dates, she rearranged the slips, trying to find common musical elements within the song—*The Song of the Manitou.*

Finally satisfied, she looked over the bizarre song sung in an unknown language. Thanks to Nanak's coy tutelage, each lesson delivered just a piece of the full score, with no clear beginning or end declared. Yet she found one section that seemed to overlap into several verses of musical cohesion.

Clearing her throat, Lily took in a breath and began releasing notes that just tickled her vocal cords. Her eyes traveled over the six pieces of paper, note-by-note, syllable by syllable, just as Nanak had taught her.

The door of her room flew open, causing her to jump with a slight squeal.

"It's you!" Winnie said with a deep sigh, clutching her chest. "I could not figure out what I was hearing. I got the chills and the hair on my arms stood on end. What is all of that?"

Lily picked up the pieces of paper in a disorganized shuffle. "Sorry, were you trying to sleep?"

"No, I was sitting by the fire warming my feet. You were singing?"

"Yes, these are my notes. Grandfather Nanak is teaching me old songs and stories about our people, and then I write them down for Guerin."

Winnie's brow wrinkled. "Our people? You might be a single coin, but you still have two sides. Remember, my ancestors walked these woods when *your* people were still along the Atlantic."

The Sioux.

"Can you tell me why the Chippewa call your people snakes?"

"Come, sit with me at the fire, and I'll share some of our tales," Winnie said, leading the way back to the fire.

Once seated, Winnie propped her bare feet up towards the fire. "The Sioux call themselves the Oceti Sakowin, the Seven Council Fires. We were allies against the dangers of the world. Our enemies called us snakes because we vigorously defended the lands of our territory, which stretched from the Great Lakes all the way to Bear Mountain in the lands of my Blackfeet people."

"Bear Mountain?"

"It is the stump of a giant tree, the world's first tree, and the Great Bear tried to destroy our people, who hid atop the stump of the fallen tree. Its claw marks can still be seen."

"You mean Devil's Tower? In Wyoming?"

Winnie smiled and shrugged. "Yes, once again, the words are twisted. Like the term Blackfeet. In the Days of the Dawn, when my people were new to the land, a great fire swept across the prairies, killing everything in its path except for a group of women, who were spared by the creator. When they returned to their village, their feet were filthy from all the ash."

"You're a long way from your homeland," Lily surmised. "Grandfather told me of the Seven Fires of the Anishinaabe, and you describe your people as the Seven Council Fires. Is there a connection?"

"Life is all about perspective. The Sioux are snakes to a people seeking their Promised Lands, yet we see ourselves as the Guardians of the Frontier, protecting our lands against enemies who seek the Unktehi, the horned serpent that lurks in the depths."

"Were they protecting the Horned Serpent?"

"Heavens no. They were protecting…peace? Do you remember the Great Bear I spoke of, just now?" At Lily's nod, her mother smiled. "Besides the creation of Bear Mountain, my mother told me another tale of the Great Bear, explaining why the Sioux fought until the day she was captured by Chief Sweating Stone. You remember the story behind your namesake?"

"Lake Tewapa Tankiyan—the Place of the Crooked Roots."

"A Blackfoot boy, who was born in the Black Hills, dreamed of the Great Bear that left the claw marks. He became so obsessed with this ancient evil that the elders in the village realized there was no choice but to let him chase after the monster from legend."

"Sounds like Migisi"

Winnie chuckled. "Yes, boys! This boy, this Wishwee, he left his home and wandered far, facing many obstacles, until finally, he came to a place called the Haunted Valley, for hidden deep in a cave of this valley was the sleeping bear, known also as No Soul. What Wishwee did not understand is that No Soul was not an ordinary bear. No Soul was an immortal shapeshifter, capable of taking any terrifying form it chose. Mortal weapons could not harm this evil monster, which is what the spirits warned Wishwee as he was about to enter the cave and face certain death."

So No Soul is another tale of the Wintermaker...

"To defeat No Soul, the spirits told him, you need to find the White Egg. I forget how Wishwee managed to acquire the egg, but it helped him defeat No Soul and release all of the victims trapped inside of the cave with him. My mother told me that this story of Wishwee and No Soul is a tale of the past as well as a tale of the future."

"Grandfather Nanak said the same thing about the Seven Fires Prophecy," Lily mused. "You said your people were guardians. Could they have been guarding an island? The one the Chippewa were seeking?"

"I am not Santee; I'm Blackfoot Lakota."

"What's the difference?"

"The old alliance of villages, the Seven Council Fires, was made up of my Lakota people in the west, the two Yankton tribes upon the plains, and the four eastern tribes. Some call the Santee the Dakota; others call them the Isanti, which means People of the Knife, but I knew them by the old word, Isanyathi, which means the Guardians of the Frontier. The Santee kept our enemies beyond the Mississippi and Great Lakes for generations before their strength finally failed. Whether they protected an island, a white egg, or even the lair of No Soul—it does not matter—my people are broken and the secrets are lost. Perhaps it is a good thing you are learning about your Chippewa heritage. I wish I knew more about my people."

For a few moments, her mother looked sad, as if she were about to cry. Then Winnie wiggled her toes, and Lily did the same.

Women of the Blackfeet.

Choosers of the Slain

Lake Manitou

December 1897

MARTIN NIELSON SAT upon the frozen lake with a whiskey bottle in his hands. Hearing the approach of a horse upon the ice, he looked down at the bottle and swallowed the last bit of whiskey. With the hoofbeats getting louder, he quickly held the empty bottle over the hole in the ice and dropped it, knocking his cork aside as it bobbed in the hole. With the top of his boot, he pushed it below the surface of the water, allowing it to fill and sink to the bottom of the lake.

Please, no more condolences. I'll throw up all over the ice if someone tries to be nice again.

Even in the darkness, the stars illuminated the frozen lake, with the patches free of snow acting like mirrors to the sky. The approaching horse was large, and it came from the east, meaning only one thing: Gustaf Forsberg.

The door of the old outhouse faced south, toward the southern shore, preventing Martin from seeing how many younger Forsbergs had come with the elder Swede. The hooves of the massive plow horse crunched loudly on the trek across the frozen lake, and as it neared, Martin could hear humming.

He also brought the girls.

Sure enough, when the horse neared, he could hear the girls singing "Children of the Heavenly Father" along with their father.

When Martin first met Gustaf at the Van Slyke Creamery, he cowered when the big Swede barked about cutting in line during morning deliveries, but since that day, he allowed the man the honor of first delivery at the creamery and learned that despite his solemn ways, the man had a tender heart. *And now, there is no line.*

At first, the whiskey helped deaden the trauma of seeing Van Slyke's death and the strange mist he'd seen. Then, whiskey helped deaden even worse pain. Now, it was all gone but the pain still grew.

The heavy hooves halted, the singing ended, and soon Martin heard the passel of children exploring the ice as their father opened up holes.

Gustaf's shack stood about fifty yards northwest of Martin's repurposed outhouse. Lantern light suddenly illuminated the outhouse, coming in through the gaps in the boards. In the middle of the winter, a day lasted only until five o'clock.

Martin heard the crunch of footsteps approaching his fish shack. Living on a farm just a few hundred yards away along the southern shore, Martin walked down with only what he could carry, but thanks to the Forsberg lantern, he could clearly see beyond his cork in the hole.

It was Signe who tentatively approached.

And then she saw it.

"Oh my goodness! Oh my goodness! Britta, Bjorn! Come here. You have to see this."

Martin smiled at how Signe reacted to the Northern Pike he had tossed upon the ice an hour earlier.

"It's a monster!" Bjorn declared nearby. "Father! You have to see this. It is bigger than Signe."

"Look at its teeth!"

Martin secured his short fishing pole, stood up, and opened the flimsy door to the outhouse.

"Did you catch that, Mr. Nielson?" Signe asked when she saw him emerge.

"The hole almost wasn't big enough. By the time he tired, I was almost too tired to lift him out."

"How big do you think he is?" Bjorn asked his father who had just joined them.

"It must be at least twenty pounds—well done, Nielson. Well done." The praise was tempered by a look of concern.

I can't do anything right. "Therese should come over and show Dolly how to pickle fish."

"I will say something, but she doesn't like going out in the cold except for church on Sundays." Gustaf paused, asking then, "How is Dolly?"

Martin bit his lip. "It's been pretty tough on her." *Please no more condolences.*

Britta's eyes began to well up with tears.

Signe looked at him, her father, and her emotional older sister, and rushed up to give Martin a hug—and then a kiss on his cheek.

Go kiss Dolly. God knows nothing I do can help her. "Thank you, Signe."

No one mentioned the miscarriage aloud, and the tears remained locked away.

Bjorn reappeared with an ice chipper in his hands, oblivious to the moment. "Do you mind if I open up some of your old holes?"

"Go right ahead, but it is no guarantee there is another monster hiding below the ice."

So Bjorn began chipping away while Gustaf led the girls to their large icehouse.

Alone again, Martin hunched his shoulders against the chill. The recent weather had matched his mood: cold. Each night, another few inches of ice grew toward the depths of the lake, just as Martin found his heart hardening to the cruelties of life.

But the Forsberg family brought renewed dreams of his own family as he listened to their singing and laughter close by.

After half an hour, Bjorn finally stopped chipping and began jigging in a series of holes that ranged from Turtle Island to the southern shore.

For the next hour, his friend asked him a dozen questions about fishing tactics and techniques before proximity took him out of range.

Finally, the lake grew quiet again. *Please, keep singing, keep asking. It helps.* Nielson stared at the hole, picturing the whiskey bottle at the bottom of the lake, until a strange glow appeared upon the ice.

At first, he flinched, thinking of the strange mist he'd seen at the creamery. Instead of the yellow colors of a lantern, strange reds and blues flickered upon the ice. Bjorn Forsberg's eyes immediately went to the heavens, forcing Martin to stand and step out of his shelter to look north also.

"Ah, the Valkyries have come to gather another soul to Valhalla," Martin said as he watched the northern lights begin to flicker.

"What are Valkyries?"

"Your pa never told you any of the old Norse legends? Maybe the old stories died off in Sweden, but my mother still knew most of them, despite being a good church-going Christian. Valkyries are like angels, I suppose, taking souls up to heaven."

"Those lights are angels?"

"I can't rightly say what those lights are for certain, but that is what my mother used to tell me."

Martin smiled, watching his friend's face fill with wonder.

Cooling ice boomed under them, causing Bjorn to look over for reassurance. "It's not going to break, is it?"

"You could drive an entire team of horses with loaded wagons over this ice and it wouldn't so much as buckle. Ice just does that from time to time."

"Good. We were fishing on Saturday afternoon and one of the Berg boys told me that there was some sort of monster that lived in the lake."

"There's no such thing as monsters," Martin said, a little harsh. His thoughts went back to the moments after Stefan Van Slyke was killed in the boiler explosion … *It was from shock. My mind playing tricks.*

"So Lake Manitou's not cursed?"

"No," Martin answered quickly. "It's just ice."

But nothing that happened in the past month supported his denial.

Stefan Van Slyke was killed in front of him, and the creamery was shut down.

Dolly miscarried.

Maybe it is cursed, Bjorn.

A LITTLE PAST nine o'clock, the Forsberg family packed up and returned home, leaving Martin to his dark thoughts.

Twenty minutes after the noisy Forsbergs left, the fish returned. Martin saw his cork jiggle once or twice and then slowly drop just an inch. Gently cranking up the excess line onto the reel, Martin waited until he felt tension in the line and then set the hook.

But the fish didn't even budge.

With the twenty-pound northern pike, the line almost cut through his gloves when the fish took off, but this fish felt more like a log.

Martin kicked the outhouse door open to get better leverage, but he could not pull any harder or risk breaking the line. "Come on, come on, come up and let me at least see you."

Could it be a sturgeon? Hand over fist, he brought the dead weight up about ten of the twenty feet. "At least show me what you are."

And then suddenly, the line broke, sending Martin sprawling backwards onto his butt.

Before he could even curse, the water within the hole began to bubble like a pot left unattended on a stove.

A pair of hairy claws came up from the hole, along with a cloud of fog.

And then a pair of red eyes fixed on him.

The dark torso began to claw and scratch at the ice; it dragged itself closer and closer to where Martin had fallen.

Martin rolled over to scramble away from the horror he'd pulled up from the lake, but something clutched at his left ankle.

"Get off me," he managed to vocalize, and at the same time, he kicked at the strange creature with his right boot—he missed.

A few months earlier, Martin had come upon an angry badger that snapped and snarled and took several blows from futile kicks before it ran off. This creature, with it long, black, oily hair, was twice as large as a badger, but when his heel struck the creature, it lifted off the ground, flying into the air with the weight of a balloon.

The long fingers of the creature desperately searched for something to grab, but within seconds, it flew a hundred yards until Martin couldn't even see it.

Am I losing my mind? Am I seeing things?

He didn't even bother picking up his belongings. Quickly walking backwards to the shore, he kept his eyes on the ice, hoping to not see the creature come rushing back at him.

CHAPTER FORTY-THREE

The Ironwood Log

Turtle Island Reservation
December 1897

LILY WEBER FELT a thousand eyes upon her each time she stepped out of her house to walk to Grandfather's cabin. With the arrival of winter, she could now see enough of the emptiness of the forest and the unblemished snow to know she was truly alone and safe, but in her mind, generations of Wijigan Chippewa and Blackfoot Lakota watched her approaching the crossroads of destiny.

Three small snowfalls, without a late season thaw, left the woods ankle-to-knee deep in snow, and the normal path became a slow, unsteady trek. Away from the woods, the wind left only a few inches of snow along the open fields.

Lily blazed a fresh trail.

Once she neared, she saw a cold sweat lodge, a dead fire, and a healthy pillar of smoke rising from Grandfather's chimney. *No Song today.*

Despite early December temperatures, the cabin was pleasantly warm, and Lily shed her heavy coat to take her place in front of the stove.

After the brief exchanges of pleasantries, Nanak got right to business. He retrieved a large fabric-wrapped bundle from his bed and carried it over to her.

"I've given you pieces of the Song of the Manitou over the past few months for your protection. Each part contains small spells, but put together, the Song of the Manitou is powerful magic," Nanak warned as he cradled the large bundle in his arms. "Do not ever sing the Song of the Manitou until you are fully prepared to battle the Wintermaker to the death. Is that clear?"

Lily swallowed hard. "I-I shouldn't sing it until I have Migisi with me."

"Do not sing it until you have the Great Thunderbird, the Water Drum, the Sacred Shell, and …"

"And what?"

"To defeat the Wintermaker, there must also be a … a … I cannot think of the proper word to use. Do you know *omodai?*"

"A jar?"

Nanakonan's face wrinkled in thought. "It matters not—one thing at a time. Let me show this to you."

He carefully unwrapped the bundle to reveal a wooden container. From the wooden container, he pulled out a leathery tube, which when unrolled, contained sheets of birch bark with ancient pictographs drawn upon the light surface.

"What are they?" Lily asked, her mind absorbing the information.

"You know what they are."

The sequence.

Each pictograph represented a separate song she'd learned over the past months, and Grandfather's random instructional order became obvious. With the pieces of paper on her bed, she'd come close with a few segments, but now, she understood how complex the full song would be. Its brilliance also became obvious.

It's a list that contains the verses of a song, but none of the lyrics are written down. Oral tradition needs a written code—only the Wijigan know the lyrics.

The scroll was beautiful and terrifying at the same time. Some pictographs were quite obvious, now that she knew the segment of the song, but others were elusive. She studied it as if preparing for one of Sister Lynch's calculus examinations.

"Questions?" Grandfather asked after several silent minutes.

"Am I supposed to memorize this like the lyrics of the song?"

"When your training is done, you will not need this."

"Wait, what is this then?"

"You know what it is, but you do not know where it is found."

"It's found right in front of me."

Nanak smirked. "Your brother searched for it but could not find it, for a good reason. When you are able to find its hiding place, you will be ready to sing the Song of the Manitou and fight the Wintermaker."

Her heartstrings plucked a sour note. *Ready? But I've been practicing since we began.* The bundle, with all of its protective layers, took up the space of a man, even though it appeared to be quite light.

Does he keep it under the floorboards? Ah, Migisi was searching for a cave. Just like in the story of No Soul. "How did *you* learn where it is kept?"

"My father told me, and his father told him, for Chief Wiyipisiw placed it in our keeping. The words of Manabozho gave you the power to lift heated stones, a clear sign of your powers as a Firehandler. While Firehandlers are rare, your gift does not make you the fulfillment of prophecy. Is that clear?"

"Yes."

"Chief Wiyipisiw gathered up enough of the Song to wake the Wintermaker, but the dark magic he unleashed turned like a serpent and bit him. In his arrogance, he thought his will was greater than that of Manabozho, and without the Sacred Shell, he tried to use the magic for his own purposes, bringing his own death along with all of his followers. It is said that Manabozho will give visions to the one who will face the Wintermaker, and when it is returned it to its resting place, it will remain safe from anyone but the one who knows the truth." He studied her; eyes narrowed. "So tell me in your words, why did Wiyipisiw fail?"

"He didn't trust Manabozho, and he didn't have the Sacred Shell."

"You will make a good teacher. You have learned much." Before she could thank him for the compliment he added, "There is still much to learn before your training is complete." Grandfather motioned towards the scroll, letting Lily look it over for a few more minutes.

Why didn't he warn me before we started? I already sung some of it … She felt as if a nun had just slapped her knuckles with a ruler. She pushed away her self-pity to study the open scroll with wonder. *I wish I could show this to Father Guerin.* Much of it looked familiar, logical—except for one section. "The spell of protection … I don't … When we practiced it, I thought …"

"Did you think the protection was for you?"

Nanak had introduced it as a spell of protection, but she assumed it'd been similar to Psalm 23. Thinking it was protection for her through the Valley of the Shadow of Death, she'd practiced it the most. "No, but I … just …"

"Before submitting to the grave, the Wintermaker learned many dark arts, including how to bind evil spirits to his will. Tak-Pei, pukwudgies … memegwesi … every village has an old woman who tells of the Little People of the forest. Forget what you think you know. The Wintermaker trapped these spirits here with him, to protect him against—”

“It protects *him*?” Lily was aghast. “The spell protects *the Wintermaker*?”

“This is not a spell to protect the Firehandler, if that’s what you were thinking. Is that what you thought?”

Why didn’t he say something first? “I assumed—”

“Hmph. What did I tell you when we began?”

She bit her lip, unsure of what angered her the most. She was angry at Nanakonan for being so reckless. She was angry at Father Guerin for condoning the pagan rituals. She was mad at Migisi for not being here. “Why would we even want to wake the Little People if they are servants of the Wintermaker?”

Grandfather remained unfazed. “The Tak-Pei-Wanikan are slaves of the Wintermaker, bound to him by the magic of the Water Drum, and their fates are bound to their master’s fate, so waking them is a necessary step in waking the Wintermaker. If an enemy comes too close, the Tak-Pei-Wanikan will wake and defend its sleeping master. Waking them also means that they will obey the Song of the Manitou, giving the Firehandler incredible powers—if they can be controlled.”

No wonder Mother was bothered by my song. It was a spell to wake evil. Lily stiffened. *Wait. Did I wake them by practicing the song?*

“Is something wrong?” Nanak asked, looking suspicious.

“No.” Lily shook off her concern. “So the parts you’ve taught me are nowhere near the beginning of the song. When will I learn the opening?”

“For you to learn those verses, you must learn them yourself.” Grandfather rolled the birchbark scroll up.

“Learn them myself?”

“Even though the Sacred Shell has been lost to us, those who once sang it are not lost—at least not to us.” Grandfather paused from packing up the scroll to glance up to a dreamcatcher hanging from his ceiling.

Lily followed his gaze. "How will a dreamcatcher teach me the rest of the song?"

"When Grandmother Spider first taught the people the art of her loom, it was to trap bad dreams, allowing only the good dreams to reach the sleeper." Grandfather smiled. "A Jessakkid, however, can find hidden truths within the webs."

Lily thought of the ghosts she'd seen in the woods. *Wiyipisiw had been trapped at my window.* "A dreamcatcher can capture memories of the dead?"

"Yes, and there are those who still linger near the waters of Lake Manitou who once knew the full Song of the Manitou," he answered. He glanced at a web with tiny pieces of snake tail tied to the loom looking thoughtful. "But to capture these old souls, you will need a powerful net. When spring comes, we will collect young branches from an old willow. At Ghost Hollow, there is a willow tree as old as the earth itself. To learn the full song, we must journey there once the weather warms. Until then, we will practice."

Not giving her a chance to reply, he rose, setting the bundle back onto his bed and reached for the supplies to make dreamcatchers he had set nearby.

TEDIOUS HOURS PASSED. When hunger ended their time together, Lily did not immediately follow her tracks back home. Instead, she looked around, trying to figure out where Grandfather would hide the large bundle. After following the foot trails, she found they only led to the cold sweat lodge and a spot between pines where he relieved himself.

A secret cave then?

Lily stood near the edge of the ravine, now understanding why Migisi had been in search of a cave. Near Nanak's cabin, the ravine was steep, but to the south, nearer Lake Manitou, it sloped down to meet the beaches.

Staying away from the edge, Lily took a short walk.

A hollow implies a depression, and willows grow by rivers and creeks. It must grow near some small inlet. At seven miles long, Lake Manitou had enough points and bays to have twenty miles of shoreline—not a quick discovery.

At the bluff, however, she stood at one of the tallest points along the shore. Her trek through the snow ended in surprise: at the bottom of the hill, a new bridge spanned the Blue Knife River. Although not fully complete, its final form had taken shape.

Something whizzed by her head, ricocheting off a nearby pine. By the time Lily understood what was happening, a piece of coal glanced off her shoulder, striking her on the cheek.

"Get off my property, you little whore!" a man bellowed from the top of the ridge. Armed with a bucket of coal, Adam Thunder Face picked up another piece.

She had wandered into the white void between property lines, and Adam Thunder Face was ready—and armed.

"I see the smoke from the sweat lodge. I know what the two of you are doing."

Lily ran.

Calm Before the Storm

Turtle Island Reservation
December 1897

A BLIZZARD ARRIVED in Hiawatha County shortly before Christmas, trapping its residents for days until the world dug out.

Lily watched the snow that had drifted in through the cracks in the mortar begin to melt, leaving little rivers that flowed across the worn pine boards. Even the frost on the windows along the eastern wall of the house began to melt as the morning sun came up over the ravine. She sat on the rocking chair with a heavy buffalo coat embracing her.

When will it stop?

As if sensing her, Winnie said, "This blizzard is nothing compared to the blizzards out on the open plains,"

"And Migisi is out there on the prairie." *He needs to be here. I can't handle this alone anymore.*

"You said the Morris School has large dormitories and giant stoves. The Sioux learned how to adapt, and Migisi has the blood of the Sioux flowing in his veins. He will adapt." Her mother's words sounded hollow. *She misses him.* "I'm just glad you are here with me this winter instead of being at White Earth. You are a good daughter."

Lily grunted. *You wouldn't say that if you knew what I'd been doing. My sins are piling up and I have no one to confess them to.*

The cast iron stove no longer gave off enough heat to justify sitting in front of it, which made the voice of Lily's full bladder even louder. The rocking chair groaned as she rose, the floorboards creaking when she walked across the room to the corner where they kept the bucket. Hoisting up her dress, she crouched over the bucket, making sure to avoid the cold wood. Once done, she walked the bucket over to the door.

A tiny avalanche of snow fell upon the floor as soon as the door opened, despite the fact that a path had already been cut in the drift that led to the outhouse.

"Mama, I'm going to go out and shovel snow before everything becomes buried again." *It's going to be a week before I can do any language lessons.*

"Bring in more coal."

"The wind undid all my hard work from yesterday, so it will be another hour before I can dig the coal shed out." Lily's breath created clouds of crystal in the cold air.

BY THE TIME she returned from shoveling snow, Winnie had opened a handful of jars and sliced some pork, producing a hearty breakfast.

"This afternoon I will clear a path to the road."

"You're still not thinking about going to Split Rock, are you?"

Lily did not answer immediately. "Father Guerin should be returning from his trip to Mankato. I need to make sure Kermit can get to us."

"Beware of all of his sugary promises. This early snow might help cool you off in more ways than one."

"What is that supposed to mean?"

"All you talk about is Father Guerin, Father Guerin, Father Guerin … He is a priest, Lily, and a priest does not take a wife like a Mide does."

Anger and shame fought for a response. "It's not like that at all."

"You are willing to shovel your way all the way to Split Rock to teach him a few words. What am I supposed to make of that?"

The accusation hurt. *What does she think of me?* "I'm just helping him learn our language and ways. Sister Inez and Father Hebert are there, along with others, and we do our lessons at the church. You act like we are doing something wrong."

"You are Big Squeak's little girl. If someone says something is wrong, he will do it anyway." Winnie shrugged. "As soon as you learn something is bad, you want to do it."

"It's not like that, Mother. Father Guerin is learning about the Chippewa so his school can teach our culture as well as their culture."

"And he thinks this is a good idea? Does he understand exactly what kind of man Nanakonan is?"

"He does, and I have all sorts of new information to share with him"

WHICH LILY DID—two days later. Clearing the drive to the reservation had taken less time than clearing the roads around Lake Manitou, but finally, they opened, and Kermit Crain was one of the first wagons on the road.

Lily found Guerin wrapped in blankets, sniffling and coughing at his desk. *Oh, dear. Once again, it's just not the right time to bring it up.* "You're sick," she said in greeting as she carefully stepped onto the balcony.

"I caught a cold on my trip to Mankato. Like a fool, I went stomping around in this weather as if I were an explorer. Sister Inez brought me soup, though."

"Why were you even in Mankato? There aren't any reservations that far south." *Just a Haunted Valley and a mysterious lake.*

"Scratching an itch."

Lily took out her lesson notes and sat down across from him. "Scratching an itch?"

"I've been investigating the investigator of an investigator."

Lily sighed, not bothering to respond to that, and flipped through her lesson notes.

"Joseph Nicollet provided some of the first accurate maps of Minnesota and South Dakota, but after reading his private journals, I realized he had a few private obsessions, including Spirit Lake, watersheds, and vitriol."

"Vitriol?"

"Yes, he seemed to go out of his way to explore a region of Minnesota a few hundred miles south of here, where rivers flow in opposite directions, where a lake produces spiritual healing, and where the earth bleeds blue—with copper vitriol. Mankato means blue earth."

And Tewapa means Lily. "Did you visit Lake Tewapa?"

Guerin chuckled. "Your namesake? No, the storm cut my trip short, so I did not have time to visit Lura Lake, as it's called now. I'm lucky I even got back. My train was stuck in Belle Plaine for a day until the tracks were cleared."

"What were you looking for?"

"I wanted to understand Nicollet's obsession. His map of Minnesota left all sorts of clues into his thoughts. Mankato, Blue Earth, Undine, and his many trips to Spirit Lakes made me curious. It turns out he went looking for a place called Fort L'Huillier, where a man named LeSueur tried to mine blue earth that he claimed to be copper. There isn't any copper at Mankato, only lots of rich farmland."

"So it was a lie?"

"That's what later explorers determined, yet LeSueur risked his life for something, and Joseph Nicollet risked his life to follow LeSueur."

"And you risked yours to follow Nicollet."

"Yes. The blind leading the blind." He smiled before coughing. "Yet one of the world's most prominent scientists crisscrossed Blue Earth County numerous times searching for this fictional copper mine. He left words like Mankato, LeSueur, Lahontan, Blue Earth, and Undine all over his map as if trying to draw attention to the myth."

Mah-kato ... blue earth. "What does Undine mean?"

"Oh, you'll like this one, Lily. Undine is most recently a Germanic legend about a man who gets seduced by a water spirit, who ultimately causes his death."

"A manido?"

"Yes, but it gets better. The older definition of Undine is more than a word for a water spirit. It is also one of the four elements in alchemy: Earth, Air, Water, and Fire. An alchemist by the name of Paracelsus used this Germanic word to describe the element of water. Besides all of his scientific discoveries, Paracelsus was obsessed with discovering the Philosopher's Stone. We have the word 'zinc' because of his study of vitriol, which alchemists used as an acronym: Visita Interiora Terrae Rectificando Invenies Occultum Lapidem."

"Is that Latin?"

"It is. It translates to: Visit the interior of the Earth; by rectification thou shalt find the hidden stone." Father Guerin smiled proudly then had to use a hanky for his nose.

"Are you running a fever?"

"No, it's just a little cold." Avoiding her gaze, Father Guerin sorted through his stacks of books until he grabbed one and held it up. "This is the private journal of Joseph Nicollet, who recorded his thoughts along with his barometric and astronomical measurements of the Upper Mississippi. Listen to what Nicollet wrote:

Saturday, August 13, 1836
Lake Manito

We had traveled only some hundred yards when a path of flowers and a garden of greenery opened before us. The surface of the water was completely concealed by the large round leaves of the white water lilies crowned with their striking flowers, the size and brilliance of which vie with those of the grandiflore magnolia. A curtain of green trees bordering the left bank protected its jagged shadows across the wide ribbon of green and white.

Everyone seemed affected by this pretty landscape. Chagobay himself, in the front of the canoe, was afraid of damaging the flowers, explaining that the roots descended into the depths. He would hold his paddle up, and the other paddlers would do the same and our galley, at the mercy of the current, would glide lightly over the bed of greenness leaving unharmed the yellow-hearted white corollas, unwinding gently their flexible stems.

As we entered into Manito Lake, Chagobay began to sing, asking that our passage through the field of water lilies be invisible.

Guerin closed the book and Lily lowered her head in shame. *I'm just a puzzle piece to him. He doesn't even see me sitting in front of him. All he sees is the great-granddaughter of a man he found in a book.*

"What's wrong Lily?"

"Am I just another clue?"

"Excuse me?"

"You're fixated on lilies. First, you go to Mankato, and then you read about my great-grandfather singing about lilies. What am I to you?

He popped up from his chair and rushed around the table to kneel beside her. He reached out for a moment as if to hug her only to immediately withdraw. "No, Lily. I'm sorry for pressing. I tend to obsess about things. It's what I do. I didn't mean to hurt your feelings, honestly."

Lily glanced at him from the corner of her eye before nodding.

Guerin seemed to sense it as well, and with a nod, returned to his chair. "You're not here to listen to my wild conspiracy theories about water spirits and the Philosopher's Stone, are you?"

She didn't answer that, asking instead a question of her own. "Do you know why Chagobay had them lift the paddles?" She didn't give him a chance to answer. "He probably thought they would wake the Horned Serpent that lived in the water. I'm named Lily after the same water lilies that grow by the outlet to this day. I'm embarrassed because it made it all feel so ... real. It's making me feel uncomfortable."

"I'm sorry, we'll focus on our lessons then."

But she didn't reach for her lesson plan. Instead, the puzzle pieces suddenly aligned in her mind. She asked, "Have you come to Lake Manitou in search of the Philosopher's Stone?"

CHAPTER FORTY-FIVE

Marked at Birth

Split Rock, MN
January 1897

THE GHOSTS WERE puppets of the Porcupine Men, Albert Fisher decided.

When the lake froze, logging shifted from the water to the wagon, which was far less effective. Strangely enough, the big wheel of the sawmill kept spinning even when men ice-fished on Lake Manitou. From the top floor of the mill, Albert could see everything, including a dead boy.

Almost hugging the pockets of his father's jacket, Albert offered only furtive glances to the window, where his inky foes, the Porcupine Men, studied him from the shadows. He chose to keep his eyes on the sinister men surrounding his father: Walter Stewart, Ozias Haggard, and Phillip Marquette.

The only ally he knew in the group was a wiry sawman by the name of Farrell Luning, whose presence was justified by opening up the sawmill after the darkness of evening. Each of the businessmen from St. John had tousled Albert's hair after he was introduced, even by the men from the east. Only Luning's leathery hand had not touched his head, and in a private moment the young man winked at their shared boredom.

After that, Albert studied the young man employed by his father. With a mousy face, Luning appeared to be in his late teens, gaunt from hard labor.

I remember seeing him working in the lagoon.

Outside of the wooden building, on the lake, a large frozen pool normally collected the logs during the spring, summer, and fall until it was time to send them into the log chute for processing. Young men gambled their lives out on the lagoon, wrangling the massive pine logs, risking drowning or being crushed.

Luning must've been lucky. Only the fat older men—the survivors—ran the saws.

When his father's bragging took him from the rear of the room to the front of the room overlooking Lake Manitou, Albert peeled away from his side to remain at the window overlooking Split Rock Creek.

Stay away from the lake, Albert reminded himself. *You don't want to end up like poor Frankie Auerbach.*

The dead boy was more annoying as a ghost than when he'd been while alive. Countless times near Lake Manitou, the creep bullied and intimidated him. None of it worked, of course, and Albert kept his distance. Although sickly, Albert was a voracious reader, and when the ghost of Frankie Auerbach appeared, biology books, not horror stories, protected him from certain danger. Even while his father talked, the ghost of Frankie lingered near the shore.

I see you for what you are, Frankie, but I also see the jaws of the monster.

Under the forced supervision of his father, Albert walked a tightrope between two worlds. Where his father and the businessmen stood—that was on the wrong side of things. The still, frozen water beneath the front window of the mill belonged to the ghosts—and to the strange new creatures. *The Porcupine Men,* he dubbed them.

During the Christmas blizzard, they'd been bold enough to come scratching at his window, whispering their lies in the wind. A real porcupine has a skirt of quills, with the head, shoulders, and spine twice as long, almost like the mane of a lion. In the same way, the creatures also had hair, but it was neither quill nor strand—just an inky darkness that covered them. While their feet and legs could barely be distinguished from their torso, the long arms and even longer fingers appeared humanoid. The haunting eyes were the only thing human on a face that had more of a snout than a nose.

The deadly waters of Lake Manitou flickered. There were now three Porcupine Men that called out his name, but Albert had only discovered two deaths in the newspapers involving the waters of Lake Manitou. Frankie Auerbach had been the first, followed by Stefan Van Slyke, but the third "victim" had not been written about, yet. And he wasn't about to be lured in to wake a fourth.

Why don't the adults see them?

His father stopped talking about the sawmill and the proper man began to ask questions. They stepped to the stairs while Farrell Luning walked around to where Albert stood. Luning took a moment to study him. "The exhibition is over, Big Al." Luning closed the observation window to the east. "Go stand with your father where it's safe."

Big Al? The unexpected nickname made him smile, and for a moment, Albert forgot all about the lurking monsters. He took a few steps closer and then turned around to study Luning. *Wait. Where it's safe? Does he see the Porcupine Men also?*

Hesitant, Albert moved next to the men as they huddled at the open window, knowing there was safety in numbers.

Ira Douglas, the skinny man, kept talking about pineries, dams, and quarries. Only the bald man took notice when Albert stepped beside his father. There was nothing soft or inquisitive about the bald man's gaze, causing Albert to hug even tighter to his father's side. The human men felt as sinister as the Porcupine Men. A few seconds later, the man's gaze returned, forcing Albert to almost stand behind his father.

The conversation came back around, and Douglas mentioned the ogre's name—Dobie.

"Now that our bridge is in place," Dobie continued, "the only thing keeping us from the next phase is the dam, which is progressing even if we've taken some wins and losses. With winter here, my attention has been further north, with the pineries near Leech Lake, but as soon as things begin to thaw, we'll play one of the three cards we've been dealt."

Albert braved a look out the window to Lake Manitou.

"Remember patience," the skinny man added. "This is a marathon, not a sprint."

They all chuckled.

"Does that satisfy everyone?" Albert's father asked. "Any more questions about my end of the operation?"

"No, no, you've done well," one of the St. John businessmen answered, and they all began to walk away from the front window and toward the stairs. Albert kept himself safely positioned, but it didn't stop Halvar Dobie's meaty hand from grabbing him by the chin.

"What is that? A birthmark?" Dobie asked.

Albert froze, but his father turned to answer. "Ah, yes, he's had it since he was born. His hair covers most of it now."

"You've done this before, huh, kid?" Dobie said, chuckling. "Maybe we should be asking you the questions."

The comment perplexed Albert's father, but Dobie let go of the boy's chin and headed for the stairs.

Done what before?

CHAPTER FORTY-SIX

Manabozho's Lodge

Turtle Island Reservation
March 1897

LILY WEBER NOW knew there was something different about her home. Even though the rest of Hiawatha County received the warmth of the spring sun, Lake Manitou seemed to hold onto winter for an extra month. The deep ravines kept the snow sheltered and preserved, and the thick ice from a long winter refused to let go of the shore.

She stood on the edge of the ravine with her hands on her hips. Below, the melting snow and ice brought the river to life, but all along the slope, months of snowpack remained. *So much for searching for the cave.*

Instead, she walked south for a better view of the lake. After weeks of training, Grandfather Nanak took a break to nurse an abscessed tooth, so she walked right past his cabin. Even though the March sun had removed much of the snow on the open field, the lake was still frozen. Gray ice meant open water soon, and with spring, Lily and Nanak would travel to Jiibay Hollow to harvest new growth from an old willow tree, and then her training would be near completion.

Just in time for Migisi's release.

Even though she'd excelled at Sacred Heart, Lily understood how they would manipulate her brother. Sending some of the students home for summer turned into both punishment and incentive. With good behavior, Father Guerin had promised, Migisi would be allowed to return home for the summer. *If I can fake being a Firehandler, Migisi can fake being a civilized Christian.*

Lily had gathered up her notes, stuffed them into a bag, and prepared herself for the first long walk of spring earlier that morning.

If Migisi does come home at the end of May, I'll need to be ready to show the young Thunderbird all that I know. Do I teach him? Or do I let these legends die with Grandfather?

She needed to rehearse and knew better than to do it in the same space as her mother, and she dared not do it at St. Marie's, so she decided to do it at the safest place around Lake Manitou—Turtle Island.

As Lily approached the island from the north, walking over puddles of water melting upon the thick ice, she could see the green hump of the shell, as well as the large rocky head and the small peninsulas that created its arms.

"Manabozho's lodge," Grandfather called it, but he did little to explain the reference to the island.

Unlike her knowledge of the life of Christ, her knowledge of Manabozho and the Midewiwin way remained amateur. Over the past few weeks, she and Father Guerin tried their best to compare the religion to their own: Good and Evil became romanticized. In Lily's mind, Manabozho looked like Jesus as he taught the original Anishinaabe the same stories Grandfather told her over the winter. Likewise, her supernatural gifts were gifts of the Holy Spirit. Holding a hot stone became as rational as St. Peter briefly walking on water, St. John speaking in tongues, or St. Stephen enduring a painless martyr's death. Her nemesis became a Horned Serpent that looked like the renaissance paintings of Satan, and the ghosts and Tak-Pei were nothing more than lowly demons worthy of being cast into a herd of pigs. Father Guerin had an answer for everything.

She pictured Father Guerin riding somewhere out in the wilderness now. The heroic image made her smile, and when he returned from his recent trip, she would impress him with the completed transcription of the Song of the Manitou.

I must be ready to do my part.

The shore of Turtle Island was miserable. The "head" was a fifteen-foot-tall solitary boulder, but the rest of the shore was a defensive wall of small boulders and stone that made transitioning from ice to solid ground awkward and dangerous.

Finally, she stood upon a golden blanket of wet pine needles. She paused long enough for her chilled feet to warm before hiking to the highest point upon the turtle shell, a mound of exposed boulders that peeked out from the pines.

From her perch, she could get a 360-degree view of the entire lake. Closest to her, she could see the shallow "tail" of the turtle that connected the island to the main shore. The almost invisible peninsula led to a wooded hill and a simple farmhouse, but on the western slope of the hill, she saw a crease in the world.

The crease was filled with trees, and even without leaves, the density of the cut hid the details under the canopy of branches, but the shore, normally hidden by the island, revealed a small stream that deposited snowmelt into Lake Manitou.

Jiibay Hollow?

Lily sat down upon the closest bare rock and bowed her head.

What am I supposed to do? Why is this happening to me?

She retrieved her cross necklace and recited prayers taught to her by Sister Lynch at Sacred Heart and Sister Inez at St. Marie's. Finished, she let go of the cross and let her bare palm rest upon the cold stone—Inyan. The creator god of the Lakota, whose corpse could be seen in the ancient stones upon the world, was neither good nor evil, so she turned her thoughts to him as she walked the fine line between Christian and Chippewa.

Receiving no answers, her hand found its way to her satchel. The Song of the Manitou was waiting for her. Since she now knew the parts to avoid, especially the waking of the Tak-Pei, she focused on another section of the Song—a call for help.

Clearing her throat, she opened her mouth and barely vocalized the foreign syllables written upon the paper. The phonetic lyrics felt warm, soothing. When Migisi returned, she'd do her duty then hide behind her cross, letting *him* deal with the paradoxical battle for humanity.

"Granddaughter?"

The voice ended her song, but she remained as still as the stone she sat upon.

Lily closed her eyes, not in fear, but to concentrate.

She knew there were ghosts, so when she opened her eyes to the crease of land known as Jiibay Hollow, it did not startle her to see a ghost standing in the shadows of the tree.

"Granddaughter?" the figure called out from under the willow. "I can hear you, but I cannot see you."

Lily began walking.

Her paternal grandmother, Nanak's wife, had died far up north while birthing a child who would have been an aunt for Lily. Her maternal grandmother, Chief Sweating Stone's slave, had died at Leech Lake several years earlier.

The ghost is not one my grandmothers.

When Lily reached the nearside of the island, she stopped several yards from the shore, keeping a safe distance. "I am here."

"Oh. I thought you were someone else. Will you come closer so I can see you with my old eyes?"

Her heart raced, but the voice did not sound sinister. "If you don't mind, I'll stay here where it's safe."

"Yes," the old woman answered. "The Tak-Pei can't harm you on the island. You ... you have questions, don't you?"

Would the Tak-Pei speak of themselves that way?

The old woman asked, "Has your grandfather taught you the story of the dreamcatcher?"

How does she know? "Yes."

"Yes, yes. Of course he has. You are here to save the children in your dreams. You would not have come if you hadn't learned the truth about the dreamcatcher," the old woman mused. "I-I think I am Grandmother Spider. I am not sure if I have become her, have always been her, or am about to become her. I am your ally in the coming battle."

Lily felt as if a teacher stood at her desk with a ruler in hand ready to smack her knuckles. According to Nanakonan, Grandmother Spider was a creator god from the dawn, so the voice did not match up to that of a deity. "What can you tell me about the coming battle?"

"Death is coming, and it is all your fault for opening your mouth to sing. You've woken the Tak-Pei, and there is nothing you can do to stop them now. Yet there is a terrible path to victory—to save the children. If you come closer, I can show you this path."

Is this a trick? Is it a demon sensing my guilt? "Why don't you come closer to me?" Lily countered.

Grandmother Spider held the lifeless fronds of the willow, which obscured seeing her better. "You know the answer and have already forgotten, but soon, when your heart is shattered into a million pieces, you will understand. What is the most important thing to you?"

"Jesus, I suppose."

The old woman cackled from the shadows. "Christ will not be in jeopardy in the coming battle. The Wintermaker will take the most precious thing to you. Do you know what it is?"

The children. Family.

"Yes, child. I know what is most precious to you, and I can still help you protect it. Do you still want my help?"

Protection for my family? "Of course."

"Then you must stand under the willow. Do not worry about ghosts or the Tak-Pei. They fear you more than you know. You are a Firehandler who has not yet held true fire. But soon you will. If you come to me right now, we can change your destiny."

She wants me to come closer? At the center of the dark shore, the arms of a great willow tree stood above the creek bed. Although the tangle of branches and the maze of trunks obscured the rest, a narrow window appeared between the rocks of the creek bed and the curtain of branches.

It's enormous, Lily realized, even though the tree was tucked into the ravine.

An old woman—not a creator god—stood in the shadows of the tree.

"You are so young and beautiful," the old woman said. "Your heart is whole. I'll see you soon at the cave, but now ... now you must run."

Low growls came from the sides, and near the shore, black shadows emerged from the ice, and as they rose, the ice groaned and cracked. Long arms like the legs of a grasshopper emerged from their bodies, and as the dark hands touched the ice, the arms flexed.

Lily felt the ice move under her feet, and a wind blew right into her face like the exhalation of a great lion.

"Run!"

Her legs obeyed the command, and soon her feet were splashing across the melting ice. Once she cleared the island, she glanced back, only to see the inky demons running after her.

The Tak-Pei.

The glance caused her to lose her balance, and she spilled onto the wet ice, but only for an instant—she clamored to her feet and ran for home rather than the island.

She said I would be safe on the island.

But it was now too late.

A hundred yards from the northern shore, she stopped.

A gray wall of figures rose in unison to block her path.

No. Not ghosts or spirits—a wall of ice.

The Tak-Pei were using their magic to push the entire ice shelf away from the southern shore, and now it came crashing into the northern shore. As it piled up, it was crushed by its own weight that turned it into a million ice fragments that grew taller by the second.

Help me. Oh please, God, help me.

She saw a solitary figure standing on the hill: Adam Thunder Face. He was surrounded by a pile of wood, transfixed, holding a still raised ax in mid-swing.

Lily did not scream for help. Nor did she run for the sandy shore, choosing instead to head for the western bank of the Blue Knife. Nearing the magically created ice wall, she heard the rumble of the annual ice out.

At the last second, she jumped onto the shifting heap, surfing the shards up one side and down the other until she found the solid ground of the northern shore under her feet.

CHAPTER FORTY-SEVEN

Retracing the Steps

Sterling Junction
March 21, 1897

KERMIT CRAIN PATIENTLY waited for his mother to come tuck him in before he snuck through his bedroom window, crawled onto the roof, and dropped onto the spongy grass beside the house. The boy waited for a few minutes next to the kitchen window until he heard his father's booming voice. His father would normally stay up for another hour, and in that time, Kermit hoped to save himself from a lashing.

Somewhere out in the darkness, his father's treasured Barlow jackknife was waiting to be found. Kermit had borrowed it earlier in the day when he went fishing along the banks of Lake Manitou. It wasn't until he returned for supper that he realized he had inexplicably lost the knife that had once belonged to his grandfather. So under the light of the rising full moon, Kermit hustled across the yard to retrace the steps he had walked earlier in the day.

The Crain farm was south of town, just off the intersection of Old Copper Road and the road leading north into St. John. His father was a blacksmith that worked at Sterling Junction, so he easily was able to find the railroad tracks that led into town.

I remember using the Barlow knife to cut the line, Kermit told himself as he walked down the tracks that passed by the lake. His heavy Dacron line had snagged in the water, and unable to break it, he'd had to cut the line and tie on new tackle.

Kermit had been in such a hurry to get himself out of trouble that he hadn't really taken the time to think his plan through completely. Now, as he walked in the darkness, he realized how foolish it was.

He shuffled his feet in the rocks between the railroad ties, hoping that the noise would be enough to scare off anything lurking in the darkness.

Normally, Kermit found that little changed about his world when the sun went down. But lately his brother Monte had been telling of ghosts that lived in the waters of Lake Manitou. As Kermit walked, he tried to dismiss thoughts of beheaded women, serpents in the water, or ghouls that wanted to drag a child into the lake.

Idiot, Kermit dismissed with a forced smirk. *Where does Monte come up with these stories?*

On the edge of town, where the railroad veered west around the area some of the oldest farmers called Assinikande, or Flat Rock, Kermit followed a worn path, made by deer and farm boys, that led directly to the shore of Lake Manitou.

The Barlow knife was sitting right on the large rock where he had set it four hours earlier. His relief at seeing it faded quickly. Feeling as if he was being watched, Kermit glanced around before snatching up the knife.

His feet echoed loudly on the ground, as if the earth itself was trying to announce his presence to whatever was watching him. The faster he walked, the louder his steps became, until Kermit realized that the sound of his own heart contributed to his betrayal.

At the end of the worn path, his pace slowed but his heart rate quickened as he saw lights where there should only be darkness.

He blinked, stopped, and then blinked again.

Lanterns?

Even if the moon had been new, Kermit would have known exactly where he stood—and where the lanterns had been set. In his ten years, he had passed by Flat Rock more than a hundred times, be it from the narrow road along the lakeshore or by walking the tracks along the west side. Smooth waves of granite, polished by untold years of erosion, poked out of the marshy area that formed the western shores of Lake Manitou. Monte and his friends would play the part of the Union while Kermit and the younger farm boys would be forced to play the Confederate side when reenacting the Battle of Gettysburg and other Civil War battles. It was during these battles of "capture the flag" that he had learned every nook and cranny of Flat Rock.

Those lanterns are lining the pit, Kermit realized, and even though a cold shudder went down his spine, he could not turn and run toward the safety of the railroad tracks.

To him, the pit could have been one of the Seven Wonders of the World. In Miss White's science class, he had learned the basic principles of geology, which could not explain how the deep bowl had formed in the field of granite—or how water refused to gather in the bowl despite any cracks or fissures to drain it.

Kermit often told himself that when he was an adult, he would answer these mysteries, but now, it seemed that other adults had taken up the cause.

The flicker of light he saw did not come from the lanterns themselves but from bodies passing by the light. Having run over the granite while being chased by Monte gave Kermit confidence in his ability to flee from whatever danger lay ahead; he began to sneak forward.

Ducking behind mounds of granite, Kermit advanced towards the bowl.

All the while, he could almost hear Monte's voice whispering in his ear. *"What if it is some sort of pagan Indian ritual where they are offering human sacrifices to their gods?"*

No, Kermit told himself. The Indians he had met were much different than the ones in the books he read. Most of them he knew even went to church.

"What if it is some sort of Ku Klux Klan ceremony?" Monte's distant voice continued to plant fear in him. *"What if they are torturing some poor Indian? They will kill you for being a witness."*

Kermit shook off that possibility, too. Miss White had explained the atrocities of the Klan following the Civil War, but she had also explained that the Klan had been suppressed by lawmakers shortly after the war ended.

He stopped when he heard voices. Near the bowl, the rolling mounds of granite were low, and Kermit pressed his face to the cool stone. His own heart pounded so loudly that he felt as if his internal drum would shine a spotlight on his position in the dark, so he opened the short two-inch blade of the Barlow to soothe his nerves.

"Gentlemen, I think we are prepared. You can assume your positions," a voice called out to the small assembly.

Conversations continued, including a pair of shadowy figures who stood closest to Kermit. The men spoke in full voices, as if standing in front of the post office.

"Any updates about the dam?"

The second man sighed. "Azero is getting impatient with Morrison and is going to apply a little pressure to get land secured for the dam. Mr. Douglas thinks he's found some legal precedent that could get us both plots of land. Soon, we'll have our dam, and then, everything you see around us will be a massive hole in the ground.

"Ah, yes. Have you seen Dobie?"

"He's not a fan of ceremonies, is he? Let's take our places."

Farther away, Kermit could hear carefully crafted words that almost reminded him of one of Father Hebert's sermons. His fear abruptly turned to curiosity.

Surrendering the last secure location for a good look, Kermit rose onto his haunches and steadily side-stepped like a crab until he could clearly see the figures standing near the light.

Although he could not clearly see any of the faces, his fears were allayed when he saw all of them dressed up in business suits. *How odd.*

The fat man who had been speaking sat at a chair, which looked as out of place as the table where the other man now knelt. A third man then took the sitting man by the arm and began leading him in circles around three candles.

He's blindfolded, Kermit realized, seeing then that all three men were wearing strange white aprons during the ceremony. *Very odd.*

From the outer edge of the lanterns, a man wearing denim and flannel suddenly interrupted the circling pair and harshly confronted the man. Although the words were deliberate and rehearsed, when Kermit heard the flannel man threaten the blindfolded man, he sat up on his haunches.

When the man said "die" and struck the blindfolded man, Kermit took two steps backward.

It's a play. This is some sort of performance.

A second man stepped into the circle, and this time, the argument sounded real, despite the fact that the blindfolded man still had his escort. The second man took the blindfolded man by the lapels of his jacket and shook him harshly.

"Grandmaster Hiram Abiff, give me the secrets of a Master Mason, or I will take your life on the spot," the newest assailant shouted, giving Kermit goose bumps.

This could not be happening. Not in my town.

This is the stuff of pulp fiction books.

I need to—The sweet smell of cigar smoke descended upon him with more terror than any ghost or ghoul could have. The supernatural did not find young Kermit—instead, it was a hand of steel upon his shoulder that reached out from the darkness.

"What have…" a man's voice began and abruptly stopped when the Barlow knife punched him in the belly. In that moment of hot blood upon his fingers, Kermit could briefly see the man's face and bald head illuminated by the cigar, which tumbled from his mouth with a groan.

Kermit ran as he had never run before. His feet floated over stone, and then tarred timber, and finally the fields of home. He gave no thought to silently entering through the window, and instead, burst through the front door of his house, causing his mother to scream in alarm. His father still sat at the rocking chair, and Kermit threw himself at his feet, clinging to them in absolute subjection.

"There's blood on him," his mother said, voice shrill. "Why is there blood on him?"

His father reached down to collect the Barlow knife that had clattered on the floor. "What happened, Kermit?"

He clung tightly to his father's legs and began to sob uncontrollably.

"Was it the Manitou?" Monte asked, coming into the room. He sounded so sincere that Kermit began to doubt everything he had seen.

Could it be true? Had the monster from the legends simply taken the shape of humans?

"Be reasonable, Monte. There is no such thing." His father pulled Kermit up by the shoulders to look him in the eyes. "Where did the blood come from, Kermit?"

Last Stand

St. John, MN
March 27, 1898

AS SOON AS the church bells finished ringing, Lily Weber prepared herself. The congregation began singing and she ascended for the balcony, discreetly slipping into a vacant pew and joining the song.

While her lips sang one song, her mind thought of another, and her inability to focus caused her to clench her hands and lower her head in frustration.

What have I done? God, forgive me.

With Nanak still sick and Father Guerin away, Lily bottled up her terror and wore a brave face, first for her mother and now for the congregation of St. Marie's. When the last song played, she stood and retreated to the school room.

Just a few minutes into the lesson, she came to a realization about the children: they were subdued. Just like she went through the motions as assistant to Sister Inez, they all played their parts yet seemed distracted. Lily saw it in their eyes, like in the days following the death of Frankie Auerbach. *They are hiding something.*

Each time Sister Inez asked a question or began a new assignment, the secret slipped below the surface. The absences of two boys, Kermit Crain and Albert Fischer, made the remaining children more introverted.

Finally, after the end of the lesson, Bjorn Forsberg broke from the stupor of routine to linger at the doorway. "Miss Weber?"

Lily stood beside Sister Inez, who paid no attention to the boy. *I hope this isn't what I think it is.* "Yes, Bjorn?"

"My father asked me if I could pick up some calving supplies this afternoon at a dairy farm west of Nimrod Crossing. I don't know your plans, but if you needed a ride, I'd be going right past your home."

Is this his way of courting me? The offer did feel like an answer to her prayers though. "When would you be leaving?"

"Soon, right after lunch."

Seeing there were still no smiles or longing eyes, she nodded. "Thank you, Bjorn. I'd appreciate it."

"Give me half an hour and I'll pull the wagon around to the front of the church."

If it was Bjorn Forsberg's way of courting, he did a poor job of it. With Samuel Thunder Face, his intentions had been obvious with each move he made. With Father Guerin, his smile and kind eyes indicated one thing, but his words and actions were quite opposite. But Bjorn treated her like an extra sack of potatoes. And once she was sitting next to him on the wagon bench, he kept his eyes on the road and horses.

Finally, as they neared Lyons, Bjorn found his voice. "What's this all about?"

She looked up, biting back a yawn. "Oh, yeah," she said, seeing the camp of tarp tents on the hill adjacent to Lyons, "all these workers showed up yesterday to finish the road and bridge."

"Nobody is going to visit Nimrod anymore," Bjorn mused. "In a few weeks, I'll be able to just cut straight across to St. John."

And then he grew silent again.

Lily tried to picture a life with Bjorn Forsberg. *Wife of a dairy farmer?* She'd have a house, a nice kitchen, a social status, but at the price of a lifetime without any meaningful conversation.

Suddenly Bjorn's hand shot up to point. "Did you see that?"

"See what?"

"Two ravens chased an owl out of the ravine and into the woods east of the Nimrod Road."

"I guess I missed it."

"I probably shouldn't be saying this on a Sunday," he began, "but ravens are Odin's messengers. Huginn and Muninn."

"Pardon me?"

"Their names. Huginn and Muninn. They would fly all over Midgard, bringing news back to Odin. Seeing them made me think of the old stories."

Well, that is interesting. "My grandfather said owls are evil birds. Our word for them is *gookooko'oo.*"

"It sounds like an owl hoot," Bjorn commented, smiling with teeth yellowed by plaque.

She looked down in panic. "Y-you don't have to drop me off at my house," she said at the corner. "It's a nice spring day, I don't mind walking the rest of the way."

"It's no trouble. Honestly."

"It's fine," she insisted, jumping from her seat. "Thanks again, Bjorn."

"Have a nice day," he called as he passed her.

Don't panic. He was just being nice. Lily glanced up, seeing some smoke in the air above her house—a sign her mother had returned and was already baking. Lily's ambitions would have to wait, but by midafternoon, she'd be exploring the ravine.

The cave must be somewhere along the eastern shore.

The fragments of three conversations gave her a starting point. She mulled over everything she knew as she walked. She'd overheard Nanak telling Father Guerin about hiding the entrance to a cave. Then there was Migisi's efforts to find said cave. Finally, her father had even mentioned finding a cave.

Grandfather does not keep the scrolls in his cabin, but how does he access them without giving away the location of the secret cave?

A strange squeal caught her ear, and she stopped mid step. Her head pivoted and she saw a far more sinister column of smoke. *Is that smoke from Nanak's cabin?*

Instead of an orderly pillar coming from his chimney, great puffs of smoke entered the clean blue sky. Before she could even process the clues, her mother's screams filled the air.

The front door of her home was open—

A roar overlapped more screams until a muffled thud brought silence.

Tentative, Lily took a few steps forward. "Mother?"

Adam Thunder Face filled the doorway, holding an ax and covered in blood.

Lily dropped her belongings on a gasp of surprise. *Run. Run!*

Bjorn and the wagon were already out of sight, yet it was impossible to outrun the ogre to the end of the road let alone all the way to Nimrod Crossing.

Run!

Remembering how clumsy he'd been in the snow, she ran from the road and into the uneven field. Her only chance to live would be getting to the little tent camp created by the team of engineers working on the new road and bridge.

I'm dead.

I'm dead.

I'm dead.

They veered off the road also and out into the open field. While Lily ran over the clods of mud from the recently plowed field, Adam Thunder Face's feet twisted and stumbled.

Lily could see the distant tents and small figures of men staring at the burning cabin in the distance. She wanted to scream but knew she needed every breath and bit of energy to run.

From behind, the ferocity of breathing taunted her, and it took every bit of her focus not to lose courage and veer off to the side.

She risked a glance back: Adam Thunder Face was only twenty yards away, approaching fast. He hurled the ax, but it sailed over her head by three feet. She stopped, frozen in terror. From the corner of her eye, she watched Adam Thunder Face, off-balance from the throw, collapsing in the dirt.

Run! Lily hesitated too long, she had only taken a few steps before a knife whizzed by her head and landed in the ground in front of her. *Run, run!*

"Help," Lily managed to call out through her heavy breathing. "Help!" she shouted a little louder. Then the adrenaline kicked in and a scream ripped through her lungs.

Men were pointing in her direction, moving towards her.

Help, please help.

She could see the wide eyes as she approached—frail men with pressed shirts and suspenders. None of them were armed. She ran past.

Lily cleared the third tent and saw a man with a revolver and fell at his feet. "Save me. Save me."

Another man appeared with shaving cream on half his face. He stopped to stand above her. "What happened, darling?"

A single pistol shot fired, followed by two more.

Guardian of the Frontier

Old Copper Road
March 28, 1898

BJORN FORSBERG SAT on the second-floor balcony connected to Britta's bedroom with his rifle on his lap. *Who'd want to hurt Lily?*

The house was boarded up, the shotgun in the kitchen with his mother and the girls. The northern side of the house was his only blind spot, but from his balcony perch, he could see three sides from a safe distance.

Winnie Weber's blood, Bjorn remembered as he studied his clean hands. He'd heard screams over the wagon wheels, and upon turning around, he'd found Lyons, the workers camp, and Turtle Island Reservation in complete chaos. Old Nanakonan and Winnie had been murdered by the Loose Goose bartender without warning or provocation. Although Lily escaped the attack, Adam Thunder Face vanished moments later, and a manhunt immediately began. Bjorn helped tend to the dead while adults tended to Lily's grief.

I should have comforted her. She didn't even know those other men.

Today, the church bells had called away his father right after morning milking and Bjorn spent the time wondering what he'd be feeling if his parents and sisters were all gone.

Finally, his father rode up on Sleipnir.

Bjorn stood on the eastern railing, watching his father go from the barn.

Gus Forsberg called to him, stopping in the yard. "He killed the Bordeaux dog."

Bjorn's lips parted to ask a question, but nothing came out. *He didn't flee north. He's near.*

"Martin Nielson saw crows this morning and found the dog near Kanaranzi Creek. There's a theory he's going south on the Crow Wing River, so Constable Graham is gathering a search party to cut him off before he reaches Staples. When Marshal Morrison arrives, we're going to form a search party to sweep the lake."

"Why did he do it?"

"Folks think it might be some old Indian feud, but now that he's killed the dog, it's obvious the man has lost his mind."

I don't care about the dog. "How's Miss Weber?"

His father shook his head. "I didn't hear anything about that. The Constable from St. John is organizing men at the reservation, so she's got a small army protecting her now. They're going to be searching the Blue Knife River." He paused, looking weary. "I'm going to get the girls situated in the root cellar, and then you and I are going to have a look around the property, agreed?"

Bjorn nodded, stealing a glance south. Less than a mile down Old Copper Road, the Bordeaux dog had been discovered. At first, it terrified and angered him to know the killer lurked near his house, but then he realized Thunder Face might be lingering for another shot at Lily.

By the time he got to the back yard, his mother stood in the opening of the root cellar, shotgun in hand.

"We'll be back in less than an hour," his father promised. "I need to know he's not hiding on our property before I join the search party."

Bjorn followed fast as his father walked away so that his mother couldn't stop him from joining his father.

THEY FOLLOWED THE trail north through the woods until they came out of the woods at Bleeding Rock. Bjorn felt his pocket for more .22 bullets, knowing his father's Winchester had been loaded to capacity.

Although spooky, the woods around Bleeding Rock held few places for a man of Adam Thunder Face's size to hide, and once they searched it, they headed to the steep cliffs.

"I want you to just sit here, looking down on the channel between us and Deadwood Island. I'm going to start searching around the north shore, so you watch for him to bolt south. If you see anything, fire a shot in the air and I'll know what's going on. Understand?"

Bjorn nodded, and once his father continued, he laid down on his belly with the barrel of the .22 hanging over the cliff edge. Stretching before him were miles of shoreline. He stoically studied the gusting winds that turned the lake into a frothy soup of whitecaps.

Although Turtle Island, with its tall pine and oak trees, provided more shelter from the elements, Deadwood Island's brush allowed a man to hunker down and hide.

That's where I'd hide.

With the Blue Knife River three miles away, Adam Thunder Face could have hidden anywhere, but Bjorn's instincts and patience paid off after sitting on the cliff's edge for only twenty minutes.

Got you.

From a brush pile, the limping killer emerged dragging a small rowboat. Clinging to the bow of the boat, Adam Thunder Face pulled it behind him until he reached the soft mud of the shore. In a matter of seconds, the rowboat was spun around, and he began plowing through the waves with powerful strokes of the oars.

Seeing the boat angling toward the outlet of Kanaranzi Creek, where the MacPherson boys guarded their farm, Bjorn took aim. In a matter of seconds, he had a view of the man's back. He had dropped a deer at such a distance, and with each dip of the oars, the killer grew larger in his sights.

But Bjorn couldn't pull the trigger.

His breathing became so labored that the tip of the rifle barrel began to fluctuate up and down. Even though his friends and family were in mortal danger because of this man, he could not bring himself to take a life.

Adam Thunder Face paused mid-stroke when a piece of his boat flipped into the air like a wooden grasshopper. Three seconds later, another piece of wood jumped off his boat.

Bjorn steadied his breathing and aimed lower.

The third shot hit right at the waterline.

The fourth shot struck with a splash of water.

This time, Adam Thunder Face looked up at the cliff right before Bjorn pumped another bullet into the chamber and took aim again.

A primal scream, stranger than anger or frustration, echoed across the water, but not before Adam Thunder Face turned his sinking vessel back toward the island.

He didn't even sound human … Could it be rabies?

A few moments later, his father came running, Winchester in hand, and joined the chorus of bullets, ruining the killer's plan of escaping down the Crow Wing River.

By the time Adam Thunder Face reached the shore, Bjorn had to open the chamber of his rifle and fumble through his pocket full of bullets to reload, allowing the killer to run into the brush.

"He's not going anywhere now," his father said moments later, appearing at his side and patting Bjorn on the back. "You did well to keep him on the island."

Three horses came galloping along the southern shore—the MacPhersons had heard the shooting.

Within the hour, the scattered posse swarmed to take position.

ADULT RIFLEMEN SITUATED themselves along the granite ridge while the men from Split Rock obtained three rowboats from the Berg, Nielson, and Bordeaux farms. All three, weighed down with six men each, plowed through the rough waters of Lake Manitou.

Having helped Martin Nielson get a rowboat, Bjorn found himself suddenly part of the armed posse paddling to the island.

In an adjacent boat, Bushy Bill Morrison studied Deadwood Island before he called out, "That Indian could have a rifle for all we know."

Before anyone could reply, a wave turned Marshal Morrison's rowboat, and a moment later, a second wave capsized it.

"Damn it all," Martin Nielson muttered, and without being told, he turned his boat to go rescue the men from the chilly water. Four figures were clamoring at the side of the overturned boat, but Marshal Morrison appeared to be struggling mightily in the water.

"Something's got my foot," Morrison shouted.

Bjorn looked into the depths for danger. He knew the stories of Lake Manitou and had grown up learning the stories from Norse mythology of the legendary Midgard Serpent battling Thor upon the water. Terror gripped his heart.

Just before Nielson's rowboat pulled up next to the wreck, Morrison disappeared.

Something's got a hold of him!

Instead of jumping in after Morrison, Nielson took a long oar and shoved it in the water where Morrison had disappeared. He stirred it until it struck something solid. Bjorn leaned closer to the water: a few feet below the water, Morrison clutched ahold of the oar.

Hand-over-hand, Nielson pulled the oar out of the water, but just as Morrison's hand reached the surface, the wooden oar was pulled back down a foot.

Martin Nielson's eyes met Bjorn's and widened with terror.

Good, maybe Morrison will get eaten alive.

"Hold onto my belt," Nielson yelled to the others, and this time, as he pulled the oar up, he leaned precariously over the edge of the boat.

"Nielson, you'll capsize us!" Bordeaux shouted.

But Nielson, with one hand on the oar, reached into the water deep enough that his face broke the surface. Bjorn moved closer, ready to grab him as the others kept the boat balanced. He saw Nielsen's left hand grabbing ahold of Morrison's hand.

Be careful. Don't let it get you!

A moment later, Morrison was hauled into the boat and ended up across Bjorn's lap.

Distracted, Bjorn ignored the terrified lawman and kept his gaze on the water, looking for a clear view of a tentacle or toothy mouth. *There's no such thing. Grow up.*

A groan had him looking towards the shore where the third rowboat landed, and the men quickly spread out to scour the woods.

"He's not breathing!" one of the men beside Bjorn snapped.

"Maybe we should—"

Suddenly Morrison vomited into the belly of the boat and began violently coughing.

He's not looking so high and mighty now. Does he remember me?

"Grab ahold of the edge of the boat," Nielson said to the other men in the water, "we'll drag you all into shore."

With a clenched jaw, Nielson fought against the wind and the drag to head for shore.

"Something grabbed me by the ankle," Morrison whispered to Bjorn, wide-eyed.

Bjorn glanced to Nielson, who remained stoic despite the terrifying story he'd told weeks earlier about a monster he saw while ice fishing.

"Probably just a sunken tree," Bordeaux offered.

"There's probably a current flowing around the island," someone else added.

Bill Morrison, with his hair flopping in his face and his big mustache drooping limply at the corners of his mouth, shook his head. "No, it brushed past me, circled me twice, and then tried to drag me to the bottom of the lake. It … it …"

Is it true? Is there a monster in the waters? Is that why I've been having such terrible dreams?

A scream filled the air.

A moment later, gunshots followed.

Adam Thunder Face came out of the brush stumbling, bleeding from multiple wounds. Yet his legs kept moving.

Two more bullets hit home, and he dropped the bloody ax.

But he kept charging.

Men followed out of the brush, taking aim and firing.

Finally, the killer fell just a few yards in front of Bjorn.

As blood spurted from the man's wounds, his body also leaked a strange, dark substance that separated itself from the red liquid and slithered for the protection of darkness.

That's not normal. Bjorn had slaughtered animals before. *The blood looks almost alive.*

Morrison continued to cough and wheeze, drawing Bjorn's attention away from the slain giant.

"Did you see it pulling me down?" Morrison asked with desperate eyes.

Bjorn had seen enough, which is why he turned to Nielson, who cautioned him with a slight shake of his head. "It was probably just a tree branch. What else could have done that?"

Nielson, who had managed to get only a dozen yards from his boat, smirked and shook his head. "I'd keep those thoughts to yourself, or people in Hiawatha County might think you've gone loony."

A few moments later, men hauled the body of Jonas Penny onto the shore and laid it on the sand beside the bullet-riddled body of Adam Thunder Face. Bjorn felt a knot forming in his belly from the gruesome deaths of both men, but before he could be consumed by the moment, Morrison vomited a second time into the bottom of the boat.

After wiping the mucous from his mouth, he turned back to Bjorn. "You saw it, didn't you, kid? I know you saw it."

Bjorn gave a slight nod, even though he'd only seen the struggle. *Whatever it was, there are four more souls whose blood are now part of Lake Manitou.*

Worked to the Bone

Split Rock, MN
March 29, 1898

LIKE A PILOT fish cleaning the teeth of a great white shark, Farrell Luning waited for the monster's mouth to open.

The roar was deafening as mighty logs from the northern pine fields were torn to pieces in front of his eyes. Every two hours, when the men working the saws took a break, he would step in with Walter Corr to remove and sharpen the blade. Having already sharpened the blades on the first floor, Farrell now waited at the second story window for the whistle to blow.

With the arrival of spring, he almost envied the younger men out on the log pond today. When he first started at the Fisher Sawmill, he too had put in his time out on Lake Manitou, wrangling the logs into the chutes. Now, after risking life and limb during his teen years, he enjoyed the safer life as a saw filer.

The ten o'clock whistle sounded, and the whirl of belts and blades softened as the saws were temporarily shifted into neutral to allow the sawmen a quick break and the filers a few minutes at the blades. George Fisher insisted that his filers rotated to different saws throughout their shift so that there were four sets of eyes upon them instead of the same two all day long, which contented Farrell, who found that each blade almost had its own personality.

Abigail, as he called her, was the fore-blade on the second floor, which allowed him a scenic view of the lake behind him. He and Walter quickly found their rhythm on the files while the men who pushed the logs through the building sipped from their jugs and grabbed a quick bite to eat. Occasionally, there were some young bucks that wanted to chat with the veteran filers, but they usually took the hint to leave them alone after a few shifts.

Compared to the big teeth of Evangeline and Rosemary downstairs, Abigail's small teeth responded quickly to his file. The large timbers were cut downstairs while the smaller timbers were cut upstairs; all of them were then sent down the chutes to the finishing wagons that ran parallel to the Crow Wing River.

Walter no longer spoke but simply nodded with a grunt as he slipped Abigail back onto her pulley. Almost finished, Farrell closed the doors of the blade house moments before the whistle sounded again and the building roared back to life.

Taking just a moment to catch their breath after such intense work, he and Walter walked down the room until they reached Elizabeth. It would be another hour and forty-five minutes before he would get a chance at Old Betsy's teeth, and while he waited, they performed basic maintenance on the peripheral equipment while men and logs passed them by.

The predictability of this routine became almost soothing after a while, so when George Fisher led a group of businessmen through the mill, it startled him.

"As you can see, the mill itself sits over Split Rock Creek," George said as he led the men to the window that looked east toward town. "The stone banks made it easy to secure the mill a safe distance above the water, and despite being so narrow, Split Rock Creek almost has as much water flow as the Crow Wing River."

"So the Nicollet Dam will help ensure a steady flow of water through this mill?" the fat man asked.

The fat man must be the big boss, Luning assumed, recognizing the other men from an earlier visit.

"It will, which is why I feel the funding of this project is so important. Not only will it help with logging on the Blue Knife, but it will help regulate water levels on the lake."

George Fisher waved at someone below the window and said something that caused them to chuckle.

One of the men, the stocky bald man, did not chuckle but grimaced, sweat beading upon his head. *Is he injured?*

The fat man frowned, asking, "Have you considered switching from water powered saws to steam powered saws? That's what they are doing throughout New York state."

"I have, Mr. Gunn, but there is a certain degree of danger and unpredictability with boilers. A boiler explosion killed a man at the local creamery. Your investment in the Nicollet Dam will provide a safer working environment for everybody here at my mill."

A moment later, the procession returned down the staircase, just as it had done before.

"What do you suppose that was about?" Walter Corr asked as he watched the men leave.

Rich men carving up the world. "That's the group of Triton businessmen I told you about. I guess George must be trying to impress the big investor."

"You figure that's why we put on a coat of paint last fall?"

"I would bet you're right."

Both men wandered to the window overlooking Split Rock Creek. Luning spotted a boy in a blue jacket, young Albert Fisher, standing along the rocks overlooking the creek. On several occasions, George had brought his heir with him.

Luning gasped as he saw the boy slip on wet granite and slide right into the roaring water of the creek. His fingers gripped the open window, and for a second, his bodyweight leaned toward the door leading to the hall.

But the boy had already been swept ten yards down the frothing, icy gauntlet.

There was no help in sight.

Nobody had seen young Albert slip into the raging creek.

The boy is going to die.

Save him!

His body shifted into motion like the gears, pulleys, and belts of the building that surrounded him. In one fluid act, he lifted his legs over the window and dropped two stories into the creek below.

In his first year at the Fisher Sawmill, the thirteen-year-old Farrell had leaned out onto the log pond to wrangle a stubborn log only to lose his footing and fall over the log and into the cold water. That was when he learned the truth about the Manitou.

Trapped below the logs, unable to find a seam in the floating prison, Farrell faced certain death. But it wasn't the million cold needles pricking his flesh, nor was it the pressure in his lungs burning for release—it was the voice in his mind that terrified him.

It knew me.

Somewhere below him, somehow deeper than the lake floor itself, he felt a malevolent presence reaching up for him like an invisible tentacle trying to pull his soul from his body. It felt as if it'd been watching all those years and waited for the right moment to strike. But then the timber parted, and the men hauled him out of the water like a load of cod.

Five years later, and once again in the frigid waters of Lake Manitou, Luning felt the hand of death. Even though he was officially an adult, his body was tossed around like a doll in the boiling water of the creek. But years of working in the mill had given him arms of steel, and he willed himself to swim through the current.

He felt a boulder brush against his shoulder, and a moment later, he found enough leverage to lift his head out of the water for a breath—and for vantage. He could see Albert's blue jacket just ten yards ahead, so he threw himself into the maelstrom. Although the current battered him, he managed to close in on the boy.

His hand brushed by the boy's leg.

A moment later, his strong hands gripped an arm.

Reaching the boy, though, almost killed him. The boy's weight created drag within the current, pulling him from the surface. He tucked the boy into his left arm and flailed frantically with his right. Twice his hand brushed against stone, but his cold fingers could not latch on.

Finally, his nails gripped stone, but the full weight of the boy and current tried to rip his arm out of the socket—but Luning refused to let the lake waters claim either of them.

He pulled the boy's head above water, but the kid was unresponsive. For a moment, he just cradled the granite outcropping until he heard voices. Hands reached down to the water and pulled the boy from his grasp.

Suddenly free, Luning almost was swept away by the current, but hands clawed at his wrists and soon he was being hauled over the sharp edges of stone.

Frantic men suddenly surrounded him, cutting off the warmth of the sun that beamed down upon him. A hollow thumping pattern ended with coughing and a vomit of water—Albert lived.

"Bloody hell, is that his bone?" One of the men asked, but it wasn't until Farrell looked down that he realized they were talking about the white root sticking out of his thigh.

"Somebody call for the doctor."

The water whispered to him again, but in defeat and agitation. He'd saved the boy. He's saved himself.

Farrell Luning didn't care about the cost. As long as he didn't die in the water, life would be tolerable.

A New Job for Job

Old Copper Road
March 29, 1898

MARTIN NIELSON DID not bother putting on a jacket or primping in front of a mirror. Three months after Dolly's miscarriage, he was a ratty mess.

Stepping out into the false warmth of the morning sun, he pulled his suspenders over his shoulders, reached into his pocket, and found his pocketknife. With the sharp blade, he shaved the stubble around his upper lip and chin, leaving a golden beard that covered his neck and jowls— a tribute to his dead firstborn.

Dolly wears her pain on her face, and so do I, in my own way.

The only reason he shaved away the hair from his mouth is that his blonde beard was easily stained by food and coffee, and if Dolly was ever to kiss him again, he could leave her no excuses not to.

Standing on the hill, he could see all of his three hundred twenty acres. His was the fifth of six farms along Old Copper Road, all of which were considered worthless. The Forsberg farm existed on a rocky ridge between the lake and the river; the MacPherson farm had no tillable land and was built entirely on slope; the Bordeaux farm sat on a low flood plain; the Larson land was level but riddled with rocks and ancient oaks; and the last plot, the Berg land, had twenty tillable acres surrounded by open fields of bedrock.

His three hundred twenty acres, including Turtle Island, had two monstrous hills with a swamp between them. He'd built his house and farm buildings on the hill closest to the lake, plucked every stone from the field, and had since raised two successful wheat crops that now fed the local dairy herds. He turned to the southern hill—an untamed Behemoth—knowing he'd have to tackle it after planting ended.

Turning back to the lake, he spotted movement near the island.

The dog pack returned.

The dog pack consisted of Lars, Hans, Elias, Nils, Agnes, Mabel, and Sylvie Berg, although Martin didn't know which name belonged to which face. Their father, Olaf, was a drunk whose erratic moods would swing from violence to ridiculous paranoia. Martin often helped with projects yet never saw help in return. Tools not locked away in the barn would often disappear, and those loaned were never returned.

"Wights must've taken them," Olaf would claim rather than blaming his children.

Now, the pack marched up the hill.

Martin met them so as not to disturb Dolly's sleep. "Good morning."

"There's something on the island," Paul began. "I didn't see it myself, but Sylvie claims it was a ghost and Nils thinks it was a banshee."

"It was a naked, singing woman," Nils added.

The death of Adam Thunder Face has them hysterical. "And you want me to check it out? It seems like this might be some sort of prank."

"God's honest truth. Pa was still sleeping or else we would've told him, and seeing the island is your property…"

The rowboat was still down by the shore, but fear crawled up his spine and into the hairs of his neck and forearms. *I don't want the kids thinking I'm a coward.* "Let's go check it out."

As the Pied Piper of Hiawatha led the children, Martin battled indecision, and by the time he reached the shore, he boldly walked out into the water. "You little ones just stay on shore. The rest of you walk where I walk."

A skinny bridge of land, the tail of the turtle, connected to the island, allowing him to keep his feet on solid ground and pass through clear, shallow water rather than the uncertainty under the depths of a rowboat. It also thinned the pack to just three.

Paul Berg talked as he walked. "Pa went to St. John yesterday, and Barnabas Hawes said somebody at the Brickyard got stabbed."

A stabbing or an accident? "You don't say."

"They brought him into the kiln room and sewed him up right there. Hawes didn't know who he was or who stabbed him. Strange, huh? I hope Nils' banshee doesn't have a knife."

Martin reached into his pocket to check for his own knife. "Anything supernatural would not be able to cause any phys—"

Nils shouted and pointed, "See! I told you I saw someone, Mr. Nielson."

A naked woman rested on her side; a plaid dress was draped as a blanket. Surrounding her, tufts of hair cut from her own head.

"Run back to your house, Nils. Fetch a blanket," Martin commanded. *It's the Weber girl.* He rushed forward, hesitating at both her condition and nudity. "Oh, my. What have you done?"

"Let me die," she muttered, the first sign she was alive.

Martin scooped her cold, naked body into his arms and began walking. By the time he finished sloshing through the water, the Berg children had found a blanket. They all chattered theories as Martin dropped to a knee to let the girls help wrap her.

Well, Dolly is in for a surprise.

THE CRISIS SEEMED to end Dolly's depression, for as soon as the Berg children left the house, Dolly focused all of her attention toward tending to Lily Weber. Dolly nursed her through hypothermia, then dressed her, fed her, and even helped shape her hair into a short bob.

Two days after finding her, Lily walked out of the bedroom built for their miscarried child.

"Come, sweetheart," Dolly called to Lily. "Have a seat. I have bacon, eggs, and bread for breakfast."

Lily's arms trembled, and her wide eyes were ringed with dark circles.

Martin sat silently with his cup of coffee. Modesty caused him to look at his plate as she sat down, even though she was now clothed in one of his wife's dresses. "The men at the camp said you bolted from the camp the day after the incident. Folks assumed you went to Leech Lake to be with your people," he said to fill the silence. "They killed the man who murdered your family."

Dolly gasped and shot him a dirty look. "Please, Martin, not at the table."

"The poor girl is terrified," he argued back. "She needs to know that there is no danger out there anymore."

Lily scoffed and then hung her head.

"I'm going to bring you to Split Rock," Martin finally said. "Sister Inez has been looking for you, and has a place prepared for you to stay."

"Has Father Guerin returned?"

"I don't know anything about Father Guerin, but I know Sister Inez is a good woman who will look after you."

Lily continued eating without responding.

AN HOUR LATER, Martin sat beside Lily on the bench of his wagon as they left the farm on the top of the grassy hill to descend into the dark woods of Old Copper Road.

Lily kept her eyes fixed on Dolly's borrowed shoes.

The poor girl is suffering. But what didn't she tell us?

Propriety and duty called for him to bring her to a place of shelter, but as he passed through the sinister woods, his mind took him to occult places. He wanted to keep her, protect her, interrogate her. Her eyes held answers.

"Try not to blame God for this," Martin said as they passed through the darkest tangle of oak branches. "'Naked I came from my mother's womb, and naked I shall depart, the Lord gives, and the Lord takes away.' That's from the Book of Job. I read it several times after my wife and I lost our child." He sighed. "Job had it pretty rough, too, and in his darkest hour, he kept his heart turned to God. I used to think it was a parable about hard times, but now I know evil can truly prey upon a man. I get it now."

Lily looked to the passing tree trunks, giving a small shrug.

The wagon turned north, the sinister oak trees giving way to another grassy meadow where Kanaranzi Creek leaked flood waters from the wild rice fields along the southeastern corner of Lake Manitou.

"Why did you scoff earlier?" Martin pressed.

Lily didn't answer.

Forming a Loop

Split Rock, MN
April 1898

AFTER TWO WEEKS in the shelter of the convent, Lily Weber sat up from her bed, determined to end her miserable life.

The pain of loss did not lessen, as the nuns had promised. Thoughts of Nanak and Winnie normally brought a torrent of tears, but Lily had finally emptied the well. The cotton sheet twisted around her thigh, and she slowly pulled it free from her weight and the rest of the bedding until it rested in a bundle between her feet. She picked up a corner and wrapped the thin fabric around her forearm.

This will do.

The nuns sacrificed the best room for their guest, giving her a nice top floor room with a balcony that overlooked the yard, the town, and the entire valley.

Dawn had not yet broken, leaving the world dark.

Like my soul.

Standing in her nightgown, Lily once again let the cold stab at her flesh as penance for her deeds. She walked over to the railing.

A jump would only break my leg, not my neck.

She sat down, not in resignation but in determination, and placed her foot against one of the square-cut railing posts. Slowly she pushed until all of her weight leaned against it. Not only did the railing push forward, but the post began to lean, slipping free from the single nail that held it into place.

The carpenter built it for appearance, not a suicide attempt.

From the depths of darkness, a shape took form, capturing her focus.

A symbolic death.

A giant willow tree stood in the front yard, its branches level with the third floor of the convent. *I used to love climbing trees as a child—when I still had a family. I could climb up into the arms of the willow, wrap the sheet around an overhanging branch, and—*

A young man approached, foiling her plan.

Under the cover of darkness, he warily jogged from the northern edge of the property, making a beeline for the willow. Once he stood under the branches, he reached down and picked up a knife on the ground. He began cutting leafless fronds down from the dormant tree.

I've seen this before …

Setting the knife back down, the young man in the black slouch hat pushed aside the curtain of the willow and stepped under its canopy.

Lily stood.

This can't be happening.

Leaving the sheet on the balcony floor, she leaned far out over it, peering to the ground below. She saw someone's feet.

My feet?

Fear did not pass through her as she climbed up onto the railing, and her toes blindly found the lattice that would act as a ladder. She didn't worry about slipping, she'd already seen herself climb down it months earlier.

When she reached the bottom, she did not turn to face the young woman now laying there. Lily knew who she was.

Instead, she followed the young man wearing her father's hat. *How did he get it? Is he one of my father's men? What's he doing under the willow?*

Lily cautiously approached, her bare feet touching the cold grass.

The fronds moved, and the young man stepped out, looking right at her. It was indeed her father's slouch hat, missing the raven wings. The young man had stolen other things as well: Migisi's mischievous smile, and eyes that belonged to—

"Lily?"

"Who are you?" she asked, but her voice spooked him, and the young man turned and ran back from where he'd come.

Willow for a dreamcatcher, Lily remembered Nanak's tutelage. *The young man came to make a dreamcatcher.* At her feet, she saw the knife, which shimmered strangely between looking rusted and new. Even holding it in her hand, the shifting reality changed. She reached up and cut a few fronds. In doing so, she noticed the other apparition.

Under the tree, an old man sat on a metal chair, its rear legs touching the trunk. He watched her approach, lifted a weak hand, and said, "You've finally come."

"Who are you?"

"Omodai," the old man answered.

"Excuse me?" Lily asked, remembering Nanak's word for jar, but the old man was not Native.

"I was marked from birth and brought to this cursed place as the main course for the feast. I've been trying to fight death my whole life, and now, at the end, I'm fighting death another way. They always say it's darkest before the dawn ..." His words trailed off. "I was beginning to think you weren't going to come." His lips quivered. "I'm afraid, Lily. I need your help. You need to find me."

"I have found you here, right now," Lily whispered. "I don't understand."

The old man lifted his hand and brushed aside the thin white hair on his scalp to reveal a birthmark. "When you sang the Song, you not only woke enemies, but you also called allies. We'll save the children together."

Lily knew the birthmark.

"Albert?"

The old man nodded. "Yes, now go make your dreamcatcher, and then we'll talk more about turning the tides of this battle. You've lost enough. Now, it's time for you to start fighting."

Old Albert faded, and Lily soon stood alone. As she stepped out from under the willow, she took the thin end of the fronds, and the cut ends, and formed a temporary loom of a new web.

Just as Grandfather taught me.

Something's Rotten

St. John, MN
April 1898

THE STAB WOUND ached, and Halvar Dobie worried the stitching might've opened up during his ride into town. As he approached the Bonnie Lass Hotel and Saloon, he pictured puss and excrement mixing together under his skin.

Beside him on horse, Walter Stewart schmoozed with locals he knew and recognized while Dobie snarled through the pain and agitation. Stewart had brought John Kirkpatrick to Dobie's new homestead on the western bank of the Blue Knife River so that they could travel together to the future location of the Nicollet Dam.

Things were happening quickly now, so Dobie tried not to be the one to slow things down. Riding around Hiawatha County all day had taken its toll, though, and he couldn't help but grunt as he dismounted his horse.

"Should I have someone fetch a doctor?" Walter Stewart asked.

"You sick, Dobie?" Kirkpatrick asked, unaware of what had happened a few weeks earlier.

Dobie scowled at Stewart for even referencing his wound in public and shook his head.

When the three men entered the saloon, everyone else was drinking at the bar. Adrianna Sinclair, the daughter and sole heir of William Sinclair, had earlier insisted her father purchase the Bonnie Lass Hotel and Saloon as part of the negotiation to visit her uncle and cousins "out west." She demanded indoor plumbing, running water, and toilets, making her hotel the most extravagant in the area while also the most raucous. Far from a classic western saloon, her saloon nevertheless had several locals sitting in booths and tables for a Saturday night meal, yet there were no prostitutes or cowboys to be seen.

Even so, Adrianna stood behind the bar, serving alcohol to her fantasized lawman Bushy Bill Morrison along with the eastern guests, Ira Douglas and Azero Gunn. All five of the Sinclair cousins had been wild during their youth back in Nova Scotia, but the youngest, Adrianna, had studied the worst behaviors of her elder cousins and perfected them. Had cousin Jack Sinclair not died in the tragic fire, Adrianna would've been a mother with children by now, but instead, she continued to host her own private party each weekend as owner and hostess of her own hotel.

Seeing her again after a few weeks, Dobie almost choked. *Oh, good God, is she pregnant?*

Independently wealthy and a thousand miles from her father, her despair after the death of Jack had turned to shameless hedonism in recent years, with Bushy Bill Morrison being the most recent to claim her bed.

Perhaps she'll go home to Nova Scotia if she's going to be a mother.

"It's good to see you looking well," Gunn greeted Dobie coyly as they reached the bar.

Does everybody know my shame?

For generations, the Dobie family served as protectors for the Grandmasters of the Order of Eos and had even served a few Scottish kings. In his youth, Dobie had participated in Highland games and could wield his family's ancestral broadsword, so it embarrassed him that he'd nearly been killed a few weeks earlier. "I certainly have regained my appetite," Dobie said, patting Azero Gunn's even larger gut. "I hope you left something for supper."

"My cooks can prepare as much supper as you can eat," Adrianna Sinclair chirped. "Shall we meet upstairs in the private lounge in an hour?"

The details were quickly decided. Walter Stewart went to go fetch his brothers-in-law while the guests retired to their second floor rooms to freshen up.

After spending the winter in the cramped hotel room, Dobie had spent the past week overseeing the construction of his new house a few miles upstream from Lake Manitou. The house was to be built on a hill between the headwaters of the Blue Knife River and the nearby Crow Wing River, with Nimrod Crossing within walking distance. The location also placed him at the center of Hiawatha County, where he could oversee all Eos business.

Back in his old room, he stripped off his riding jacket, his vest, and shirt to inspect the wound. Surprisingly, despite the pain, the wound looked secure. His fingers pressed around the scar tissue with no visible issues.

If only I'd grabbed the kid, all this talk of monsters in the water could be put to rest, Dobie thought as stripped off his shirt. He splashed some water on his face, took off his shoes, and flopped back down on his bed to collect himself for a few minutes.

With the return of Ira Douglas and Azero Gunn, the final stage of the project would begin—building the Nicollet Dam. On paper, Dobie would supervise the construction of the dam with John Kirkpatrick running it when finished. Strangely, the Nicollet Dam project had brought the two sides of the fractured family together, and Dobie could keep hotheads like Pierre Delhut from his aggressive nature and dullards like Walter Stewart from his own stupidity.

The brief rest allowed Dobie to recover, and after slipping on his vest, he checked his pocket watch.

Time to eat.

Dobie slipped on a pair of casual shoes instead of his riding boots and stepped out into the hallway of the Bonnie Lass Hotel and Saloon. He knocked on the doors of Azero Gunn, Ira Douglas, and Bill Morrison before continuing down the hall to the private dining room.

Adrianna Sinclair's blonde hair flowed over her shoulders and green velvet ballroom dress that not only revealed her ample cleavage but also the bulge at her belly.

She's indeed pregnant and too carefree to hide it.

Even though she was a woman, Adrianna was allowed to sit at the head of the table and listen to all Eos discussions. Her father William had raised her to worship the old gods and withheld nothing from his daughter.

Halvar Dobie sat at the other end of the table.

On his left, Ozias Haggard, Philip Marquette, and Walter Stewart sat in rank while on his right, Azero Gunn, Ira Douglas, John Kirkpatrick, and Bill Morrison filled the long table.

"Our generation will lay the foundation for the final stages of this grand plan," Ira Douglas explained during the main course. To the public, Triton Corporation would transform the Blue Knife River into a new logging corridor, with the dam controlling water levels to transfer product from the pine forests in the north to the saw mill in Split Rock. "Of course, our true purpose is to ensure flooding doesn't threaten our mining at Haggard Quarry."

Haggard would run the excavation and sale of quartzite products in the county, with Marquette's business branching off into gravestones and monuments—"a modest business that'll draw no attention."

"What about the Chippewa?" Morrison dramatically shifted the conversation. "We can't forget about them"

Ira Douglas shrugged and turned to Dobie, "Is there an issue still? The bridge and the dam are happening. There's no turning back now."

Keep it together, Morrison.

Something had happened to Morrison the day the posse shot and killed Andrew Thunder Face. "It's not the rest of Turtle Island Reservation that worries me," Morrison continued "As long as the Chippewa are still living in Minnesota in large numbers, we need to worry."

"We're not living in 1862 any more, Bill," Stewart said. "What's the population of Hiawatha County now?"

Azero Gunn cleared his throat. "When I began, it was about 160, but now we're well over 10,000 souls. It's more than doubled in the past ten years alone."

"I'm more than aware of the efforts of the Mahkahta Settlement Claim Association's efforts," Morrison muttered bitterly. "I got a first hand taste of it when I fell into the fucking lake. Thanks to Gunn, we're sitting on a powder keg, gentlemen, and you all act as if there's no threat to us just because we've put the matches in a drawer and locked it. Do you not know the history of this place? The Chippewa know how to start a fire, too."

God damn it, Morrison. Keep your mouth shut. Halvar Dobie not only knew where all the bodies were buried but he also knew the truth behind the settlement of Hiawatha County. Back in Albany, Azero Gunn had become a wealthy man selling land, but through his company, he determined who lived there. Azero Gunn had chosen the name of St. John and Nimrod Crossing after his father had taken the liberty of naming Hiawatha County. "Our politicians will take care of the Chippewa if you just let them do their job."

"Where there's smoke, there's fire," Morrison continued loudly. "And if none of us woke the dark spirits, then our enemies must be responsible. If you won't let me kill the Jesuit, then let me deal with the Chippewa."

"Easy, Bill," Walter Stewart added.

"Slow and steady, Morrison," Ozias Haggard joined.

Dobie could tell none of the locals understood Morrison's point except that of a racist bigot bent on genocide.

"The dark shadows are stirring," Morrison continued. "You all rejoice in the bloody deeds of Andrew Thunder Face because you can now build your dam. A man I'd known for a decade lost his mind. He didn't kill Nanak because of your bribe. Something happened to him."

Walter Stewart smirked and looked down.

"Your names are on Gunn's list, too," Morrison shouted. "Do you think it was good fortune your fathers all received such prime lots?"

"Morrison!" Dobie barked and pounded the table with a clenched fist. "That's enough."

Instead of ambition, fear motivated Morrison now. Adrianna Sinclair, who knew the true power of Eos, swept in to whisper in Morrison's ear. His anger subsided, and he composed himself. "I apologize, gentlemen. If you don't mind, I'll excuse myself and remain your humble servant. Dobie…don't underestimate our enemies."

With that, Bushy Bill Morrison retreated, and for the next hour, the story of the murder of Nanakonan was rehashed from a legal perspective, moral perspective, and finally, from a spiritual perspective.

"I didn't mean to insult Morrison," Stewart said. "If anything, I meant it as a compliment to the job he's done in obtaining those lots. I know the tales about this place. I'm not a fool."

And this is the reason I'm building a house in Hiawatha County. I just hope I don't have to kill any of these men to keep our secrets.

"Morrison serves a different purpose, just as you serve a specific purpose for Triton Corporation and also the Order of Eos. Continue to prove your loyalty, and Eos will lift your children into higher and higher positions of authority—and knowledge. Trust what we are doing, and you will be rewarded."

They all nodded, but Ozias Haggard dared to ask a question, "I'm not questioning or showing a lack of trust, but how deep do you want the quarry by 1910?"

Azero Gunn chuckled and raised his glass. "That's the spirit, Oz. That's the spirit."

TWO HOURS LATER, Halvar Dobie rested on his bed thinking of blood. His family joined the Sinclair family tree back in the 1300s, making him relatively fresh blood. Other families, however, went back to the days of the dawn.

On the other side of the wall, the Morrison and Sinclair bloodlines giggled, gossipped, and groaned. *Did Adrianna tell Morrison about the purpose of the Mahkahta Settlement Claim Association's purpose? Now she really has to go back to Nova Scotia.*

Am I dooming my own children by moving here?

Am I to be part of the great buffet?

A scream tossed Dobie from his bed.

Adrianna.

His hand found his pistol, and even though he only wore cotton drawers, he burst into the lit hallway. He put a shoulder into the locked door, and when he stumbled into the room, he found a nude Adrianna huddled in a corner of the candlelit bathroom and a nude Morrison looking down at the clawfoot bathtub.

Seeing Dobie, she scrambled from the corner and ran over to his protection, immediately hiding herself under the safety of his left arm. His gun pointed to Morrison, who kept his focus on the bathtub.

"It's gone," he muttered. "It went right back down the drain."

"It had black fingers," Adrianna added. "They reached out and took hold of my ankle. What was it? What was it?"

Dobie pushed her aside for a moment. "Get dressed," he said softly and stepped forward to confront the threat. He pointed the pistol at Morrison's chest. "Bill?"

Morrison mumbled, "It swirled around in the water for a minute and then just vanished."

Dobie studied Morrison's eyes for any signs or symptoms but only saw terror and confusion. "Get some clothes on, Bill."

There was nothing but soap suds to shoot in the tub, and as Dobie eyed the dark drain, he heard sloshing and splashing.

Azero?

"You gotta believe me," Morrison said. "Something came up out of the water."

I think I believe you.

Dobie rushed from Morrison's room to find Ira Douglas standing in the hallway. "What's happening?"

Azero Gunn hadn't bothered latching his door, but inside the bathroom door was closed. When Dobie opened it, he looked into the drowned, dead eyes of a murdered man.

Venom from the serpent's fangs.

While the Cat's Away

Split Rock, MN
April 1898

THE NEXT MORNING, Lily woke to find the three harvested lengths of willow beside her bed. With her room filled with natural light, she found a small piece of yarn, which allowed her to cross the narrow and wide end of the stick she'd taken and secure them together.

Let's see if old Albert is right …

Quickly she prepared herself for the day and sat on the edge of the bed with the loop on her lap.

The old man had spoken of loops: her loop began when Bushy Bill Morrison knocked her upside the head, resulting in her being placed upon the porch. It ended with thoughts of suicide following the trauma she'd seemingly caused, resulting in her climbing down the trellis.

Nothing can change it now. She looked in the webless loom. *It's all in the past.*

To fill the loom, Lily needed the right supplies, and nothing at Good Counsel could give her what she needed. Only home could—

She hunched forward, the pain pulsing through her body, but like wringing a wet towel, not a drop remained.

Footsteps sounded and Lily straightened as Sister Inez gently opened the door, peeked in, then stepped through. "It's good to see you awake."

Bitter thoughts bubbled in Lily's mind, but her thoughts of suicide had also been wrung dry. She nodded.

Sister Inez moved to sit beside her.

When nothing was said, Lily filled the silence, asking, "When can I go home?"

Sister Inez gulped. "Y-You're welcome to stay here as long as you need. We're all here to help you get through these dark days."

Yet more dark days are ahead. "I can't stay in this room all day."

"It appears as if God has already made plans for you," Sister Inez said, her tone hesitant. "There was an accident at the sawmill."

Lily's heart leapt. "Was it Albert?"

Sister Inez went on to speak of a man named Farrell Luning who had suffered an accident while working at the sawmill that stood over Split Rock Creek. He'd broken both legs and needed extra care that his wife Florence could not provide alone.

He broke his legs saving Albert. Young Albert.

"Would you be interested in taking on the position to help care for Mr. Luning?"

Is he one of the allies Old Albert mentioned? Lily nodded and the details came pouring out faster than Lily could process. Sister Inez left with a hug and a smug look of contentment.

It'll take more than a job to fix me.

Lily returned to her mourning, even though she could now see the end of the dark tunnel.

THAT NIGHT, BEFORE bed, she hung the frame of the dreamcatcher on the trellis railing.

Old Albert was a man of his word.

"The magic is in the willow," his voice came to her dreams. "The old tree outlived me, didn't it? Its roots connect the past, present, and future—where I am trying to help you find the right path. Let me teach you."

Lily sat up in bed, even though it was unclear if it was for real or just in her dream.

Through the frame, she saw the old man's face. "Very soon, a young man will face a critical choice. You can control the narrative. Farrell Luning will be given a choice to leave Lake Manitou, and if he does leave, the loop will be destroyed, and I will become just a dream. You can shape the future, and by doing so, you can fight the Wintermaker. This will be your first battle."

INSTEAD OF BATTLING the Wintermaker, Lily battled the Luning kitchen. A list of tasks given by Florence helped keep her mind from wandering. When Mrs. Luning returned from the mercantile store, she gasped twice upon entering her home. The first gasp came when she saw how clean her kitchen had become since earlier in the morning. The second gasp came when she saw Lily's hands.

"Oh, Lily, you have worked your hands raw!"

Lily looked down. *Red from scrubbing yet impervious to heat.* "I don't mind."

"Well I do. Farrell will think less of me if he sees how clean you have made my kitchen. I asked you to tidy up a little—I didn't expect this."

"I am sorry, Mrs. Luning."

"Don't apologize. Help me unpack these groceries."

Lily snatched up the sacks of food and set them on the kitchen table.

"You would think Kaiser Wilhelm was coming to visit," Florence commented under her breath.

"So I did well?"

"Of course you did. This is far more than I bargained for when I told Sister Inez I'd hire you to help around the house."

"I know, but work helps keep my mind off things," Lily admitted. "Besides, you have an important guest coming tonight."

"Minetta Fisher will probably try to steal you away from me, but she won't have you without a fight," Florence joked. "Is Farrell sleeping?"

Lily nodded.

"Good. I hope tonight does not tire him too much."

FOR THE REST of the afternoon, Lily helped Florence prepare the meal for the evening's festivities. It had taken only a few days for her to meet all the friends and family of the Lunings as they stopped by to call on Farrell. She knew who was to come tonight and what each of them were particular about.

At four o'clock, while the food cooked in the oven, Lily helped Florence dress her husband for the evening. What had been awkward the first few days had become second nature after a week. Soon, Farrell was buttoned and belted and carried out into the living room, where his legs were propped up in front of his chair.

And when the guests arrived, Lily hustled from the kitchen to answer the door.

"Good evening, Lily," Dr. Jenkins said, his wife silent at his side. "Could you tell Mr. Luning that Dr. Jenkins and his wife are here?"

I'm not a child. Lily submitted with a nod and motioned them inside to the dining room.

"Farrell Luning, you are not following doctor's orders very well," Dr. Jenkins declared upon seeing Farrell in a chair. "You were supposed to stay off those legs for a month."

"I couldn't entertain guests from my bed. Besides, I am quite sick of staring at that ceiling."

While Dr. Jenkins laughed, Lily decided that Florence had found herself a good man. Although Farrell looked rugged and fierce, he'd shown grace and manners during his darkest moments. He even insisted Lily call him Farrell instead of Mr. Luning, reminding Lily only a few years separated them.

"Florence, if I'm not mistaken?" Mrs. Jenkins politely greeted when Florence entered the room. "I've heard all about your husband's heroism at the mill. You must be proud."

"I couldn't be prouder."

Suddenly, all eyes turned to Lily, and she almost ran.

"Lily has been taking care of me, as you can see." Farrell smiled.

"Young lady, it is a tragedy what happened to your family," Dr. Jenkins sympathized. "What a horrible, horrible situation."

Two horribles. Lily bowed her head, unsure of what to say.

"We thank the Lord for bringing Lily into our lives. He has seen fit to test both of us, and Lily has been more than up to the challenge."

"Did you hear about the latest death?" Mrs. Jenkins asked, looking for a bit of gossip now that the pleasantries were exchanged. "George Fisher's business partner."

"Ira Douglas?" Farrell asked.

"No, the fat one," Mrs. Jenkins whispered.

"Azero Gunn?" Farrell tossed out another name Lily thought she knew.

"That's the name. Apparently, he had a heart attack and drowned to death in his hotel bathtub."

The battle rages without me. The darkness is spreading.

"That's terrible," Florence repeated, and when she put a hand upon Lily's shoulder, Lily jumped.

Hearing the names of Douglas and Gunn, she finally remembered them being mentioned in passing by either the St. John businessmen or Marshal Morrison the previous summer.

Now one of them, Azero Gunn, was dead.

Is that my fault too?

Her guilt doubled when what happened to Farrell Luning and Albert Fisher at the sawmill was retold, so when the Fisher family arrived for dinner, including Albert, Lily stayed in the kitchen, unable to face young Albert.

If I ran out of the house, my destiny would change. I have the power to destroy the loom before it has even begun.

After supper, George Fisher announced, "I came here tonight to properly thank you for saving my son's life and to reward you for your dedicated service at the mill. Dr. Jenkins said that although he managed to save your legs, you are going to struggle returning to your former abilities."

"Ah, I'm still young, I'll bounce back in no time. I can do my job with one leg, if need be. The sooner I get back to my girls, the better."

"Your girls?" Minetta Fisher asked curiously.

Farrell smiled. "My saw blades: Old Betsy, Abigail, Evangeline, and Rosemary. I need to make sure Walter Corr is brushing their teeth properly."

"You will always have a job at the Fisher Sawmill, but I want to speak to you about other opportunities."

"Oh?"

Lily peeked in from the kitchen, her eyes finding Albert.

"As you've probably heard, Triton will soon begin work on the construction of the Nicollet Dam, which means that by this fall, production at the sawmill will improve. I know how fond you are of your saws, and I hope you will take your love of mechanization into a new area. I intend to expand the lumber mill into a much larger operation that can provide all of Hiawatha County with inexpensive lumber. To do this, I need a man who could oversee the expansion of the facilities."

Behind the kitchen door, Lily slumped against the wall. *Nicollet Dam? Is my home already gone? How can they do this?*

"I appreciate your faith in me; I can take things apart and put them back together again, but I can't design machines," Farrell said humbly.

"I understand. It will take a few months for your legs to heal, and during that time, I would like to send you and Florence to Chicago to learn about some of the lumber mills there. I would pay for your travel expenses, of course, with the hope that you return next spring and oversee the changes that need to happen."

"Mr. Fisher, you offer us too much."

Lily returned to the doorway. The choice of Farrell Luning was the first string upon which everything else was built on the loom. Accepting the job would likely destroy the future described by Old Albert—he had said as much in her dream.

"I still have Albert, thanks to you. The rest of this is meaningless without him. What do you say, Farrell?"

"We have a deal, Mr. Fisher."

Albert suddenly pushed away from his spot at the table.

"Albert, are you feeling alright?" his mother asked.

The boy shook his head and bolted for the door.

Lily began to follow. "I will fetch him," she offered when his mother went for the door.

ALBERT FISHER HAD almost reached Market Street by the time Lily spotted him. Even in a dress, she easily ran him down.

"You must come back."

"I don't want to die," Albert wheezed.

"Neither do I."

He shook his head. "If I stay, it will get me."

"What will get you?"

"The Porcupine Men are hunting me. They want to give me to the monster in the lake, but they are afraid of Mr. Luning."

Just like the children in my dream. "What do you mean?" Lily asked, even as she thought of Old Albert's mention of allies and her suspicions of Luning being one were confirmed.

"Someone let them out. Now I hear them every night when I dream. They are afraid of Mr. Luning. If he leaves, they'll drag me down to the monster in the water, I know it."

"Then stay away from the water."

"What?" he asked in a whimper.

Lily moved his hair, studying the hidden birthmark. "Don't go near the lake. Dreams can't hurt you, but the water can."

"You believe me?" Albert's eyes grew wide, hopeful.

"I do," she soothed. "I did see a ghost that day when I saw you by the banks of the creek, but I think something far worse is waiting in Lake Manitou."

"What does it want?"

"I don't know yet, but I promise you, I am going to find out and stop it." Lily knew the terror in the boy's eyes was real. She was afraid too. "Have you heard of the Great Thunderbird?"

He shook his head.

"The Great Thunderbird is the enemy of the monster you saw. It flies high above Lake Manitou, waiting for the monster to come out. When it does, it will strike the monster with its bolts of lightning."

"Really?"

Lily felt Nanak's voice whispering in her mind as she replied, "The monster is a coward, which is why it tried to pick on a little boy like you." She paused and looked up to the heavens. "But the Great Thunderbird is hunting it right now, waiting for the water monster to make a mistake. And then … zap!"

Albert smiled at Lily's dramatic thunderbolt reenactment. "How do you know?"

I didn't. I'm trusting you. You saved yourself. "I learned about it from my grandfather right before he died. I'll make sure the monster goes back down from where it came, agreed, Albert?" At his nod, she added, "My friend, Father Guerin, is out there looking for answers, and when my brother Migisi gets back from his school, all of us will find a way to stop this. Do you believe me?"

He smiled.

But do I believe myself?

"There's something else I need to tell you. I had a dream about you, and others. When I first dreamed it, I didn't even know whose faces I saw, but one by one, I met the others. I think the people in the dream are protectors. I think we've been chosen to protect you from this monster."

Together we can save the children.

The faces of Bjorn Forsberg, Martin Nielson, and Kermit Crain came to her mind, joining Albert Fisher and Farrell Luning.

"I think we need to keep Luning here; don't you agree?"

Albert nodded again.

"You're not alone, Albert, and I think once I figure out a plan, you're going to live to be an old man, so don't worry about these things that are hunting you." She sighed. "But for now, you just stay away from the lake, understand?"

If my magic woke them, then I should be able to put them back where they came from. All I need is a little time to figure it out.

"Can you keep this a secret for now?"

Albert took her by the hand. "Yes, I'm glad I'm not alone."

"Until Father Guerin returns, we're going to hold steady. Agreed?"

"Agreed."

WHEN LILY OPENED the door, Mrs. Fisher and Mrs. Luning fawned all over Albert.

"Thank you, Lily," Florence whispered and gave her shoulder a squeeze.

"Mr. Luning has something for you," Minetta Fisher said to Albert once she stopped hugging him.

Albert cautiously approached the wounded lumberjack. "I wanted you to have this. I was wearing it when I jumped into the water after you."

Albert turned over the light package wrapped in tissue.

"Go ahead, open it."

The boy tore through the tissue to discover a polished wooden cross on a leather band. "I—"

"I know it doesn't look like much, but it has saved my life twice in the water. When I was a young man at your daddy's mill, I saw the largest oak tree I'd ever seen. While it was going down the chute, the old oak tree stopped the saws dead. The workers tried again, and it would go no further. Inside of this old oak was wood so dense that the metal teeth of our best blades couldn't cut it. We had to pull it out and hack around this core. I kept the heart of this tree and whittled a crucifix from it. I wanted you to have it to keep you safe."

"Can I keep it?" Albert asked with a grin, and then turned to show Lily.

Albert's mother sniffled, sharing a look with Mr. Fisher.

"Absolutely, pal."

Albert slipped the leather over his neck. He looked up at Farrell, and then over at Lily.

Lily felt jealous but tried to smile.

LATER THAT NIGHT, Lily helped Florence ease Farrell back into his bed. Although she usually kept her mouth shut and did her duty, she lingered before leaving to return to the nuns at Good Counsel.

"Albert seemed to like that gift," she said softly.

"I wasn't sure a boy of ten would appreciate it," Farrell admitted with a laugh. "That was a true story about the old oak. It really was the hardest old tree I'd ever come across."

Now, I must do my part to keep him here. "You said the crucifix saved your life twice. What happened the other time?"

Farrell's eyes widened, and for a moment, he gave her the same look Albert had given earlier. The toughened sawman turned into a frightened child. "I'd rather not talk about it."

And even though Lily nodded and joined Florence in the doorway, she knew.

Farrell Luning knows about the Manitou … Welcome to the team.

CHAPTER FIFTY-FIVE

Darkest Before the Dawn

Split Rock, MN
April 1898

WITHIN A WEEK, the new dreamcatcher was finished. After working at the Luning home, instead of walking up the hill to the convent, Lily walked toward Old Copper Road.

And now I need some answers.

Part of her wanted to find Winnie's spirit. If the spirits of the Sioux women were strong enough to haunt that road a century after their deaths, then she hoped something of her mother still existed so that she could beg for forgiveness.

Will she forgive me for what I did? Or Grandfather?

On the southern end of Split Rock, Lily walked past George Fisher's new lumber mill. She paused to measure how the landscape had been changed. The Fisher mansion once stood alone, but now acres of trees had been cleared for the big buildings. A small house had also been built—for Farrell Luning.

After Lily told him a few Chippewa tales, Luning began to connect the dots. His confession came the next day, and the following, he rejected George Fisher's offer to travel. Then Luning agreed to oversee the construction, an assistant to the hired engineer. When his wife was out of the room, Lily and Farrell shared the truths they knew.

Now I need to tell Father Guerin.

Just behind the new lumber mill and the Van Slyke creamery, the dirt road followed the slope of the Crow Wing River bank to the new trestle bridge. On the north side of town, a big, wooden covered bridge spanned the junction of Split Rock Creek and the Crow Wing River, but this bridge was built of riveted iron beams.

As Lily walked up to the trestle bridge for the first time, she noticed the pine boards placed over the metal framework were still white and full of sap. She slipped through the long metal rods that acted as a horizontal railing and sat on the edge of the deck with her feet dangling twenty feet above the Crow Wing River.

The edge of the threshold.

After weeks of respite from dreams, Tak-Pei, and the Manitou, she formed a theory that the Crow Wing River was some sort of barrier. And her Old Testament studies confirmed this theory. The Hebrews had a watery underworld called Sheol, which explained to her what happened to Jonah the prophet when he drowned. Behind the Gates of Sheol, the righteous dead were separated into something later known as Abraham's Bosom, or Paradise. The Greeks and Egyptians had a similar concept where the spirits of the dead journeyed upon this watery conduit until it led them to the Land of the Dead. Nanak had Jibay-ziibi, the River of Souls, which leads to the Land of the Midnight Sun, where her people spent eternity.

Crow Wing River flowed south, where it would join the Mississippi River, which flowed to the Gulf of Mexico and the

Greek Oceanus, where the four rivers would guide souls to the Underworld.

For everybody but the souls who die near Lake Manitou.

On the other side of the granite ridge, the souls that died in or near Lake Manitou stayed, only able to materialize as ghosts and wander a few yards from the shore before some black magic pulled them back.

Like a fur trader setting traps for wary animals, Lily hung her dreamcatcher on one of the iron beams and left it overnight to see what she would find the next morning.

Please … I need answers.

THE AIR WAS cool enough that she could see her breath when she climbed over the railing to retrieve her dreamcatcher the next morning.

A wave of disappointment overcame her when Nanak's lessons failed to produce results. She wasn't sure why it didn't work. The willow hoop that hung on the metal beam had a web similar to every other dreamcatcher Nanak made, meaning there were almost a hundred little squares and crooked rectangles formed by the threads. *Had I forgotten a step? A loop he made?*

Frustrated, Lily was about to drop the dreamcatcher into the water when she paused, hands curling around the dew-covered webs.

There, in the magical threshold that separated Lake Manitou from the rest of the world, her dreamcatcher became a window: instead of seeing right through the web, a hundred windows appeared. It confused Lily at first because the physical world remained mostly the same regardless of how she held it.

If she held it over the river, she'd see windows to the river— but not all of them were the same. In one window, she could see raging water: in another, a frozen sheet of ice.

The same thing happened when she turned it toward the trees. In the present, she would see a mighty oak along the shore, but in another, the oak would appear as a seedling. In another, it was a gnarled old log.

Then there was an eye.

She almost dropped the loom and ran, but she steadied her nerves, found the bottom window marked by one of the beads she'd obtained from the nuns, and peered right back.

Moving her face closer to the window, Lily found herself staring at a woman in her late thirties. Her auburn hair was pulled back in a ponytail. The right side of the woman's tawny face had a scarred patch of skin where her eye should have been. The one-eyed woman wore a tight-fitting undershirt, with the icon of a fierce bird upon her chest—*the Great Thunderbird*. Her eye was the color of lightning.

"Aaniin, Lily. It is nice to finally find you," the woman greeted with carefully formed syllables.

"W-who are you?"

"You shouldn't know my name. Time is very delicate," she replied, struggling through her slurred speech. "Call me … Future Spider."

Spider. "Are you a relative of mine?" Lily thought of all the children she'd seen who shared her eyes.

The woman shook her head. "No, but I do share the blood of the Wintermaker with you, which is why I am able to speak with you here. I know what the Wintermaker has done to your family, and I am here to offer my help. As you can see, he has hurt me also, physically and emotionally. Alone, we are not strong enough, but together, we can defeat him, Grandmother Spider."

"I'm not—"

"Oh, but you are, even if you don't know it yet. You are Past Spider, the one who wakes Present Spider." A smile appeared, but only on the left side of the woman's face. The muscles on the right side only pulled her face into a horrible mockery of a smile. "Look at the bead above this one. Look into that window."

Lily listened, finding a young blonde girl sitting on the deck of the bridge. In her hands, she held a brunette doll.

"Are you Grandmother Spider also?" the young girl asked.

Lily shook her head, but then heard slurred words answering the little girl: "She is the same person, Little Spider. Tell her what happened to you."

The little blonde girl showed no fear as she talked to the two women separated by time. "I rode my bike down to the bridge so I could drop rocks into the water when an old lady in a canoe came down the river."

"Tell Lily about the old woman."

"She wore a great big hat and had bright green pants. She was so old that she couldn't even climb out of the canoe. I had to come down to where she was."

The apparition I saw at Jiibay Hollow, Lily reflected. *The one holding onto the willow tree.*

"And what did she give you, Little Spider?"

"She gave me a dreamcatcher and told me that I was Grandmother Spider now."

"What else?"

"That she closed that loop and that I had to help fight the Wintermaker."

There was a short pause before the green-eyed woman asked, "Do you now understand, Lily?"

No. Have I lost my mind? "The two of you have come to help me fight the ... uh ... Horned Serpent?"

Little Spider giggled and even Future Spider found a little humor in it. "No, Grandmother Spider. We are not able to help you in the past. Unfortunately, the past is written. We are here to get your help in the present. She is the one with the plan."

The blonde girl nodded.

Future Spider wiped away the drool from the corner of her mouth. "Both of us know how you woke the Tak-Pei. We also know how you will face the Wintermaker in a few months. In the era of the Seventh Fire, a choice will be made that will determine whether the world will be destroyed or if an Eighth Fire will be lit, allowing mankind to survive. Your actions—the choice you will soon make—will ripple into the future, forcing our hands."

"We're here to make you feel better," Little Spider said with youthful enthusiasm.

"Together, the three of us—the past, present, and future—can defeat the Wintermaker, but only if we manage to trick him into thinking he has won," Future Spider explained. "The web of the dreamcatcher is complex, and there is only one thread that leads to victory, but many threads that lead to defeat. We are here to assure you of your choices."

"What sort of choices?" Lily asked.

"If we tell you too much, the Wintermaker might use it against us, resulting in even more death and darkness between us. Just like a dreamcatcher, time is a loop. You've already seen one of these loops, haven't you?"

The willow tree at Good Counsel.

"Since you crafted this loop in the past, you have the ability to break the loop and destroy all of these visions you see."

"When you're old," Little Spider added.

"We certainly hope you don't make that choice though," Future Spider added. "There are things only you are powerful enough to accomplish. We want you to know you are on the right path—and to trust the path you are on. Since both of us understand how tricky the Wintermaker can be, we want to give you something that will not only assure you but will guide you to us in the future. Would you like this gift?"

Lily had to force herself to take a breath. "I don't understand the gift."

"We will give you a secret from the future, something that will assure you in your darkest hours. It will give you faith to persevere."

"Yes, I could use a little hope."

"Go ahead, Little Spider. Tell Lily what she needs to know."

The little blonde girl gripped her doll tightly and scooted forward to whisper into the dreamcatcher. "You will visit me in the year 1986."

Lily's mind spun, realizing how old she would become and how any dangers she faced, she would somehow overcome—if she made the right choice.

Little Spider wasn't finished. "When we meet, I will ask you your name. You tell me your name is Lily Guerin." The girl smiled. "You're Joey's great-grandma."

A Wolf in Sheep's Clothing

Buffalo, NY
April 1898

JEAN NICHOLAS GUERIN walked the final twelve miles of his thousand-mile journey from Duluth to Buffalo, New York. On his right, the waters of the Niagara River grew placid as they entered Lake Ontario. Wearing a light jacket and derby hat, he twirled his walking stick feeling temporarily liberated as no one in the world knew who he was. He'd left the priestly garb of the Jesuit spy back at his hotel room, and now, for the first time since he was Lily's age, he walked as his true self.

Old Fort Niagara loomed in the distance, with its stone buildings guarding the passageway against the French, Iroquois, and English ghosts from the past. Jean knew the reason the retired fort still guarded the Great Lakes, even though the rest of the world now saw it as a tourist attraction. He looked away from the fort, finding the lighthouse, which could be seen through the budding trees that lined the river.

He came to a stop, standing, hands on hips, studying the gray door on the landward side, hearing the crash of waves on the shore along with his own breath. *I have no other choice.*

He headed across the open field and knocked on the door. A wide-eyed young man in his late teens answered, his posture one of uncertainty.

"I'm here to speak with the keeper. I'm a custodian from upriver."

"A custodian … yes, of course, come in."

The first floor of the lighthouse was a cozy combination of white stone and stained wood, with heavy beams crossing the ceiling. "I'll tell Ray you're here. He's up in the tower, probably reading. There is some leftover stew over on the stove, if you'd like it."

"I had a hearty breakfast," Jean told the young apprentice. A moment later, a portly, balding man wearing suspenders and an unbuttoned dress shirt came rushing through the doorway to the staircase. "I hear you're a custodian from upstream aways. Ray Pfarr, I'm the keeper, and this is Hugh Burns, my assistant. Can we offer you anything to eat or drink?"

"No, Hugh already graciously offered. I left a bit of a mess back where I came from, and the sooner I can get some help cleaning up, the quicker I can get back."

"Absolutely," Ray said, tidying his unkempt shirt. "Hugh, go get the horses ready, in case we need to send you out on errands."

This brought a broad grin to the young man's face, and Jean turned away. *I was thrown to the wolves at his age.*

Ray led Jean to the stairs. As they climbed, the keeper gave Jean a quick narrative of the lighthouse, which had been built in 1823, with major modifications done in 1872. "… of course, this location has been in use by custodians like yourself since, oh, the 1680s, if I remember rightly."

Ray stepped aside to let Jean take in the full view of Lake Ontario from the three-story structure. Jean took a courtesy glance before saying, "I think I'm in over my head."

"Are you now?" Ray asked. "Tell me about your mission."

My mission.

The ability to talk to another Periphery agent after so much time in isolation caught Jean by surprise, resulting in a release of sobs. He leaned forward, hands on his knees, crying so hard that he thought he might vomit. After a few minutes, the keeper's hand patted him once upon his shoulder, and the moment ended. Jean wiped his face and gritted his teeth, suppressing the emotions with a couple deep breaths.

"My apologies," he said, his head bowed.

Ray took it in stride. "I'm here to help and provide resources, but to do that, I need to understand your assignment."

Where do I even begin? "I've been deep undercover for almost a decade. My initial assignment was to investigate the Jesuit Order, which was mostly research and library work. I had access to internal documents and information going back centuries."

"For what purpose?"

Jean sighed. "A few miles from here, the Jesuits built a mission in order to evangelize the indigenous population. It was one of hundreds of missions, churches, and outposts, which was why the purpose was so easily hidden. Between the Atlantic and Minnesota, where I am stationed, the Jesuit Church created missions at Montreal, Niagara Falls, Detroit, Manitoulin Island, Sault Ste. Marie, and Madeline Island. Does that mean anything to you?"

Ray's face held honest consternation. "Well, um, they're all along the Great Lakes corridor, aren't they?"

He's in the dark about my mission. "They are the exact location of the Chippewa's westward migration, known to them as the Seven Stopping Places. You see, the Jesuit Order became obsessed with a prophecy known as the Seven Fires Prophecy, and as soon as they got a footing on the new continent, they sent many of their brightest and best to study it."

"And the Periphery sent you to find out why."

Jean shook his head. "Our superiors understood their obsession, but two hundred years ago, things went wrong, and neither ally nor enemy understood what happened. Some believed the prize was claimed; others believed the hoaxes and coverups. Regardless, the names of LeSueur and Lahontan were quickly forgotten. My interest in the matter was discovered, and I was sent from the libraries in Rome to a mountain village in the Philippines. I almost lost my life, twice, in service to the Jesuits—but I did my duty. After I almost died in Cuba, my two missions aligned. The Jesuit Order sent me to Minnesota to investigate the crisis happening with Indian reservations."

Ray sighed and shook his head. "You'll have to excuse my ignorance on the matter. What crisis?"

"It began with the Dawes Act in 1887, which is an attempt to break up tribal lands by giving them to the individual so that pressure can be applied by local businessmen to acquire the land privately. It's happening all across the nation, but once again, the Jesuit Order became fixated on the lands of the Seventh Stopping Place—Minnesota."

"You sound like you're on top of this. Why do you think you're in over your head?"

"When I came, I thought it would be similar to my mission in the Philippines and Cuba, where I was to organize local support and, if needed, militarize the oppressed population to fight against the turning of the tide. But I've encountered a formidable enemy."

Triton. The international network of companies went far beyond the local businessmen in St. John and had enough clout to buy politicians at the national level. While the eyes of the nation focused on how the law impacted tribes in Oklahoma, the center of the attack came in Minnesota.

"So you've come to me for help," Ray answered. "What do you need?"

"I've made a real mess of things. Lives have been lost. Innocent lives." Jean had been in Detroit when he received the telegram about the murders of Nanakonan and Winnie. *How can I ever face Lily again?* "I had to break cover to come here. I needed to let someone in the Periphery know."

"Know what, exactly?"

The Philosopher's Stone is hidden somewhere in Hiawatha County. "I need a scholar, an expert in Anishinaabe beliefs. I don't even know if we have an agent like that … If we did, what was the point of sending me? To make a mess of things?" Guerin felt all of his mistakes twisting in his gut. "I need a man who can come to this school I'm building without raising suspicions in the Catholic Church. If the Jesuits get cold feet and withdraw their funds for the school, I have no play remaining. I need someone who can act as a guardian after this crisis ends. Our enemy is moving quickly."

And Lily is all that remains.

"Why not ask for more than one Periphery agent then?"

Jean thought back to his earliest training in the depths of Rome. "How much did the Periphery teach you about the Order of Eos?"

The enthusiasm in Ray's face faded. "Eos? That's your enemy?"

Jean nodded. "It's like a spider web spread over the whole place. If I touch one thread, the entire web vibrates. Even by myself, I've gotten stuck at times, but if I bring too much help, all the traps set by Eos will be sprung."

"Yes, I understand your reason to be cautious. Are you sure it's Eos and not other forms of … villainy?"

Jean nodded his head. "Yes, the Order of Eos has been interested in the region for … generations. If we rush this, or have a sudden show of force, they might panic and do something catastrophic. And then where will we be? My predecessor Nicollet went charging in a generation ago, unaware that he was aiding the

Order of Eos. While he didn't acquire the asset, his actions told them enough. If we don't act quickly, I believe the Order of Eos will not only kill the remaining family members but might threaten the entire Ojibwe nation."

Ray's jovial face grew solemn. "Well, this is the most excitement this old lighthouse has seen in years."

"The Jesuit Order is still trying to understand what went wrong two centuries ago, but I couldn't risk involving them more, nor could I risk attempting correspondence with the Periphery. I knew this place was a safehouse, a place of extraction, which is why I came here."

"Of course. Yes. I understand … some of it. But you plan on returning?"

"As soon as the Jesuit Order sent me to Hiawatha County, Eos was already there, watching my every move, so as long as I react to their moves, I doubt they worry about me too much. To these local businessmen, I'm just a pebble in their shoe. They're ramping up operations, though, from the legal measures to remove the Chippewa to damming the river and developing a quarry, they are about to do the most ambitious excavation since Pierre-Charles LeSueur went to King Louis to fund a copper mine."

"Son, you'll have to excuse my ignorance. The Periphery has agents out on all sorts of missions, which I never understand. I'm just the keeper of this lighthouse. If you need out, I'll get you out. If you need aid, we'll make the request to provide it. I have no idea what you're talking about, but I can see how you're rattled by your discovery. Tell me what I'm supposed to do."

I need to get back to her, to protect her because Triton waited until I left to begin wiping out the family.

Jean quickly regrouped. "Start with finding an agent well-versed in Anishinaabe lore. I can't rely on a sixteen-year-old girl for my decisions."

Yet Lily knew about the Philosopher's Stone, or Water Drum, as she called it. Numerous names, multiple mythologies, but it was the same object. *If Joseph Nicollet had managed to gain access to the cave, things would be so different now.* Instead, Jean was left with the scattered pieces of the puzzle, which only now were taking form.

"Anything else?" Ray asked.

What happens if I do find it? Do I bring it back to Rome? Will it be hidden again? Do I hand it over to the Jesuits and let them decide? "I need an extraction plan, starting in Hiawatha County. If it all falls apart, I might need to move the girl and the asset at the drop of a hat."

Lily… Nanakonan and Winnie were lost, Migisi taken, and Big Squeak was in custody. *She's the only link to the Philosopher's Stone now. But if I whisk her away into protective custody, it will only affirm matters to Eos.*

"And I'll need an invisible flow of cash. The Catholic Church has funded my new Jesuit school, but I need it to be a stronghold for our fight to come. I can't wait for bids and paperwork to be processed. I want that school built as fast as possible with workers I can trust."

If it's not too late already.

What's in a Name?

Split Rock, MN
May 1898

LILY GUERIN? THE idea festered in Lily Weber's brain. It disgusted her. It angered her. It intrigued her. *Am I destined to fall in love with a priest? Am I already in love?*

Each day after finishing her work at the Luning house, she would sit out on the balcony, look up at the stars, and ponder her future.

Each night, the same greeted her—

Venus, the Roman goddess of love.

Lucifer, the Hebrew Light-bearer, or Satan.

Ikwe'anung, the Women's Star.

Waabun'anung, the Morning Star.

Ningobi'anung, the Evening Star.

Stars connected her to the past, and she felt a strange assurance knowing that despite how the world changed, the stars would remain the same. These same stars could also be seen in the present by her brother Migisi, the last of her family. Lily also knew that whatever happened in the coming months, the stars would be the same in her future—a future with Jean Guerin?

Mother sensed it. She saw the way I acted around him.

Whore, Jezebel, Delilah. The seduction of a priest had to bring some sort of damnation with it, even though Lily had no plans of seducing him.

To the north, Lily saw a shimmer of color: Jiibayag niimi'idiway—Spirits Dancing. She pondered the scientific phenomenon known as the Northern Lights, wondering if it was a good or bad omen. Or if they were just electrical charges in the atmosphere.

Her eyes next found the Milky Way, which her people referred to as the River of Souls. The River led to the Pleiades, which the nuns in Morris taught were named after seven sisters from Greek mythology, but to Nanak, it was the hole in the sky, the gate to the afterlife.

Winnie took pride in being a Catholic, and her expectation was to join her savior in Heaven … Yet what if she was imprisoned in the waters of Lake Manitou? Suddenly the thought of saving the children went beyond the present and future.

Is that my quest? To save all souls trapped in this forsaken place?

Thinking first of her mother and then of the trapped souls, her eyes wandered to the far north and Ursa Major, the Great Bear. She usually remembered the story of Wishwee and the Great Bear from her mother when seeing Ursa Major, but it was the story of the Fisher Cat that entertained her mind now.

She remembered Nanak's intensity as he tried to explain to her the importance of the relationship of the Fisher Constellation and the North Star. In the legend, the Fisher Cat battled the Wintermaker of the North to help free the trapped souls.

The Fisher Cat, the triumphant hero who freed the souls from captivity.

Hero … Now I'm supposed to be the hero.

Both the past and the future looked to her. Were waiting on her.

Beside her on the balcony, the dreamcatcher remained silent. The magic within the loom had been used to speak with the Spiders. In front of her, hundreds of branches from the willow tree held answers, but Lily had no desire to crawl under it again.

The apparition of Old Albert had been right about Farrell Luning's decision, and if the rest was true, dark days loomed ahead.

LILY WOKE TO the sound of a horse galloping up the hill to Good Counsel. The heavy hooves were urgent and stopped suddenly.

By the time she sat up and peered over the balcony, the horse she heard was already tied to the post at the north side of the building.

Moments later, she heard voices from the hallway, the door opened, and one of the nuns stood, baffled for a moment, until she saw Lily on the balcony. "Father Guerin has returned," she said. "He needs to speak to you downstairs."

My hero has returned, but I don't want it to be true.

I can't …

Lily paused for a moment, collecting her strength, then bolted out of the bedroom, down the stairs, and rushed into the foyer.

Guerin stood waiting, his riding cassock filthy from the muddy roads. Lily realized she wore only her sleeping gown right before she threw her arms around him.

She embraced the dream.

She held on to a promise.

She clung to her destiny.

From the doorway to the foyer, Sister Inez cleared her throat with disapproval, but Lily held on until she felt her tears soaking the black fabric on his chest. Guerin's body seemed tense, but he gently patted her back and didn't push her away.

"I'm sorry," Lily finally said and stepped back to wipe her face. "I'm just so happy to see you."

"We need to talk," Guerin said somberly, and his lack of emotion felt like a kick in the stomach. "Go get dressed, and I will tell you."

I already know. Lily nodded and obediently walked to where Sister Inez motioned her.

A few minutes later, she joined him in the foyer again.

Guerin held a black hat. "On my return home, I received some horrible news. Your father died in prison."

Lily curled her legs to her chest, wrapped her arms around them, and leaned into the cushion of the couch.

"The circumstances behind it—"

"Stop. Just stop talking," Lily muttered. Closing her eyes, she sank into the depths of darkness for several minutes.

'When you sang the Song, you not only woke enemies, but you also called allies.'

Lily pulled the reminder close to her heart.

I am not alone in this fight.

The spiders had answered the call, but instead of a small loop, they previewed future decades in the making. *I will find a way through this.*

When she swam back to the surface, she asked, "My brother is in danger, isn't he?"

Guerin nodded. "That is why you won't be staying here any longer. I'm bringing you back to the Turtle Island Reservation with me."

"I'm not going back there," Lily snapped. "You don't know what happened."

"I understand some of it," he countered, which caused her to sigh and look away from his sincere but naive face.

Lily couldn't find the words to tell him about the Wintermaker.

Or the Tak-Pei.

Or the ghosts.

Or the Song.

"What do you think you know?" she asked, weary.

Guerin looked to confirm the nuns had left the room before he spoke softly, "A rumor has gone out through the reservations that the blood of the Wijigan Clan has been found."

The words cut right to the core, but Lily tried to protect what remained. "What does that mean?"

"A religious revival has been taking place in Canada by a Mide who believes a messiah figure will come to lead the people to a great victory, but there are people who will do anything to stop this from happening. Dangerous people."

Did one of those people kill my father in his prison cell?

"As soon as I get you back to the school, I am going to Morris to get Migisi and bring him back."

"School?"

"Construction began two weeks ago," he replied and tried to smile. "I have men there that can protect you and your brother while I get to the bottom of all of this."

"But how can you …?"

"Take him?" Guerin supplied, looking over his circular spectacles at her. "On my way east, I spoke to your father while he was in prison. He understood the danger you and your brother were in. He signed papers making you and Migisi wards of the church."

"Wards?"

"I have become your legal guardian, in a way, which allows me to get Migisi and bring him home."

Fool, Lily thought to herself. *He's not going to be your husband. He sees you as a child, still. Lily Guerin? Is that how … Is that what the young Spider meant?*

Father Guerin suddenly leaned forward but instead of launching himself from his chair, he doubled over, putting his elbows on his knees and his face in his hands. He sat like that motionless for a minute or so until Lily realized he was crying.

It surprised her to see her champion showing such unexpected vulnerability.

Shouldn't I be the one crying?

What does he have to cry about?

She watched the priest slowly pull himself together after a few minutes.

"I never knew my parents, so I cannot possibly fathom your loss, Lily. But I also grew up as a ward of the church, so I do grasp what it feels like to have no one." He made a frustrated sound. "I came to Minnesota because I wanted to protect your people, but now my efforts seemed to have spun out of control. I may have revealed your family as the last of the Wijigan."

That's why he cries? "This isn't your fault," Lily told him but again could not find a way to talk openly about the Wintermaker. "There were three elders who visited Nanakonan last summer. Any of them could have spread these rumors."

"The world has learned you and Migisi have the blood of the Wijigan, and I will do everything I can to protect you, but to best protect you, I think it is time you tell me about what your grandfather taught you."

Now?

He leaned closer, eyes intent.

How did I entertain thoughts of loving him? He just wants my secrets.

Lily looked away. "Bring my brother safely back to me, and then I will tell you everything."

Transformation

Turtle Island Reservation
May 1898

IN THE SPAN of a few short months, Lily's world had changed.

At Lyons, the grass had already reached up from the earth to surround the saloon, house, and other buildings. The camp of engineers had doubled in number, and the road continued straight for the Blue Knife River, where a bridge spanned it.

Sitting beside Guerin, Lily followed the curve in the road that led to Nimrod Crossing far to the north. She closed her eyes as they passed by her grandfather's property, but when they neared her home, Guerin explained why the wagon did not stop.

"I had all of your belongings brought to DeSmet Hall, where they are safe and dry. Once the girls' dormitory is built, we can bring them down there."

Even from a mile away, Lily could see the new buildings of the school. In her dreams, she had hoped for a simple white building with a bell, but Guerin obviously had grander plans, as he explained to her during the tour.

Turtle Island Jesuit School was a campus of flags and stakes. The Superintendent's Office was a three-room brick building in the middle of campus built under a big oak tree. Three separate crews of men worked on three different areas.

On the north edge of campus, a crew finished the roof of DeSmet Dormitory, which would eventually house nearly a hundred boys. In the middle of campus, near the edge of the wooded ravine, another crew of a dozen men dug the foundation for the Academic Building. Two hundred yards to the south, walls and rafters were being raised for Vandevelde Dormitory, which would house fifty girls. A fourth building, the stable, had been built along the edge of the ravine.

Guerin explained every stake and flag of what would become a community of thirty buildings when finished.

At the time, the membership of Turtle Island Reservation was one—Lily.

FROM THE SUPERINTENDENT'S Office came Paul White Wolf. "You must be Lily. I'm pleased to meet you. Father Guerin has told me so much about you."

Paul White Wolf looked the part of a school superintendent, with his monocle, pleated trousers, and shiny shoes. He was a Potawatomi Indian who'd left Michigan for a formal education in England.

His right-hand man, and quite obviously, a spy of sorts.

"Mr. White Wolf will run the school this fall, and while I am gone, you can rest assured knowing you are safe in his care."

They spent a few minutes exchanging pleasantries before Guerin motioned for her to follow him. "Let me show you to your temporary room."

He brought Lily to DeSmet Hall, which despite not being finished yet, was complete enough to hold her belongings.

"I'll leave tomorrow morning for Morris to get Migisi. You can take some time to sort through these belongings from your house."

"What about Nanak's belongings?"

Guerin froze, averting eye contact when she looked at him. "Mr. White Wolf scoured through the ruins and collected them. He has what could be salvaged in a chest at his office. The dam construction is happening just downstream from his old cabin, but the land is now claimed by Triton Corporation."

"How?"

"The lawyers from Triton are using some antiquated laws that claim the land passed to the Dakota tribe due to conquest."

"Conquest? It was murder." Lily pictured the crazed eyes of Adam Thunder Face, seeing an evil spirit within him—a spirit she'd woken. Now, she wondered if he'd simply been hired by Triton.

"The courts saw it differently. It's fallen into legal limbo. Technically, the land still remains part of the Turtle Island Reservation, but privately, it is claimed by Triton. Possession is nine tenths of the law, and Triton is wasting no time as we try to fight this in court." He glanced at her. "Is there anything I need to know about Nanak's property?"

So ... he already knows. Or suspects something. Lily lowered her head. "Yes. Somewhere on his property, he had a secret hiding place. I just don't know where it is."

"What kind of secret hiding place?"

A hiding place for the Philosopher's Stone. Lily shot him a cold glare, staying silent. *Do you need me to say it aloud?*

Her time away from home had also given her a better understanding of the legend from across the Atlantic. For thousands of years, the Philosopher's Stone drove men to madness. From kings to scientists, the quest for the enigmatic stone ranged from spiritual enlightenment to frenzied greed. Most legends described it simply: a stone that could transform lead into gold. Yet other legends connected it to darker spiritual purposes, including immortality—Lily's connection to her legends of the Wintermaker and Wishwee.

Guerin did not press. "While I'm away collecting your brother, I'd like you to give Mr. White Wolf a tour of the property, from your perspective. Mr. White Wolf and the other men here will protect you. They understand."

No. No, they don't understand. And neither do you.

GUERIN LEFT THE next morning for Morris, a hundred miles away near the border of South Dakota. To distract herself from his departure, she went to find her family's belongings.

Sorting through what remained proved painful, and after hours of crying, Lily found herself knocking on the door of Paul White Wolf.

I've summoned allies, too. "I need your help," Lily began when the door opened.

"What kind of help?"

"I know you belong to the same people that sent Father Guerin, and I think I understand what you're looking for, but if we're going to be allies, I need a few things to prepare for the fight. You're more than just a school superintendent, right?"

He studied her, making Lily suddenly feel naked in front of him. Finally, his eyebrows raised. "'Better the devil you know than the devil you don't know.' You want to get to know me?" At her nod, he sighed. "Yes, Miss Lily, I belong to the 'same people' that sent Jean Nicholas to seminary school, even though I only met him a few weeks ago. And yes, I am more than just a school superintendent, but then again, you are more than just an aspiring schoolteacher, are you not?"

He let go of the door, leaving it ajar. He circled her where she'd stopped in the center of the room. "I am not new to this quest, even though I have become one of your knights sworn to defend you. I don't need you to explain the Seven Fires, the symbolism of the Water Drum, or even the truth about the Wijigan. While Father Guerin recovered in a Georgetown Hospital, he read my studies and reports of the Anishinaabe, from my Potawatomi perspective, of course. In the old Grail legends, the most experienced knights failed while the pure of heart managed to find the Cup of Christ and save the kingdom. And if I'm going to play the role of Paul White Wolf, I need to know if Lancelot and Guinevere are sleeping together."

"Excuse me?"

"I can't allow a priest to sleep with one of my teachers. Is that clear?"

"Yes. But … but … no, it's not like that at all." Lily felt as if her ears were on fire and her heart would pound right out of her chest. *Is it really that obvious?*

"Then explain the nature of your relationship so I can understand it. From the way he talks about you, I can tell he's holding back, and it's quite obvious that you no longer see him as a religious authority. We can't have this in the days to come." At her silence, he prodded. "So?"

She shook as she released the breath she was holding. "I can't … I've … Nothing has happened, nothing even close. No kisses. Nothing like that. I've just had …"

White Wolf nodded for her to continue.

"I've had dreams, and not improper dreams like a schoolgirl with a crush." She raised her chin, defiant now against the implications he had made. "If you know the truth about the Wijigan, then you know the truth about my family. I've seen things that I can't unsee. I've had visions while I'm wide awake. These dreams I have, some of them have come true already, but I don't know if I'm forcing them to come true of if they are destined."

White Wolf's piercing eyes held focus for a few moments later, and then the kindly superintendent returned as his stance relaxed.

"I see. I apologize for throwing these accusations at you, but I need you to understand that—"

"Oh, I understand," Lily interrupted. "And I'm glad you brought it up. It's not like I want to feel this way about him … if I did. I can talk to him about some things but then I can't act—"

"You are right. We are allies, but if I am to do my job properly, I can't let this relationship continue, or else things will unravel when the school opens. Do you understand?"

"I do."

"Now tell me more about these dreams of yours."

A FEW MINUTES later, Paul White Wolf sat in the back of the birchbark canoe as Lily gave him a tour down the river.

Immediately she had noticed the footings for the dam were already in place, yet the water continued to flow around them. A bit farther, the new bridge passed over the river on its way to St. John, leaving Lily a bit speechless.

When the canoe entered the open waters of the lake, Mr. White Wolf asked, "Where are we going?"

Wordlessly, she took him to Jiibay Hollow.

"I don't know the extent of your skillset, but I figure Father Guerin hired you for a reason. Pay attention to anything you see or hear. The last time I came here, they tried to murder me."

"They?"

Lily did not try to explain the Tak-Pei, and as she stepped ashore, she felt secure, leading White Wolf along the trickling stream. At the sound of wings, her heart leapt until she saw a flock of ravens lift into the sky, their eyes upon her.

I must be close.

From both sides of the rocky ravine, the branches of the trees touched, making a tunnel of foliage. The ascent of the creek was almost as steep as its banks, and each step forward meant climbing over boulders.

Finally, Lily stopped in front of the grand willow.

It was twice the size as the one at Good Counsel, and its branches filled the space of the ravine, from the roots sunk into the creek bed to its canopy that almost blocked out the sun.

"Impressive old tree," White Wolf said, catching his breath with his hands on his hips.

You have no idea.

Lily quickly harvested the descending branches, avoiding whatever might be lurking in the shadows near the trunk.

"For making dreamcatchers," White Wolf surmised as she worked.

"We're going to need all the help we can get," Lily explained.

A SHORT TIME later, her father's canoe was secure back near her old home, but the expedition was not over. "Let me show you the place where we found the megis shells."

Near the place where Migisi battled the big snapping turtle, Lily brought her new ally. Her fingers began to comb the ground for another, but in doing so, she thought of all she'd lost.

I'm sorry. So sorry.

She began to cry.

Paul White Wolf let out a long sigh, as if annoyed, but a second later, she heard a metallic click. Turning, she saw him holding a cocked pistol in his hands. Her eyes followed the barrel to the opposite shore.

"Don't shoot," Lily said through her tears. "I know him."

Kermit Crain stood, slack-jawed, with a small pocketknife extended. He wore rugged denim and thick flannel. He tilted his head like a curious puppy and then a half-smile formed on his face. "Miss Lily? Is that you?"

"Why are you holding a knife, Kermit?"

His dark eyebrows almost joined, and his square jaw clenched tightly. "I followed it here." Kermit turned and pointed to the western shore in reference to his home at Sterling Junction.

"What did you follow?"

A bit of boyishness returned as he wrinkled his forehead a little, avoiding her question to ask, "Who's that with you?"

"This is Mr. White Wolf. He's the new superintendent of the school. He's a friend."

White Wolf carried the same somber curiosity as he asked, "What were you following?"

Kermit looked up and down the river before sighing in resignation. "I was hunting the Manitou."

Lily glanced at White Wolf and saw how he didn't laugh or smirk. "But the Manitou isn't real."

"Yes, it is. I saw it. It tried to kill me while I was fishing along the cattails on the western shore. My dad said I was only dreaming, but I know what I saw."

Hesitantly she asked, "What did you see?"

"I didn't see it well—just one tentacle, I think. It tried to pull me into the water, but I stabbed it."

"You stabbed it?"

"It bled all over me. I stayed away from the lake after that, but it kept showing up in my dreams." He looked at the knife he still held. "Once, there was a boy who picked on me at school. He was a lot bigger, and I was scared of him for the longest time. My father told me the only thing to do with a bully is punch him in the nose when he's least expecting it, so I've been hunting it before it decides to hunt for me."

"But you can't punch the Manitou in the nose."

Kermit smiled and nodded. "Yes, you can. I snuck into St. Marie's Catholic Church and stole water from the baptismal fountain. I soaked my castration knife in the water and sprinkled it over my clothes. I went back to the same spot in the reeds to face the Manitou, but it was afraid to face me." He grinned. "I even pissed in the water to show him I wasn't afraid."

A fearless ally. Lily's thoughts then turned to Migisi's boasts of using a turtle shell as a shield against the Manitou. "You followed the Manitou here?"

"No, it sent the Lucharachain after me."

"I don't know what that word means."

Kermit shrugged, finally lowering his curved blade. "Little gray demon men?"

The Tak-Pei.

"I was afraid of them at first," Kermit tucked the knife into a belt loop, "but then I realized they could only stand near the water, so I tracked them from land … Now I'm hunting them too."

How can he be so flippant? So unconcerned? "But they are spirits. How can you hurt a spirit?"

"I thought they were spirits too, but a spirit can't leave footprints, can it?"

Footprints?

White Wolf walked down to the very edge of the water and studied the bank. "What do you mean?"

"I tracked the Little People here after the last rain. They're small but have big feet."

"Show me," White Wolf commanded, and began crossing the water to the other side.

Kermit knelt.

Curious, cautious, Lily moved to join them.

And there, along the soft mud collected between the rocks, was a real footprint.

"See? I followed it from the edge of the quarry all the way to here. It led me right up the hill, but I lost its trail in the rocks. I think it crossed the river."

A few minutes later, the three picked up the tracks again.

They headed north, to the school.

CHAPTER FIFTY-NINE

The Freckled Bear

Turtle Island Jesuit School
May 1898

BY EVENING, THE threat was determined to be real, and despite the absence of Father Guerin, the entire school transformed from workers to warriors.

Lily found herself alone in the backroom of the Superintendent's Office for the rest of the day, but she was able to peek out the office window to watch the search.

Finally, at supper, White Wolf returned with an explanation. "It turns out your friend's leprechaun is most likely an adult Chippewa, from the type of moccasin prints we found going north."

"Where's Kermit?"

"Oh, he left a while ago, with the promise to stop being so foolish. I want you to be a soul of caution also. Stay where we can see you. While the person seems to have gone north, we still need to be careful."

"Who am I supposed to be afraid of? Who was it?"

"My first thought is that Triton hired somebody to put on moccasins to throw us off the trail. But they own the new quarry and dam and have little reason to harass us now that they have what they want. Most likely, it is just some curious loner who heard about the new school."

Noticing his hesitation to answer, she prompted, "Or?"

"It's probably nothing. Father Guerin ordered me to keep you safe, and that's what I plan on doing. For tonight, you can take my quarters and I'll sleep out here. Just to be sure."

Pillagers?

Lily went to bed thinking of the old blood feud between her family and the Pillagers who once took the Nicollet Expedition prisoner and later killed her great-grandfather. Chief Sweating Stone now fought to preserve the ancestral lands of Leech Lake. *Is the school a problem for him?*

Torches and rifles were set down the next morning for saws and hammers, yet Lily was instructed to still stay put.

A wagon full of lumber sent the men into motion, and when the hammering began, she went out to sit on the porch of the Superintendent's Office.

That was when Bjorn Forsberg came strolling across the yard. The freckled, red-haired Swede wore denim overalls and a plaid shirt, but he stood so straight he looked more soldier than farmer, and when he stopped in front of her, she half expected him to salute.

"Is Mr. White Wolf inside? He has to sign a slip for me."

"He's busy doing paperwork right now."

Lily tried to lock eyes with him, but he looked down as he walked past her. *A Sioux marrying a Chippewa is one thing, but a Native marrying a Swede?* Both Lily and Bjorn were now sixteen, and courtship and marriage were expected of both of them.

She shook her head. *No, I can't marry Bjorn or anybody else. I'm either going to marry Jean Guerin or…take his last name? Is that what the vision meant? In becoming a ward, do I take on his last name? Lily Guerin? No, that's adoption. He didn't adopt us. He's only our legal guardian. This is all too much.*

After getting his signature from Mr. White Wolf, Bjorn's heavy boots crossed the covered porch, but when he reached the stairs, he paused. "How've you been?"

In all honesty, Lily found him to be one of the most unattractive boys she knew. His freckled neck had caked-on grime of barn dust and dirt from the road. His short-sleeved shirt was stained yellow under the armpits, and even at a distance of ten feet, she could smell his body odor.

She'd stopped helping with Sunday school after the attack, and she hadn't been to Split Rock since Guerin brought her to the school. She missed her children. She missed her family. "I've been well, Bjorn, how about you?"

Lily studied his face. Bjorn was nervous, as if he wanted to say something she might not appreciate. "I bought a new shotgun for hunting birds in the fall. I've been making lots of money hauling lumber for Mr. Fisher."

"Do you ever see Albert?"

Bjorn shook his head, after his blue-gray eyes searched for something in her expression he turned away. "Have a pleasant day."

That's it? "You too, Bjorn."

Lily watched him slowly walk back to his wagon. "Wait!"

Bjorn pivoted; his hands clenched in front of his belly. She took a few steps forward and stopped. "Thank you for … everything. I'm glad you're my friend."

Her words straightened Bjorn's back and his chest inflated. "Of course, Miss Weber."

She was relieved at his words yet angered. *Why can't anyone see me for who I am? To Guerin, I'm a child. To Bjorn, I'm just a teacher.*

Bjorn's empty wagon headed down the long driveway before turning north toward the Nimrod Crossing road and she turned away. *Perhaps I'm not destined to find love? It hurts just waking up each day.* Neither the thought of curious Bjorn nor dashing Guerin could rekindle her heart to feel what she'd once felt for Samuel Thunder Face.

Then how can I ever have a great-grandchild?

The young spider said a name … Joey.

When Lily went to head back inside, she stopped, watching: two men came walking around DeSmet hall and into the open yard. There was hammering coming from inside the nearly finished dormitory, but as they grew closer, she noticed two peculiarities. First, they carried a big burlap sack that obviously looked empty as it lightly flapped between them. Second, their faces were strangely white.

So white, in fact, that Lily didn't even notice they were Chippewa until it was too late. Their painted faces were meant to resemble skulls, and as her mind tried to process it, all she could do was stand up.

That was when another man jumped onto the porch, slipped a strong hand over her mouth, and pulled her off the porch where the two other men waited.

With one quick punch, a smaller man hit her so hard in the belly that Lily thought she'd never breathe again. She would have collapsed into a ball if the third man hadn't covered her mouth while keeping her upright.

A moment later, she was being lifted and dropped into the big burlap sack.

She couldn't scream.

She couldn't kick.

She couldn't even see.

But Lily felt herself bouncing along as the men began to run.

Then she heard a gunshot and a strange grunt beside her. *White Wolf had been filing the paperwork. He must've seen something.*

Still she bounced along, listening to the breathing of three men until she heard a horse and felt things grow darker. *I'm in the woods of the ravine.*

Then her shoulder struck the ground, and a moment later, she was rolling, allowing the burlap sack to come off partly.

When hands reached for her feet, Lily kicked, and kicked, and kicked. Again, she felt herself being lifted, but this time, instead of just being carried, she felt herself being thrown over a man's shoulders—

A school bell rang in the distance.

A moment later, Lily was dropped again. She felt a wobble that turned into a smooth glide; she was in a canoe.

To get across the Blue Knife, her abductors would need to paddle. As soon as the pressure on her legs eased, she kicked and wiggled to reposition her body—not to run but to roll.

Long ago, when the local Pillagers learned a Wijigan priest brought a zhaaganaash to the Blue Knife River, they risked the wrath of the government to stop him. *Will these men burn me at the stake, too?*

She swung all of her weight to a single side, and before even she knew what was happening, the shock of the water had her gasping.

Struggling, she wiggled until she was free of the burlap bag and kicked towards the surface. Two men in a second canoe immediately appeared beside her but Lily took a deep breath before sinking into the current. Then she kicked and kicked and kicked like a snapping turtle avoiding capture until her hands struck rocks.

A moment later, she was scrambling onto shore as her abductors floated in the current.

Lily managed to scramble up ten yards of shore before two Chippewa men sprang from their canoe to give chase. She glanced back and fought the wave of helplessness already—

Turning around, her eyes caught a flash of color, causing her to duck.

Bjorn Forsberg appeared from behind a tree, and in one quick motion, swung his shotgun like a broadsword to catch the closest attacker in the face, spinning him wildly in an explosion of blood and teeth. Flipping the shotgun around, he pointed it right at the second attacker, who immediately turned and leapt into the current of the river. Bjorn turned the shotgun again, and with the stock of the rifle, landed two heavy blows to the midsection of the man wiggling on the ground.

Moments later, half a dozen men carrying guns appeared at the top of the ravine.

Exhausted, Lily wrapped her arms around Bjorn's smelly plaid shirt and hugged him tight. *This is the third time he's saved my life.*

It didn't take long for Mr. White Wolf and the other men to peel her away from Bjorn, who received a flood of congratulations.

"I'll get Constable Graham," someone suggested.

"No," White Wolf answered bitterly. "Not him. He can't be trusted. Clark, I need you to ride to Wadena and find Sheriff John Eddy. If you see Marshall Morrison or any other unfamiliar lawman when you arrive, walk away, understand?"

"I understand."

But I don't understand. I don't understand any of it.

THAT EVENING, SHORTLY after Lily ate supper, a familiar wagon pulled into the school yard. The construction workers watched as Guerin's wagon came to an abrupt halt. Instead of running to it, she felt her knees weaken as she sank onto the floor of the porch. She couldn't take any more bad news. *What if something bad has happened to Migisi?*

Lily, unable to stand, still tried to remain optimistic, thinking of everything the apparitions had told.

But what if ...

"Hey, Tew."

Confession

Turtle Island Jesuit School

June 1898

THE SOUND OF construction woke Lily from her sleep. With each passing hour, the school grew—a promise fulfilled. Just as the brick buildings were built upon secure foundations, she knew her spiritual alliance was built on a foundation of lies that would crumble later if she didn't do something soon.

On the other side of the room, Migisi slept, his belongings strewn in a space intended for a dozen boys. In the days since his return, Migisi grew more solemn. Lily reminded herself that he was also dealing with the loss of his family, but the glances he gave her were hurtful, and he seemed to avoid her on purpose.

When he slept, though, he remained the same boy who had been taken so long ago.

He's finally home—but is it too late? Even though she wanted to smother Migisi in more hugs, she let him sleep. She quickly dressed and waited on the front steps of the dormitory.

Lily had no choice. She had to tell Guerin everything.

Guerin and White Wolf both came out of the office at the same time, already in the middle of a conversation. When they noticed her, it was Guerin who hesitated.

How to begin?

The choices overwhelmed her, and her plan changed with each long stride he took towards her. Nearing her, White Wolf slowed, calling out a greeting as he passed. "Good morning, Miss Lily."

"Good morning," Guerin said next, his toes in front of her. *No more half-truths. Talk to him.* "Do you have time to talk?"

"I do."

Lily hummed. "Do you have a pistol?"

"I do."

"Then let's go find a place at the river."

She stood, leading him back to the place where Bjorn Forsberg had saved her days earlier from an abduction attempt. Although White Wolf and Sheriff Eddy had been baffled by the skull-faced prisoner, Guerin immediately interpreted what it meant and who sent them—Triton. Lily trusted his knowledge of villains.

Upon reaching the Blue Knife River, Lily found a large, bench-sized stone to sit upon, prompting Guerin to join her.

"Do you believe in prophecy?" she began.

"Yes, I do, however slippery it might be."

"Do you believe in destiny?"

"In a manner of speaking, yes."

"And do you believe in God?"

He scoffed. "He is known by many names and qualities, but yes, I believe in God."

Lily took a deep breath. "I don't fully understand how or why, but I was visited by apparitions from the future. Maybe I'm having a mental breakdown, but I think they were real." She paused. "How can you tell if you're insane?" she mused. "When the Seven Fires prophets visited my people, or when angels visited Moses and Abraham, they all had to trust in their sanity to receive the message … Do you know Albert Fisher?"

"The son of the local lumber baron."

Lily nodded. "I was visited by him, except he was very old. I think he came to me from the future, to guide me and to give me a purpose."

Guerin reflected before prompting, "What purpose?"

"To save the children."

"So you see this school as a fulfillment of prophecy?"

Lily shook her head. "No, it was different than that." *Lily Guerin.* "The children had my eyes. I think I am fighting now to protect the future. Does that make sense?"

"I understand. It's why I wanted to build this school, and why I wanted your help."

He's not listening. She made a sound of exasperation. "The children I dreamt about are threatened by the Horned Serpent. To fight the Horned Serpent, there must be three: a Firehandler, the Great Thunderbird, and the Omodai."

Guerin motioned for her to continue.

"Omodai is an empty vessel. I think the plan of the Wintermaker is to rise from his tomb, take on new flesh, and defy the will of God. The dark magic that surrounds this place keeps his soul, and any other soul, from drifting to the place where all souls must go—until his fated day."

The River of Souls. The Land of the Midnight Sun. Heaven. Hell. Sheol. Valhalla. The Underworld. "The Omodai is both victory and defeat. For us, it is bait to draw him up from the depths, and once vulnerable, we can kill him."

"How do you kill something that isn't alive?"

"I don't have all of the answers yet, but the Tak-Pei have woken up and now go about their master's business. We need to protect young Albert. The old Albert told me as much."

Guerin frowned. "His father is a respectable businessman, with business ties to Triton. I'm not quite sure how I would bring it up in conversation."

"Albert knows, and so do others. You heard about Kermit Crain. I think the Tak-Pei are going after any threat to their master, I think ... God ... has sent people who can help in this fight."

Lily studied Guerin's face to anticipate how he was taking it. Again, he seemed sincere and ponderous. "Kermit Crain was sent to help? He's just a boy like Albert."

And Bjorn Forsberg, and Martin Nielson, and Farrell Luning. "I know, it almost sounds silly talking about it aloud. In the old stories, there were always groups of people who guided the heroes, just like in the Bible. Jesus had disciples that ..."

You blasphemous sinner! Did you just compare yourself to Christ?

Guerin didn't speak, only nodded.

A foundation of lies to be torn down so I can start over. "I have to tell you what happened in White Earth," Lily whispered.

This time, Guerin seemed surprised by her words. His brow wrinkled and his mouth opened.

She held a hand up for him to stay silent. "As you know, things are much different there than they are here or at Morris. Even inside the school room, things were so tense and hostile. My first few weeks, I was so happy to be teaching that I ignored the signs. There was a ..."

Lily couldn't even decide how to describe him. "His Christian name was Jacob Bright Sky, and he decided I should be his wife. He was seventeen already and would linger outside the school room in the afternoons. I'd ended my relationship with Samuel Thunder Face, so I was flattered to have a beau as soon as I came to White Earth. But Jacob Bright Sky did not want a relationship."

"Lily—"

Don't let him interrupt. "It was a Wednesday, and I'd stayed late to finish grading, and in December, the sun disappears before five o'clock. His voice caught my attention, and when I stopped to talk to him, he dragged me by the wrist into some dark alley. It all happened so quickly, and he was so strong."

"Oh, Lily," Guerin murmured.

She couldn't say the words. "When it was over, I crawled out of the alley, only to be found by one of my students, William. He was just a boy, like Albert, or Bjorn, or Kermit. I was scared, I was hurt, and I was angry. I ... I ... didn't just accept William's help, I enlisted him."

Lily took a deep breath. "I turned him into a weapon. First William, and then the other young boys. I unleashed them, even though I still held their chains. Within a few weeks, Jacob Bright Sky was found dead, beaten to death. The boys returned to me like a pack of dogs, tails wagging, seeking my approval. I didn't understand it then, but I understand it now—I had enchanted them. The old blanket men were right—I bewitched them. Whatever gifts God bestowed upon me, I turned it into something evil, so now, I don't trust myself to do what is right."

Lily began crying, and when it was over, she realized Guerin had put his arm around her shoulder to comfort her.

She scooted over and shook off his pity.

Now he knows. Yet the weight of her deed did not lessen.

Guerin cleared his throat. "We can aspire to be like Christ, but all men, and women, fall short. On the road to Damascus, Christ chose a man who hunted his disciples. The man who had been Saul transformed into the apostle Paul, who never forgot his former sins yet still became a great evangelist for God." He patted her knee. "You don't have to remain the person who went to White Earth. You don't have to remain the person you were yesterday. All you need to do is become the person you need to be tomorrow."

I'm not sure I can. With the backside of her wrist, Lily wiped her tears away. "If we find it, what happens then?"

His mouth opened for a moment as if to protest.

"You didn't come to listen to me cry and didn't come here for my people. You came to investigate the stories about the Philosopher's Stone. What happens if we find it?"

"I honestly don't know. I'm glad God has sent you allies. I, too, have allies. Your grandfather knew these allies existed. I brought Paul White Wolf here because he knows the history of the quest better than I do. There are only a handful of people alive that know why I'm here, and I have no specific orders on what to do if … I find anything. But know this: my first priority is to make sure it doesn't fall into the hands of our enemies—and to protect you."

Lily found herself breathing heavily. *My chaste knight of the Round Table.* Knowing she had a protector was thrilling, but knowing real villains lurked terrified her.

Triton. The nefarious company owned pineries, a new quarry, and the Nicollet dam, and despite White Wolf's best efforts, they even claimed Lily's abductor from the city jail before answers could be found.

What does Triton want? Is it just the Philosopher's Stone, or do they serve the Wintermaker also? Aloud, she asked, "But if we do find it, what then?"

"We prepare for a fight. Our school can also serve as a fortress, but only against physical threats. I don't know how to fight the paranormal."

"Neither do I." Lily shrugged at his skeptical stare. "I didn't get to finish my training. There are pieces missing."

"How do we finish?"

"Nanak called for help with Migisi. There were three blanket men, secret members of the Wijigan Clan, who answered the call."

"Give me their names and I can find them."

"Clyde Speaks First, Joseph Little Toad, and James Grey Sky. They are the last of the Wijigan Elders."

CHAPTER SIXTY-ONE

Sound of the Water Drum

Turtle Island Jesuit School

June 1898

AFTER DAYS OF hugging, laughing, and crying, the Great Thunderbird wrapped his fingers around the throat of Migisi Weber and choked the orphan boy to death, just a few feet from where his sister Tew slept.

Adopted by the priest? I don't think so. I will always be Migisi Asibikaashi!

Tew had tried to explain her dreams, something about her last name, but Migisi refused to listen after he understood what adoption meant. He didn't get a choice in being a ward, and that ended all talk of changing their last name.

As soon as Migisi stepped out of the unfinished dormitory, he could breathe again, and standing barefoot upon the land of his ancestors gave him strength for the coming battle. He still remembered every square inch of the property, but under the blanket of darkness, he walked to a place he'd rarely stood.

Even though it was too dark to read the English letters, Migisi knew which headstone belonged to his mother. Tew twisted the skills taught to her by Nanak for her own purposes—a willow dreamcatcher hung on their mother's grave in hopes of a final conversation. Migisi lifted the dreamcatcher and stepped back from the graves.

The grass was cold under his toes.

Big Squeak's body had been transported home, to be placed beside a woman who despised him. *The coward!* And not only had Big Squeak failed to follow his own destiny, but he'd also interrupted Migisi's destiny, assaulting the elders who'd come to help with his Vision Quest.

Grandfather, Mother, and Father were now placed in the ground—casualties in the war. A war he played a part in.

And now I must do my part—even if I die.

Migisi had to sift through all of the lies to understand the truth. If Tew could be believed, she'd learned the Song of the Manitou and had carried fire, affirming her destiny as a Wabeno, a Firehandler. One person alone, however, could not defeat the Horned Serpent. Even though his hands were scarred, he could still serve another role—the role of the Great Thunderbird.

In the tales, the enemy of the Horned Serpent was the Thunderbird, a supernatural creature somewhere between a storm cloud and an actual eagle. Migisi particularly remembered the tale involving the boy Iyash, trapped on the island, and how the boy offered his eyes to the Horned Serpent, only to betray it, leading it into shallow waters, and laughing as the Thunderbird came to destroy it.

The Wintermaker and his Tak-Pei might be laughing now, but soon, I will stand over their corpses.

To do that, Migisi needed a weapon stronger than a turtle shield.

Holding the dreamcatcher, he walked south until he found the place where Nanak's cabin and sweat lodge had once stood. The foundation of the cabin remained, knee deep rubble, and the place where the sweat lodge had been built, a promontory of stone above the Blue Knife—also destroyed.

Just a few yards upstream, the foundations of a dam were in place, and soon the entire river valley all the way to Nimrod would be flooded.

Great Spirit, hear me. Show me the truth, Manabozho, Migisi prayed.

Whether ten minutes, an hour, or several hours passed, Migisi did not know, but his prayers ended with the beginning note of the Song of the Manitou.

A man's voice sang the foreign syllables, commanding the Tak-Pei. Like a lens, the dreamcatcher's loom held pieces of the past, showing him countless ordinary nights except for one, when the fires of the Wijigan burned across the lake at Assinikande, the Flat Rock.

The singer, the horned priest Wiyipisiw, soon found himself surrounded by a horde of Tak Pai, who paid no attention to the dozens of other Wijigan warriors gathered around the priest listening to his words. A younger man, Makadewaa, the priest's son, rested upon the flat rock, his arms and legs spread and his eyes to the stars.

The Omodai.

In front of the horned priest Wiyipisiw, a brilliant white rock sat upon a burning fire, soaking up heat and energy.

The Water Drum.

During Migisi's testing, the old priest Joseph Little Toad had pulled him aside for a private lesson: "Let me tell you about the mystery of the Water Drum." He had then procured the dissembled pieces of his lesson. "In the days of the dawn, the original Water Drum sounded. It was used for the creation of life, both physical and spiritual. While the first Water Drum was lost to man, we remember it through symbols."

Joseph Little Toad showed Migisi the components: a hollowed-out log to serve as a vessel, a symbol for a body imbued with soul.

The water within represented the blood given by Mother Earth to create life. Over the top of the drum, a deerskin represented how man was clothed with flesh. Securing the hide to the drum, seven stones represented the wisdom and prophecy given to the Original Man.

Once assembled, Joseph Little Toad had whispered words and breathed upon the surface of the drum. "The sound of the drum represents a heartbeat. Once you are fully trained, you will learn why the Water Drum is needed."

Can I still be fully trained? Or have the lessons been lost?

Now, peering through the willow dreamcatcher, Migisi looked to the past and understood a simple truth—Wiyipisiw had indeed found the original Water Drum.

In front of Wiyipisiw, the white rock sat upon the fire, soaking up heat and energy.

Then, a gunshot sounded in the distance.

Followed by several more blasts.

War cries and barbarous yawps sent the camp of Wijigan followers into disarray. Makadewaa's tethers were cut free, just as a war party of white men and Indians came crashing in from the west. A moment later, another war party came in from the north, where the town of St. John would be one day. Joining the scattered white men and Sioux were a party of Pillagers.

Then something strange happened.

Makadewaa reached down to pick up the White Egg, and the skin on his hands immediately sizzled and burned, sloughing off in a bloody mess. He screamed in agony until Wiyipisiw rushed over, pushed his son aside, and with mitts of deerskin hide, lifted the stone and set it in the middle of a canoe.

Crying, Makadewaa followed Wiyipisiw to the canoe, where a heavy chest had already been placed. Even with bloody hands, he grabbed a paddle and fled Assinikande. Father and son paddled across Lake Manitou toward the Blue Knife River. A half-dozen canoes with armed white men as well as more native warriors tried to cut off the escape, but Migisi's ancestors reached the river before they did.

Just as they passed the tall mouth of the Blue Knife, four snipers fired down from the top of the ravine. The escorting canoes veered off to engage the snipers, allowing Wiyipisiw and Makadewaa to continue.

As father and son passed through the Nicollet Rapids, Wiyipisiw beached the canoe. "Makadewaa, go ahead without me. You must hide the Water Drum and the Ironwood Log where no one can find them and then flee to the north."

"I won't leave you, Father," Makadewaa answered.

"You must! It is our destiny. Go on ahead, I will give you time to hide the sacred treasures."

So Makadewaa paddled upstream alone.

Could it be … and so close … Migisi followed the past, through the dreamcatcher, to a cave.

The White Egg, which Wiyipisiw had called the Water Drum, had already burned the leather mitts, but the mitts gave the boy enough protection to haul the heavy object into the cave, setting it far in the back away from the light. Next, he dragged the heavy chest out of the canoe and up the rocky slope, pausing halfway from exhaustion.

In the distance, gunshots could be heard.

Makadewaa took a moment to open the thick metal hinges to peek inside. Inside the velvet-lined chest, rested dozens of artifacts and scrolls similar to what Nanakonan had used while introducing him to the Song of the Manitou.

Once the treasures were hidden, Makadewaa used a short log to pry away at the bank to bring a small avalanche of rock and dirt down on the cave opening.

The memory vanished, leaving Migisi touching a silent dreamcatcher.

CHAPTER SIXTY-TWO

A Fair Trade

Turtle Island Reservation
July 1898

FAWN CHEVREUIL SAT in the back of the wagon and finally understood where she was being taken—Lake Manitou. The other children either slept or stared off in a daze, but even in darkness, she recognized the headwaters of the Blue Knife.

The armed men guarding the children remained somber, and if not for the figure sitting on the wagon bench, Fawn would have believed she was being sold into some sort of slavery. Worrying kept her awake while the others slept on.

A single lantern led the wagon down the road reserved for the zhaaganaash during the day. White Earth had become a boiling pot of hostility, and the thought of leaving, however uncertain, filled Fawn with optimism. During each day, when the wagon was hidden in undergrowth, she tried to determine where she was being taken. Now that she spotted the Nimrod Crossing bridge, she knew.

Black Fish wasn't lying.

Eldest of the children, she sat in the best spot, the back corner near the bench. It provided her with physical security and also a position nearest the leader of the adults—Chief Sweating Stone.

"Why are you doing this?"

Chief Sweating Stone flinched, as if returning from a far-off place, but then he slowly turned to look over his shoulder at her.

"I told the elders I was purging our ranks of the unwanted, including the daughter of a traitor," the old man began. "I am not a religious man. I come from the Loon Clan of the Leech Lake Pillagers, and since I was a child, I prepared to be a leader of my people. Yet I know the old stories, even the ones that are whispered. Traitors often do what they think is best. Traitors can be selfish and lack foresight, but their intentions are often for those they love."

Did my father betray Big Squeak for love or profit?

"Why am I doing this?" the warrior mused aloud. "To make right a betrayal. When our people began, when Manabozho walked among the Daybreak People, we were visited by prophets to guide our way. Do you know this story, girl?"

"The Seven Fires."

"Yes, and I have often ignored the dramatic claims and supernatural promises given in these stories. But I still listened. And I counted. Seven Fires, Seven Stopping Places, Seven Prophecies, yet eight prophets. Eight prophets guided our people, yet, as a young leader, I was taught that Anishinaabe culture was guided by seven clans. Today, it is only six, but I pondered the actions of my predecessors." He let out a sigh. "Do you know where I am taking you?"

"Lake Manitou."

"Do you know why I am taking you there?"

Be bold. Be brave. "I hope the rumors of a school being built are true because if they are not, I worry a wagon full of children might be used for something much worse."

Chief Sweating Stone's mouth pursed and puckered, filling Fawn with fear. "The Chippewa have always been the Faith Keepers, but during those dark days of war, our people divided. I was taught that there once was an eighth clan, the Wijigan Clan, but that the people of the skull turned to dark magic and were cast out. The Pillagers were tasked with driving them out, but the Great Spirit refuses to let them perish."

Did the children at Bleeding Rock know they were going to be sacrificed? Is he going to kill all the children? Fawn prepared her legs to leap from the wagon. "So why are you taking me to Lake Manitou?"

"As I said, I am not a religious man, but I can look around and see that an illness has come over the entire nation. When our people were united, we defeated all enemies in our path. Now, we are only six clans and might lose the last of our reservations. In fear, my ancestors once turned against the Wijigan Clan, but now my grandchildren are the last of the Wijigan. I will not turn my back on them in their hour of need."

Good … Fawn relaxed. *But something is still not right about this.*

The wagon continued through the night.

A FEW HOURS later, the trek ended when another lantern appeared.

Fawn woke the children, fearing the unknown. She didn't know the other man holding the second lantern, or the men surrounding the wagon, but she did know the robed man sitting on the bench of the second wagon—Father Guerin.

"Do you have them?" Father Guerin asked.

"I have the Chevreuil girl, as well as a handful of orphans. I couldn't find the LeDuc children or their father, though. For now, this will have to do. Do we have a deal?"

"Find the LeDuc children, and I'll bring another wagon. Remember, I want these crates spread out to the other reservations. Is that clear?"

"They will soon vanish in the wind."

Father Guerin nodded, and from the back of his wagon came crates that looked like skinny coffins—the length of a man yet only eighteen inches wide. The gate of her wagon opened, and their escorts began helping the children down. No sooner had the first of the children vacated than the crate slid onto Chief Sweating Stone's wagon. One of the Chippewa men opened the crate to reveal brand new rifles.

Fawn remained in the back of the wagon until it was emptied. At the approach of one of Father Guerin's men, she relented and got out. On her way to the priest, she saw more crates being transferred, clearing the back of the wagon for more children.

Once the deal was complete, Father Guerin walked over to Chief Sweating Stone, where they had a private conversation between the two wagons.

The other man holding the lantern began to speak. "Welcome children, I am Superintendent Paul White Wolf, of the Fire People, the Potawatomi of Michigan. By dawn, you'll be home on Anishinaabe land at the Turtle Island Jesuit School. We'll give you food, shelter, and an education, and if you choose, a new home."

THE PROMISE TURNED out to be true, and as the wagon reached the place where Winnie's house had once been, a new campus of brick buildings, most still under construction, greeted them. Workers and faculty also greeted them, along with a handful of other children, including Fawn's relatives, Migisi and Lily, both of whom seemed to be carrying dark secrets despite their welcoming smiles. Their eyes are both haunted.

Something is wrong. This is all too good to be true.

CHAPTER SIXTY-THREE

Man of Valor

Split Rock, MN
July 1898

THE PAIN DID not fade, as the doctors had promised Farrell Luning, and after two hours of listening to his wife sleep, he commanded his crippled legs to move to the side of the bed.

Pain reminds a fella he is still alive … I'm about to be very alive.

Both legs were braced to let the bones heal, although his left could support enough weight for him to use crutches. As soon as they slid off the bed, the downward rush of blood heightened the pain until he felt his heart pounding in his temples. He silently and steadily collected the two crutches and leaned forward onto them.

I need to get out of this house.

Despite wearing only a nightshirt, Farrell hobbled his way from his front door and out into the yard. His eyes looked to the sky. In the cosmos above, he found the familiar constellations—the Big Dipper, the Little Dipper, Draco, and Cassiopeia— along with the swathe of stars forming the Milky Way.

What am I supposed to do now?

Dr. Jenkins told him the truth without even using the words— he was now a cripple. Yes, he could eventually stand with braces and a crutch, but without support, he'd topple with the simplest tasks. The goodwill built up for saving Albert Fisher had also been wasted after he rejected George Fisher's offer to become an engineer for the new lumber mill.

"Did they wake you up too?"

Farrell flinched at the unexpected voice, and almost lost his balance upon his crutches. The voice came from Albert Fisher, who like himself, stood in the darkness wearing his nightshirt.

"You should be in bed," Farrell told the boy in a whisper.

Albert turned around to the three-story house where his parents slept. He shrugged and walked across the big yard. After clearing the land for the lumberyard, Farrell could now clearly see how his boss's home contrasted with his simple square house on the other side of the unbuilt factory. "I can't sleep with them making noise."

Them? Farrell looked around self-consciously, hoping no one saw him in his bedclothes and crutches. "I don't hear anything, Albert." While initially true, a loon now called out from the lake, its shrill cry barely audible from across the river valley.

"If you come, maybe they'll go away."

"What are you talking about, buddy?"

"Don't you remember what Lily told you? They're calling out to me, trying to confuse me."

The Little People? Farrell couldn't remember the word Lily had used, but having seen and felt them twice, he had listened to her full explanation of the evil that hunted Albert. He'd been so taken by the story that he stayed home instead of taking Mr. Fisher's offer. "Did you see them in your dream?"

Albert shook his head. "I saw them across the river."

The damned river. It had almost taken his life, and now, it was trying to take his common sense. "Show me."

Albert walked toward the river. By the time Farrell reached it, he was breathing heavily but unable to wipe the sweat from his forehead due to his crutches, ignoring as it dripped through his brows.

"Son of a bitch," he said in full volume, his eyes adjusting to fully see within the darkness. *Is the boy fearless?* Farrell felt his heart pounding in his chest. Once, years earlier, his father had taken him hunting, only to be surrounded by a pack of wolves. Then, like now, there was only one obvious choice—stand still until it passes.

"My mother couldn't see them, so I thought they were just in my head. But you can see them?"

"Those ugly bastards? Yeah, kid, I see them." Even though an adult and married, Farrell felt like a child as his mind tried to comprehend the reality of the boogeyman. With red eyes, shadowy faces, elongated arms, and bodies covered in wispy quills, the creatures stood on the edge of the water. "So they won't cross the water?"

"Lily is right. This is as far as they can go. Normally, they stay at the lake, but something has made them angry."

Terror turned to machismo. "Hand me a rock."

"What?"

"Pick up a rock; hand it to me."

Fight or flight, his father had taught him. That day in the woods, the two yelled and screamed, sending the wolves running. Placing his weight on his right armpit, and using only his strong arm, he chucked the rock across the water, sending it crashing into the opposite shore. The closest creature snarled and retreated.

"Have there always been this many?" Farrell asked, counting seven others that remained.

"No, but each time somebody dies near the water, another Tak-Pei wakes."

How does he know this? Has he been talking to Lily? "Wakes?"

"Lily said they are servants of the Wintermaker, but I think they might be some sort of demon, like from the Bible."

Albert's simplification didn't help. "Demons, huh? Maybe now's a good time to get my cross back."

Albert shook his head. "I think something really bad is going to happen. I worry about Lily. I think she needs us."

Farrell had tried to put the beautiful young woman out of his mind. At first, his pain blinded him, but as he healed, he became aware of how intoxicated he'd been by her beauty and paranormal stories. When Father Guerin returned, Farrell felt relieved that the temptation was gone.

Is she in danger? "The two of us? I think we'd lose a fight to a rabid dog."

"There's a reason we can see them and nobody else can."

Farrell bit his lip as he conquered his fear. "Good point. Get me another rock. A handful, actually. I don't like the way they're looking at me."

After three tosses, the rest of the Tak-Pei vanished into the darkness. "Well, maybe now you can sleep. I've chased them away."

"All you did was drive them back toward Lily."

Farrell realized both of them stood on the eastern shore while the creatures stood on the side nearer Lake Manitou and Lily.

Well shit. "I tell you what, you go get some sleep, and I'll try to do the same, and when morning comes, come help me get my wagon ready and the two of us will ride over to the reservation and see how she's doing."

He made sure Albert returned home before he turned back. Halfway to his new home, Farrell turned to face the darkness. *If they've always been there*—he thought of his near-drowning in the lagoon and recently in Split Rock Creek—*why are they suddenly awake?*

Vision Quest

Turtle Island Jesuit School
August 1898

ILY WEBER WOKE, disoriented. She didn't wake in her childhood home, nor did she wake in the dormitory. Instead of the well-lit upstairs room at Good Counsel, she was surrounded by darkness and smoke.

The sweat lodge...

Instead of seeing wise Nanak on the other side of the fire, she saw a stranger—Clyde Speaks First. Gathering her strength, she sat up. Suddenly, all eyes were on her—including those of Guerin.

She could not keep from studying the pink scars upon his visible flesh for he, too, laid on his side upon the cool earth, his cheek pressed to the ground. He was seeking his own answers.

The blanket men also sat in the lodge, each in his ceremonial location, waiting.

This is wrong. The people are all wrong.

She'd dreamed of being in a boat, with Bjorn Forsberg in the bow, keeping watch, with Albert, Farrell, Migisi, Fawn, Kermit, Martin Nielson, and Guerin. Lily had a shepherd's hook to pull drowning children from the water, as the Horned Serpent and foul

Tak-Pei swirled around in the waters, plucking the children away from her.

Now, she was surrounded by strange men.

It was the fourth day since the ceremony began, but now there were fewer than had started, and she worried it would ruin things.

James Grey Sky, who sat at the western position of the Cedar Man, snored through the day, somehow sleeping in a sitting position with his chin resting upon his chest. Clyde Speaks First also slept, sitting in the southern position of the Bird Man.

Superintendent White Wolf served as Conductor, sharing his Potawatomi version of the ritual as the guide for the group. He even had his own replica of the Water Drum, which he used for the opening of the ceremony.

Two newly hired teachers served as Doorman and Fireman, and even though Lily had forgotten their names, she'd never forget their expressions as she proved to all of them that she was indeed an authentic Wabeno, a Firehandler.

Now, we'll see if I am granted my vision.

For most of the fourth day, Lily found herself alternating between staring at Guerin or staring at the construction of the sweat lodge: the willow branches, basswood, and cedar bark. Grandfather taught her about the sacred qualities of the willow, but now, in the witness of adults, she'd revealed the sacred magic.

I've always been a good student. I hope you are proud, Grandfather.

Light still came through the seams in the construction but night was coming and with it the journey she'd take to the spirit world. Soon, her destiny would be fully revealed.

Or so she hoped.

Lily looked down at her black palms, studying the lines and creases upon them. Migisi had run away from the ceremony shortly after it started, followed by Fawn, who excused herself to check on him. When Lily picked up the first stone, she saw their faces change, too. By the time she lifted the second stone from the coals, Guerin also looked at her differently, but not in the same way as the children.

Seven stones now rested upon the womb of the earth, and beside the small pit, Lily counted the minutes, waiting for sleep and magic.

And I also wait for purification and guidance.

She blinked, and when she opened her eyes, the elders were sitting in position, prepared.

"Take this piece of cedar," Clyde Speaks First instructed, "and place it in your mouth. Let it guide your tongue as you speak to the spirits sent to you."

The gritty piece of wood immediately adhered to her tongue, drawing the little moisture remaining into the bark. The flavor made her hungry, and her stomach twisted and gurgled at the cruel trick.

The Doorman opened the flap, and the sweat lodge exhaled into the night sky. At the crescent altar, a new fire heated more stones for the final night of the ritual. Lily saw that Fawn watched her with wide eyes, peeking into the lodge with a smile and confidant nod.

Migisi must be fine if she has returned.

One by one, the heated stones were brought into the lodge, and once the door was closed, Lily passed out.

WHEN SHE WOKE, others were in the lodge with her.

"Why are you doing this to me?" a man whimpered. The voice came from beside her, a couple of feet from the pile of stones.

He's not lying down. It's just ... his head.

Lily propped her own head under her arms to confirm what she saw: the head was not severed but the body appeared to be buried in stone.

"Please, kill me or let me go," the head spoke, weak and disoriented. No one else even seemed to see it, and in the blink of an eye, it was gone.

The western door of the sweat lodge opened, and for a moment, she thought the ghost of her father had entered. Even though constructed with four doors, only the eastern door was functional in a lodge. The western door was reserved for spirits.

No, he's not my father. He's too young.

"Hmph," the young man said, sitting cross-legged upon the ground in front of where Guerin appeared to be frozen in time. None of the other participants appeared to move either.

I know him. I saw him leave the willow tree.

"What a tangled web you've woven, Lily," the young man said as if pleased with himself. "How did you do this?"

"I'm in a sweat lodge," Lily answered. "It's the fourth day..."

"...so you're communicating with spirits." He looked above his head. "Under the willow? Same place, same tree, just different branches. Death magic surrounds us. It's just like you said."

"Who are you?" Lily asked.

The young man shook his head. "Not yet. Today, I need your help. I'm just the binding holding two branches together. Give me your hand."

Lily still laid upon the ground on her side, but she managed to extend her hand to the apparition of the young man. When she wrapped her fingers around his, Lily saw another apparition holding his other hand.

The young man turned to the new apparition. "Go ahead, speak to Lily. She's listening."

The second apparition sat on the other side of the stones, opposite of Lily, but when she spoke, Lily recognized her from the vision at the trestle bridge.

"Grandmother Spider?" the voice was slurred just as before. "I need your help. I've found it, but I don't know what to do. If you can help me, then I can help you. Can you sing this for me?"

With her free hand, the apparition reached across the timeless fire to display a strange notebook with pictographs written upon it. In doing so, the woman blocked the radiance from the heat, revealing her deformed face and her dark clothing marked with a drawing of a fierce thunderbird.

It's the Song of the Manitou.

It was only a fragment, but it was similar to what Grandfather had shown her.

"If you can help me with this one section," the scarred woman said with a lisp, "I can do the rest on my own."

With her last bit of strength, Lily drew in a breath and began to sing. She didn't even need to look at the paper. In her mind, she saw Grandfather's birchbark, and the Song came flowing up from her belly and out of her mouth. While her voice traveled an unseen path, her fingers touched the grit and mulch, keeping her body grounded to the solid stone beneath her. Yet instead of the heat coming from the sweating stones, she felt warmth growing at the tips of her fingers.

Is this what White Wolf meant about the womb of the earth?

Am I being purified by heat?

All the tension in the past few months vanished as she bent to the will of her destiny. Her Vision Quest had come. The spirits answered the call.

But then her face grew cold.

The young man's hand was gone.

She heard excited voices.

Felt their panic.

A hand upon her bare shoulder, shaking her. Shaking.

"Lily, stop it. Stop it, Lily!"

Then a hand covered her mouth, smothering her for just a moment.

The hand belonged to Guerin, his face illuminated by torch as he sat over her, his eyes full of terror and wonder.

"What happened?" she asked, turning to see the others.

Clyde Speaks First answered, "You began to sing the Song of the Manitou."

The woman, the young man, and even the head were gone. But so too was the source of the insufferable heat.

The pile of stones was gone.

JAMES GRAY SKY sat with his left hand covering his own mouth. Clyde Speaks First shook as he wept.

Paul White Wolf, illuminated by a torch at the doorway, said in disbelief, "I've never seen such a thing."

The womb of the earth…

For four nights, twenty-eight stones collected upon the womb, but now, they were gone, swallowed. A space the size of a badger hole remained, and just a few inches from the rim, the largest of the stones could be seen wedged in the descending chasm.

I'm a witch.

James Gray Sky stood and walked out through the opened doorway. He couldn't meet her gaze.

Even these men are repulsed by me. What sort of evil dwells in me? "I don't understand," Lily whispered. "What just happened?"

No one answered; Paul White Wolf asked his own question to Guerin, "So are you convinced now?"

Guerin stood and draped a cotton blanket over Lily. "I am."

The Gentle Poet

Turtle Island Jesuit School

August 1898

AFTER THE VISION Quest, Father Guerin and Superintendent White Wolf resumed construction and preparation of the school, leaving Fawn Chevreuil to guess at what was going to happen next.

Lily didn't want to talk about it.

Migisi sulked also.

The Blanket Men stayed, but their conversations with Father Guerin were always in private. For Fawn, much of August was spent watching the boys playing games while the girls worked on ornamental regalia.

She sat now with three of her new friends, sewing beads onto leather as the adults gathered together in the main office while Migisi taught the game of "Four Sticks" to the new boys living with them at the school. Lily sat apart from the girls who watched for their own entertainment, forcing Fawn to break a rule: chatting publicly with Miss Weber like she was Lily. Everyone now walked on eggshells around her, especially after the Vision Quest, but Fawn had waited long enough.

"Why are we all just sitting around waiting for something terrible to happen?"

Lily chuckled wetly and patted the ground for her to sit. "Nobody knows what to do. Too many priests; too many interpretations."

"Is that why you're crying?"

"I'm crying because I'm the one who made this mess."

"Why do you say that?"

"Because Migisi keeps blaming me for everything. He acts like I killed everyone with my bare hands."

Fawn leaned into Lily, putting her head against her shoulder. *Both of you changed.* "You can't blame yourself for any of this. We're dealing with things that shouldn't exist."

"But Migisi is right. I didn't listen to Grandfather. I sang and woke the evil that slumbers in Lake Manitou. It's not stopping, either. We have to figure something out."

"What do you mean it's not stopping?"

"Do you remember the farmer who visited yesterday?"

"The one with the broken legs?"

"No, that was Farrell and Albert. Yesterday, the blonde farmer, Martin Nielson."

The cute one. "What about him?"

"He said there was a house fire that took the lives of two little girls. They lived near the lake, by Sterling Junction. I could see in his eyes what he wanted to say, but he didn't. Kermit said the same thing, how there was an accident that killed two workers."

"You can't blame yourself for everyone that dies. Bad stuff happens, Lily."

"No, it is my fault, and with each death, the Tak-Pei get stronger, and when they get strong enough, then …"

"Then what? What aren't you telling me?"

"Clyde Speaks First believes that it is only a matter of time before the Wintermaker wakes, too. He told Guer—Father Guerin that the Tak-Pei are the servants of the Wintermaker, and that the reason the old Wijigan made sacrifices was to wake their master. He thinks the Tak-Pei will soon take matters into their own hands, with or without us."

"Soon? Like how soon?"

Lily shrugged. "Father Guerin says that all the blame should be put onto Triton. He thinks the dam is some sort of gambit by these men, who have their own twisted interpretations of the Wintermaker. He thinks they intend to dig so they can unearth the evil that dwells here, with or without any rituals."

"I mean, the Seven Fires do talk about a boy making a choice in the time of the Seventh Fire. It would make sense that white men would mess things up for everybody."

Lily chuckled again, her tears slowing. "Grey Sky thinks it'll be even sooner. Our people remember the story of the Wintermaker with the constellation Orion. He's literally called the Wintermaker because when the earth's axis tilts away from the sun, Orion reappears with the arrival of winter."

"So the Wintermaker's coming this fall?"

"The Autumnal Equinox is the third week of September, and when it arrives, the spirits will be at their strongest. So ... the clock is ticking, Fawn."

"But how do you fight something like this? What is the Wintermaker, exactly? Is it a real water serpent or what?"

"I listened to Father Guerin, Mr. White Wolf, and James Gray Sky all agree that in both religions, the Horned Serpent represents the same thing, which means I'm going to be facing some sort of demonic spirit looking to rise from the grave. The River of Souls and Heaven are synonymous with the 'up place' and thus water, in both religions, is the 'down place.' This evil sorcerer has managed to keep his soul from moving on, and with it stuck here, the plan is to once again come back to life. I guess that's where I step in."

The rest of the children played, unaware of the dark conversation. "To do what?" Fawn asked in a whisper.

Lily looked around at the students. "That's the terrifying part. We think I'm supposed to unleash the magic of the Song of the Manitou upon the Wintermaker, but we need other things: the Sacred Shell, the original Water Drum, and the Omodai."

"What do they do?"

"The Sacred Shell, we think, is a written version of the original Song of the Manitou. Nanakonan passed down much of it orally, but this is the oldest, most accurate version. According to tradition, it was lost generations ago, but …"

"But?"

"I think I've found a way around it. In my Vision Quest, and a few times before that, I've encountered apparitions. One of the apparitions is ... uh ... from the future. She's reached back through time to me and during my Vision Quest, she sang a new part of the Song of the Manitou, the one that—"

"Turned solid stone to pudding," Fawn interrupted, having seen the melted depression. "What about the Water Drum?"

"James Gray Sky told me that every Mide makes a symbolic representation of the original Water Drum, which was some sort of tool that the Great Creator used when making the world and bringing life. The Seven Fires speak of it being used, and in order to defeat the Wintermaker, the original needs to be found."

"Where is it?"

"Nobody knows. Father Guerin believes it is more than just a drum. He thinks the Water Drum is at the center of each religion's creation story." Lily glanced at her, a small smile on her face. "You were right about him, he's not here just to help our people.

"I knew it!"

"He calls the Water Drum 'the Philosopher's Stone' and says that folks from around the world are looking for it, and that our family is both blessed and cursed as guardians of this secret."

"But you said no one knows where it is."

"If you believe the Seven Fires prophecy, which it is hard *not* to believe now, it says that a young boy will receive a vision showing where it is hidden."

Fawn turned to the boys playing "Four Sticks" in the distance. "Migisi?"

"I don't know if the boy has to be part of the Wijigan Clan, but if it does, he's one of the only blood heirs left, aside from the old Blanket Men."

"Have you talked to him about it?"

"I've tried, but since he's returned, he's not been the same. First, he blames me for what has happened, and second, he— where are you going?"

Fawn marched across the yard, and as she neared, she noticed how the boys stiffened. "Migisi, we need to talk."

"I'm busy."

"Now, Migisi," she ordered, and it was the other boy's inaction for the game that forced him to rise. As they walked, she scolded: "We're dealing with matters of life and death and you're playing games."

"Lily doesn't know what she's doing."

"Yeah, yeah, yeah. Listen, have you had any visions about a lost drum or stone?"

Migisi's step faltered.

He has. "What do you know?"

"Nothing."

"Tell me, Migisi." She took him by the arm, pinching with her fingertips.

"I saw it through the Dream Catcher. I had a vision of a great battle, and the survivors hid something in a cave."

"A cave? Along the Blue Knife?"

Migisi nodded.

What is wrong with my cousins? Fawn let go of his shoulder only to smack him. "And you were just going to keep this to yourself?"

The two stood halfway across the yard, but close enough that Lily and others could possibly hear the conversation. Migisi rubbed his arm and then pulled Fawn to a stop and stepped closer. "I don't want her to use it."

"We're family, Migisi. If we don't stick together, we're going to get picked off one by one." When he averted his eyes, she added, "Now, you don't have to tell Father Guerin or the others, but you need to let Lily—*us*—know what you've seen. Agreed?"

SEVERAL MINUTES LATER, the three stood at the river's edge.

Fawn didn't even need to see the opening of the cave to know it was there. A trickle of water seeped out of the cliff, bringing with it a distinct blue stain. She stood between the two siblings. "So what's in there?"

"Trouble," Migisi said, prompting another quick smack from Fawn.

Lily answered this time: "Grandfather taught me that the Wintermaker, when he was a man, used the power of the Water Drum to keep his soul from drifting away to its final destination. The Water Drum is a two-edged sword. It can give him his victory over death, or we can use it to undo the magic surrounding this place and send him, and all the other souls, to their resting places."

Migisi shook his head.

"What?"

"I'm not saying she's wrong, but ... never mind."

"What, Migisi?"

Lily looked like she could cry. "Just say it."

"Nanakonan told me that we were only keepers of the tradition, that we were supposed to pass down our knowledge, not use it."

"Well, it's too late, isn't it, Migisi?" Lily snapped.

Migisi began to pull away, but Fawn held him steady by the shoulder. "Finish your point."

"My point is ... well ... when Nanakonan was a boy, a star with a tail appeared in the sky. His father told him it was the Serpent Star, a comet. This comet comes to earth once a generation, and Nanak said it is counting down the eras of the Seven Fires."

"So when's it coming back?"

"1910."

Fawn suddenly understood the problem. Too many interpretations of the same legend. Lily expected a battle in just a few weeks, and Migisi expected it in another thirteen years. "Well, it's better to be safe than sorry. Do we try to get it out?"

"No," Migisi said immediately. "It needs to stay hidden until needed." He glanced at his sister then away. "If Lily really is the one who's meant to wield it, and I'm the true Thunderbird, then she'll be able to speak to it in her hour of need."

"Do we tell the Blanket Men about it?" Fawn asked when Lily didn't reply.

"Of course not," Migisi snapped. "Everybody's looking for it, and if somebody else finds it, the prophecy will unravel."

"Don't we want the Wintermaker to stay sleeping?"

"He needs to die—all the way," Migisi countered.

"He's right," Lily said softly. "Letting him win or letting him stay sleeping is a victory for the bad guys, so if somebody else gets the stone, there's no way we can possibly fight him." She turned away from the cave. "Until it's time, we leave it alone."

"Well, good. I'm glad that's settled," Fawn said. "Now, can the two of you stop acting like infants and start working together?"

They both nodded.

Then why don't I believe either of you?

When they reached the top of the ravine, Fawn felt a kick in the stomach at what she saw—the Blanket Men were leaving the school.

CHAPTER SIXTY-SIX

The Midewiwin Lodge

Turtle Island Jesuit School
September 1898

THE SPIRITUAL TRAINING for Lily Weber came to a sudden halt.

September brought harmony to the Turtle Island Jesuit School, even though August had ended in conflict when Chief Sweating Stone had brought another load of students in exchange for rifles. The transaction, however, had been interrupted by Clyde Speaks First's sentries, and tempers had quickly flared. Within minutes, each Blanket Man had charged Guerin with betrayal, giving different reasons before disbanding with shouts and threats.

Then life grew quiet again.

For Lily, she quickly became lost in the routine of classes, a distraction that allowed her to forget what existed just beyond the borders of campus. Her day began at the girls' dormitory, where she lived with a dozen girls. Plans for staff cabins existed, but with the dormitory still half-empty, Lily found plenty of room and good company.

After breakfast, both dormitories released the children out into the yard, where the kids could run off some energy. At this time,

Lily crossed to the school building, keeping an eye out for either Fawn or Migisi.

Guerin had made her dreams come true, and after preparing a lesson in her classroom during the first period of the day, she taught grammar to a classroom of girls, and then had two periods of teaching to the boys. After lunch break, Lily's day was complete, leaving her to grade assignments or to wander campus.

Today, like many days prior, she wandered into the back of Superintendent White Wolf's classroom to listen to him teach Indigenous History. Even though he did not come from the Wijigan tradition, he was a master of both the oral and written traditions of the eastern tribes. His curriculum began with creation stories, with an emphasis on the Seven Grandfathers, a moral code similar to what the nuns at Morris taught about the Ten Commandments.

"The boy who received the lessons of the Seven Grandfathers," White Wolf said, "eventually became the oldest man in his village, and as he passed on his knowledge to the next generations, one of the brightest boys grew ill to the point of death. To save this boy, the old man taught his people the secrets of the Midewiwin Lodge, which I will now share with you."

As White Wolf explained the building of the rectangular lodge, Lily's mind wandered to the apparition of the old woman she'd seen in her own visions, which had also grown quiet in recent days.

"Despite all these preparations," White Wolf continued, "the boy grew closer to death. The old man, reflecting on his prior lessons, understood what was missing: the Water Drum."

Lily's mind spun as she listened to him explain the symbolism of a water drum, with the original Water Drum hidden just a few hundred yards away along the Blue Knife River. In the story, the old man used the drum to pull the boy's spirit back inside of his body, restoring him to health.

Is that what will happen to the Wintermaker? Is that how he will rise from death?

White Wolf spoke as if the world was not coming to an end in a few more weeks, and thus, quickly transitioned to the symbolism of the Midewiwin Lodge itself, focusing on the role played by each clan, involving the familial heritage of his students. Unlike the sweat lodge, which was used for a Vision Quest, the Midewiwin Lodge had an open framework ceiling, allowing the priests to communicate with the River of Souls and the Land of the Midnight Sun. On his chalkboard, White Wolf marked, from east to west, where each clan would sit within the lodge.

Will I need a lodge full of people when I face the Wintermaker?

Just like a sweat lodge, the Midewiwin also had Fire Keepers along with a place for the Water Drum.

Physical fire and spiritual fire?

Lily had too many questions.

Yet as she started to look away, the images within the crude clan labels began to change. Instead of simple circles to represent the clans, faces began to appear. *I'm having a vision while wide awake—don't act like a fool in front of the students.* Lily bit her lower lip, hoping the pain would make the faces go away, but it didn't.

Where White Wolf had drawn the Bear Clan outside of the lodge's eastern door, she began to see the face of Bjorn Forsberg. At the western end of the lodge, she saw the face of Martin Nielson in one of the circles.

Before she recognized any more faces, Lily rose and left, betrayed by the loud latches of the heavy door. She marched out of the academic building until she stood alone on the grassy field.

I just need a minute. She put her hands on her hips and lowered her head at the sight in the distance. Her Creator was surely laughing at her, for standing with Guerin at the school office was Martin Nielson. The two shook hands before Nielson returned to his horse. Seeing Lily standing alone, he tipped his hat to her and rode away.

A premonition? Is something important about to happen with Nielson?

Guerin also saw her and headed toward her. "Miss Lily, how was your day?"

"I think you've made a big mistake."

"Oh? Care to explain?"

"I know your reasons for building this school." *You gave me my heart's desire.* "But I can feel something growing. I feel it in the tips of the fingers and toes, getting stronger by the day. I'm not a coward, and I'm not going to run from a fight, or from a responsibility, but by bringing all these children here, I worry that we've put their lives in jeopardy."

"How so?"

"What if things go wrong? I know when Jesus sent out his disciples, they were able to cast out demons and heal the sick, but what if I fail? What if the Wintermaker wins? Then we will have set up a buffet table for him to choose from."

Guerin put both of his hands on her shoulders, as if to steady her. Looking up at him, Lily found herself staring at his clean-shaven upper lip. She leaned up and—shame caused her to pull away.

"Tell me what you need. Tell me, and I'll make sure you have it."

"I don't know, I don't know what to do!" Lily shouted so loudly that construction workers from the distant buildings looked up.

It wasn't quite the truth; she suspected what to do. Her mind went back to the drawing of the lodge and the chalk faces.

CHAPTER SIXTY-SEVEN

Bad Dreams

Turtle Island Jesuit School
September 29, 1898

AN ANSWER CAME to Migisi Asibikaashi in his dream. His unconscious spirit hovered over a group of warriors, including a young man he recognized from earlier visions—*Wiyipisiw.*

In the dream, it was night, with only the flashes of lightning from a growing thunderstorm providing light to see. A small fleet of long canoes rested along the low bank of a sandy river, each of them with a hatchet-sized hole in the hull. In the tall grass, the slain bodies of the young men guarding them were hidden, with only the Thunderbird able to see the victims.

Wiyipisiw was younger than in the previous vision involving Flat Rock at Lake Manitou. Now, he was a strong war captain, his skin smeared black. He let the cold rain fall upon his back as he laid in the tall grass, his face just feet from the closest canoe.

In the distance, a different type of thunder filled the air— gunfire. Even though miles away to the south, the pop and crackle of it indicated the ferocity of a battle that contrasted with the heavy breathing in the tall grass.

"They will use the thunderstorm to flee," Wiyipisiw told his warriors in a whisper. "Prepare yourselves for my command."

Moments later, the sound of moccasins upon the mud grew louder: Wiyipisiw had placed himself between the Detroit River and Lake Michigan, leaving no way out but victory.

The small creek emptying into the Detroit River exploded into froth as a dozen figures crossed the knee-deep water. Wiyipisiw tightened his grip on his ax. The splashing ended as soon as it began, and when the lightning flashed, the fleeing warriors stood at the opposite end of the canoes.

Although wet and harried, the features of the warriors were distinct—Meskwaki, or as the French knew them, the Fox. No sooner had the closest Meskwaki warrior laid hands on the nose of the canoe than Wiyipisiw burst from the tall grass at the stern—a signal for his men to attack.

In his dream, Migisi watched as the hidden Chippewa warriors ambushed the fleeing Meskwaki warriors, the storm and suddenness of the attack swirling together in chaos and carnage.

In less than a minute, the Chippewa prevailed.

"Don't touch it!" Wiyipisiw shouted as he surveyed the slaughter. He rushed over to where one of his men stood with bloody hands. "It is the White Egg of the Snake People, and it will bite the hand that touches it."

Migisi felt his own palms ache.

"Quickly, wrap it in leather and place it into the chest I've prepared. We must flee before the rest of the Meskwaki find out we've taken it."

The Water Drum—Father Guerin's Philosopher's Stone.

The dream ended, giving Migisi one answer while creating several more questions. He sat up in his dormitory bed, surrounded by other boys with simple dreams. His headmaster, also asleep, was a worldly twenty-two-year-old from Saint Croix, but Migisi knew he could provide no counsel.

With bare feet, Migisi tiptoed out of the building and sat down upon the front steps. In what had been a field a year ago there now stood a dozen buildings, dark silhouettes under the night sky.

He looked past them to the stars. *Where are you, Serpent Star?*

Grandfather told him all about how the Serpent Star ushered in a new era back in 1835. Wiyipisiw would have been alive during a previous appearance in 1758. Despite what Lily and Father Guerin thought, the return of the star would not be rushed. It would return right on schedule in 1910 and again in 1986. *Just like clockwork.* The school was the only thing they got right.

We will train a generation to fight against the Horned Serpent.

He rubbed his eyes and squinted. He studied the distant sky, searching for the Wintermaker. Instead, he saw a group of adults walking across the yard toward him.

I guess I'm in trouble for being out of bed.

A clicking noise sounded to his side, and after seeing the metallic glint of the pistol, he understood it was the cock of a hammer. Migisi didn't move as another man came from around the other corner.

"Is this the one?" a man whispered to another as several adults converged at the steps. None of them were Father Guerin's hired thugs.

"See, the Great Spirit has seen fit to deliver him to us without incident," another said.

I know him, Migisi thought seconds before a rough hand covered his mouth.

The Enemy of My Enemy

Turtle Island Jesuit School
September 30, 1898

FAWN CHEVREUIL KEPT her theories to herself as the rest of the girls talked about the abduction of Migisi. After finding several adult moccasin footprints, a frantic search of the Blue Knife River provided no answers.

Was it Triton again?

Fawn knew how a group of Chippewa men had tried to take Lily, and that, before they could be brought to justice, the abductors had all but vanished before anything could be learned. Because of this, Father Guerin and the adults did not make the news known to anyone off campus.

Was it the Tak-Pei?

The paranormal explanation terrified her, but she understood the reality of the threat. *The Wintermaker is coming, and the Tak-Pei are growing stronger.* If they used their magic to snatch the strongest boy at the school, what chance did the rest of them have?

All of Saturday, allies on horses rode in and out of camp to update Father Guerin, who sat on the porch with Superintendent

White Wolf. Lily sat with him like Mary Magdalene at the feet of Jesus.

All this Fawn watched from the dorm window.

After lunch, during activity time, she crossed the field to the Superintendent's office, keeping herself visible to her teacher while also catching Lily's attention, who finally left the porch to join her.

"How are you holding up?" Fawn asked.

Lily had old eyes, dull from too many burdens and heartache. "I'm afraid something terrible is going to happen to him."

Fawn could not deny what she felt also. "Migisi is strong and clever. Whoever took him is about to find out he's a handful."

Lily squinted, but not in frustration or thought. Turning, Fawn saw what caught her attention: on the southern edge of the school, a man on a horse appeared out of the wooded ravine, flanked by one of Father Guerin's workers. Father Guerin and White Wolf saw the man also and stood.

Even from a distance, Fawn could see the man's head was as bald as a cue ball and had twice the girth of a normal man.

Lily whispered, "Halvar Dobie."

"Who?"

"Triton."

The black horse stopped in front of the Superintendent's office, but Dobie did not dismount. "It appears we share a problem," he said in greeting.

Lily and Fawn moved closer.

"Did you take him?" Father Guerin asked. Fawn could see him reaching for his revolver ready at his hip.

Dobie slowly shook his head. "We took someone, but not the boy. I want to make something else clear: we had nothing to do with Adam Thunder Face killing the old medicine man or the woman either. Whatever happened, it was between them."

Liar. What about Big Squeak?

Father Guerin appeared unconvinced. "Yet your lawyers were ready to claim the land. Life is so ironic."

Halvar Dobie pursed his lips, making his thick mustache squirm. "As the Nicollet Dam supervisor, I'm tasked with security of the facility, and one of our greatest concerns is domestic terrorism, chiefly, a threat from your Chippewa revolutionaries."

Fawn turned to see Father Guerin's reaction, but he was stone faced.

"So a while back," Dobie continued, "when my security team found moccasin prints, we asked to question your kidnappers ourselves."

The men who tried to abduct Lily.

"You mean tortured," Father Guerin clarified.

"Honestly, Father Guerin, I'm surprised a man such as yourself even trusted civil authorities." He scoffed. "I work for Triton and protect all of its interests, and you stand in our way on several of those issues. But now that the business with the dam has mostly been resolved, my focus is this new threat."

"And what threat is that?"

Dobie winced, putting a hand upon his side. "The man we interrogated was from Isle Royal. He'd been part of that fracas you certainly read about in the newspapers. This malcontent later came to the Bad River Reservation, where he received new orders from the crazed zealot who sent him to Lake Manitou to abduct the children of Big Squeak."

Halvar Dobie turned his eyes to Lily, then away.

"You know who I am, and I know who you are, Father Guerin, and as much as I admire this little chess game we've been playing with the pineries in the north, we can't have a third player ruining our game, can we?"

"Do you know where our third player might be found?"

"Yes, I've been keeping an eye on him since this summer. I know what you're planning this winter, but this fellow plans on stealing your revolution, just as he stole the boy from your camp. If you don't stop him, I'm going to have to do it, and you won't like the methods I employ."

Where did this guy come from? Fawn took a step closer, wanting to ask the questions Father Guerin failed to, but Lily took her by the arm.

Father Guerin glanced at them and then asked, "Where is Migisi?"

"Where else would he be? All the scattered Chippewa will gather at Onigum to collect their annuity payments, along with your man Chief Sweating Stone, and that's when this zealot will turn your protest into a bloodbath." His eyes swept the area before he added, "You've been warned."

Halvar Dobie turned his horse around and trotted toward the dam site.

Father Guerin watched him leave before bursting into anger with a series of kicks to the chair he'd been sitting on. "I invited the fox right into the hen house."

"No," White Wolf said quickly. "Who didn't come? Who's from Bad River? This is the work of Joseph Little Toad."

Superintendent White Wolf walked to a group of concerned staff members while Father Guerin charged into the office leaving Fawn as stupefied as Lily. "Were they talking about Migisi? Is Migisi at Leech Lake?"

Lily's eyes dropped, dejected. "I think so."

"I don't understand," Fawn muttered. "Who took Migisi?"

"It wasn't Triton. It was our people. Our own clan."

"Joseph Little Toad?"

"Yes," Lily said and headed for the porch at a fast walk. "He still thinks Migisi is the one."

Fawn followed, and when she reached the porch, she could see Father Guerin already packing to leave, including his gun. Lily crossed right past the threshold and into his private chambers.

Fawn flinched with surprise. *There are no longer barriers for these two.*

Lily took no notice of being in his bedroom. "You have a responsibility to protect the children here at the school."

"Paul knows what he's doing. He'll keep you safe."

"You can't go to Leech Lake alone," Lily snapped. "Let me come with you."

Father Guerin paused, glancing at her. "Don't worry, I'll find your brother."

"Little Toad's men won't let you near him or the boy, especially after how it all ended," Superintendent White Wolf explained, coming to stand behind Fawn.

Little Toad had remained in the north woods … *And now he has Migisi*

"What if this is a ploy just to draw you away?" Lily countered.

"That's why I must go alone. You'll be safe here, I promise."

Anger and heartache flashed over Lily's face. *Losing him would be the end of her. How much more can a person take?*

Father Guerin would not be swayed, even though his face held concern. "I've prepared a bonfire up north. I've stuffed the kindling between the logs, and now, Joseph Little Toad holds a match to it. I have to stop him before he uses the fire against us."

Fawn heard horses galloping hard down the road, and she stepped back from the porch to see two Chippewa men heading towards them.

Superintendent White Wolf turned towards them, his hands fisted at his sides.

A moment later, Father Guerin and Lily stepped out of the office.

Fawn's heart first constricted at the worry of receiving more bad news, but when she saw the faces of the men, her heart swelled with relief.

Blackfish and Pierre LeDuc drove their horses right up to the office, stopping with such fury that dust and dirt created a sudden cloud around them.

"What is it?" Father Guerin asked.

"We bring news from Leech Lake."

So maybe it was bad news after all.

CHAPTER SIXTY-NINE

The Battle of Bear Island

Turtle Island Jesuit School
October 5, 1898

ILY WEBER WATCHED for a lynch mob. Outside the Superintendent's office, Paul White Wolf had transformed the staff of Turtle Island Jesuit School into an armed platoon that patrolled the campus. Blackfish sat so close to Lily that she could smell him and even hear the rumblings of his stomach. Pistol and knife were ready, as well as a rifle propped next to his chair.

Halvar Dobie's warnings had come too late.

An entire state had turned against them.

Forty miles north, at Leech Lake, a war had begun. Hundreds of Chippewa men, women, and children had gathered to receive their annuity payments from the government, but when government agents tried to arrest one of the hereditary chiefs on charges of bootlegging, violence erupted.

These details were described in newspapers from Brainerd to New York. What the world didn't know was that dozens of the Chippewa men were well armed, ready to create an incident worthy of the papers. Yet there was something that neither the U.S. government nor the armed Chippewa understood.

Two Chippewa spies, Blackfish and Pierre LeDuc, had witnessed Joseph Little Toad preparing a ritual on Bear Island involving a young boy—the son of their best friend.

Migisi.

"Are they going to kill Migisi?" Lily asked Blackfish, breaking the silence.

Blackfish wiped his entire face with his palm before shaking his head. "Joseph Little Toad believes he is a great prophet sent to help the people, but he believes another will lead the people to a glorious awakening. His camp has hundreds of followers who believe they will defeat the government in a great war and restore the world to how it once was."

"Is he insane?"

"No, he thinks he is a Firehandler who will wake a manido that will guide a young boy to victory."

The Omodai.

On the heels of Blackfish and LeDuc, news traveled by telegram, newspaper, and courier to all the outlying towns in Minnesota about the rumors of a violent uprising. Many of the older generation still remembered the Dakota War of 1862, when Chief Little Crow attacked cities, burned farms, slaughtered innocent civilians, and took hundreds of women and children prisoner.

As Guerin rode north with LeDuc to try to stop Joseph Little Toad, Blackfish joined the armed teachers to protect the children from something unexpected—a mob.

"Your grandfather Chief Sweating Stone is a reasonable man that trusts Father Guerin. Together, they will find a path through the chaos."

"What if he doesn't get there in time?"

Blackfish didn't reply but Lily already knew the answer: *The best outcome is that my brother is killed by government troops … The worst outcome is that Little Toad performs the Song of the Manitou.*

The truth was now known. Nanakonan served a different purpose than Joseph Little Toad, although both were descended from the Wijigan Clan. Grandfather believed that one day the Wintermaker would rise, yet would be defeated, cast into the depths of the underworld to fix a great schism in the natural world. Joseph Little Toad believed he could wake the Wintermaker as a savior to the people in their time of need.

"Why am I being guarded if all Little Toad needs is my brother?"

"As I said, Little Toad believes he is a prophet, but he is a false prophet. Your family has kept the truth through the generations, and when Little Toad fails, he will come looking for what is missing—and only you know the truth."

Little Toad doesn't have the full Song. But then again, neither do I. And the only thing I could give him is…

Ride of the Valkyries

Hiawatha County
October 7, 1898

BJORN FORSBERG KEPT his attention on the tall, dry grass along the Nimrod road, waiting to pull the trigger. He kept his horse at a slow walk, knowing that the pheasants would either run or take flight when he got too close. And once he reached the turn in the road, the pheasants would have no choice but to take flight.

His plan was foiled as a rider came down the road. *Hey, I know that horse—Grim.*

Martin Nielson slowed his horse for a moment and then waved at Bjorn who returned the wave and beckoned him over. *I guess the pheasants will have to wait.*

He spurred his horse out of the ditch and up onto the road. "Hey."

"Things still quiet down here?"

Bjorn nodded. "You just come from up north?"

"Utter chaos up there. I'm just relaying news to Superintendent White Wolf."

"Oh yeah? What's happening?"

"By the time Father Guerin got to Walker, it was already a shit show. To put the Chippewa in their place, the locals sent a platoon of soldiers to Bear Island to arrest the bootleggers and those who resisted arrest are at Onigum. Not only had the bootlegger suspects fled to Bear Island but the troops came across a religious ceremony as well. So when a shot was fired, the scene turned to chaos and the soldiers were immediately pinned down by sniper fire and an unexpected number of Chippewa warriors."

"How's Father Guerin?"

"By the time he got there, General Bacon showed up by train with a couple hundred soldiers. They loaded them up on steamers to surround the island."

"Like they did at Gull Lake."

"Except this time, the steamers were sitting ducks, and the ships were turned into target practice for the Chippewa marksmen hidden in the woods. By the time the shooting stopped, almost two-dozen men were killed or wounded, with almost seventy men pinned down on the island."

"A shit show," Bjorn repeated. "But what about Father Guerin? And Migisi?"

"Father Guerin was on the steamers. He wanted to talk sense into the Chippewa, but it was more than just the bootleggers on the island. There are hundreds of angry Chippewa camped across the channel at Sugar Point as well."

Will this spill over to Lake Manitou? "It's like Custer's Last Stand all over again."

Martin Nielson's eyes drifted off to the distance, but his hands found their way to Grim's saddlebags, and with a flick of his fingers, he freed his rifle. "Don't move."

"What is it?" Bjorn felt the hairs on his neck standing on end. His mind pictured the ghost of Adam Thunder Face on Deadwood Island.

"Just now, as we were talking, I saw almost a bunch of Chippewa come out of the woods, cross the road, and go down the bank to Lake Manitou."

Nielson squinted as he scanned the rest of the woods.

"What should we do?"

"It looked like they were armed but—"

This is bad. This is very bad. "But what?"

"They were carrying one of the canoes right side up, as if they had cargo in it."

"What if—"

Martin tensed and nodded at the unfinished statement.

Bjorn turned his head to look, keeping his horse calm. "They're going to Deadwood Island. We need to do something." *And we should make sure Lily is safe.*

"Where the hell is Father Guerin when you need him?" Nielson looked west. "We need to keep White Wolf informed. The worst thing we can do is cause a panic and have this thing turn into a bloodbath here in Hiawatha County. You come with me. We're going to the school."

AS THE TWO rode up to the school, they put away their guns prior to being intercepted by the school's security. The road to the school was blockaded with wagons, and even beyond the sentries, more men held fortified positions.

"State your business," one of the new staff members shouted.

"You have a new problem," Nielson began, then explained what he knew.

A few minutes later, Bjorn and Nielson repeated the story to Paul White Wolf, with Lily standing in the doorway of the office.

White Wolf rejected plans that divided his strength as he debated the dangers of involving corrupt law enforcement to play the offense.

"We could rally the folks along Old Copper Road," Bjorn offered when White Wolf went back to pacing. "With the Bergs and MacPhersons, we could have our own platoon in an hour or two."

Before anything could be decided, a rider galloped full speed into camp.

Lily gasped and went running.

Even though everyone else acted in relief, Bjorn's heart sank.

CHAPTER SEVENTY-ONE

Detention

Turtle Island Jesuit School
October 8, 1898

LILY WEBER SAT on Guerin's bed, surrounded by all of his belongings, guarded by men pledged to protect her, and yet never had she felt so alone. Her solitude gave her time to reflect, and just like the storm front that rolled over Hiawatha County, tears of regret began to pour down her cheeks.

He met me, and I ruined his life.

Two hours earlier, Lily had watched her gallant knights ride from the castle on their private quests. Martin Nielson had departed for the southern shore of Lake Manitou to gather a private posse of local men who could be trusted. Like a blonde Paul Revere, he would ride down Old Copper Road until he reached the Forsberg farm, where they would gather in force.

Bjorn Forsberg and Guerin had left for the eastern shore of Lake Manitou, where the Swedes kept a rowboat that would allow Guerin access to Deadwood Island.

"General Bacon spooked Little Toad," Guerin had earlier explained. "We've separated the head of the snake from his body of followers. If we can stop him now, things might be better controlled."

So her knights had scattered across the kingdom, leaving Paul White Wolf armed on the front porch and the rest of the adults patrolling the school grounds.

White Wolf refused to look at her, especially after what she'd done earlier.

I can't believe I did that in front of everyone.

By the light of the lantern, Lily paced around the room, but when she ventured out into the main office, White Wolf sent her retreating with a simple, "Stay away from the windows. I don't want you seen."

Which means he doesn't want to look at me either. Lily wiped at her cheeks.

It had happened so unexpectedly.

As soon as Guerin slid off his horse, she'd rushed up, thrown her arms around him in relief, but as she pulled away, in sight of everyone, she kissed his cheek.

While the priest had acted as if nothing had happened, and as everyone exchanged information, Lily withered upon seeing White Wolf, hands on hips, shaking his head, pointing back to the office building.

Is that why the apparitions knew me as Lily Guerin?

Am I destined to marry him?

Oh, God! Why do I keep ruining everything?

Lightning lit the sky, and a roll of thunder had her jumping at the noise. A gust of wind made the structure creak, and a moment later, rain began to pound against the small pane of glass. Her head turned when a flash of lightning filled the room.

Migisi is out there somewhere. Will they burn him? Or use his blood?

Lily turned her face to the bed's lone pillow and tried to smother her fears. *What am I supposed to do, Grandmother Spider? Guide me. Show me the path to the future, where I can fix this mess.*

Thunder and lightning exploded simultaneously as the big oak outside the office broke in half, and a branch crashed into the back wall of the building, hitting it with the force of a freight train.

Lily stepped out into the cold rain.

I'm coming.

The '72 Colt

Split Rock, MN
October 8, 1898

FATHER JEAN GUERIN slowed his horse to a trot and flipped open the leather latch of his holster. A covered wagon parked on the Split Rock Bridge; a lantern cast shadows upon the tarp.

"What's wrong?" Bjorn Forsberg asked as his horse drew even.

I shouldn't have risked his life. "It's a checkpoint. Stay here, wait for me to pass by, and then come through on your own. Tell them you were hunting and got home late. Understand?"

The boy nodded and obeyed.

Jean spurred his horse forward onto the bridge.

Four armed men stepped out of the wagon, holding shotguns and lanterns. "State your business."

"Father Guerin. I've just returned from Leech Lake with news."

"It's that Jesuit Priest," a sentry mumbled.

One threw back the hood of his rain jacket to reveal Constable Graham. "You're just back from Leech Lake? What's happening?"

"It's a bit of a mess," Jean admitted. *A mess I made.* He gave a muddied account of what sparked the riot at Onigum during the annuity distribution, and then he downplayed the violence that happened later on Bear Island. He made no mention of the Wijigan zealots, but instead focused on how General Bacon had arrived to bring law and order to the situation.

"Why are you in Split Rock?" Constable Graham questioned. "Shouldn't you be up there negotiating with the two sides?"

Little Toad has Migisi. "Yes, in fact, that's why I returned. I have correspondence from Washington that should aid in the negotiations. If the violence is indeed over, I want to be prepared to help negotiate the peace."

"We've heard rumors of insurrections spreading to other communities."

"Simply rumors," Jean countered quickly.

"You might be a priest, but we know you're an Indian lover, too. If anything happens here in our community, I know who to blame."

Trust me, I'm here to stop a lynch mob as much as you. "I understand. By morning, I'll be riding back north to Leech Lake to help settle this."

Jean rode past the checkpoint, turned his horse up the hill toward the church, but once out of sight, he doubled back to head down Market Street, where Bjorn already appeared.

Together, they rode to the south end of town, crossed the trestle bridge, and explained everything to Gus Forsberg, who immediately understood the combustible situation.

As Gus went out to Old Copper Road to join Martin Nielson's attempt to gather allies, Bjorn led Jean down to the shore where the boat was kept. Bjorn carried an unlit lantern and the two huddled under the boughs of a pine tree while they waited for the others. Across the channel, Deadwood Island loomed, silent and sinister.

Even though the cold October weather numbed his skin, he could still feel the spot where Lily kissed him. *I didn't mean to mislead her.* Just like in Manilla and Havana, everything was now unraveling, and his finger slipped inside of his jacket to hold his pistol. The 1872 Colt Open Top revolver had come into the world the same time he had, and it had traveled with him around the world. He'd faced danger in the Philippines and in Cuba, but those were political threats. Now, a child's life was in danger, and another, Bjorn, followed him into the madness.

Bjorn Forsberg squinted at the island, not saying a word.

Where are the adults? Why didn't I send Bjorn to gather the others?

He knew the flawed plan. Martin Nielson rode southwest, first to the Crain farm before moving onward, spreading the word that help was needed. Waiting on Old Copper Road, Gus Forsberg would then lead them to the rowboat.

But what am I doing here? From one of General Bacon's steamships, Jean had seen Little Toad's canoe leave Bear Island, but with Chief Sweating Stone and dozens of other Chippewa still on the island, the single canoe was ignored by the soldiers during the fracas. *Constable Gordon was right. My duty to the Jesuit Order is back at Leech Lake.*

Am I doing this because of a promise I never made?

Or am I trying to impress Lily?

His fingers felt the revolver's chamber, which held six bullets. Although Little Toad was an old man, his henchmen were young and strong. From Nielson and Forsberg's account, there had not been more than several zealots heading for the island. *This is my mess, and I should deal with it. Bjorn and the others can make sure no one gets off the island.*

Long before Lily confirmed his worst fears, Jean understood the nature of the Wijigan as well as the Order of Eos. His puppet masters had chosen the mask for the orphan boy to wear, but he placed it on his face with full awareness of the lie.

"We need to understand," the puppet masters had said back in the Georgetown hospital. "Discover the truth about Lake Manitou."

Now, a madman had Migisi and threatened more than the boy's life.

Jean moved his hand from his pistol to his neck, tugging at the priestly collar until he ripped it free and threw it onto the wet ground. "I just can't sit here and wait," he muttered. "Stay here with the rowboat and lantern. I'm going ahead to scout the situation." Standing, he stripped off his wool trench coat, removing the Colt 1872 Open Top from its holster.

"Shouldn't we wait…?"

Not answering, Jean stepped out of his riding boots. He double-checked that his knife was still strapped to his right leg.

One way or another, this is the end of Father Guerin. He glanced down at the remains of his former self. His first step sunk the collar in the mud. *The Periphery saved the life of an orphan just so I could jump in front of a moving train.*

"Stay here until the others arrive, no matter what you hear," Jean commanded and walked away from Bjorn before he could reply.

ALTHOUGH THE WILD rice fields were thick south of the island and the water remained shallow, a slight current flowed around the inside of the island. At first, the water was warmer than the air, but soon the cold water pierced deep to his core. A hundred yards from shore, Jean began kicking a strange sideways backstroke that allowed him to keep his head and pistol above water, but as he grew closer, he saw flickers of light coming from the center of the island.

The others can't be witnesses to this. I have to do this myself.

Crawling ashore, Jean heard the first harmonic syllables on the wind. He tucked tight to a tree, holding his pistol against his chest.

The light from where the sound emanated turned out to be several small torches stuck into the ground.

What ... He saw Migisi stretched out with cords held down by spikes in the ground. *Poor kid looks like he's been crucified.*

Above Migisi, Joseph Little Toad shook his rattles and sang to the storm while the rest of the painted Wijigan zealots watched with slack jaws and wide eyes.

They're attempting the ritual.

Not in another decade.

It's happening now. Jean carefully cocked back the hammer for a quick first shot and readied himself.

From the edge of the camp, he stepped fully into the light with a drawn pistol—"God forgive me."

The first bullet hit Joseph Little Toad squarely in the chest, knocking him off his feet. The next two bullets struck the heads of the two closest men. Advancing on the four remaining men, Jean waited for one of them to scramble after a weapon before firing his fourth bullet into the man's torso. When the man nearest to Migisi made a move, Jean squeezed off his fifth bullet, before standing between Migisi and the last two zealots.

Both men froze, terrified, unsure of what he'd do next.

Five bullets, five men killed.

But two remained, even though they probably had not done the math yet. Jean leveled the pistol in their faces, taking turns as to which looked down the barrel.

I can't let either of them live.

One look into their rain-streaked skull faces told Jean all he needed—*these men will not surrender.* He reached for his knife.

"Father Guerin?" a voice called out from the shore. "Where are you?"

Too soon, Bjorn. Too soon. Yet the uncertainty of knifing a man to death caused him to delay instead of act. He lost his nerve.

"Over here!" Jean shouted, gun extended.

"Over there, I see light," another voice came through the brush.

Jean knew the second voice immediately, and it wasn't the voice of Forsberg or Nielson. The voice belonged to Constable Gordon Graham, and the figure beside him was also unmistakable— Marshal Bushy Bill Morrison.

Did Morrison track the Wijigan all the way from Leech Lake?

Or did he leave shortly after I left?

Now, the remaining zealots were outnumbered.

"Good Lord," Gordon Graham said when he saw the scene.

"Put a gun on those two over there," Jean instructed, taking his eyes off the two to look over at Migisi.

A sixth shot filled the air, with a flash of crimson joining it where Gordon Graham's head had once been.

Startled at the source of the shot, Jean pointed his pistol back to the two zealots, who shared a look of confusion. Both were still unarmed. They hadn't shot Graham.

Morrison?

And then there was nothing but pain as Jean spun and fell face first into mud.

CHAPTER SEVENTY-THREE

The Summons

Turtle Island Jesuit School
October 8, 1898

NOT A STORM—*magic unleashed.* Fawn Chevreuil's ears still rang after the shockwave finished echoing across the campus of Turtle Island Jesuit School. The lightning that split the big oak tree in half left red embers where it had passed. A large branch rested against the Superintendent's office, crumbling the brick wall. A moment later, Lily had stepped over the fallen branches to run toward the wooded ravine of the Blue Knife River.

Now, Superintendent White Wolf stood looking at the tree, and a dozen adults converged around it, including the headmistress of the girls' dorm.

Sensing her opportunity, Fawn opened the window, climbed out backwards, and then dropped to the ground, unseen. *Lily needs me*—she ran into the darkness wearing nothing but her nightgown.

When she had closed her eyes to sleep hours earlier, she had seen the battle with clarity: the Tak-Pei gathered together at Deadwood Island with the souls of the dead, and the Jiibay rose from the depths of Lake Manitou like moths drawn to the flame.

Now awake, alert, Fawn ran in the darkness, seeing nothing except the occasional trunk of a tree. *Why does Lily run away from the fight? Migisi is in the other direction.*

A dragging noise provided the answer.

It quickly stopped, replaced only by the sound of Fawn's own lungs. "Lily?"

"Oh, thank God, it's you."

Fawn advanced to the sound of her voice. Near the river, the canopy of trees parted, allowing the flickering lightning to show her where Lily stood beside Big Squeak's birchbark canoe.

Without even asking, Fawn took hold of one of the ends and helped drag it to the water's edge. In the distance, Superintendent White Wolf began calling Lily's name.

Lily set her end down, but it was not the call that stopped her.

At first, Fawn didn't understand what was wrong.

"No, no, no," Lily muttered. "It's done. They finished it."

"What?"

"The water!"

The canoe was stored on top of the ravine, yet there had not been a steep descent. It was as if magic had caused the entire body of water to rise up to kill them all ... *Oh. The dam.*

"They closed the dam earlier in the week," Lily reminded. "The reservoir has filled up because of the rains."

"We can portage around the dam—"

"No, that's not the point. It'll be lost."

Voices grew nearer.

"Climb in. We need to go."

Obeying, Fawn began padding from the front of the canoe, giving her a view of the changed river. With each paddle, she began to understand what had been lost.

There were no rocks or boulders. Nor did the current pull her along through tight channels.

The dam had been closed, filling the ravine with forty feet of placid water.

"Did you hear that?" Lily asked in a whisper.

Fawn stopped paddling and shook her head. "What is it?"

"I heard a boy's voice."

"Migisi?"

"No. It came from…"

Lily looked over the side of the canoe, and Fawn prepared herself to be devoured by some terrible water monster when she looked, but she didn't see anything but the dark surface. "What did you hear?"

"I heard the word 'Clay' and when I looked down, I could see them."

"See what?"

"The two brothers in our canoe. They're looking for it also. We need to follow them. Don't you see them?"

This is insane, Fawn thought but obediently obeyed, paddling so that Lily could navigate. Lily kept her gaze on the water as if following a school of fish.

Finally, they veered toward the shore and Fawn immediately knew where she was. The big bald stone marked the place where they had built the sweat lodge for Lily's Vision Quest. It had been the visible landmark showing the line between sweet Winnie's property and crazy Nanakonan's property. A short distance away, the charred cabin remained, along with the concrete monstrosity of the roaring dam.

After getting out of the canoe, Lily frantically turned back toward the river. Fawn had no other choice than to join her, blind to the hysteria. *This is like being in a dream while awake.*

"They found it. They led me right to it. I can see them down below, climbing out of the rocks," Lily said in awe. "Do you remember the blue vitriol in the rocks? They can still see it. They know where the cave is."

The cave…

Fawn stared into the water, but still saw nothing, but then—closing her eyes, she saw two brothers climbing out of a canoe identical to the one beached at the top of the ravine. Through the rumbles of thunder and the roar of the wind buffeting the pines, she heard a faint voice speaking: "Right over there in the rocks. It's blue, just like you said, Pewabic."

Fawn realized the voice was coming from deep within the water below her. Her eyes opened and she looked down. She saw a boy that appeared to be the same age as Lily, the other was in the front of the canoe, pointing to the same place where Migisi had once hunted for the Horned Serpent.

The boys, buried by water, began to climb up the rocky slopes toward them.

"What do we do?" Fawn took Lily's hand in terror and anticipation.

"We let them show us the way. I've seen him before in my visions. He's the young man from the future."

Fawn looked back down.

The younger boy stayed at the canoe while the older boy climbed toward them. The young man had Father Guerin's lean face with a leather headband to keep his long hair out of his eyes, which made him look like Lily's father. But he wore strangely painted blue jeans and a black shirt with the word "Metallica" written upon it. *Is that Latin?* He swung his elbows round his knees as he sat down, tapping his gray snakeskin boots nervously.

"I know where the Water Drum can be found," he said aloud. "I can help you save him. It's over here."

The younger, short-haired boy stopped, standing on the rubble pile just below the cave.

Lily whispered to Fawn, "Are you seeing this?"

Fawn nodded. *This is happening too fast.*

"Do I trust him?"

Something seems wrong. Unable to discern why she felt worried, Fawn nodded again.

Taking a deep breath, Lily let go of her hand and pushed herself off of the granite ledge. She fell neck deep into the water.

Fawn found herself sitting with the apparition of the young man, who also looked down at Lily, but instead of speaking to her, he spoke to the younger boy in the water. "I need you to lead Lily back down to the cave."

The young boy's head frantically looked around him.

"I need you to do this, Joey. I need you to go in there first," the older boy said.

Joey! The name spoken by the Spiders to Lily.

"I'm scared, Levi."

Levi—the other great-grandson. This is a vision from the future.

"Don't be," Levi said. "I'm doing this to protect you. I'd never let anything bad happen to you. Now, go down there and crawl into that cave."

When he dove, Lily vanished in the water, leaving Fawn alone with the older boy's spirit.

For several minutes, Fawn sat shivering, trying to control her senses. Finally, she controlled her fears to ask, "Why are you here?"

"I'm closing the loop that Lily created. She called out for help, and we answered. What choice do I have? If I deny her, she fails and my world crumbles away." He paused, his expression hardening. "I need your help, though."

"Me?" Fawn clarified, surprised. A fresh wave of fear ran through her when he nodded.

"I don't have time to explain now, but we have to help her and stop her all at the same time."

"Why?"

"Lily is about to doom us all—for in victory, she will bring us defeat."

Fawn looked down at the dark, still water. *I-I think I've known that for a while now. But I know and love Lily. I don't know anything about this strange young man.* Aloud she asked, "What is happening to her?"

"My brother helped her find the opening to the cave, which has an air pocket. Our ancestors hid something in it long ago, and Lily needs it to fight the Wintermaker. I couldn't find any other way but to let it come true." He sighed. "She has to find it."

A moment later, Lily appeared, struggling to swim and gasping for air when she broke the surface. She carried something heavy at her side, which she set upon the granite.

"What is it?" Fawn asked.

Lily and the young man Levi answered simultaneously, "The Water Drum."

A moment later, Lily caught her breath and returned to her spot beside Fawn, setting the wrapped object between her feet.

"What are you going to do?" Fawn asked.

"I need help," Lily explained. "I need the rest of the Song of the Manitou, the parts that Grandfather never taught me."

More ghosts? Fawn wondered. "How can you learn something that was lost?"

Levi was the one who answered this time. "In the future, the Song of the Manitou is found. You can call out to the one who finds it. She knows what you need."

"Who is she?" Lily asked.

"She's an ally," Levi said, glancing briefly at Fawn. "She's from the future, and she told me that you must hear the lost verses to save your loved ones. Do you want me to call her?"

Fawn looked away. *What does he mean by "in victory, she will bring us defeat?" Am I supposed to stop Lily?*

"Yes, call her for me," Lily said.

A moment later, another apparition sat beside the young man in snakeskin boots. Fawn saw a woman in her thirties, the side of her head shaved, with a gruesome pink scar above her brow. Where her right eye should have been, she only saw a smooth patch of skin. On her chest, she wore a strange emblem of a mighty bird—the Great Thunderbird.

"I need you to teach her the secrets of the Water Drum," Levi said to the scarred woman. "Sing the missing verses to Lily so she can save him."

Migisi? Has something happened to Migisi?

And then the boys vanished over the edge of the cliff and into the waters of the Blue Knife River.

Wait! You didn't tell me what to do!

You said Lily will doom us...

The scarred woman sighed. "If I teach you the missing verses of the Song of the Manitou," the woman began, "you will be able to save him today, but you will only delay the inevitable."

Is this what Levi meant? The inevitable doom?

"I love him," Lily said.

Is she talking about Migisi or Father Guerin?

The woman nodded. "If I teach you the rest of the Song, you will have to swear an oath."

"Anything. Whatever you want."

The wounded woman cackled, her laughter spilling out of her paralyzed mouth. "It isn't an oath to me. It will be an oath to the Wintermaker."

"I will do anything."

Fawn winced. *Oh Lily, you can't possibly mean that.*

Despite the woman's misshapen mouth, soon lyrics came from her lips, and as she sang, Fawn could feel the stone grow warmer and warmer at Lily's feet.

And then it began to pulse.

Thump...

Thump....

Thump...

Fawn thought she understood now why it had been called the Water Drum.

Thump, thump, thump...

And then she realized the stone had begun to beat like a heart.

It was a heart.

My God. Lily, what are you doing?

CHAPTER SEVENTY-FOUR

Magic From the Dawn

Deadwood Island
October 8, 1898

MIGISI ASIBIKAASHI LAY spread-eagle upon the muddy sand, his hands and feet bound with leather straps tied to stakes pounded into the wet earth.

Surrounding him, his abductors sat in positions representing the different clans of creation, with Joseph Little Toad conducting the ritual. In front of the old sorcerer, an ornate water drum echoed, calling out to the spirits in Lake Manitou.

He doesn't have the real water drum, Migisi told himself, trying to give himself an emotion other than terror. *And he doesn't have the Ironwood Scrolls or the Sacred Shell.*

Yet with each passing minute, the situation grew worse.

No, Joseph Little Toad did not have the full Song, but as a surviving member of the Wijigan Clan, he'd inherited some of it, and from what he'd gleaned from Lily, he had enough.

He's calling out to the Tak-Pei.

Back at Leech Lake, Little Toad had put Migisi through the same ritual, strapping him to the earth, thumping the water drum, and singing the verses of the Song of the Manitou. While the ancient magic did summon a storm, Little Toad's belief that Leech Lake's Bear Island was the Seventh Stopping Place was wrong.

The shells, Migisi had thought. *The sacred megis shells will guide the way.*

Little Toad's blunder had become obvious, and for a brief moment, Migisi thought the ordeal had ended. A platoon of U.S. soldiers had marched right up to their ritual, but instead of saving him or arresting Little Toad, they froze for a few moments before retreating from where they'd come.

That was three days ago, and now, Little Toad understood his mistake in choosing Leech Lake. This time, when he thumped his drum and sang the old words, the magic responded.

The stars did not shine, and just like with Leech Lake, the old conjurer summoned another storm to blanket the sky, hiding the deeds from the eyes of their ancestors.

What about the Serpent Star? Nanak had been emphatic—*the Wintermaker can only be defeated at a time when the Serpent Star returns.*

Migisi turned his head away from the vacant heavens, pressing his cheek against the mud to witness eight foul creatures climbing out of the depths of Lake Manitou. His body shivered uncontrollably, from both the cold and terror.

Like a curious wolf pack, the Tak-Pei approached. Lily had woken them while he'd been away at Morris, and since then, each death along the shores of the lake strengthened them to the point where they now glistened with oily quills and rippled with paranormal strength as they circled around the humans who'd called out in the ancient language.

Having spent the last few days with Little Toad and his zealots, Migisi understood what would happen next: he would be sacrificed. The edge of a knife did not frighten him, but what Little Toad intended was far worse than death. His blood, the blood of the Wijigan, was not to be sacrificed to the Wintermaker. No, instead, it was meant to entice the sleeping sorcerer. The Tak-Pei would rip his soul from his flesh so that the ancient spirit of the Wintermaker could take his flesh and wear it like a robe. Joseph Little Toad wanted a messianic figure to lead the people into a great war, and the Wintermaker would be his new god on earth.

I thought I was the Thunderbird, destined to destroy him. I don't want to become him. Migisi rolled his head away in anguish.

Little Toad's hoarse voice continued singing a verse that Migisi had never heard before from Nanak or Lily, and even though he did not understand the old language, he understood one of the words, which pierced his soul like a cold knife.

The true name of the Wintermaker.

From the depths, a shadow moved, and the island felt as if it quivered. Just behind Little Toad, a dark shadow took the form of a human man, but when it took a step closer, it had the face of Father Guerin.

Then death flashed in his hand, killing Little Toad and a few of the others.

Father Guerin's pistol stopped on two surviving acolytes, but Migisi could only watch in horror as the events spun out of control. Bushy Bill Morrison appeared, as if providing support, only to shoot down Graham, Father Guerin, and the remaining acolytes.

Father Guerin's death had come so suddenly that when his body flopped down upon the ground near Migisi, the priest's body was almost immediately lifeless.

Get up. You can't be dead. You need to save me.

Bushy Bill Morrison advanced, pistol ready. "Nothing personal, kid. I'm just following orders. I didn't want to kill the priest, or Graham, but I couldn't let them be witness to this. Nor could I let this ritual continue. My people have been patient for far too long to let Little Toad steal the future away from us. You understand?"

Bushy Bill now stood over him, and with sympathetic eyes, he lifted the pistol.

Migisi's eyes darted to the side and he struggled against his bonds.

The Tak-Pei, fed by the blood of the slain, had absorbed all the magic found in death and doubled in density, now no longer little figures the size of dogs but looming monsters each larger than a man.

Bushy Bill Morrison had no clue.

But the U.S. Marshal did sense the other threat, and when the hammer of a pheasant rifle clicked back, his eyes and pistol drifted away from the death blow.

A red-headed white boy stood on the edge of the shadows, with a shotgun pointed at the back of Morrison—*Bjorn Forsberg*.

Having been witness to the horror, the farm boy stepped out of the shadows to prevent Migisi's cold-blooded murder. The young hero, however, had not counted on the shadows coming to life around him.

"Run!" Migisi screamed.

Bushy Bill was preparing to shoot the fleeing farm boy in the back when black, oily hands grabbed ahold of him, and like a pack of wolf pups playing with a dead squirrel, the Tak-Pei tossed the body of Morrison into the air, batting it around for a short while as the man screamed in abject horror.

His body was ripped limb from limb, bile and gore filling the air as pieces of his body landed in branches and bushes surrounding the clearing.

On the edge of the light, Bjorn Forsberg had disappeared, the shotgun resting where he'd dropped it before taking flight.

Then the Tak-Pei closed in on Migisi.

He jerked his arms and legs violently, hoping the bonds would break, which they didn't. *Just kill me. Don't let me be the Omodai. Please, please.*

When the first oily hand touched his flesh, it felt cold as ice water, but then the sharp pain turned into the tingle of a leg that had fallen asleep. The tingling grew, a million tiny needles prickling in his flesh.

And … it all stopped.

Am I dead?

The Tak-Pei still held onto him, but now…

Is that my body? Migisi saw his own miserable form, his heart still beating, lungs still breathing, pinned to the ground.

Lake Manitou changed immediately. No longer was he on an island in a lake, but he stood atop a mountain with a deep ravine. At the bottom of the ravine, no longer hidden by sediment or muck, there was the rectangular shape of a doorway, and standing in the passage, was a man.

It isn't supposed to happen like this, Migisi thought, desperate.

I agree, the Wintermaker answered from the doorway. *Something is not right.*

The Elixir of Life

Lake Manitou
October 8, 1898

*T*HERE IS NO *turning back now.* Lily Weber held tight to the Philosopher's Stone in her lap as Fawn paddled hard for shore.

"I see light ahead," Fawn reported. "Deep in the island."

As soon as the nose of the canoe grated against the muck, Fawn was out, pulling the canoe forward so Lily could disembark.

Looking down, Lily realized why the stone was so light. *It's holding on to me more than I'm holding onto it.* She could see the color of the stone swirl with red, as if it had blood within it.

A voice whispered in her brain—*Don't sing it yet. Wait until they all gather.*

So Lily waited, letting Fawn help her out of the canoe so both of them could rush toward the faint light at the center of the island.

Nothing could have prepared Lily for what she discovered: from the bile dripping from the trees to the scattered corpses illuminated by torch to her still brother tied to the earth in the middle of it all.

Fawn was running, pausing only to step over a body before dropping beside Migisi. "He's alive."

Lily cautiously advanced but stopped when Fawn turned back around and gasped. Lily saw the black cassock.

No!

Rushing forward, she soon stood over the still body. His circular glasses were twisted on the sand, his eyes open, unblinking. His mouth slightly ajar, as if death caught him by surprise.

The Philosopher's Stone again rested on her thighs—*Don't let go. I'm the only thing that can save you now.*

Fawn turned from Migisi and joined Lily at the corpse. "I'm pretty sure he's dead, Lily."

He can't be dead. What about the apparitions? The little boy knew me as his great-grandmother. How can I become Lily Guerin if he's—

"Lily?"

Fawn's voice turned into a grunt as black arms took hold of her and pulled her away like a leaf in the wind.

No!

The stone spoke again. *Now. Sing the Song. I'm the only thing that can stop them.*

Lily opened her mouth, and the Tak-Pei immediately paused their attack on Fawn upon hearing the first few notes.

The stone responded with a pulse of heat, wrapping itself around her fingers and over the top of her hands, merging the two of them together—the Firehandler and the Philosopher's Stone.

Although the Tak-Pei sensed the magic, they did not flee. The one holding Fawn flung her aside, with Fawn making a grunting noise as she hit the ground, followed by a slight moan.

Unleash me, the stone called to Lily. *These foul demons are no match for us.*

More syllables poured out of her mouth, and the words written in the past and discovered in the future filled the air. The stone expanded from her lap, doubling in size until with one punctuated note, the bubble burst and the stone transformed into liquid. Lily felt some of it still gripping her hands, but the rest rose like steam from a boiling pot.

What should I do now? Lily asked of it.

It answered immediately, *First, defend yourself.*

The vapor from the stone constricted, and like a whip, lashed out at the closest Tak-Pei, striking its flesh with such force that the oily creature lost its form as it hurdled into the woods of the island.

The other Tak-Pei rushed at her, but the Philosopher's Stone responded first like a blanket that wrapped around her and then like the snapping mouth of a serpent. Lily and the stone were one, the stone acting as a spiritual and physical extension of her mind.

One by one, the stone lashed out at the Tak-Pei until Lily secured the island.

In the silence, Lily took measure of the scene. Fawn was unconscious but breathing, the only injury a scrape on her right temple. Migisi also lived, and with her focused mind, the ties that bound him were dissolved away, but even freed, Migisi did not respond. Guerin, however, did not move at all.

He can't be dead. I need to save him.

Don't worry about the priest, the stone soothed. *His soul isn't going anywhere. The fools have woken my master, and now we must destroy him.*

Lily peered into the depths of Lake Manitou, and her eyes saw what had once terrified her great-grandfather Chagobay. The roots of the water lily reached down to the depths, and there, the Wintermaker looked up at her. It wasn't a Horned Serpent or a water monster, though—it was the spirit of a man.

"You are not the one who woke me," the Wintermaker said to her across the void, "yet you hold the key to my resurrection."

Resurrection? Lily looked over at the cold body of Jean Guerin as the stone hummed. She'd seen the future, a future where she'd become Lily Guerin. *I'll have great-grandchildren. How do I protect that future?* She pictured the faces of the children from her dream—the ones who shared her eyes. *Of course, they are my descendants.* Two of them she knew: Levi and Joey.

"It was an accident."

"Yes, your voice woke my servants, didn't it? But it was not you who woke me. Why do you hold the key in your hand if you do not intend on freeing me?"

"This wasn't supposed to happen. None of this."

"You are right, child, none of this was supposed to happen—not now, at least. My hour has not yet come, yet here you are."

He's afraid of us, the stone murmured. *He knows we hold the knife to his throat.*

At her hesitance, it snapped, *Use it!*

In the Seven Fires Prophecy, the fate of mankind came down to a choice. One choice would bring destruction, and the other would bring an Eighth Fire of peace and harmony. *Free will mixed with fate.* Lily had seen her future, but was yet to reach it; a million decisions had to be made before destiny could arrive.

"If you haven't come to fight," the Wintermaker continued, "then perhaps we can negotiate. We can pretend none of this happened … especially since I have something that you might want."

Two spirits appeared next to the Wintermaker: Migisi and Jean. Lily looked at her little brother first. Unlike Jean, whose body was pale and lifeless, Migisi still breathed.

It's a trick, the stone said.

Unsure, she looked around for help and saw Fawn. Her cousin's spirit sat beside her own unconscious body. In her hand, she held a glowing megis shell, but her eyes were closed.

I need help! Why isn't anyone helping me?

Even the stone was silent now.

"It's a simple choice, Noozhishenh," the Wintermaker said, speaking the Chippewa word for granddaughter.

The loop must be closed. I have to do my part. I have to protect the future for the children—my children. "Give him back to me."

The Wintermaker smiled. "The waters are filled with souls, some fresh and some as old as the dawn. Be clear, what are you asking, child?"

In her dreams, both Migisi and Jean had boldly sacrificed themselves like the knights of old battling a dragon, yet Migisi still breathed while Jean's body rested upon the cold sand.

No adoption.

No marriage.

No Lily Guerin

"He can't be dead. It wasn't supposed to happen this way."

"The priest?" the Wintermaker clarified, his smile widening.

It's a bluff. Migisi is fine.

"Yes. Give Jean back to me."

"And why would I do that?" Lily's anger grew.

Yes, the stone whispered, *threaten him. He will understand the threat.*

"Because I have the original Water Drum, your precious key. I command it, and it obeys, and instead of using it to bring you back to life, I could use it to destroy the magic that protects you and then cast you to the depths where you belong."

"You remind me of my daughter in so many ways," the Wintermaker replied, a small but genuine smile now on his face. "But in order to give you the soul of the priest, you must do your part first. Only then can we begin to negotiate."

What part? Lily wondered.

The stone knew—*We must heal his body first. I can help. I can give this to you.*

Even though her hands never touched him, Lily nevertheless felt Jean's cold flesh through the Philosopher's Stone ...

... and a thousand little needles went into motion.

CHAPTER SEVENTY-SIX

Rekindling of Old Flames

Deadwood Island
October 8, 1898

FAWN CHEVREUIL DREAMT of the boy Iyash standing on the island as the Horned Serpent left a wake in the water of the channel between the island and the safety of the mainland. On the mainland, she was surrounded by animals that stepped out of the forest as if answering the boy's call: a large buck, a bald eagle, a black raven, a sly fisher cat, a spotted loon, a brilliantly white crane, a muddy catfish, and a massive bear.

"This is the beginning," Iyash said to her from the other side of the channel. "But before you can save me, you have to reach the end of the journey."

"Isn't *this* the Seventh Stopping Place?" Her hold tightening on the megis shell she'd found in the mud of the Blue Knife.

"It *is* the Seventh Stopping Place, but it is *not* the end of the journey."

The horns of the water serpent shot away from the channel and out into the depths of the open sea. As soon as they vanished, the water of the channel boiled until a dark object appeared. As it rose, water poured off the rounded surface. Finally, Fawn understood what she saw: a massive turtle, its shell covered in sediment and moss as if it'd laid dormant for a thousand years.

"For you to reach me, you must find the place on the shell where the water divides," Iyash instructed. "Do you see the place?"

Fawn saw a tiny light. In fact, the closer she looked at the shell, the more detail it revealed, until it became obvious that she looked at the landscape of the continent. She was sitting on the edge of the shell and looked at the island where Iyash waited. Behind her, rivers were flowing off the back of the turtle that looked like the St. Lawrence, the Mississippi, and the Red River. Even farther behind her, she saw the ridge of the turtle's back, as if high mountains. And there, hidden in the ridges, she saw the light referenced by Iyash.

"What is it?"

"You must rekindle the flame before you can show the others how to retrace the path back to me. You must light the way for them in their darkest hour. Do you remember what you were told at the cave?"

She did: *'Lily is about to doom us all—for in victory, she will bring us defeat.'*

Levi asked for her help.

The boy Iyash also asked for her help. "Can you do this?"

I must rekindle the flame. "Yes," she said, her eyes fixed on the tiny point of light until it was the only thing she could see. *I must help them in their darkest hour.*

"Good."

AS SHE PASSED from dream to consciousness, the light remained as she opened her eyes.

Back on Deadwood Island, the light transformed into a lantern, and the man who held it had a kind face and a beard that ringed his jaw but left his mouth shaved clean. "There's a girl over here. She's alive."

I'm alive? But how?

It was still dark, yet the nightmare seemed over for the singing had stopped, and the living shadows had vanished.

Fawn's eyes studied the tree above her and its twisted branches. Another face appeared to loom over her, a white boy's face.

"Hi, you're safe now, I think."

She knew the boy, but the throbbing in her skull kept the name from reaching her tongue. "What happened?"

"I don't know. We just got here."

Albert Fisher—that was the boy's name. Over the last few weeks, he'd come to the school to speak with Lily and …

Oh, God.

Fawn sat up, bringing twice as much pain to her head. She remembered how the devils had tossed her around, and then how Lily's voice cut the darkness like a sword. But before that, she'd been at the side of Migisi and had seen the lifeless body of Father Guerin.

It can't be true.

"Father Guerin is—" Her words failed her when she saw Father Guerin sitting up with Bjorn Forsberg and Martin Nielson flanking him. Although quite shaken, Father Guerin looked very much alive.

What? How …

"Hold still, sweetheart," Farrell Luning said to Fawn. "Let me look at your head."

With a grimace, Farrell tended to the bloody spot on the back of her head as pain and nausea churned in her gut.

I don't understand.

Father Guerin was opening his shirt, revealing his pale chest, unblemished. If not for the hole in his cassock and shirt, Fawn might have believed it to all be a nightmare.

Once Luning finished his examination, he winced as he rose to his feet, and in doing so, revealed another baffling scene.

Lily was alive, sitting on the ground with Migisi cradled in her lap, his head leaning against her chest. His eyes were closed, and he appeared unharmed. Kermit Crain sat beside her with a hand on her shoulder as she wept.

"Help me up. I need to see Lily," Fawn demanded. When she stood, she saw spots so intense that it felt as if the Tak-Pei had rushed in for another attack.

"Easy," Albert whispered, still holding her hand.

Catching her breath, she looked around to the canopy of trees illuminated by the lanterns. There was no sign of a water serpent, the Tak-Pei, or the sinister Wintermaker, but something still felt wrong.

The island seemed inert. *What then*—a new horror presented itself.

She looked to the site of the ritual, where the Wijigan acolytes and Joseph Little Toad had gathered around a prone Migisi to perform the Song of the Manitou. Not only were the bodies gone but not a drop of blood remained.

But it *had* happened.

Even the dismembered body of Bushy Bill Morrison had vanished.

The answer to it all rested at Lily's feet.

The Water Drum.

"To Lily, please." Fawn put her weight upon Albert's shoulder as Father Guerin's private search party congealed together. Lily was focused on nothing but Migisi, and Father Guerin remained transfixed on his chest. Nearing him, she could hear his mumbling.

"I saw it," he said to Martin Nielson. "Once my soul left my body, I saw all of them. Dozens and dozens of souls trapped in the waters of Lake Manitou. All the stories are true, but ... but ... at the bottom of it all, I saw the dragon itself."

Fawn had seen it too—but only the beginning.

"It's the wounded head," Father Guerin said, gripping Nielson's arm. "It's right out of scripture. I saw the wounded head, which was healed." His hand returned to his exposed chest, studying the miracle again. "I don't—"

Seeing Fawn, Father Guerin stopped speaking and used the others for help to stand.

Wordlessly, they all gathered around Lily and Migisi.

"I don't know what to do," Lily whispered.

"Where did they go, Lily?" Fawn asked sharply.

Lily looked to the Philosopher's Stone at her feet. "I used all the magic I knew to put them back to sleep. I fixed all the mistakes I'd made but one—I thought it was just a bluff."

"What's wrong with him?" Martin Nielson asked.

"They took him," Lily said, shaking her head. "They took hold of Migisi and pulled him down into the depths. Everything happened so quickly. He was unharmed, and Jean, you were ... you were..."

"I'm here now, Lily," Father Guerin said, kneeling down beside her to hold one of her hands. "Tell us what we need to do."

"I don't know."

"Someone is coming," Farrell Luning called out, gesturing to the west.

Bjorn Forsberg stepped forward with his shotgun, and Kermit turned, holding a large, curved blade.

"Albert, go fetch my pistol," Father Guerin commanded, standing.

Fawn watched as two birchbark canoes approached from the northwest. Even before the uplifted noses of the canoes slid onto the soft shore, she knew the dark silhouettes: Pierre LeDuc and Blackfish LaBiche.

Both men hopped from the canoes and walked to Lily. The introductions and explanations were brief, and the attention quickly returned to Lily and Migisi.

"They took his soul," Lily said, despondent, "and I don't know how to put it back."

"Let's get everyone back to the school," Luning said when LeDuc and LaBiche didn't respond. "Your brother has been through quite an ordeal. Let's get him in front of a fire."

No. Dreams of Iyash stuck on the island filled her mind, along with the animals that waited upon the shore.

It's a sign. It must be.

This is my part.

This is how I'll help Iyash.

"No," Fawn said aloud. "I think ... I think I know where he is, and what we must do."

Everyone, including Lily, looked at her.

So she told them her dream.

The Isanti Lodge

Turtle Island
October 8, 1898

THE *MANITOU IS real.* Kermit Crain sat, a slight smile on his face, his curved castration knife upon his lap as he watched the ritual begin.

They now gathered on Turtle Island, which was only an island by a few inches of water, connected by a peninsula to Martin Nielson's land. A fire burned at the center, illuminating all of them. Hastily hewn pine branches marked the foundation of the roofless lodge, with the team of believers sitting inside.

Martin Nielson sat at the western door, with Bjorn Forsberg, Albert Fisher, and Farrell Luning sitting along the southern wall. Fawn Chevreuil, Father Guerin, Lily, and he sat along the northern wall. Migisi's body rested on one side of the fire and the Philosopher's Stone rested opposite of it. Outside of the bough foundation, Pierre LeDuc and Blackfish guarded the eastern door, just as Fawn insisted.

Ironically, although Kermit had been the first to see the Manitou months earlier, he'd missed most of what happened on Deadwood Island. *It must've been pretty scary, though.*

The evidence was on their faces. Bold Lily had seemingly deflated with an outpouring of tears as they traveled toward the island. And Father Guerin's hands had not stopped trembling since they sat. Fawn Chevreuil's wide eyes reminded him of a gopher about to be snatched up by a hawk. Even stern Bjorn Forsberg looked shaken, his freckled forehead creased.

"What happened?" Kermit had asked Bjorn privately as they rowed across the lake to Turtle Island.

"I saw him die," Bjorn said, glancing over at Father Guerin. "Now the others are all gone, and he's alive."

They who?

Kermit had been watching the storm when Martin Nielson rode by, looking for help. Instead of finding armed Indians, he and Martin arrived at the island to find weeping and chaos. Albert and Farrell had heard the shooting too, but not a body remained to be found, except for an unconscious Migisi.

"Now what?" Lily asked, sniffling.

Fawn answered calmly, "We need to sanctify this place. Use the Water Drum to cleanse it from the magic of the Wintermaker. The Great Spirit, your God, has brought all of us here today to fight against evil. First, begin with that."

Lily opened her mouth, and the words that came out sounded more angelic than human. The stone responded and pulsed as if alive; it transformed from solid into liquid.

For a moment, Kermit lifted his knife, thinking the stone might transform into the water serpent, its rivulets flowing outward like fingers. Then the liquid transformed into vapor, and Lily's words sent it out into the darkness of the island.

Eleven of them gathered upon the rocky ridge of the island, just as Fawn had insisted, to fight a final battle before the break of dawn. Already, the stars were beginning to diminish, and a glow began to appear in the east.

To think … I used to be just worried about Pa's wrath.

The vapor returned to the fire.

"I'm finished," Lily whispered.

"Is there a song of protection?" Fawn asked.

"Yes."

"Then sing it, marking all of us. We are the ones who will stand against the Wintermaker. All of us, together."

Lily nodded, and the ritual continued.

This is good. Kermit remembered the occult ritual he'd observed at Flat Rock the previous year. Although his family didn't believe him about a secret society in St. John, perhaps now he'd found a pool of believers that would. *Good versus evil.*

Kermit paused as the vapor passed over him. Whatever it was, the Philosopher's Stone did not seem to be something made by God, and as a result, it felt sinister, even if Lily was using it for good.

It can't hurt me … us … right?

At the end of the second song, Lily sighed heavily. "Now what?"

"Now, you go find your brother."

Lily crumbled, looking away. "I don't know what that means."

Fawn hissed. "Yes, you do. You've driven the Tak-Pei back into slumber, and you've thwarted the Wintermaker, closing him back in his hole. Little Toad tried to offer Migisi as an omodai, a vessel, for the taking. He's down in the depths, lost with the other spirits. Call out to the spirits, ask them for aid in finding your brother."

Lily nodded and began to sing.

The Place of Souls, Kermit reflected. Since his attack, he'd picked up every book on Indians he could get his hands on, reading all about the legends of the Chippewa and Sioux. Before the Chippewa settled along the Blue Knife, the Sioux once held the area, and instead of Lake Manitou, they called it *Wanagiyata.*

It's always been cursed.

The evil that slumbered went beyond cultures.

The answers were in the distant past.

If the tales were true, the Sioux had a band of warriors sworn to guard the area—the Santee. In some books, they were known as the Isanyanthi, or Guardians of the Frontier. Yet Kermit found a third spelling of the same band, Isanti, which meant People of the Knife. He looked down at the knife he held and smiled.

Guardians.

The Blue Knife River.

Lake Manitou.

Place of Souls.

This is my destiny. I'm meant to be part of this group.

Kermit jumped along with the others when Migisi abruptly began to swing his arms and kick his legs, all while taking deep breaths like that of a drowning victim. Both Father Guerin and Lily left their spots, rushing forward to hold him.

I don't even know what we just did.

But it obviously worked.

Migisi opened his eyes, twisting his head to look around at those surrounding him. Terror filled his eyes. Fawn reached out to hold his hand.

"You're safe now," Lily soothed, crying tears of relief.

He's seen the Manitou. I know the look in his eyes.

From outside the lodge, Blackfish declared, "We should return. The sun is coming up and soon the world will also wake up."

Lily nodded, and everyone began to rise, including Migisi, who sat up with his own strength. With squinted eyes, he looked around at those gathered around him, and when the answers became obvious, he looked at Lily with abject horror, "What did you do?"

"We saved you, little brother."

"No, I was there. I was with the Wintermaker. I heard you. You picked *him!*" Migisi shoved her away when she reached for him, disgust on his face.

"I fixed it. I fixed everything," she replied, her voice breaking. "You're fine. I knew you were strong. I knew you would fight. Look … Father Guerin's fine. We won the day. You're here now."

Migisi shook. "How could you? You left me down there!"

He pushed away Father Guerin when he reached for him, tripping on the boughs as he left the lodge. He headed to Pierre LeDuc. "I want to go home."

"I think we all need to go home, to sort this out," Father Guerin declared, putting a comforting hand on Lily's shoulder.

Kermit wanted to comfort Lily too, but she buried her face in Father Guerin's chest when Migisi ran off.

In the silence, no one else knew what to do. He watched the group begin to divide, with some returning east to Split Rock and the rest returning north to the school. Kermit decided to walk with Martin Nielson.

"Well, that was the strangest night of my life," Nielson declared, tussling Kermit's hair.

"I suppose we're not going to talk about this to other folks," Kermit said. "My family wouldn't believe me anyway."

"I don't think my wife will either. You can come talk to me about it any time you want, but yes, I think we should keep this to ourselves for the time being."

FOR A WHILE, Kermit walked the high ground toward Old Copper Road, which would take him home to Sterling Junction, but then he heard the angry calls of ravens. When he stopped, he could see them circling above a tree in the ravine.

A willow tree.

Weaving a Web

Turtle Island
October 19, 1898

JEAN GUERIN STOOD with his hands on his hips as the delegation of politicians and Indian agents left the school. *They think the war is over—it's only begun.*

He turned, reviewing all that he had built. Dozens of children were safe inside of a school built to protect them from all sorts of dangers. Even though conflict at Leech Lake had dissipated, the victory was hollow.

I shouldn't be here right now. Why am I even alive?

He turned to the Superintendent's office where another conflict waited to be resolved.

Opening the door, he found his two closest allies.

Lily Weber sat cross-legged on the corner chair, the soiled cassock still draped over her legs. In her fingers, she held a needle and thread, ready to patch the bullet hole in the back of the garment. She'd claimed it without asking.

Paul White Wolf stood at the window of his office, looking out at the delegation that was departing.

Now what am I supposed to do? What can I say?

"So now what?" White Wolf asked, his gaze still fixed outward.

Lily glanced at White Wolf and then over to him.

Collapsing in a chair, Jean looked up at the ceiling. "Now the war will be waged by newspaper writers, politicians, and lawyers, but for all intents and purposes, the Battle of Sugar Point is over. Winter has a way of cooling tensions, and by spring, the government, the Bureau of Indian Affairs, and the tribal leaders will fight from behind tables. A truce doesn't mean victory, but it does mean there is a little hope."

White Wolf grunted, causing Jean to look at him. He shook his head before glancing at Lily. "No, Jean. *Now* what?"

The kiss…

Long before swearing his vows, Jean had known self-control. In the Philippines, he'd been offered the daughters of a mountain chieftain, and in Cuba, he had a flock of girls that followed him wherever he went. Even in the quiet moments of the balcony, as the two had smiled and laughed, he knew how to ignore the feelings he had for the beautiful young woman. Now the smiles and laughter were gone, and the trauma of recent events blanketed them all. More than once in recent days, Lily had crossed the line with her feelings. If he stayed much longer, he'd not be able to resist her.

Jean looked to Lily, who kept her eyes to the hole in the jacket where Bushy Bill Morrison's bullet had taken his life.

Now, Jean no longer wore his priestly collar.

Now he too had feelings.

Jean cleared his throat. "A strategy? Is that what you want to discuss?"

White Wolf shifted but did not answer.

"Well, we need to focus on defense. Our enemies have been revealed, and we know their weaknesses now, as well as what they are waiting for. We have a decade before Halley's Comet, the Serpent Star, returns to us, and in that time, we're going to turn Turtle Island Jesuit School into the preeminent center of

Indigenous Studies in the United States while we compare the legends of the Philosopher's Stone with the tales of the sacred Water Drum."

Two weeks had passed since the Battle of Sugar Point began, and the 3rd US Infantry Regiment, the Minnesota National Guard, and local militias were all ordered home. A council of Chippewa chiefs, free from the taint of Little Toad, won more than a military victory, which is what Jean's Jesuit superiors had informed him of moments earlier.

My mission succeeded. So what has White Wolf upset?

"You still don't understand," White Wolf answered. "Those men came today to tell us that the conflict between the Chippewa and the government is over. Politicians are changing policy about reservations and land rights. If I'm being optimistic, I'd even guess that some of what was lost might be given back."

"Yes, that's what I heard too. Is there a problem?"

What does he want from me?

"Your assignment here is over, Jean. It's a matter of weeks before your Jesuit superiors realize it and call you back—while you're talking about waiting for a comet to come in another ten years."

No one else would understand what I've seen. No one else would protect this family. "You heard Migisi. There's no denying the Serpent Star is anything other than Halley's Comet." *And it's returning soon.*

"The Society of Jesus is going to send for you. Your time here at the school is over. While everyone else marked by Lily can stay here and wait for the coming storm, your official mission here is complete. Plus, Eos has wised up to your strategy."

Triton will find better politicians. How can I leave when I still understand so little about them? I know the truth about this place, but what do my enemies want with it?

Lily was closing the hole in the back of the cassock. White Wolf was standing with arms crossed, waiting.

Can't he see the obvious truth? "I've already made my choice. When I was up at Bear Island, I could have stayed with Chief Sweating Stone and the other tribal leaders to help them through the crisis, but instead, I chose to follow Little Toad in order to save Migisi. When I drew my pistol on Deadwood Island, I effectively resigned my position in the Jesuit Order. Ironically, I've never believed more than I do now, and I'm no longer a part of the Church."

White Wolf shook his head. "That doesn't work. Staying here will only draw attention, suspicion. Without an explanation, the Catholic Church and the Jesuits will see it as a betrayal, and our enemies, like Triton, will know you've learned something significant. Our superiors won't allow you to stay under these circumstances."

Lily glanced at him with panicked eyes.

"I've been part of three active conflicts in the past five years," Jean countered. "I've been shot and stabbed twice. I'm lucky to be alive, so I'll invent some story about needing to clear my head and soothe my nerves."

"At a haunted lake?"

"Fine, then I'll play the altruistic angle. I'll gush about how much I enjoy the school, and how I've found a new love in education. I'll stay as a teacher or administrator."

"Your idea for a school was a stroke of genius, allowing me to be here, but as much as I'd like you by my side, the Periphery is not going to allow you to stay if they've got me. Your presence will be red flags for all to see."

How can I leave Lily after all of this? A small globe sat on the corner of White Wolf's desk, and Jean swept it off so violently that when it crashed onto the floor, it broke free from its axis and rolled all the way over to the door. "Then what do you suggest? I was all but born into the Periphery, and when I was Lily's age, I joined the Jesuits on the request of my supervisors. The head custodian himself told me I was born for this assignment. The Periphery understands my true loyalties and the importance of—"

Lily had given his cassock a dramatic snap. In silence, she stood and walked from her spot in the corner and over to where he sat.

"Lily, I—" His heart raced as she drew near.

She shook her head, folding the long riding jacket into quarters before setting it down on his lap. She leaned over and kissed him on the cheek. "There is only one path now." She turned to White Wolf to say, "He can stay for love."

Jean dropped his head in his hands.

When he looked up, only White Wolf remained. His eyes were wide but not in condemnation. "Lily's right. A scandal would be believed. Tender your resignation from the Jesuit Order, and then as a private citizen, buy a small plot of land nearby. You can't stay at the school, but we need you to shepherd us through the days to come, even in an unofficial capacity."

Am I staying for the Periphery?

Or for love?

Miss Weber

Turtle Island
October 19, 1898

WHEN THE BELL rang, ending Lily Weber's hour of grammar lessons, she stood in front of her desk to collect the assignments after the students left. Despite her instruction, the sheets were handed to her in all manners of angles, leaving an unkempt pile. The instructions about the grammar books were also ignored, with some left wide open, one knocked to the floor, and yet one book remained exactly where it had been set prior to the period.

Migisi's spot.

How do I fix my brother?

As if noticing the same book, Fawn cleared her throat as she walked forward to turn in her assignment.

"Do you know where he is?"

Fawn nodded. "He's down by the river again."

He shouldn't be skipping school. "I thought we were past all of this."

"I heard some of the boys talking about his nightmares and wetting the bed. It's gotten worse since Father Guerin left. Do you want me to tell Superintendent White Wolf?"

"No, but do you mind coming with me? He'll at least speak with you."

Fawn smiled. "Absolutely."

Walking out of the building, Lily was greeted by a cool autumn day, with drifts of maple leaves blowing across the yard and a blanket of gray over their heads.

They found Migisi on the southern border of the school. He sat on the bluff, sharpening his knife, looking down at the still reservoir created by the Nicollet Dam. The construction workers hired by Triton built a log chute that ran from the outlet of the dam to the waiting lake.

If he's afraid, do I lie to him to help him through this? "Why are you sharpening a knife?" Lily asked.

Her brother grunted. "Because it makes me feel better."

Lily could smell the urine on her brother, and combined with his messy hair, her brother looked a mess. "I need you to be part of the Isanti Lodge."

"That's a stupid name," Migisi said bitterly. "Why did you pick a Dakota word?"

"Kermit chose the word."

"Kermit didn't stab the Manitou. I've seen the real thing. The Wintermaker isn't some giant snake swimming in the water. It's down in the depths, waiting."

"And we defeated him," Lily boasted.

"Did we?" Migisi snapped. "Your story doesn't make sense, Tew, especially the part about Father Guerin. I saw him get killed."

When she looked at Fawn, her cousin shared the same wrinkled brow. *Neither of them knows what really happened.* "I ... when I ... I'm not a sorceress. I don't understand how any of this works, and I still don't even know what I said. When Fawn and I got to the island, we found you unconscious and Jean ... wounded. I just let my heart guide me from that point."

When her brother scoffed, Lily added, "I was given help, Migisi. Is that what you want to hear? Apparitions guided your stupid sister in my fight against the Wintermaker."

Fawn came to her aid then. "I was there when that happened. There was a boy with snakeskin boots, and a woman with a deformed face, and others who came to help."

Migisi shook his head. "Can you trust them?"

"They helped save your life and Jean's life," Lily countered, frustrated. "How can I not trust them? Now listen to me, Migisi, I know you're scared but—"

"I'm not scared!"

Don't argue. Don't tear him down. Build him up. "You're right, Migisi. I didn't defeat the Wintermaker."

He turned; his eyes filled with concern.

"I used the power of the Water Drum against its maker, but I only delayed the inevitable. Nanakonan was right. The Wintermaker will only get stronger, and when the Serpent Star returns, the Tak-Pei will wake, and the real battle will begin."

Migisi softened. "Is that why Father Guerin left?"

"No, no, that's not … he just moved off campus. He bought the Bordeaux farm south of Split Rock because to help us finish the fight. You know when the Serpent Star is coming, don't you?"

Migisi nodded. "Nanak told me all about it. Mr. White Wolf said it is Halley's Comet, and that it'll be here in 1910."

"Twelve years from now. Do you know what we're going to do in those twelve years? The Isanti Lodge is going to prepare. We're going to train. We're going to learn. We're going to prepare ourselves for battle with the Horned Serpent, just like Nanakonan would have wanted. He believed you were the Great Thunderbird, and I need you to play that role for us."

"What role?"

"You are going to be trained to be a warrior. We've found the sacred Water Drum and Ironwood Scrolls, and once we find the

Sacred Shell, and learn how to light the Sacred Fire, we'll be able to defeat the Wintermaker once and for all."

"Your sister's right, Migisi," Fawn added. "I had a vision of you. It's how we knew how to pull you back up from the depths. I saw Iyash trapped on an island, with the Horned Serpent swimming around it. But I also saw the buck, the eagle, the raven, the fisher cat, the loon, the crane, the catfish, and the bear."

"I don't understand what—"

Lily explained, "Fawn is the deer, you are the eagle, Father Guerin is the black raven, the fisher cat is Martin Nielson, the loon is Farrell Luning, the white crane is Kermit Crain, the muddy catfish is Albert Fisher, and the massive bear is Bjorn Forsberg. Together, we can defeat the Wintermaker."

"But I thought I was the boy on the island."

"You were, but you're also the eagle, the Great Thunderbird. Now do you see? We need you to learn all you can from Paul White Wolf and get strong for what's coming. You'll be a strong warrior when evil rises, and with your help, we'll fulfill our destiny and send the Wintermaker into the Land of the Midnight Sun where he belongs."

"So what part do you play?" Migisi asked.

Lily shrugged. "I'm the Firehandler, the one who plays the Water Drum. I made a terrible mistake when I sang the Song of the Manitou, but next time, I will be prepared. We will all be prepared."

Lily watched her brother ponder it all for several minutes.

He began to nod before finally saying, "Even though I think you're stupid sometimes, you're still my sister. I'll protect you."

I know you will. Lily gave her brother a kiss on his cheek. "You'll always be my hero." She gave him a little push, adding, "Now, go back to class where you belong."

Migisi put away his knife and picked up his turtle shell shield. "Coming?"

"Lily and I are going to talk for a bit," Fawn said.

Migisi isn't the only one with questions, apparently.

Fawn waited until Migisi was far enough away before she commented, "With Migisi on one side and Jean on the other, no wonder you live to be an old lady. I wish I had guys willing to fight and die for me."

Lily chuckled sadly. "Oh, Fawn. What am I supposed to do now?"

"You need to go talk to Jean."

"And say what?"

"Does it matter? Whether you come right out and tell him you love him or just flirt around the truth, it's still your destiny, isn't it? There's no changing it."

"I think he already knows," Lily said.

"Even so, you need to be careful, Lily. I worry that your future is more fragile than you think. Maybe Migisi is right. How do you know you're not being misled?"

Not you too. "Why do you say that?"

"What is it that you think we saw? The night Father Guerin died? When we were here at the river?"

"I saw the future," Lily answered. *Is it lying if it is a half-truth?* "There have been clues for quite a while now: the time I saw the young man under the willow, the little girl on the bridge, the old woman off the shore of Turtle Island, and especially when we came to look for the stone. These apparitions were not ghosts; they were visitors from the future. They came from the future to set me on the right path. But in talking to them, I realized something. That old lady ... she was me."

"You saw yourself?" Fawn asked.

"After Nanak and my parents died, I prayed. I didn't know what to do, and an old version of myself answered."

"How old?" Fawn asked.

"Why does it matter?"

"Could you have been over a hundred?"

Lily smirked. "Considering how wrinkled and hideous I looked, yeah, I'd guess I could be that old." Lily lowered her head. "I think the young man in the snakeskin boots is my grandchild."

Fawn shook her head. "Something is wrong."

She suspects something. "Why do you say that?"

"While you were in the water, retrieving the … stone, I spoke with the apparition, the boy in the snakeskin boots. He said something strange. He said that your victory will actually be a defeat. What do you think he meant?"

He knows … Did he try to warn Fawn from the future? "The only thing I know is that my victory ensured that there would be children, grandchildren, and great-grandchildren. If I failed, everything would have been destroyed."

"But if we're going to fight the Wintermaker in just twelve years, why is it that an old woman visited your dreams? In twelve years, the boy in the snakeskin boots won't even be born yet. Were you lying to Migisi about facing the Wintermaker when the comet comes again?"

Lily forced a laugh. "I'm going to go insane trying to understand all of this. All I know is that with the comet, the Wintermaker grows stronger, but if we can all stay together, we have enough magic to fight him. We held together, didn't we? We saved Jean, and Migisi, and … Do you trust me, Fawn?"

Fawn nodded.

"Then what do I do?"

"You're done teaching for the day. Instead of grading papers, just go talk to him."

I can't stop the comet from coming, nor can I undo what I've done. "Alright," Lily decided. "You're right. I don't really have a choice now. What happens will happen. I'll go talk to Jean."

Waiting at the Willow

Split Rock, MN
1961

THE RINGING PHONE startled Albert Fisher, stealing him from an old memory. By the second ring, he realized it was not the main house phone in Eunice's parlor but the one in his office. *The private line.* With a groan, he rose from the plush chair and slipped his feet into his slippers, which still held the warmth given off by the fireplace.

Has something happened? Is that why I heard sirens earlier?

He passed by the grandfather clock in the long hall, noting that it was well past midnight. Fumbling for lights in the den, he reached the phone by the sixth ring.

He cleared his throat and answered, "Yes?"

The caller was breathing heavily. "Albert, it's Ed Nielson. I just returned from a house fire."

No more tragedies. "Yes, I heard the sirens and saw the lights going south. Whose house?"

Ed Nielson hesitated. "The Guerin farm ... It was Lily's house."

Impossible. That can't be. "How is she?"

"She's been burned, badly, and so was her son Louis when he rushed in to get her out. Glen Forsberg worries she might not live through the night. As soon as we got back to the firehouse, he drove out to the hospital in Brainerd. He'll be calling to give you an update."

"Yes, yes. I understand. I'm just struggling to—"

"Understand what it means? I'll leave those questions for you to figure out. I just knew you had to hear right away."

"You did well, Edward. What about her grandchildren?"

"They were in the big house, and the fire didn't affect it. But there is one more thing. The girl, Nicole, she told Forsberg there were some sinister-looking men that stopped by earlier in the day wanting to speak to Lily. The girl was hysterical, but she thinks they might be responsible for the fire."

Servants of the Wintermaker. "Look into it and see what you can learn."

"I already called Wally Crain. I'll have him call you in the morning once he looks into it. Is there anything else you need me to do?"

Lily can't die. It's too early.

"Albert? Do you need anything from me?"

"No, thank you, Ed. It's late, and I'm sure you're exhausted. Get some sleep. I'll gather the others for a meeting tomorrow after supper." He paused. "Please … pray for Lily."

After the call ended, Albert had to steady himself against the desk. *How can we go on without her? If she dies, how can …* He shook off his fear. *I must have faith she'll survive.*

He reached for the "heart of the oak" crucifix that had been given to him by Farrell Luning long ago. Holding it over his heart, he prayed for Lily Guerin and also for himself. He knew what slept in Lake Manitou and who protected them from it.

Holding the wooden pendant brought back another old memory. *Could it be now? Is she going to be waiting there for me?*

Outside the windows of his mansion, a majestic willow stood as a shadow against the soft glow of the Split Rock streetlights. Nothing remained of Good Counsel Convent, even though Albert had reused the old brick to help build his mansion on the retired property. The original willow tree had rotted and died, only to be replaced by one he'd personally propagated and grown from the original. Since attaining maturity a decade earlier, visiting it had become part of his routine.

He slipped on a jacket and quietly stepped outside.

Above his head, the stars filled the night sky, obscuring the tiny point of light from Halley's Comet. He'd seen it brush by earth in 1910, when it brought death and mayhem to Lake Manitou. *It's turned around and is coming back, but it won't return for another two decades. How can Lily die? It's not time.*

Under the willow, he found his folding chair, where he once again waited for the promised loop to close.

You were there for me, my old friend, and now I'll be there for you.

It was an old thought that he'd reminded himself of countless times, but on the night where Lily's life again hung in the balance, everything felt aligned. This time, he reached up and grabbed a handful of willow branches.

Moments later, when a figure parted the willow branches, Albert didn't flinch, but the face did not belong to Lily. "Who are you?"

A young man wore the black slouch hat that once belonged to Big Squeak Weber, and he carried the curved castration knife that'd belonged to Kermit Crain. "Whoa… You're … you're Albert Fisher."

"Do I know you?"

"No, you've been dead for years. She told me you'd be here, but I didn't think I'd actually find you here. I'm Levi MacPherson, Lily Guerin's great-grandson."

"Lily sent you to me?"

"No. She doesn't even know that I—Hey, do you know anything about Robin? She told me all about the Omodai."

Omodai? Albert shook his head. "No. Who is she?"

"I'm not sure," Levi said. "She's been haunting my dreams lately, so I'm not even sure if she's real. But she obviously knew about you. I'm supposed to give you a message. She said that someone betrays us to the Wintermaker, and now, he is trying to attack the past. Something about loops? She said that without Lily protecting the lake, the loops can be broken, and the future destroyed."

"How? What am I supposed to do?" Albert asked.

"This is some heavy stuff, isn't it?" Levi smirked. "First, Robin said you need to stay under the willow until Lily comes. I'm not sure how long that means. But then, Robin said you face the Wintermaker at the place where you almost died. She said life and death will again hang in the balance. Got it?"

The sawmill. How could I forget? "I'm supposed to wait here for Lily?"

"I'd like to talk more, but I think Lily's coming. Good luck, Albert, I'll be rooting for you from the future. I have to assume you'll remember all this, otherwise, I won't exist, will I?"

Levi cut a few branches from the tree, then looked around cautiously before calling out, "Lily?"

He must have heard something for, with a nod, Levi vanished into the darkness.

In the distance, Albert heard Lily's voice calling out. A moment later, she stepped under the willow, young and beautiful still.

"You've finally come."

Lily's eyes widened at his words. "Who are you?"

He almost rushed to hug her, to tell her everything that had happened to Jean Guerin, Fawn Chevreuil, Kermit Crain, Bjorn Forsberg, Martin Nielson, and Farrell Luning. *If I tell her, she could change things. She could stop their deaths if she knew about the details.*

Albert opened his mouth in a moment of weakness, and then closed it again. *The boy was trying to warn me. I need to close the loop. He knows.* "Omodai."

"Excuse me?" Lily asked.

The children are still in danger. I'm a fool to believe I was the Omodai. "I was marked from birth and brought to this cursed place as the main course for the feast. I've been trying to fight death my whole life, and now, at the end, I'm fighting death another way. They always say it's darkest before the dawn ... I was beginning to think you weren't going to come." *She's so young and beautiful, yet now she's dying of burns in a hospital.* "I'm afraid, Lily. I need your help. You need to find me."

"I have found you here, right now," Lily whispered. "I don't understand."

Close a loop. Create a loop. Albert lifted his free hand and brushed aside the thin white hair on his scalp to reveal a birthmark. "When you sang the Song, you not only woke enemies, but you also called allies. We'll save the children together."

"Albert?"

There's so much I want to tell you, sweet Lily. I could stop all your pain with a word. "Yes, now go make your dreamcatcher, and then we'll talk more about turning the tides of this battle. You've lost enough. Now, it's time for you to start fighting."

Albert let go of the willow fronds, and Lily vanished into the past.

I'm sorry, Lily. So sorry.

The Wintermaker was waiting.

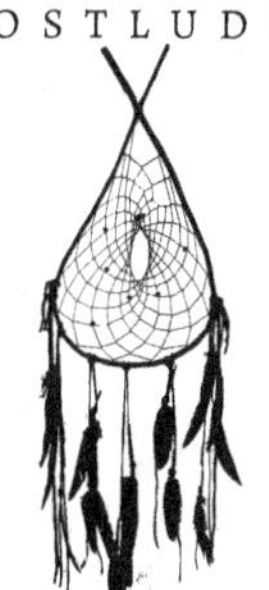

The Two-Faced Terror

Brainerd, MN
May 2029

ROBIN BERG STARED into the eyes of Hell—or at least that's who she assumed visited her dreams.

After the visit from the raven at school, the world of Hiawatha County stayed right where it belonged—in her dream journal. She had boldly rescued it from oblivion several hours earlier when she stormed back into Mr. Allen's classroom to snatch it away from the kid who took her spot in the front row. Now, the dream journal rested on her end table while she left the harsh world of her reality to visit her imaginary friends in Hiawatha County.

Instead of heroic Lily, bold Fawn, or noble Migisi, a horrific face floated up from the dark abyss for a visit. In Norse mythology, Hell wasn't a place but a person. The daughter of the trickster god Loki, Hell (or Hel or Hela) also lived in a frozen hell like Minnesota (albeit a bit colder). The ruler of the dead was easily identified: half of her face was that of a beautiful young maiden while the other half of her visage was a rotting corpse.

"The raven was real," Hela whispered. "Everyone else heard it, didn't they? You're not crazy. You're special."

"I don't know you," Robin answered the face that visited from never-never-land. "Why have I never dreamed about you before?"

"I'm the last one," Hela answered. "Your mind began with Nanakonan and is working its way through the years. You'll find me at the end of it all. They keep trying and failing to kill me, and this time, I'm going to make them pay. Will you be my vengeance, Robin? They destroyed my world, so I will destroy theirs."

"Don't bullies suck," Robin mused, unafraid. The real monsters lived in the dank locker rooms and meth kitchens of her world. Her imaginary goddess of death didn't frighten her. In fact, Hela's pink scar tissue held no maggots nor did the empty eye socket contain any slithering snakes—just smoothed skin where an eyeball should've been found. "Wait…I know you. You're the one who taught Lily the song, weren't you? Oh, I get it. You're wearing a Baltimore Ravens sweatshirt. Edgar Allan Poe's hometown. So that was *you* that crashed into the glass earlier today?"

"I think I'm dying under the willow, and the only way to contact you was through a raven," Hela explained. "Ravens are messengers, remember?"

"That's cool," Robin said. "It sure explains all of my dreams about Lily."

"And now I need your help to stop Lily from destroying the world."

"Is that all?" Robin teased. "I mean, I know I'm dreaming right now. I know you're not real."

"You're right. You're either crazy or a hero. Which would you rather be?"

Robin laughed. "You forget the option where I do the bidding of the Goddess of Death and become the villain who destroys the world. I have a hard time believing Lily is a villain."

"If I could convince you that Hiawatha County is real, along with all the people you know and love who live within it, would you trust me then?"

"Just don't make me do anything that'll make them put me on meds, okay? I like hiding from the real world in Hiawatha County. So how am I supposed to find you? Or Lily?"

"Use your dream journal," Hela answered. "Hiawatha County is not imaginary—it's just hidden. If you can find it, you'll know where to find me."

Under the willow.

ONCE ROBIN WOKE from her dream, her hand quickly found her phone and the dream journal to jot down what Hela had just told her. Once she was done scribbling it down, she pulled up Google Maps and followed the line of Highway 10 west into the green expanse of nothingness. South of Nimrod, a green blob labeled "Lyons State Forest" mocked the idea of finding the mysterious Lake Manitou.

It's just not real.

But it was worth taking a look.

THE END

The Dreamcatcher Chronicles
will continue with Book Two:
THE WINTERMAKER

<u>Robin Berg's Dream Journal</u>
"Who's Who in Hiawatha County"
#1898 People

<u>Those Along the Blue Knife River:</u>
NANAKONAN—a Chippewa elder given a land allotment
along the Blue Knife River in 1851. #boyinthecanoe
    —Chagobay, his father, who guided Nicollet's
    expedition to Lake Manitou in #1836.
    —Makadewaa, his grandfather. #1758
    —Wiyipisiw, his great-grandfather. #wijigan
BIG SQUEAK, his son. —a notorious bootlegger and
    leader of the Black Hat Gang. Landowner along
    the eastern shore of the Blue Knife River.
    —Pierre LeDuc, a Black Hat gang member.
    —Blackfish Labiche, a Black Hat gang member.
    —Michael Chevreuil, A Black Hat gang member.
      —Fawn, his daughter. #cousins
WINNIE, his daughter-in-law. #lakotablood
    —Sweating Stone, her father. #Pillager
TEWAPA, his granddaughter. #prefers Lily #prefers
    Weber #firehandler #teacher
MIGISI, his grandson. #eagle

BIG MARTEN, Teddy—former landowner along eastern
    shore of the Blue Knife River. (d. 1896)
GRAY HERON, Fred—a former landowner along the
    eastern shore of the Blue Knife River.
    —Rose, his wife
THUNDER FACE, Adam—a Dakota man of obscure
    origins. #bully #possessed? #100-year lease??
    —Samuel, his son
    —Evangeline, his daughter

<u>Those From the Big Woods and Beyond:</u>
    GRAY SKY, James—a Chippewa elder from Mille Lacs
    LITTLE TOAD, Joseph—a Chippewa elder from Bad
        River, Wisconsin. #wijigan
    SPEAKS FIRST, Clyde—A Chippewa elder from Fond du
        Lac. #wijigan
    SWEATING STONE—an ancestral chieftain from Leech
        Lake.
        —Tall Birch, his personal guard
        —Cut Ear, his personal guard
        —Wichapi, his former Lakota wife.

<u>Those who Live on Old Copper Road (Starting at Split Rock)</u>
    The Forsberg Family: #bearclan #guardians
        BJORN—the smelly hero. #norwegianforbear
        Gustaf, his father, a dairy farmer. #bighorses
        Britta, his sister.
        Signe, his sister
    The MacPherson Family: #sonoftheparson
        Donald—a Scottish farmer
        Willem, his son
        Emily, his daughter
    The Bordeaux Family: #everybodymatters
        Jermie Bordeaux—a pig farmer living near
        Kanaranzi Creek on Lake Manitou.
        Margerie, his wife.
    The Larson Family: #houseinthewoods
        Hans, a first-generation farmer from Wisconsin.
        Why does their farm seem familiar?
    The Nielson Family: #martenclan #warrior
        MARTIN—A Norwegian farmer. #fasthorse
        Dolly, his wife.
    The Berg Family: #poorwhitetrash
        Olaf, Norwegian farmer along the far side of
        Jiibay Hollow.

Ida, his wife

Agnes, Elias, Hans, Lars, Mabel, Nils, Paul, Syvia-kids

The Crain Family: #craneclan #leaders

Charles-An English blacksmith from Sterling Junction.

Monte, his eldest son

KERMIT-his son. #knife

The Order of Eos: #menofthedawn #badguys

THE SINCLAIR FAMILY: the English branch of Eos.

William-current Grandmaster #novascotia

Adrianna, his daughter #bunintheoven

Scott, his older brother (d. 1896) #stjohn

Sara Delhut, his daughter

Jack, his only son. #Hinckley Fire

Molly Stewart, his daughter.

Erin Haggard, his daughter

Lilly Marquette, his daughter

Halvar Dobie- Albany businessman #henchman.

Azero Gunn- Mahkahta Settlement Claim Association

Ira Douglas- private attorney for Triton Corporation

THE DELHUT FAMILY: #American branch #Detroit

PIERRE DELHUT- wealthy Detroit steel tycoon. Grandson of Solomon Delhut. One of the three families running Triton Corporation. #marriedsinclair #sara

Ozias Haggard, his brother-in-law

Walter Stewart, his brother-in-law

Phillip Marquette, his brother-in-law

THE TERRONT FAMILY: #French branch

Edouard Terront- a French Industrialist.

<u>Those who Live Near Split Rock:</u>

The Fisher Family: #Fishclan #intellectuals
GEORGE FISHER—owner of the Split Rock
sawmill.
—Minnetta, his wife
—Albert, his son. #fish #omodai?

The Luning Family: #Loonclan #leaders
Farrell Luning—A local lumberjack
—Florence, his wife

Everybody Else:

APPLE, Christopher—a farmer near the Turtle Island
Reservation.

AUERBACH, John—a Split Rock businessman.
—Christine, his wife.
—Frankie, his son

BARROW, Minister—the presbyterian minister in
St. John.

CORR, Walter—a saw operator at Fisher Mills

GRAHAM, Gordon—constable of Split Rock.

GRANT, Delbert—a local mailman.

HASKINS, Matt—a local dairy farmer.

HAWES, Barnabas—masonry worker at Haggard Quarry.

HEBERT, Father—Catholic Priest assigned to St.
Marie's in Split Rock.

INEZ, Sister—a Catholic nun who does missionary
work with the local poor.

JENKINS, "Doc"—the local doctor in Split Rock.

PENNY, Jonas—the local milkman

VAN SLYKE, STEVEN—owner of Dutch Boy Dairy
—Burt, his son
—Stefan, his son

ROBIN BERG'S DREAM JOURNAL
"LEGENDS AND LORE"
#1898

<u>Anishinaabe</u>—Some say the word means "Beings Made out of Nothing" and others "the Original Man," so don't quote me on this. Also known as the <u>Chippewa</u> and <u>Ojibwe</u>. Their religion is known as the Midewiwin Way (Migisi) and they kinda have something like God (Gitche Manito), and even an earthly mediator similar to Jesus (Manabozho). Despite not having the stone tablets of the Ten Commandments, they have a moral code known as the Seven Grandfathers. Despite slight variations between regions (Ottawa, Potawatomi, etc.), their society is built upon a clan system, taught to them long ago.

    A.   Ah-ja-jawk (Crane)—the chieftains
    B.   Mahng (Loon)—the chieftains
    C.   Gi-Goon (Fish)—the intellectuals
    D.   Mu-kwa (Bear)—the police
    E.   Wa-bi-zha-shi (Marten)—the warriors
    F.   Be-nays (Bird)—Spiritual Leaders
    G.   Wa-wa-shesh-she (Deer)—Gentle People

<u>Asibikaashi</u>—the Chippewa word for spider.

<u>Blanket Men</u>—slang for older generation who still practiced the Midēwiwin religion . #Nanakonan #Littletoad #Clyde

<u>Dreamcatcher</u>—a loop of willow with a sinew web created long ago by Grandmother Spider, a creation deity (Lily coincidence?) and decorated with beads and feathers. The most common tale about the Dreamcatcher is that it keeps evil spirits away from sleeping children.

<u>Fire Keeper</u>—a position of social and religious importance, similar to the way a priest conducts various social and religious ceremonies.

<u>Gitchi-Animikii</u>—translates as Great Thunderbird (Migisi). The enemy of the water serpent known as the Horned Serpent. Literally, it seems to be some sort of eagle. #guardian angel #opposes evil

<u>Gitche Manito</u>—The Great Spirit. #God?

<u>Gookooko-oo</u>—the owl. There is a unique belief that owls are harbingers of death and should be avoided at all costs.

<u>Hela</u>—the Goddess of Death in Norse mythology, whose two-faces have the appearance of a young woman on one half, and the other is a rotting face of a corpse.

<u>Horned Serpent</u>—Literally, a water serpent. Also found in a ton of other myths. Nidhogg is a Norse dragon that guards the world tree. Jormungandr is another Norse water serpent. At times, it is synonymous with a watery manitou. Its enemy is the Thunderbird.

<u>Inyan</u>—an Oceti Sakowin creator god. Since Inyan sacrificed himself to help shape the world, rock formations are seen as holy by the Seven Council Fires people. The unique rock formations around Lake Manitou are seen as sacred. #God? #Norse creation?

<u>Ironwood Log</u>—a relic mentioned in the Seven Fires Prophecies. The Ironwood Log is the container for the sacred scrolls (most likely birch bark) that held the prophecies. Generations prior, the Ironwood Log was hidden. Prophecy believed this sacred container will one day be found, and its secrets revealed. #whatsinthebox? #cave

<u>Iyash</u>—a mythic hero in Anishinaabe folklore. These tales range from the Atlantic to the plains and feature a hero who stands against the evil Horned Serpent.

<u>Jessakkid</u>—a gift from the Great Spirit. Comparable to Seers, Exorcists, Necromancers, or Prophets.

<u>Jiibay</u>—Anishinaabe word for ghost. Typically, the dead travel the River of Souls but nothing's typical in Lake Manitou. #riverstyx #sheol #valhala

Land of the Midnight Sun—the final resting place in Chippewa Culture. #heaven

Lærad—An alternative name for the Norse world tree, also known as Yggdrasil. The roots of Lærad are found in three locations: Hvergelmir, the bubbling, boiling spring; Urðarbrunnr, the Well of Fates; and Mímisbrunnr, in the land of the Giants.

Manabozho—the Mediator. A physical embodiment of the Great Spirit, who came to earth in human form to teach the people. The name varies widely (Hiawatha, Glooscap, Nanabush) but the tales seem to indicate a shape-shifting ability. #Jesus #godonearth

Mide—a priest in the Midewiwin religion.

No Soul—a mythic figure in Dakota Culture about a shapeshifting, immortal monster that lives in a cave. The hero Wishwee is able to destroy the monster with a "white egg."

Nokomis—the Chippewa word for grandmother.
Noozhishenh—the Chippewa word for granddaughter.

Oceti Sakowin—the Seven Council Fires. Also known by their enemies as the Sioux. This alliance of seven tribes once stretched from the Great Lakes all the way to the Black Hills. For almost a century, northern Minnesota was a battleground between the migrating Anishinaabe and the Oceti Sakowin, until sometime around 1750 when the Dakota departed their sacred lands for southern Minnesota.
The Dakota (or Eastern Sioux). Also known as Isanyathi "Guardians of the Frontier"
    —Mdewakanton "Dwellers of Spirit Lake"
    —Wahpekute
    —Wahpeton
    —Sisseton
The Middle Sioux
    —Yankton
    —Yanktonai
The Western Sioux
    —The Lakota (or Teton Sioux)

<u>**Ojiig**</u>—the legendary hero (a marten/Fisher Cat) that frees the Summerbirds trapped by the evil Wintermaker. Now represented by the Big Dipper constellation.

<u>**Omodai**</u>—the Chippewa word for a container, like a bowl, cup, or vessel.

<u>**Pewabic**</u>—the Chippewa word for clay or vitriol.

<u>**Philosopher's Stone**</u>—the European term for an object sought after for thousands of years. Known commonly as the substance that can turn lead into gold, the scientific lore goes far beyond a simple alkahest that can transform matter into being the key or origin to all matter. The word vitriol, for example, is a Latin phrase used during the quest to find the original stone, which transforms anything it touches into ormus, a blue-green byproduct similar to copper.

<u>**Pillagers**</u>—a group of Chippewa living around central Minnesota and Leech Lake.

<u>**Potowatomi**</u>—the Fire People. Eastern cousins of the Chippewa.

<u>**River of Souls**</u>—it is the way a soul travels to its final resting place. It is seen as the Milky Way, with the entrance to the Land of the Midnight Sun found at the Pleiades, which the Chippewa refer to as the Sweating Stones.

<u>**The Sacred Fire**</u>—a concept found in the Seven Fire Prophecy. It is the goal of the Chippewa (and humanity) to light this Sacred Fire following the fulfillment of the Seven Fire Prophecy. With the lighting of the Sacred Fire, humanity is doomed to destruction. The spiritual answers needed to light this Sacred Fire will be revealed in the era of the Seventh Fire.

<u>**The Sacred Shell**</u>—a concept found in the Seven Fire Prophecy. As a symbol, it is literally the megis shell (cowry shell) that guided the

Anishinaabe along the Seven Stopping Places. The lore suggests that the Sacred Shell was lost during the early years of the migration, and although the Chippewa found their way to the Seventh Stopping Place without it, it will be key during the era of the Seventh Fire to understanding the truth behind the original prophecies.

The Serpent Star—a unique term used to describe Halley's Comet. Although the belief is not held by most Mide, it is believed by some that the arrival of the Serpent Star was a harbinger for the arrival of a new era. #1456 #1532 #1607 #1682 #1758 #1835 #1910? #1986 #2061

The Seven Fires—a sacred prophecy given to the Anishinaabe generations ago that prompted their departure from their brothers in Nova Scotia to their sacred lands in Minnesota. The exact language of this prophecy varies from region to region. This is the account told by the elders in Hiawatha County:

The First Fire: A warning to leave the east
- Midewiwin Lodge established
- The Anishinaabe became a "new" people
- Follow the sacred Megis shell
- Seek a Turtle-Shaped Island
- Seek a Land Where Food Grows on the Water

The Second Fire: A Lost People
- The Sacred Shell was lost
- Camped by a Great Body of Water
- A Boy Will Show the Path

The Third Fire: Finding the Path
- The way is learned
- A Land to the West

The Fourth Fire: Two Prophets Warn
- Beware the Light-skinned race
- Face of Brotherhood
- Face of Death
- Bringing poison and pollution

The Fifth Fire: A Great Struggle
- All Native Peoples Struggle
- Abandoning the old teachings

The Sixth Fire: Deceived by a Promise
- Grandchildren will turn against the elders

- Light-skinned race will take the lands
- Near destruction of the Native people

<u>The Seventh Fire: Retracing the Steps</u>

- A young prophet with a strange light in his eyes
- Elders will help them retrace their steps
- A New People will appear
- The Water Drum will sound its voice.
- The Sacred Fire will again be lit
- The Light-Skinned race will have a choice between:
  An Eighth Eternal Fire, or...
  Destruction of earth

<u>The Seven Stopping Places:</u>

1. Montreal Island
2. Niagara Falls
3. Lake St. Clair
4. Manitoulin Island
5. Sault Ste. Marie
6. Madeline Island
7. Lake Manitou?

<u>Song of the Manitou</u>—a verbal chant taught to the Wijigan Clan to be used with the Water Drum. It is rumored that the original text was kept in the Sacred Shell so that the Sacred Fire could be lit in the era of the Seventh Fire.

<u>Summerbirds</u>—from the tale of Ojiig and the Wintermaker. In the story, the Wintermaker collected the Summerbirds in snares, refusing to allow them free, and thus, preventing the seasons from ever changing. Because of this, the hero Fisher Cat went to the lands of the north, freed the Summerbirds, and was chased into the stars by the Wintermaker, who hunts him still.

<u>Sweat Lodge Ceremony</u>—When a child approached adulthood, they would enter a sweat lodge for a "vision quest." After four days of fasting, it is believed that the spirit of the individual travels from the lodge to the crescent moon and the star world. The lodge is built of willow and covers a pit where hot stones are collected. The four doors of the lodge are manned by representatives of the Cedar Man,

Bird Man, Bear Man, and the Door Man. Outside a fire is kept to heat the stones, which the Fire Man oversees. The Conductor oversees the ceremony, often including an apprentice for the purposes of training.

The Tak-Pei—the Little Men of the Forest. Known by names all over the world (Canotila, gnomes, fossegrim, Pukwudgies, memegwesi), the sinister spirits near Lake Manitou often appear in the shape of an oily porcupine.

Tewapa Tankiyan—Lake with the Crooked Lily Roots. The illustrious mapmaker Joseph Nicollet visited present day Lura Lake in Blue Earth County, where the mystical qualities of the lily root were harvested for use in vision quests. Coincidentally, the man who dubbed the Undine Region with the moniker "Blue Earth" also traveled north of the mouth of the Crow Wing River, where he also noted blue earth and lily pads near Lake Manitou.

Turtle Island—akin to the Promised Land of the Hebrews, in some tales, the turtle is symbolic for the whole of North America as well as an Ark symbol in flood tales. Yet for the Anishinaabe, Turtle Island is the distinctive island at the end of the Seven Fires quest. While other Chippewa communities believe the ultimate Turtle Island could be Spirit Island near Duluth, Madeline Island of the Apostle Islands, or even Turtle Mountain in North Dakota, the Chippewa in Hiawatha County believe it to be found in Lake Manitou.

Undine—the Water Spirit in alchemy. Other terms: the mermaid, water nymph, and siren. During his mapping of Minnesota, Joseph Nicollet labeled present day Blue Earth County (where he noted the copper vitriol) as the Undine Region.

Wabeno—the Firehandler. Like the Jessikkid, little is known about this exotic priesthood of the Anishinaabe. The adherents of this secretive religious society are known as the "Dawn Society" and are considered servants of Manabozho, blessed with the ability to handle fire and perform other feats of magic.

<u>**Wanagiyata**</u>—the original Sioux word for Lake Manitou, which translates as Place of Souls.

<u>**Water Drum**</u>—found in the Seven Fires Prophecies. The concept of the Water Drum has been woven into Anishinaabe culture in the same way the symbol of the cross has found its way in Christian ceremony. Although commonly found, the typical Mide had a symbolic representation of the original Water Drum in the same way Catholic Priest carry only a symbolic cross. The original Water Drum was part of creation, representing all that was spiritually and physically needed for life. In the tale of its creation, it was used to bring health and life back to a sick boy, who went on to teach the Midewiwin way to future generations. #philosopher's stone?

<u>**Wijigan**</u>—The Skull Clan. For generations, this Anishinaabe clan was supported by the community, but following dark deeds at Madeline Island and Lake Manitou, the Chippewa purged this clan from their society.

<u>**Wintermaker**</u>—the mythical villain now represented by the constellation Orion. Possible connection to the Dakota tales of "Red Horn." When this constellation appears at the horizon, he brings winter and death with him. His enemy is the Fisher Cat. His goal was to prevent the changing of the seasons, which is why he used his magic to trap the Summerbirds.

Zhaaganaash—The Light-Skinned Race.

ABOUT THE AUTHOR

Imagine the love child of Rambo and Ma Ingalls. That's Jason Lee Willis. Overly nurtured by his Vietnam War veteran father and Lutheran church secretary mother, he grew up in the fantasy realm of South Dakota before his exodus brought him to mysterious Minnesota for college.

His love of mythology and storytelling led him to a career as a high school English teacher, where he guided his students in writing poetry, short stories, and even screenplays. As a professional storyteller, he now works as a journalist and blogger, does historical lectures, book talks, radio segments, podcasts, and maintains a video channel on YouTube, The Minnesota Alchemist.

Willis currently lives in Minnesota, where he lives the life of a hobbit by gardening, writing, walking around barefoot, wearing vests, fishing, and going on adventures with his wife, Julie.